THE
ROCKETS'
RED GLARE

THE
ROCKETS'
RED GLARE

Forecast Fiction by

John Darrin
Dr. Michael Gresalfi

BIBLIOQUE
Baltimore Maryland USA

THE ROCKETS' RED GLARE

Copyright © 2013 John Darrin

Co-author: Dr. Michael Gresalfi
Editor: Nicole Gresalfi
Cover Art: Print Designer
Cover Design: Rob Zarharychuk
Book Design: John Darrin

ISBN 978-0-692-41890-1

Published by Biblioque LLC, Baltimore, MD, USA
www.biblioque.com

Publisher's Cataloging-in-Publication Data

Darrin, John.
The rockets' red glare / John Darrin [and] Michael Gresalfi.
pages cm
ISBN: 978-0-692-41890-1 (pbk.)
ISBN: 978-0-615-87002-1 (e-book)
1. Dirty bombs—Fiction. 2. Terrorists—Fiction. 3.
Terrorism—Prevention—Fiction . 4. United States—Politics and
government—Fiction.   I. Gresalfi, Michael. II. Title.
PS3604.A767 R63 2015
813`.6—dc23
            2015906335

DEDICATIONS

JOHN DARRIN

For Josh, because he is a gift to me and an inspiration. And possibly support in my old age.

And for Claire, for letting me be a part of her life even while I was immersed in this book. Honey, I'm home!

MICHAEL GRESALFI

I dedicate this book to the Grisafi families of Caltabellotta, Sicily - the ancestral home of the American Gresalfi clan, and to 22 year old Calogero, and his wife Maria, who arrived at Ellis Island, New York on October 6, 1906 on the immigrant transport ship, the Italia, and kicked-off this New World journey for us all!

SECURITY DISCLAIMER

As required by national security protocols, prior to publication Dr. Gresalfi submitted this manuscript to the appropriate U.S Government authority for both a National Security Review and an Intellectual Property Review. He has been granted approval to proceed with its publication as revised.

When our land is illumined with liberty's smile,
    If a foe from within strikes a blow at her glory,
Down, down with the traitor that tries to defile
    The flag of the stars, and the page of her story!
By the millions unchained,
    Who their birthright have gained
    We will keep her bright blazon forever unstained;
And the star-spangled banner in triumph shall wave,
    While the land of the free is the home of the brave.

5th stanza to the Star Spangled Banner
Written by Oliver Wendell Holmes, 1861

Table of Contents

Part Eight – The Search

Part Nine – Independence Day

Part Ten – Retribution

Foreword

John Darrin and Dr. Michael Gresalfi weave a tale that is believable to any individual, including those knowledgeable of radiological/nuclear weapon designs, terrorist threat capabilities, and how our nation responds to such incidents, whether perpetrated by an adversary or the result of an accident. Likewise, this novel will ring true to those readers that have only seen, read, or heard about the threat, as well as resonate with those who fear the release of radiation from such a dirty bomb explosion.

This isn't a horror story; but, nonetheless, it can and will make the hair stand up on the back of your neck. It is so realistic that you will forget that it is just a story. Terrorism, however, is real, and it is not out of the realm of possibility that an individual or group might be able to use nuclear material in a nefarious manner, as realistically portrayed here. This book will leave you telling yourself it's just a story; but, is it, really?

The Honorable Ronald C Williams
Former Special Assistant to the President
   for Nuclear Defense Policy
Homeland Security Council
The White House

Preface

We called this book Forecast Fiction for a very powerful reason – the events and consequences portrayed here could happen tomorrow and while we would certainly be shocked, we would not be surprised. We share this viewpoint with many other homeland security and counterterrorism professionals working daily against this possibility.

Our apocalyptic premise that two hated enemies with opposing strategic goals — one distorting American fundamental Christian roots with insipid racial purity objectives and the other a North American branch of Al-Qaida steeped in a radicalized Islamic terrorist foundation — could find a temporary alliance when sharing a common enemy is strikingly parallel to what we are seeing all over the Middle East today in an even more entangled context.

Within Syria and Iraq, for example, the so-called Islamic State is presently focused on building the social-political foundation for the Fifth Caliphate, and this objective resonates deeply with many millions of stateless and politically disenfranchised followers of The Prophet Mohammed. There are perhaps more than ten thousand European-born young Muslim men and women from the prisons and ghettos of France, Belgium and elsewhere, ready to martyr themselves to fight for this idealized anti-Western end state.

The growth and strengthening of our own homegrown radical religious and racial extremists foresees a similar goal here, a separate state-within-a-state where their beliefs in religious, racial, and cultural purity can grow unblemished by what they perceive as degenerate, unsustainable, and ungodly sectarian social democracy and multi-culturalism.

Yes, this is a work of fiction, and we present it for entertainment, and also for your understanding of just how serious and possible is this "single biggest threat to U.S. security."

Introduction

This is a complex story in a genre that we call Forecast Fiction. Forecast Fiction is influenced and driven by today's global information network. It tells a non-fiction story that hasn't happened. Yet.

Forecast Fiction is fact-based, using current events, characters, technologies, geo-politics, circumstances, and history, and extrapolating them into the immediate future.

Forecast Fiction is not the distant future, it is today. It could happen before your next birthday and you wouldn't be surprised.

Forecast Fiction is as real as it can get and not be fact.

As a techno-thriller striving for realism, this book of necessity includes many acronyms and technical terms. A Glossary of these is included in Appendix 1 for your reference. For the most part, these are either well-known (FBI, CIA, DOE), or not critical to the understanding and enjoyment of the book. Knowing that AMS means Airborne Monitoring System isn't important - the context will make the meaning clear. Skip these acronyms unless you are really interested in that type of thing.

Given the broad scope of the cataclysmic events described in this book, there are many characters who would be involved in the various aspects of the story. Most of the characters are designated as minor, and their names are less important to the story than to the smooth telling of it. A Cast of Characters is included in Appendix 2, including their designation as Main, Supporting, or Minor, and a reference to their first appearance in the book.

Prologue

BALIL TOWN, ABBOTTABAD, PAKISTAN

Ibrahim al Hasan sat comfortably in the rear seat of the air conditioned Cadillac limousine he had leased in Islamabad. They had been driving for over two hours since leaving Pakistan's capital city very early in the morning and were now approaching the outskirts of Bilal Town, a wealthy northeastern suburb of Abbottabad. His destination was the Bilal Jamia Masjid Mosque, and his instructions were to do as he was told when he got there.

When he arrived a few minutes later and went inside, he was met by two men who led him through a back exit to a waiting car. They followed what seemed to be a circuitous route for thirty minutes with the man in the passenger seat constantly scanning front, rear, sideways, and even up. Finally, the car slipped through the security gates and into the walled fortress known locally at the Waziristan Haveli, the mansion, less than two miles from their starting point at the mosque.

The 38,000 square-foot compound was surrounded by 18-foot concrete walls topped with barbed wire. The 3-story house was new, the walls freshly white-washed, and the turmoil of moving-in still evident. Ibrahim noted an inordinate number of armed men, some watching him, others watching outward, and still others walking the grounds. While he understood the need for such security, he himself did not feel secure. Being this close to Osama bin Laden was inviting an American missile.

He was led inside and delivered into what appeared to be a library or office in the making. Computers were set up on tables with video monitors and speakers and cables running between them. Standing by the window, Osama bin Laden turned as they entered.

"Welcome, my cousin. Welcome to my new home. It is fortuitous that you are here to join us in breaking the fast of Ashura."

Ibrahim, a distant cousin to the Saudi Royal Family and therefore to bin Laden, smiled and bowed slightly, perspiring despite the cool winter weather. The trip had been long, and the need for secrecy, the subterfuge of hiding his plans and destination from his superiors at the Saudi Ministry of Foreign Affairs, had frayed his already exposed nerves. Why was he here? Why would his cousin summon him at all, let alone at a time of such danger? Nine years younger than bin Laden, he had not even seen him in the twenty-eight years since his exile. And Ibrahim had been just 12 years-old at the time.

Women in the household served them a substantial breakfast of boiled eggs, loaf and flat bread, jellies and honey, minced meat, and, because it was the breaking of a holiday fast, *halwa poori* and *choley*. After eating, they sipped *al-Qahwa*, Saudi-style coffee, and bin Laden dismissed the women.

"You are wondering why you are here, is that right? Of course it is. How could you not? You see my cousin, I have followed your growth all these years. Your Oxford education, your successful business, and now your government service."

"Thank you, *sayyid*. I am honored."

"And I wonder why you would risk all that you have accomplished, why you would consort with such *almooharej*, such clowns? These people you talk to, they are not serious Muslims. They will bring you trouble."

Ibrahim was stunned. Watching him from afar all these years was one thing, but to be aware of his recent clandestine meetings with several radical Salafi Muslims was frightening. How did he know such things? The little group had only met twice, and they were very careful.

"I do not understand," Ibrahim said. "These men are serious about our cause. They would join you in a minute."

"And yet I have not asked for their allegiance. Do you know why? Because they are too foolish, too interested in acting like *jihadists*, and not being one. Where were they when the Afghanis called for help? They were nowhere. They will abandon the cause the first time their lives and wealth are threatened. But you, Ibrahim. I sense that you are a serious Muslim. I have been watching, and I have heard very good things about you. And if you are truly as I believe, then I ask you to join with me. I have a very important task that only you can accomplish."

With the door to his office closed, and everyone in the household aware that he was not to be disturbed, Ibrahim watched the live coverage on CNN as President Obama spoke.

"Tonight I can report to the American people and the world - the United States has conducted an operation that killed Osama bin Laden, the leader of al Qaeda and a terrorist who has been responsible for the murder of thousands of men, women, and children."

Ibrahim didn't hear the rest; it would be just propaganda and justification, anyway. *What about your murders, Mr. President*, he thought. What about the thousands of Iraqis and Afghanis and Pakistanis and Somalis and others from across the globe who do not kowtow to the wishes of the great United States? Where are their defenders who can sneak into your country in the middle of the night and kill Americans without any accountability? Without justice. Why are your American lives so precious while Arabs and Muslims everywhere are murdered with impunity?

I have failed. My sacred task was to create al Qaeda of North America to bring the jihad to these infidels. And what have I accomplished? Four trusted lieutenants, a few capable soldiers. Nothing like the army I was entrusted to build.

And so Ibrahim started to plan.

Part One – The Incident

SATURDAY, JUNE 19

1.01 PASTOR TECHNOLOGY, INC., OAK RIDGE, TN

The tenants at 10529 Szilard Court in Oak Ridge, Tennessee, had installed a security camera to surveil their front door and parking lot as a means to lower insurance premiums. In the corner of that image, part of the parking lot and the front door of their neighbor's building could be seen. 10527 didn't have any surveillance, the theory being that the no one would want to break in and steal its contents. Before 9/11/2001, that was a pretty good theory.

The building at 10527 was owned by Pastor Technology, Inc., and licensed by the State of Tennessee to possess and use up to one million curies of various radioactive elements. At any given moment, it contained that much, and occasionally more, although Kenneth Pastor, Sr., the founder and owner, would never admit that. He had a record of minor regulatory infractions and was much less concerned with strict compliance than he was with making a dollar.

As Kenneth, his preferred name, told the rare visitor to illustrate the danger and enhance his image, if you were to put a teaspoon of Cesium-137 in your pocket, you would have a greater than 50% chance of dying in three hours. At any given time, he had about 10,000 teaspoons in his inventory. In his thirty-seven years in business, there had never been a radiological injury to anyone in his employ. That was the record he stood on, not the twenty-three significant license violations he had accumulated from various state and

Federal agencies over the years. If they had been traffic tickets, he would have been taking the bus to work.

The camera at 10529 did the digital equivalent of a click at 5:29:42 PM, catching Kenneth in mid-stride between the just-locked and alarmed front door, and his Buick LaCrosse parked directly in front. It clicked again six seconds later, and repeated the process in six-second intervals, catching a staccato record of Kenneth's departure for home for the weekend. The images were written to a hot-swappable hard disk on one of the twenty-two servers at the security company who owned and monitored the system. The disk was scheduled to be pulled at 5 AM the next morning, and a new, clean one installed. It would be. It was then scheduled to be stored for seven days before being erased and recycled into the surveillance system. It wouldn't be.

Exactly 5,141 images later, at 2:04:24 AM, an identical Buick LaCrosse pulled into the same reserved parking spot, now dimly lit by the parking lot streetlights. A similar-looking man got out and returned to the front door, unlocking it and entering the building. The camera recorded a very low-quality image of the event.

After entering the building through the front door with the key he'd been given, the man, code-named Fida, entered the security code he'd memorized and watched as the green "Armed" light flicked off and the red "Unarmed" one lit. Without turning on any lights, he removed several precut heavy black fabric pieces, edged in elastic, from his briefcase and proceeded to fit these over the four front windows working by the dim illumination from the outside lights. Satisfied that he was now invisible from outside, he reached back into the same briefcase, removed a flashlight, and examined the room. It was just as he'd been told.

He took the throwaway, pre-paid cell phone from his pocket and keyed a text message that simply read "OK" and sent it to a stored phone number, and then he sat down to await the response. It came just over fifteen minutes later, reading the identical "OK" indicating that there had been no security response to his 2 AM entry. He left the building as he came, repeating the process Kenneth had done nine hours earlier, skipping only the alarm reset and leaving the building unsecure.

The security camera recorded the departure in six images. As far as the camera was concerned, nothing else happened that weekend.

On the far side of the building, out of sight of the camera, four large panel vans drove up to a roll-up truck door located at the middle of the building's side. A man using the name Hadi got out of the driver's side of the first van and went to the keypad on the left side of the door and entered a code. When he pushed the final key in the seven-digit code, an electric motor growled, the door jerked once and then rolled up smoothly. Hadi returned to his van and drove in while the building door was still rising, missing it by fractions of an inch. After all four vans had entered and were lined up in the large, open truck bay, Hadi got out and pushed the close button on the inside door frame, and the door unwound downward from the spool above the opening.

Only when it had fully closed did Hadi turn on the lights, finding the switch just where he'd been trained it would be. The large, open area took up about three-quarters of a simple rectangular building, about ninety feet from end to end, and sixty feet front to back. The exterior walls were twenty-four feet high, rising slightly to thirty-two feet at the center where the sloping roof peaked. A bridge crane that could traverse the open area dominated the overhead view. There was no ceiling, just steel framework and electrical conduit and lights and ventilation ducts. At the far side, another roll-up door allowed drive-through loading and unloading of vehicles.

A wall divided the building from side-to-side, separating the open, industrial space from the offices in front. A long, concrete bunker ran along this wall, eight feet high and extending twelve feet into the open space like a huge step. Five concrete doors were irregularly spaced along it, identifiable only by the joint in the concrete where the heavy doors ended and the wall began. They had no handle nor hinges, electric motors behind access panels driving them outward on tracks instead of swiveling open.

This bunker was the reason for the entire building, the source of work for all the employees – five heavily shielded "hot cells" equipped for working safely and remotely with the huge amounts of radioactive material that Pastor Technology used to fuel the medical and industrial irradiators that they made to sterilize anything put in their beam of photons, from food to human blood to critical space-shuttle experiments that couldn't be contaminated by even the tiniest bacteria.

In the high-bay area where Hadi and his team were parked, trucks could drive in, be loaded or unloaded by crane, and drive out the door at the other end. Along the back wall was a machine shop with all kinds of metal cutting and forming machines, hand tools of every size and description, and piles of steel and lead and other metals and plastics and wood. And there were two-dozen or so irradiators themselves, some new and some used, stored in a locked wire mesh cage in the far corner, awaiting delivery or service, and isolated to prevent accidents.

All of this Hadi knew from his training and his one clandestine visit several weeks earlier, and he felt familiar in the room, ready to go about his work with confidence in the outcome. His cell phone hummed an almost silent alert, and he looked at the screen. A text message read simply, "Here." Hadi turned off the lights and pushed the "open" button on the door control panel. When the door had risen about four feet, the nose of the LaCrosse slid under, and the car entered as the truck had, just clearing the door's bottom edge. Hadi pressed "close" and turned the lights back on.

The driver's doors opened on the remaining four vehicles. Fida got out of the Buick, and Jalal, Dhakir, and Mahdi each got out of the trucks they had driven in and parked to the side, leaving the middle open for the anticipated traffic. Somewhere outside, equipped with press-to-talk cell phones and Kalashnikov AK-47 assault rifles, Rasul and Sajid patrolled, remaining unseen by any passer-by. The names, like the cell phones and weapons and vehicles, were temporary, all acquired for this one operation and to be discarded immediately after.

Fida went to the crane controls, a metal box attached to a cable dangling from the crane itself, twenty-five feet above the floor. He pressed the button marked with an arrow pointed toward the bottom of the control box, and the hook from the crane lowered slowly. Jalal went to the assortment of cables and shackles hanging on the rear wall and selected a four-point lift – four separate cables attached to one ten-inch oval steel ring with large-diameter shackles attached to their loose ends. Dhakir and Mahdi climbed the metal stairs to the top of the hot cells and positioned themselves at the near end and waited.

All were re-enacting moves they had learned and practiced many times. These four men were Hadi's cell, all carefully recruited and trained by him. Two came from his own mosque and he'd found the others on the Internet using videos of attacks on Americans to attract comments from sympathizers, Facebook entries to get acquainted, and friends-of-friends at other mosques to vet each and every recruit.

The guards outside were unknown to Hadi, a different cell, probably organized in a similar manner. He knew there were four of them, patrolling in two-man teams on four-hour shifts, but he had only their code names for reference.

Inside, Fida had slung the ring over the massive crane hook and Jalal pushed the up-arrow button. He maneuvered the cables to where Dhakir and Mahdi waited and they shackled each of the cables to eyebolts embedded in the hot-cell roof plug. Once locked in, Jalal raised the crane hook again, this time lifting out a four-foot square concrete block, built with several steps around the perimeter, like a three-tiered wedding cake, only upside down. Hadi, the only one of the men trained in the risks of handling radioactive materials, knew these supported the weight of the removable roof plug, and also eliminated any straight-line gap where radiation could leak out and be a danger to anyone in its path.

When the plug was removed and unhooked, they repeated the procedure at the two neighboring hot cells and soon had all three open from above. Anyone standing on the roof above these holes was now in danger. But there was no one there, and the dangerous beams of radiation streamed upward, where their power would dissipate quickly with distance from the source of the radiation, the hundreds of thousands of curies of radioactive cesium and cobalt and americium and strontium and yttrium and other very dangerous radioisotopes.

Jalal and Fida began unloading equipment from the vans. Hadi led Dhakir and Mahdi through the shower and locker and storage rooms to the front of the building where a full-length hall ran past the front of the hot cells. This was the operator area. Each hot cell was equipped with a thick, glass window, tinted yellow from the lead oxides used to make the glass even more dense to shield the gamma radiation. Sticking out of the wall above the windows were seven pairs of remote-control manipulators, articulated aluminum tubes full of cables and pulleys that extended two feet out from the wall to an "elbow" joint and then down to a "wrist" that was attached to a pistol-handled grip.

Inside the hot cells, the manipulator "hands" were simply clamps mounted at the end of some very sophisticated robotic arms that mirrored the ones outside. The operator could hold the handles on the outside, and by twisting and moving and squeezing his hands, control the two-prong clamps at the end of the arms inside. Dhakir and Mahdi knew from their training that while it looked easy enough, two-handed operations like cutting metal and pouring granules and closing lids all required a patience and touch that only came with practice, and they had done hours of it, simulating the exact tasks they would now need to perform for real.

Dhakir went to the wall-mounted file holder at the front of the cell and sorted through the papers he found there. He stopped at the second sheet and told Mahdi, "17-205." In the far left corner of the cell, Mahdi spotted a lead cylinder with these same numbers on a large, yellow plastic tag attached to the lid. Using the manipulator, he lifted the lid and set it aside and carefully clamped the handle on the basket inside and lifted it out. In the basket were three silver metal capsules, each about one inch in diameter and three inches long, arranged upright. According to Dhakir's paperwork, these were eight-year-old blood irradiator sources and currently contained about 1,500 curies each of cesium-137 in a pressed-powder form.

Extraction would be difficult and time-consuming. The silver capsules they could see were just the outside stainless steel shell. Inside was another just like it, and both of these would have to be carefully opened using high-speed cutting tools. And then, the fine granular powder that had been hard-pressed into the shell, forming a solid cylinder of cesium, would need to be removed. There were a number of safe extraction methods, including dissolving the cesium salt in water and then boiling the water off, but these took a lot of time and that was something in very short supply for Hadi's team. They had a faster and cruder method - simply drilling into each capsule, breaching the shell and breaking up the cesium powder in one operation. The large, shallow pan under the drill press would catch the powder.

The potential for spills and for airborne particles to spread contamination was great, but Hadi and his team weren't trying to comply with safety regulations, they were trying to move as much material in as short a time a possible. If they inhaled cesium, that was of small concern. If they spread contamination inside the cells, that was not important. If enough escaped the cells to set off radiation alarms in the building, that was a concern, and the reason Hadi had turned all of them off.

1.02   SAN PABLO AVENUE, OAKLAND, CA

Cops in the rear-view mirror started Kenny Pastor's hands shaking, and he gripped the wheel harder to make them stop. At 4:50 AM with no traffic on a Saturday morning, San Pablo Avenue was a straight shot south to his job, and today he was speeding. Really speeding, distracted by the nervous tension that had dogged him for days, angry that he had taken it out on Patsy, frustrated he had to work the weekend.

He pulled over just past MacArthur Boulevard, almost under the freeway overpass, and waited, hands on the steering wheel, in plain sight. The Oakland Police Department officer approached, one hand loosely on his holster and the other holding a flashlight that he used to light Kenny while keeping himself in the dark. Kenny rolled his window down and the officer asked for his license, registration, and proof of insurance. Kenny moved slowly and deliberately, taking his wallet from his left rear pocket and removing the license.

"The papers are in the glove compartment. OK if I get them?" He was struggling to remain calm and polite, taking no chances, his previous experience with the OPD having been very uncomfortable and resulting in his three-year prison sentence for drug distribution. The two kilograms of marijuana he'd had in the fake windshield washer fluid container of his previous car didn't qualify as personal use.

There was a moment's hesitation while the cop used the flashlight to illuminate the license. "Kenneth Pastor, Jr.," he read out loud. "Mr. Pastor, do you have any weapons in there?"

"No, of course not. Just the papers and some junk."

"Fine. Go ahead and get it."

The policeman took one step back and kept the light on Kenny as he got out the plastic folder with the owner's manual and all the old registrations and insurance cards that he never threw away. He leafed through these until he found the current ones and handed them to the officer, who told him to wait in the car.

After some moments, the officer spoke to him over the car's loudspeaker, from behind the open door of his black and white cruiser.

"Please step out of the car, Mr. Pastor. Slowly. And keep your hands where I can see them."

Kenny did as directed, fully expecting this once the cop ran a check on his record.

"Now, please keep your hands raised and walk backwards towards me. Good. Stop there. Turn to your right and put your hands on the car and spread your legs. Good. Do you have any weapons or drugs on you?"

Kenny said no, and the officer got out of the cruiser and circled around. Approaching Kenny from behind, talking to him the whole time, telling him he was going to pat him down and then cuff him while he asked some questions. The officer sat Kenny in the back seat of the cruiser and talked to him through the open door, asking what he was doing out before 5 AM.

"I'm on my way to work. I drive a delivery truck for Coastal Produce and I have to get the orders ready, load the truck, and make my deliveries to local restaurants before they open. My supervisor's name is Carlson and you can call him to verify that. They know I'm a parolee."

"OK if I search your car," the officer asked.

"Yeah, go ahead. I'm clean."

When he returned from searching the car, he helped Kenny out of the back seat and removed the cuffs.

"I'm ticketing you for forty-four in a thirty-five zone, even though I clocked you at fifty-seven. Your parole officer will be notified, of course, but nine miles over doesn't constitute any parole violation. No traffic this early makes it tempting to drive too fast, but any screw up, even a traffic accident with someone injured, could send you right back to prison. You slow down and remember that. The other people who are out here at this time of the morning are half asleep."

The ticket just added to his frustration. That would cost him $275 and a couple of points on his license. Neither mattered, not with the cash he had stashed in the offshore account. He still had over $90,000 left from the down payment he'd gotten, and the balance in the escrow account would set him and his family up comfortably somewhere he wouldn't need a California license.

The frustration was from the uncertainty about what was going on back East at that very moment, and what would be happening in the near future. And most of all, keeping his name out of it.

It was his name that had gotten him involved in the first place. He never did find out how they had discovered his relationship to Pastor Tech, but the guys who had approached him in prison had made no secret of their connections outside, and of the interest those connections had in his relationship to his father's company. That Kenny hadn't seen or talked to his father in over two years didn't bother them. That he hadn't been inside Pastor Tech in all that time didn't bother them. That he still had his old keys and knew his father's unchanging password protocol interested them. That he had worked there and knew the layout and equipment and safety procedures excited them. Kenny's interests were simple – survive his time in prison and take care of his family when it was over. These guys could arrange both, and that overcame his initial reluctance.

He had written a sort of manual on how to get into Pastor Tech, and what to do once you were inside. He didn't want to know why they wanted the information, or what they were going to do with it. He was content to pretend it was all academic, just writing down what he knew. If someone else chose to use that information, well, that wasn't his fault. He'd broken no laws. And besides, his father would suffer, and that was almost payment enough. Almost. The $1 million promised covered the rest.

This weekend was show time, and that was all he knew about them and their plans. He had gained access to Pastor the first night of his trip to Tennessee that the parole officer had allowed so he could get his family and bring them back to California. He'd never met the man he took with him that night, and couldn't identify him now because of the balaclava the man had worn over his head the whole time. They had spent two hours touring the facility, verifying everything Kenny had told them, and with Kenny making notes of the new equipment and new radioactive sources and any other changes. He'd revised his document to include these, and then gone back to California with Patsy and his new daughter to start their new life.

Showtime. After this weekend, the remainder of the $1 million would be transferred from the escrow account, and he would serve out his parole and then disappear.

So he was nervous and anxious as he drove off, leaving the cop to do whatever it was they did after issuing a traffic ticket. He decided he'd better calm down and not do anything else that would draw attention to him on this very important weekend.

1.03   PASTOR TECHNOLOGY, INC., OAK RIDGE, TN

Hadi's cell phone vibrated in his pocket, awakening him instantly. He took it out and glanced at the message before erasing it. He waited for another minute and the phone vibrated again, this time with the confirming message. As dawn was breaking, his guards were changing shifts, the overnight pair leaving to get rest, and two new ones – Ubaid and Tawfiq – taking their place. If Hadi didn't get both messages, he knew something was wrong, and their contingency plan, basically every man for himself and scatter cesium everywhere, would go into effect.

It was time to get started for the day, a busy Saturday for certain. They had eight loads to package and ship, and the first truck would be arriving within thirty minutes. Overnight they had prepared three canisters for shipment. While Jalal and Fida were to handle loading each truck as they arrived, Mahdi and Dhakir would continue working at the manipulators to make more canisters, staying ahead of the arrival and departure schedule so there would always be a full canister ready when an empty truck arrived.

Empty was not an accurate description of how the trucks would look to any observer. Each pickup truck would be loaded with miscellaneous gear, some trucks looking like scrap-metal collectors heading for the recycle center and others looking like delivery trucks hauling drums of materials and others like service trucks ready to provide welding or repair work. The common factor would be the 55-gallon drum mounted dead-center between the sides and a little ahead of the rear axle. Each drum would have stencils or graphics or just rust appropriate to the seeming purpose of the truck, but inside they were all identical, built in Mexico to a special design.

Hadi's cell was working through the weekend in the Pastor facility, enduring the risk of discovery, because the handling facilities and equipment for the huge amounts of deadly radioactive material were there, and duplicating it somewhere else would have been too apparent to anyone searching for the missing cesium after the theft was discovered.

Hadi rousted each team member with a single nudge of his foot. All were sleeping on air mattresses on the floor near the roll-up door. Without any conversation, Fida and Jalal prepared a simple breakfast starting with hot, thick coffee from a brewer they had brought. They also had a small refrigerator for meats and cheeses, and several loaves of bread. Mahdi and Dhakir cleared all the sleeping gear and prepared for the arrival of the first truck.

They had just finished cleaning up from breakfast when Hadi's cell phone vibrated and he read the message. From their gear, Fida handed each person a black silk hood, a "balaclava," which they pulled over their heads, covering their faces and concealing their identity. Hadi would be the only one speaking, and his English was as flawless as someone born and raised in Detroit could speak it.

The vans they had brought with them were parked to the side, leaving the aisle clear for the pickup trucks to enter and exit. As soon as everyone was covered, Fida opened the roll-up and the first truck drove in, directed to stop by Jalal when it was within range of the overhead crane. The truck was painted in the colors and logo of something called Kwik-Lube with an address in Seattle, and had three 55-gallon drums in the back, all from a well-known oil refiner. The driver and passenger, both wearing balaclavas themselves, waited as the roll-up door descended.

Without a word, Hadi nodded and his team went to work. Fida climbed into the back of the truck and removed the locking ring that clamped the lid to the middle drum. Once open, he could see inside, with everything arranged just as he'd seen many times in their training.

Centered in the drum by a wooden framework was a thirteen-inch diameter lead cylinder with a one-and-a-half-inch diameter steel pipe embedded in the middle like it was the axle for a lead wheel. The pipe was the mortar, the barrel that would launch the cesium projectile. Three eye-bolts protruded from the cylinder for lifting the 1,287 pound lead container into the hot cell where they would load the cesium.

Jalal appreciated the irony of the lead cylinder. It was intended to shield the contents from radiation detectors, and it was called a *pig*. Perfect, he thought, an unclean container named after an unclean animal for the ultimate unclean weapon, a dirty bomb. Once the lead shield was in place, the drum would be filled with lubricating oil that would hide the true contents in the unlikely event that anyone opened and examined the drums.

There would be eleven more pickup trucks arriving throughout the weekend and all of them would be loaded in the same way. The last of the sixteen cesium containers would be loaded in identical drums and placed in the four cargo vans that they had brought with them. His men would take two of the vans, and the four guards from the other cell would drive the other two. Hadi would take the Buick. Everything would be put back in place before they left, and with luck, it would be lunch time or after on Monday before anyone knew there was a problem.

1.04   INTERSTATE 40 WEST, HARRIMAN, TN

The female voice with a vaguely European accent told Roger Aikens where to go.

"Right turn ahead. Then, take the motorway."

"Did you hear that," his passenger, Bill Morse, asked.

Roger nodded his head just once without taking his eyes off the road and said, "Yup. Turn right."

"Not that. Shit, the sign tells us that. No, I meant 'motorway.' What the hell is a motorway? It's a fuckin' British interstate highway. Except, of course, Britain doesn't have states so they can't have inter-states, can they? They have counties. So they call it a motorway. Couldn't very well call it an inter-county highway, could they? This is some Belgian's idea of how Americans talk. Did you know that these GPS's are made by a Belgian company? Why can't they get the language right? Better yet, why didn't we buy an American GPS instead of this foreign crap?"

Roger said nothing, familiar with Morse's constant rants, his know-it-all attitude, and his impatience with anything non-American. Roger thought of him as a *wefe*, world's expert on fucking everything. Roger was Morse's perfect foil – imperturbable, quiet, patient, and mostly silent. He just continued to listen as he angled up the entrance ramp onto I-40 West, thirty minutes into their fifty-two hour trip to Seattle. To Roger, Morse was something like talk radio, but with good reception no matter where they were.

He'd listened to Morse all the way from Boise, two days of constant chatter on every conceivable subject. Billboards and road signs were like cue cards to Morse, sending him off on verbal tangents that quickly digressed from the original subject into unpredictable new realms, all of them entertaining if only for the curiosity of where he would go next.

"So, what the hell do you suppose is in that drum back there?"

Morse had obsessed on the purpose of the trip for most of the drive east from Boise, and now that they sort of knew they were simply hauling cargo, it looked like he was going to obsess on the drum for the whole trip back.

They'd been given the pick-up truck the previous Wednesday, painted with a Kwik-Lube company logo on the doors and three 55-gallon drums in back. They had no idea what was in them, but the way the truck crouched on its rear springs and sloshed through corners they knew they were heavy. The instructions were simple – drive to Knoxville, Tennessee, check into the Super 8 Motel, and press 1 on the speed-dial of the cell phone that came with the truck. After resting for the day and sleeping at the motel, they were given an address to put into the GPS, to arrive there at 6 AM Saturday morning, and to press 2 on the speed-dial once they got there.

At their destination, they put on the black hoods, like ski masks, only a lighter fabric, and drove into the building. Instructed not to talk or leave the truck, they watched similarly hooded men open one of the drums, attach a crane to its contents, and lift out what looked like a dull metal cylinder. About an hour later it had been re-loaded into the drum and the lid attached. One of the hooded figures, the apparent leader of the group, directed them to exit through a roll-up door on the opposite side of the building. Once clear, they'd pressed 3 on their speed-dial and received a Seattle address that they'd entered into their GPS.

"Did you see the sign on that building," Morse continued as they drove west toward Nashville. "It said Pastor Technology. Technology. Get it? We've got some high-tech weapon back there. I'll bet it's a bomb. No, why would they need high-tech to make a bomb? Unless it's an atomic bomb. Now that's high-tech. But who would make an atomic bomb in Nowhere, Tennessee? All that shit is done in secret army bases, or maybe in them FEMA death camps with slave labor!"

Roger listened to the monologue, somewhat curious himself. Morse riffed through every high-tech weapon he could imagine that would fit in a metal cylinder, and he finally said, "I've got it! That Pastor place is a secret government lab and they've developed some designer virus that only attacks specific DNA, like if you're a nigger or a kike or something. You know they have different DNA, don't you? Things that are wrong, you know, at some microscopic level and that's why they come out black or all hook-nosed or whatever. I'll bet they want to use it on those A-rabs, too, and get all that oil. This is probably some test to see if it works in the real environment, not just in some lab. She-it. How cool is that?"

Roger spoke for the first time since entering the interstate.

"Can't be no government lab. No way they'd give it to us."

"You're right," Morse said, snapping his fingers. "The Army'd be testing it on some Mexicans or something. It's got to be one of ours. That's why they put it in East Podunk, Tennessee. No one would expect us to be there. Hell, they think we all live in Montana or Mississippi. They just don't get it, do they? We're fucking everywhere, and now we've got a secret weapon. And we're taking it to Seattle. You know why that is, don't you? What do they do in Seattle? They ship shit to China, that's what. Maybe this is going over there and we're going to melt some chinks. Fuck! This is great shit."

The GPS interrupted Morse, instructing Roger to exit in two miles and then follow the motorway. He wondered what the next program on Radio Morse would be.

SUNDAY, JUNE 20

1.05   INTERSTATE 59, PICAYUNE, MS

Billy Ray Jr. was driving his three-hour shift in the big pickup truck when his father awoke and simply said, "I'm hungry. Get off at the next exit," and went back to sleep. Junior was tired. They had been driving non-stop for eleven hours since picking up the mysterious drum in Tennessee the day before, and a break would be welcome. Nine miles later, at the Memorial Boulevard exit in Picayune, Mississippi, he did as he was told, that being the only possible choice in the family of Billy Ray Ebbers, Sr.

"We're getting off, sir," Junior said in a normal voice, knowing that it would be enough to instantly rouse his father, and that he would immediately be fully awake and attentive.

"Good." Billy Ray Sr. glanced around and said, "Turn left and head for that Chevron station."

At just before 7 AM on a Sunday morning, there was little traffic and few customers at the station.

"Gas it up," Senior said, handing Junior two twenties, "then park over there at the Waffle House across the street and wait for me. See that spot right in front? That spot. Don't leave the truck, and keep your gun handy and hidden. Any trouble, you shoot and keep on shootin' till I get here. No one gets near them drums. Got that?"

"Yes sir, I do."

And he did. They were on a mission. A military mission, and Billy Ray Sr. was in command. Junior didn't understand the mission – he didn't need to. He only needed to understand that his father, the local commander of the White

Aryan Resistance in Southern Texas, had been given this mission and he had chosen Junior as his accomplice.

"I'm gonna eat in there," Senior continued. "I'll bring you somethin' and I'll take over drivin'."

Inside the Waffle House, Billy Ray Sr. took a booth at the window where he could watch the truck and Junior without turning his head. The waitress, a young, African-American, handed him the plastic-laminated menu and asked if he wanted the coffee she was already pouring into his cup. Billy Ray waited until she had filled it and then said, "No."

The waitress – her nametag read Sushonna – glanced up, almost jerking to attention like someone had poked her from behind.

"Just kiddin'," Billy Ray said without a smile. "Shush hoe nah. Is that a African name?"

"It's the name my momma gave me," Sushonna answered, familiar with the Billy Ray's of the world and ignoring the mis-pronunciation, still trying to be civil and salvage a tip.

"You a Christian girl?"

Sushonna didn't answer, instead pulling out the gold cross that hung on a chain around her neck.

"Good. I'll have the steak and eggs. Both done hard. No pink, no runny. Dry white toast with honey on the side. Grapefruit juice. That's for here. Then I'll have one of those egg sandwich things and coffee to go."

"How do you want your egg sandwich?"

"I don't care. However you do it."

Billy Ray watched Sushonna leave and then turned his attention to the truck, backed into the parking spot so it faced the Waffle House window where he sat, just as he knew Junior would do because he'd taught him these things. Junior sat in the driver's seat, glancing around constantly and looking at Billy Ray every few glances, making sure he was still there and he was seeing Junior be alert and ready for anything.

The dawn service at the Covenant of Faith and Truth Apostolic Assembly in Goliad, Texas would be over by now, Billy Ray knew, the first service he'd missed in three years. His senior Deacon would have given the Bible lesson that Billy Ray had written, without any deviation from the text. *Just one more to go*, he thought with profound satisfaction. He could hardly wait for that last sermon, the one that would announce the coming apocalypse. Well, not announce it. Foretell it. That was better.

And once foretold, there would be no turning back.

He finished his breakfast and got the check, calculating a 10% tip and leaving a penny less. It was his standard statement, and he didn't care that no one ever understood it. You are expected to do a good job, he believed, and you shouldn't have to be bribed to do it. 10% was what his small congregation tithed from their income to pay him to run and maintain their church, and the penny less simply acknowledged that no one got more from Billy Ray Ebbers, Sr. than God did.

Taking Junior's sandwich and coffee, he paid the bill at the register and left without a word.

Junior saw all of this and knew the 10%-less-a-penny story by heart. He struggled to climb over the center console into the passenger seat rather than get out and go around because Senior had told him to stay in the truck. In silence, Senior handed him the sandwich and the now slightly cool coffee and started the truck back to I-59 south, heading toward New Orleans.

The silence continued for sixteen miles while they passed Nicholson and Pearl River, turning west on I-12 and passing Slidell, Louisiana and Lacombe and Mandeville. Outside Covington, Junior asked the question that had been on his mind since 4:30 AM that morning when his father had picked him up at Days Inn in Knoxville where they'd stayed the night before.

The question was the culmination of all the questions that had been congregating in Junior's head ever since his father had arrived home on Friday in the strange pickup truck with the sign that said *Rig Services Inc. Houston, Texas*, and the three oil drums in the back. Those questions went unasked on the trip north, along with the new questions about where they were going and why. And now this new information, this escalation that made the drums in the truck a life and death urgency. "Shoot and keep shootin," Billy Ray, Sr. had told him. Not a new directive. In fact, one he'd heard many times before in the context of government and Jews and niggers and such. But not one ever delivered over a 55-gallon drum.

It was finally too much even for Junior's regimented relationship with his father.

"What's in the drums, sir?"

The silence resumed for the seventy-two miles past Hammond and Walker and Baton Rouge, and finally, near someplace called Grosse Tete, Billy Ray told him.

"The wrath of God, son, that's what's in the drum. The day of reckoning is near."

The GPS had indicated 954 miles to their destination when they'd left Pastor, and it had clicked off the miles on I-75 as regularly as a metronome. It read 783 when they decided to get off at Exit 113 for fuel and a break. They had been up and going since 5 AM, and some coffee and food would help get them past the doldrums they were experiencing thirteen hours later.

The four vans that they had brought with them to Pastor and were now using to get to their targets were all heavy-duty panel vans, different from the pick-up trucks in almost all ways. Different design, different drivers, different plans. Same cargo. Sajid was driving and would be the videographer when they got there, recording the event for display on al Jezeera television news. Rasul would wear the vest of C-4 and cesium, and he would be the event. They used a van instead of a pick-up for privacy. The cesium would have to remain in the shield right up until the last minute to avoid detection, and then Rasul would load the vest and put it on inside the van without being seen. He would have only minutes to get to his assigned location and detonate the weapon before he would succumb to the intense radiation.

The gas station was on their left at the T-intersection at the end of the exit ramp. Sajid waited, first in line to turn left on Paris Pike. When the light turned green, he looked left to be sure the intersection was clear, and then drove across the two southbound lanes of the divided highway. He had just started his left onto the northbound lanes when a black Toyota pick-up truck shot out from behind the U-Haul truck stopped on the right. Sajid jerked the steering wheel hard to the left to avoid a collision. The Toyota driver seemed unaware, and suddenly turned left himself, forcing Sajid into the median.

Rasul was thrown into the passenger-side door and as he struggled to recover, he noticed that the heavy drum, tied down in the back, had shifted slightly to the right, but he had no time to consider that. The van slid into the grassy median dividing the lanes and came to an abrupt stop. Both men looked around quickly, trying to orient themselves and absorb the sudden events and process these into their plans. Rasul recovered first and said, "Go." Sajid glanced at him, and then ahead to be sure the way was clear, and jammed the accelerator to the floor, spinning the wheels on the grass and fishtailing back onto Paris Pike, heading away from I-75.

Rasul grabbed the GPS while it recalculated their route and said, "Turn left in 2.4 miles." Sajid had the van up to seventy-five before Rasul told him the turn was half a mile ahead and he started to slow down. After the turn, Rasul said, "In seven miles, take the entrance back onto I-75. And slow down. We don't want to attract any more attention."

The two straps they had used to tie down their very heavy drum were arranged in an X pattern across the top of the drum, hooked to the floor at four points, but not to the drum itself. After Sajid got them back on I-75, Rasul climbed into the cargo area and found it had shifted only a couple of inches, and the straps were all tight. It was too heavy to move, so all he could do was keep the straps tight and hope for the best.

"Rasul," Sajid called, his voice urgent, "there is a police car following us."

Rasul looked over his passenger seat to see the flashing red and blue lights through the rearview mirror, closing fast from behind.

"It came from the rest area back there," Sajid explained. "They were watching for us! What do I do?"

"There is nothing we can do now, my brother. We cannot escape the police on this highway. Our mission is to avoid capture and release the weapon. Drive. Keep us ahead for a few minutes. I will open the container. *Allahu Akbar.*"

Sajid didn't reply, he just pushed the accelerator all the way to the floor and concentrated on keeping the van on the road. Rasul opened the small tool box they had for emergencies and, using his pliers, opened the bung hole in the side of the drum to drain the oil so he could remove the lead plug and get the cesium jar. As soon as he did that, he realized his mistake – the oil on the floor made it impossible to get any footing to open the drum lid. *Fool*, he thought, and tried anyway.

The drum lid was sealed by a locking ring – a circumferential hoop split at one point and held together by a single bolt. Removal was just a matter of undoing the bolt. In a moving van with a slick floor, it became almost impossible. After repeatedly sliding away, Rasul braced himself between the drum and the wall of the van and succeeded in getting the bolt off. He then used the box cutter to cut both nylon straps freeing the lid and exposing the lead plug. He grabbed it with both hands and started rocking and twisting it, like he was trying to uncork a very large champagne bottle.

"Hold on," Sajid called as the van swerved to the right. The now loose drum slid left in reaction, violently throwing off the balance of the van. Sajid jerked the steering wheel left to compensate, and the drum, skating on a fully-lubricated floor, slid back to the right. Rasul didn't even have time to repeat his entreaty to Allah before it slammed into him, crushing him against the wall.

The 1,300 pounds hitting the wall of the already-teetering van was all that was necessary to topple it over, and it landed on its right side, sliding for over 180 feet before coming to a stop facing mostly forward and straddling the right lane and shoulder. The air bag discharged at the impact of the rollover, and the noise deafened Sajid, but left him alive and conscious, held in place by his seat belt and shoulder harness. He looked behind and saw Rasul's upper body protruding from under the drum, now laying on its side, open.

Sajid released his seat belt and fell into the passenger door and seat. Reaching behind, he recovered their duffel bag and then kicked out the shattered windshield. Once outside, he could see the police car stopped some fifty or sixty feet behind, and several other cars off the road or in the median, no doubt because of his accident. In front of the van, he was out of the police vision while he opened the bag and took out both AK-47's and the first of four doubled banana clips, two regular clips taped together for easy reloading. He prayed as he stood and looked over the van at the single trooper, approaching slowly with his pistol drawn. He was saying something – Sajid could see his mouth moving – but his hearing was gone, and he didn't care to listen anyway.

He brought the assault rifle to his shoulder and fired a disciplined three rounds, and Allah answered his prayer as the policeman died without firing a shot. With no immediate threats to him, Sajid emerged from behind the van and went to the closest vehicle, an SUV in the median. The lone occupant, a young man, just stared as Sajid shot him in the head. He started toward a Japanese sedan behind it and two people jumped out and started to run away. Sajid aimed carefully and dropped them both with three shots.

By now, the other car occupants realized what was happening and were running away. The northbound lanes were stopped, cars abandoned as people ran south. The southbound lanes were becoming jammed as drivers gawked and then sped away. At a minivan, he found a woman driver clutching a small child to her breast, crying and imploring him with words he couldn't hear and wouldn't care about anyway. He shot the child in the back, the bullet passing through and hitting the woman in her heart.

Most targets were now out of range and Sajid turned west, setting up for more carnage. The highway was divided by a low concrete wall, low enough that he had a good field of fire across the road. Establishing his firing stance, he put a three-shot burst into a southbound car, and it immediately swerved off the road, uncontrolled by the dead driver. There was no barrier on that side, and it continued across the grassy area and into a wide ditch that separated the road from some houses nearby. He repeated the shot with the next car, and it crashed into the center barrier and skidded to a stop several car lengths past him.

There was chaos now – cars trying to avoid the wreckage and still escape once they understood the cause. He shot and halted three more vehicles while several others escaped, using up the thirty rounds in the first clip. As he released it and turned it over to insert the one taped to it, he saw flashing blue and red lights coming toward him on his side of the road. It was time to seek cover back at the van where the remainder of his ammunition was still in the duffel bag.

He jogged back, pausing to fire at several more southbound cars that had been foolish enough to try to negotiate the wreckage he'd caused there. Traffic was stopped on both sides now, and his targets would come harder, he knew. And there would be police and return fire. He guessed he'd killed fourteen people so far, and he hoped he could kill a few more before he died. There were no houses on his side of the road, just open land and a large, two-story building in the distance. Too far to run. Getting across the street to the houses on the other side would be his best option, providing some cover and possible targets before the police inevitably cornered and killed him.

Grabbing the duffel bag, he ran across the road and vaulted the concrete divider, crossed the southbound lanes, heading for a group of one-story brick houses about 400 feet away. A few people had gathered in their back yards to see what was causing the noise and commotion, and he stopped behind a large evergreen and opened fire. They were well within the range and he hit two before the others scattered back into their houses. Picking up the duffel, he ran toward the nearest house and crashed through the rear door.

He heard noises in the room to his right and started there, kicking open doors and finding an empty den and bathroom. At the first bedroom, he kicked the door open and was surprised when three shots were fired, bullets passing close and hitting the wall behind him. He fired three blind shots into the room to harass whoever was shooting and ran out the front door, looking for less dangerous targets.

He ran across the street to the house there, figuring the further he got from the scene, the less aware people would be and therefore less cautious. The front door was locked, but he solved that with a single shot to the latch and a good kick. He heard the back door slam closed and followed the sound out onto a cement patio where he saw two adults and two children running away. Knowing that he would run out of targets and time before he ran out of ammunition, he fired four three-shot bursts and hit all of them.

The yards of these houses were very large, and he had over 300 feet to cross to get to the back of another row of houses. His hearing still impaired, he didn't hear the helicopter so much as feel the shock waves from the rotating blades and looked up. It was a news chopper, the WLEX Channel 18 logo prominent on the undercarriage. He let it hover unmolested, not caring that the police would have an excellent view of his location if they were smart enough to turn on their TV. News attention, and hopefully some good video for his brother jihadists to see and rejoice at, were all that was left to him. That, and as many more dead infidels as he could manage.

He was tiring, and walked across the lawn. There was no one in sight, and at the next house, he found the back door open and unlocked. He entered and walked through a small kitchen into a large room with a dining area and a living area. On the couch, a surprised woman of about forty looked up from the television and started to say something just before he shot her.

Not stopping to search further, he exited the front door and was crossing a narrow street when the police car came roaring from an intersection to his right. He dropped the bag and emptied the remaining seventeen rounds in the clip into it. The car immediately slowed and drove across the lawn to his right, coming to a halt when it hit the side of the house he'd just vacated. Sajid had lost count, but guessed that was about number twenty.

After inserting a fresh clip, he started down the middle of the road in the direction the police car had come from, figuring that was the most likely area for more traffic and targets. The street signs told him he was at the corner of Mariner Drive and Agena Road, and that was where he died, the bullet from the police marksman at the north end of Mariner Drive, about 700 feet away, entering his chest just to the right of the sternum and about an inch higher than the shooter had intended, but instantly lethal just the same.

***

"Shooter is down. I say again – the shooter is down."

Lt. Alan Slocumb exhaled. As far as he could remember, for the first time since he'd arrived and directed pursuit of the gunman.

"Roger, Sniper 1. Send your SWAT team in to secure."

Slocumb clipped the radio back on his belt and turned to the SWAT team commander. They were in the Mobile Command Vehicle, a twenty-four foot RV equipped with communications equipment and computers and space to work. It was parked on the northbound side of I-75, along with dozens of State Police and Scott County Sheriff vehicles, and many more abandoned private vehicles. The only time Slocumb had ever seen so much chaos was in a movie.

"Witnesses said there were two people in the van. We'll send the robot in to see if the other one is holed up or what."

The radio-controlled Talon robot sped up I-75 at 5.2 mph, easily the fastest moving vehicle on the seven-mile stretch between Exits 129 and 136, where traffic was at a standstill while police tried to gain control and understanding of the situation. The operator had moved to an abandoned vehicle about 500 yards from the overturned van, well within the operating range of his hand-held controller and the wireless signal from the optical and thermal cameras mounted on the articulated arm.

The operator also set up a repeater to transmit the signal back to the Command Vehicle, another 500 yards behind him. In the vehicle, Lt. Slocumb and his team watched the road slide by and the van expand on their screen as the camera got closer. The robot turned slightly left, paralleling the van while the camera swiveled to watch it. It reached the front and the viewers saw the kicked-out windshield hanging by one edge, looking like a flap on the entrance to a tent. The Talon slowed further, approaching the front carefully for a look inside.

The front seats of the van were clearly visible and empty. The cargo area behind was harder to see without any windows. The operator turned on the LED spotlight and extended the arm to peer between the front seats. Slocumb could now see a drum tipped over on its side with someone pinned underneath in a several-inch deep pool of the dark liquid.

"See if you can get a response from him," Slocumb said to the operator.

Through the speaker on the Talon, the operator said, "You there! Can you hear me?" There was no response or movement, even after the command was repeated several times.

"OK. Continue around the van and then we'll decide what to do," Slocumb said.

The operator withdrew, swiveled left, and continued the clockwise circumnavigation. Other than the liquid on the ground with an AK-47 in it, there was nothing unusual.

"Set up in front where you can see both inside the van and the far side. I'm sending SWAT in to check it out."

A three-man team, fully armed and armored, moved in from three different angles. When they reached the van, one moved to the front where he could keep the body under surveillance, and the other two approached the cargo doors in the rear, one positioned further back to provide cover, and the other up close to open them. When everyone was in position, he opened the door and stepped back to the shoulder of the road, out of sight from inside the van. The door slammed into the pavement, and nothing moved inside. Again, the operator hailed the body with no response.

Using hand signals, the SWAT team moved in and with very little time and effort, concluded the man was dead, mostly relying on the fact that he seemed about a quarter-inch thick where the drum lay on top of him.

"We're clear here," he said, climbing out. "He's dead, looks like he got crushed in the accident."

With the threat of armed resistance gone, and with two dead perpetrators and a lot of victims, the crime scene became a scramble between the police trying to preserve evidence and medical personnel performing triage. A perimeter was set up and one of the cops stationed just off the shoulder of the road, about twelve feet from the top of the van. He had been standing there for several minutes when a medical technician walked toward him, intending to get to one of the vehicles further ahead to look for victims. As he passed by, a small pager-like device on his belt suddenly squealed, and both men jumped, startled by the abrasive sound.

"What the hell is that," the cop asked.

But the EMT's attention was on his device, and then on the van, a look of shock on his face.

"Oh, shit. Get out of there," he waved frantically and shouted at the cop as he started running back toward the command vehicle. "Everybody get back," he yelled as he ran. "There's a nuclear bomb or something in the van! Get back! Now!"

A police sergeant grabbed him as he ran by and said, "What are you talking about?"

"My pager went off! There's a shit load of radiation coming out of the van. You need to get everyone out of here! Now!" And with that he took off.

The sergeant keyed his radio and said, "Lieutenant, one of the med techs says his radiation pager went off. We need to pull everyone back."

The call went out on all the radios and several loudspeakers, some mounted on police vehicles and some handheld. The scene, already chaotic, turned to pandemonium with the approximately eighty police, fire and rescue and medical responders moving away from the van, victims in tow, in whichever direction got them the furthest, fastest. As they reached the scene perimeter, they had to in turn move the civilians, stacked up in jammed vehicles on both sides of the highway, and approaching on foot from the nearby community of Moon Lake Estates.

Slocumb called in for the HazMat team, owners of a Talon robot of their own, this one equipped with chemical, biological, and radiological detectors, and they soon had their robot at the van. The fire department operator provided commentary on the readings he was getting at his control station.

"There's nothing so far, maybe just a little above background," he said as the robot moved around the open rear doors of the van and started along the shoulder next to the roof.

"Wait, I'm getting something. Still less than 10 microrem, nothing really serious."

The monitor from the police video showed the fire department robot moving along the roof line of the van, maybe one foot away and still at the rear corner. As it moved slowly toward the front, the operator read off the readings.

"I've got about 40 microrem now. Definitely something here but no biggie. OK, it's climbing, at about 60 now ... up to 100 microrem ... wow up to almost 1000 ... it's now over 1 millirem. Climbing faster, up to over twenty millirem, now! Wow, up to almost 1,000 here, and still increasing. Shit! Wait, can that be right? It just pegged. This thing reads up to 350 rem per hour. That's 350,000 millirem, and it just pegged!"

Slocumb understood something bad was happening, but he had no frame of reference.

"Tell me what that means. In plain English!"

"Well, if that was you standing there in a 350 rem field, you'd be dead in maybe three hours, and dying long before that. But the reading must be much higher because my meter is in overload, there's too much radiation and it won't go any higher. Best I can do is back off and find a place where I can get a reading and then use inverse square to estimate a dose rate."

"I don't know what you're talking about, but if you can, give me some numbers. Then I can call the radiation experts and get some support here."

While the operator relocated his robot, Slocumb went to his computer and pulled up his RAP contacts and emergency notification procedures. RAP stood for Radiological Assistance Program and was run by the Department of Energy's National Nuclear Security Administration. RAP teams, working out of nine regional offices, were on-call 24/7 to assist state and local authorities in any radiological emergency. They had the best technology available to monitor and analyze a radioactive accident or terrorist event. The closest RAP team was based in Oak Ridge, Tennessee, and normal procedures would have them on the way within four hours of notification.

"Lieutenant? I think I've got the best estimate I'll be able to come up with. I'm about two feet from the roof, and I'm getting just under the max reading on my meter, about 350 rem per hour. I'm no expert, and these things depend a lot on the size and shape and configuration of the source of the radiation and any shielding, but if it's in that drum, then there's a lot of lead or something around it except for this one hole, so we're getting a beam of radiation, like a flashlight. That's why we didn't notice it until the tech walked into the beam. I'd say you've got something in there that reads twenty, maybe thirty thousand rem per hour on contact. In your terms, you wouldn't last ten minutes next to it. We've got us a situation here. Oh, and we need to know if it's leaking. I haven't got that kind of equipment."

"Leaking? Leaking what? Aren't you monitoring the leak?"

"Radioactive material. Look, it's like dog shit – I'm just monitoring the smell. I don't know what the shit looks like. If this is a solid piece of cobalt metal or something, then that's one problem. You just can't go near it. But if it's a powder or liquid, well then you need air samplers and soil samples 'cause it's gonna be coming out of there and spreading all over. You know, like Chernobyl."

Part Two – The Response

SUNDAY, JUNE 20

2.01 BELLOTTA RESIDENCE, KENT ISLAND, MD

Looking west over the Chesapeake Bay, the sun was still high enough in the sky that yellow dominated its aura, tinting to orange the closer it got to the horizon. Cal Bellotta knew the orange would soon transition to red as dusk got closer, maybe an hour away. He and his wife, Claire, were enjoying the remnants of a cookout with their neighbors on the patio of their home south of Stevensville on Maryland's Eastern Shore.

Married 27 years, Cal and Claire had bought the home when his government consulting work had taken off and he needed to be near Washington. Neither of them wanted to be in DC or its suburbs, and the Eastern Shore was as close as they could get and still be on the water, something they both wanted. His work took him into the city at times, and all over the country and the world, but much of it could be done in his home office, away from the craziness of DC politics and posturing. Cal's practical approach to problems, his need to analyze and resolve them instead of suppress them, were as much at odds with Washington-think as his wardrobe was with the standard government blue suit. The bureaucrats he worked with every day didn't understand *sprezzatura*, the studied nonchalance of Italian culture, and of Cal with his Sicilian heritage.

They were into the standard end-of-a-crab-feast ritual – picking at crab shells for remnants of meat, dragging dinner rolls through Old Bay spices clinging to paper plates, pouring the last of the homemade black & tan from the pitcher before the ice cubes totally diluted the rich, dark Heavy Seas Peg Leg Imperial Stout mixed half and half with Flying Dog Brewery's Raging Bitch Belgian-Style IPA. Sitting around, pleasantly full and relaxed, the talk turned to Cal's recent trip to Vienna.

"It was not a keynote speech," he said in answer to one of the wives overstating his role at the conference on the growing problem of so-called "orphan" sources — old, discarded radioactive capsules that had served their purpose and were now just a nuisance to their owners and a danger to everyone else. "I was one of a dozen speakers, and I just brought them up to date on the programs we have here to find and secure these. It's a growing problem, and many countries don't have the resources we do. In the wrong hands, just one of these could cause huge problems."

"Well, even so," the wife continued, "a trip to Vienna is so exciting. You really should have taken Claire."

"Yeah, so she could see the sights while I sat in a conference hall all day with a bunch of middle-aged nerds. That would have been fun!"

The smart phone that everyone joked was surgically attached to his waist vibrated, making a sound like a giant mosquito with an on/off switch being cycled to annoy. Cal started – it was the second of his two cell phones, the one with the encryption capability so he could talk with full assurance that no one could intercept the call, the one that never rang with good news. He didn't answer, just looked at the message on the screen.

Claire could differentiate between his two phones, and the look on her face showed she knew which had rung. His guests couldn't, so they paused their conversation politely, waiting for him to take or ignore the call.

"I'm very sorry, everyone, but I have to go. And no, Bill, before you say it, I'm not trying to avoid clean-up."

His friends were aware that Cal worked as a consultant for the Department of Homeland Security, and other, more mysterious clients, and that his training and experience all centered around radioactivity, in all its forms, peaceful or otherwise. They just had no idea how pivotal his job was to thwarting radiological WMD threats. His trip to Vienna had more to do with terrorists and rogue nations than with someone's discarded radio-therapy device.

"Sorry, hon. It's a SVTC in thirty minutes," he said quietly, pronouncing it *sivitz*. "Something is up and I'll no doubt have to go to DC afterward. The Bay Bridge will be impossible with the traffic at this hour, so I'll take the boat to the Academy while it's still daylight and catch a ride from there. I'll call you as soon as I know a schedule."

A SVTC was a Secure Video Tele-Conference, and while Cal could have done that from his home office, the message left no doubt that he would be needed in Washington that night. He waved to his guests as he trotted into the house. He quickly changed from crab-feast casual to business-casual and unplugged his laptop and tossed it and the power supply into his ready bag, a knapsack with basic toiletries, a change of clothes, a digital camera, and a wireless card for a computer so he could get securely online virtually anywhere. As he carried it to the garage, he hit a speed dial code on his personal phone and it was answered quickly.

"Willy? It's Cal. Can you gas up *Oh! Claire* post haste and turn her on and face her out? I've got to fly."

He got an affirmative as he put the knapsack into the vintage Alfa Romeo Spyder Veloce for the short trip to the marina. When he got there he tossed the keys to Willy, the manager on duty, and jumped aboard without stopping. Like Claire, Willy was accustomed to his hurried comings and goings. Usually, though, he was hurrying away from the boat, cutting some cruise short.

The marina was a hundred or so feet off the Bay, and the channel was a strict no-wake zone. Cal's hurried exit rocked a twenty-four-foot sloop, returning under power, that belonged to someone Cal vaguely knew, and he gave an apologetic wave but made no effort to slow down as he launched out of the creek and into the Bay. Willy would explain, he hoped.

Thirty minutes and a ten mile trip across the Bay were not normally compatible, even in a Marlago Sport Cuddy with its twin 250 hp Evinrude outboard motors and a top speed of about sixty mph. Getting to the U.S Naval Academy at the mouth of the Severn River would require negotiating a lot of boat traffic, and after docking it would still be a half-mile trek to Ward Hall, the location of the Information Resource Center where he would find the SVTC facility. He could run it in under three minutes, but he wouldn't be good for talking when he stopped.

But first there was the matter of navigating the mouth of the river and getting upstream to the Academy docks. Late in the day on a beautiful summer Sunday, it would be jammed with power boats and, more worrisome, sailboats of every size, manned by sailors ranging from old salts to students in dinghies. Unlike civilian meetings, SVTC started on time with no preambles, and Cal was pretty certain he was going to be late.

He didn't like being late as a general rule, and certainly not to a work-related meeting. As a consultant, an outsider, he already started every new work relationship as a test, the professional law enforcement and security types being automatically skeptical of anyone who wasn't trained in and married to the program, especially if he came with a Department of Homeland Security label.

The Marlago was up on plane and slicing from wave crest to wave crest at its maximum speed. The Bay was fairly calm with a constant breeze kicking up one-foot swells, and the Marlago handled those like they were expansion joints on an Interstate highway. But there was plenty of traffic even this far out, and he knew that was just the beginning.

Before he got past the midway point and joined the floating rush hour, he decided to clear the traffic he would encounter once he entered the Academy waters. Using his secure cell phone this time, he called the DHS Emergency Operations Center and told the duty officer who he was, where he was, where he was going, and why, and asked that someone make the calls to the security office at the Academy to expedite his arrival, maybe even get him a ride.

The traffic thickened as some amateur regatta finished and all the weekend sailors headed for port to drink beer and tell lies. A squad of teens learning to sail in twelve-foot dinghies played bumper-boat as they tried to organize themselves in the breeze, their teacher standing in his slightly-larger boat shouting instructions and encouragement through his bullhorn. Sport fisherman, most with more empty beverage containers than caught fish, wove in and out, their perception dangerously distorted by sun and alcohol. Cal thought briefly of just shushing through the whole mess at full-throttle like a downhill skier through the slalom gates. Instead, he slowed to a polite no-wake speed and drove like a New York cabby, ignoring anything not directly in front of him.

As he tried to move as quickly as possible without causing harm, his phone rang. The secure one. Caller ID said Unknown Number, but since the only people who had this cell number didn't need to be known to get attention, he answered.

"Is this Dr. Bellotta," someone asked.

"Yes. Who's this?"

"Dr. Bellotta, please give me your full name and the last four digits of your social security number for verification."

"Calogero Taddeo Bellotta. 0602. Now, who is this, and what do you need? I'm in kind of a sticky situation at the moment and talking is going to be difficult."

"Yes, sir, I'm aware of the sticky situation. That's why I'm calling."

Cal was tempted to look around and see if someone had a camera on him. How else would they be aware of his situation? And as quickly as he thought that, he realized the caller was talking about the SVTC, and whatever its subject matter was.

"Make that two sticky situations, then. I'm in the middle of a boating catastrophe waiting to happen and trying to navigate my way clear. Please be brief."

"This is Special Agent in Charge Ted Banks from the Knoxville, Tennessee FBI Field Office. Mitch Wiley over at Oak Ridge gave me your name. Are you aware of the events taking place in Kentucky as we speak?"

"No, I've heard nothing. I've been called to a SVTC that starts in," he glanced at his watch and continued, "four minutes. A SVTC I'm going to be late for. I don't know anything about Kentucky."

"Same one I'm waiting to join. I'll let everyone know you're on the way. When will you arrive?"

"I can call in on-time, but it will slow me down trying to get through this traffic. It'll be twelve, maybe fourteen minutes before I get to the video facility if I don't."

"We've had what looks to be like an aborted RDD attack in Kentucky. A big one. Thousands of curies. I'll be putting teams out shortly canvassing licensees to see if something's missing. I'll need you here fast to provide operational support. My agents will each have a rad-tech from Oak Ridge with them, but I need someone who knows the commercial side of things. I understand you've got a lot of experience and you can guide my guys and tell them what to look for at these different businesses, and maybe even go to any that seem interesting. Where are you and when can you get here?"

"I'm in Annapolis, at the Naval Academy. I can get a commercial flight out of Baltimore or Washington tonight."

"Forget that. Get over to Andrews right after the SVTC. I'll have something that flies standing by. Can't promise what, though."

2.02   FBI Fusion Center, Frankfort, KY

Eileen Daler was dozing in the passenger seat while her husband, Travis, drove east on I-64, just outside of Frankfort, Kentucky. Her long, auburn hair, usually an exclamation point on any sentence describing the striking former college track star, hadn't been washed in two-and-a-half days, and she'd wrapped it up and clamped it to the top of her head with a big, ugly, yellow plastic clip. Her boots were a little muddy and she smelled vaguely of smoke and ash from putting out the campfire after they had packed up the trailer and camping gear to head home from the weekend in Taylorsville Lake State Park. She planned a long, hot bath and a restaurant-delivered dinner when they got there.

Toby Keith was singing when the broadcast from WLLX in Lexington was interrupted by a news bulletin. She sat up straight before the newscaster had finished his first sentence, and looked around, trying to get her bearings. She saw they were just crossing the Kentucky River.

"Get off on 60," she told Travis. "I've got to get to the office."

He didn't argue – he'd heard the news and was anticipating just this.

Climbing awkwardly on the seat, she groped for her go-bag in the back and pulled out her FBI Blackberry and pager. Both were flashing an alert and she cursed silently, remonstrating herself for stuffing them in the bottom of the bag while de-camping. She hadn't heard them ring and so hadn't answered, a breach of protocol. She saw that she'd missed the alerts by forty-two minutes and hoped there would be no repercussions.

The office was in the Kentucky Transportation Cabinet building, about eight miles from their location and a normal fifteen-minute drive. Without any encouragement, Travis made it in eleven.

"I'll call you when I can," she said after a brief kiss. She jumped out of their Toyota Highlander and ran into the modern, three-sometimes-four-story building, fishing out her FBI identification card to open the electronic lock and then wave at the security guard who recognized her anyway, even when she looked like a fugitive in flight.

She stopped in her office to get a pen and notepad and was heading for the Secure Compartmentalized Information Facility, the on-site access point for all FBI computer systems, when her cell phone rang.

"Where are you?" It was Neal Heneryt, her presumptive boss and more accurately, her partner at the Kentucky Intelligence Fusion Center, the regional joint venture between the FBI, the Department of Homeland Security, several other Federal agencies, and all the significant local law enforcement and public safety agencies in Kentucky. Neal and Eileen were the Kentucky FIG, Field Intelligence Group, for the FBI.

"On my way to the SCIF." She pronounced it *skiff*. "Just got here and was going to get updated."

"Come to the EOC. We've got live video and I'll brief you."

The Emergency Operations Center was the size of a small auditorium with four banks of computer workstations facing a wall dominated by eighteen traffic video monitors and three large flat-panel screens, all arranged in one large checkerboard that could be switched to any video feed, commercial or private, from several of the control stations. After dropping her cell phone and pager in a secure locker, she entered and focused on the screens that were showing local news feeds of the accident scene, two from the ground and one from a helicopter.

Neal was at the back of the room, watching the activity and listening to the live audio feed from the Kentucky State Police on the scene. Only a few of the workstations were occupied, and Eileen knew it would fill quickly as the news spread.

He gave her a quick once-over, his eyebrows acknowledging her unusual look, and said, "They've pulled everyone way back. RAP has been called. They're on an N-plus-4 hour protocol, but they're apparently running ahead of schedule and will be leaving Oak Ridge in under two hours from notification. The Louisville Field Office has taken lead and are deploying their Special Agent Bomb Tech team and other assets. HQ is also in the loop and their HazMat HQ is alerted and sending a response unit to assist. The automated alerts have been sent so everyone up to the White House knows by now."

The FBI's nearest Hazardous Materials Response Unit, or HMRU, was based in Quantico, about 500 miles and five hours away, including the time it would take them to load their UH-60 Blackhawk helicopter and travel to the scene.

"The locals are thinking dirty bomb," he continued, "and they're probably right. The radiation readings they were able to get are off the chart, several thousands of curies at a minimum. The shooter was carrying ID as Patrice Abi Nader, Illinois driver's license and University of Illinois student ID. The other one is dead, trapped under the bomb, so we don't have any ID or pictures yet."

"What's the preliminary assessment?"

"Islamic terrorists. Witnesses at the original traffic accident reported the van occupants as 'Arabic-looking.' The shooter is definitely middle-Eastern."

"Do we know anything about the radioactive material?"

"No – only that it's a very strong gamma-emitter. Probably cesium or cobalt. Let's hope for cobalt."

"Yeah, cobalt metal is going to be easier to contain than cesium salt. Any idea where it came from? I haven't seen anything on the LEO Alert."

She referred to the FBI-operated Law Enforcement Online system, designed to provide time-critical national alerts and information sharing to public safety, law enforcement, anti-terrorism and intelligence agencies involved in the war on terrorism.

"No, nothing reported in the last seven months, and even that one was too small. It's either foreign, an old loss, or undiscovered. Not likely foreign as we would have seen that much on our border or transit monitors. And these guys don't keep weapons like this hanging around unused for long, so it's probably not old. My guess is that someone's missing something, and they don't know it yet."

"Oak Ridge is just down the road. They would seem to be a likely source. The security at the National Lab is good. Any commercial sources?"

"In Atomic City? I would guess there's one on every block."

Everyone in the FBI involved in counter-terrorism knew the history, and the attraction of Oak Ridge to the targets of their work. In 1939, Albert Einstein and Leó Szilárd wrote a letter to President Franklin Roosevelt describing the possibilities of Germany developing an atomic bomb, and advising the U.S. embark on a program of its own. The result was the Manhattan Project, and in 1942, the Army Corps of Engineers turned Oak Ridge, Tennessee into one of its main research bases. Over the years, the technology and the knowledge developed there had propagated into many commercial ventures built around the atom, and it became the region's economic foundation.

"I guess I'd better get started, then. I'll contact Nashville."

Nashville was the site of the Tennessee Fusion Center, their counterpart in the region, located at the Tennessee Bureau of Investigation headquarters. By the time Eileen called them, they were already up to speed and monitoring the activity in their own EOC.

"I've got over 700 licensees in Tennessee," Jimmy Reasens told Eileen when she called. "Between them, that's over 800 different locations where radioactive materials are stored and used. Knoxville is organizing a canvass of all of them, but even with state and local help, it's going to take a week or two to cover everything."

"That's too long. And we don't even know it came from there."

"I know," Reasens answered. "We're prioritizing by the type and amount. The information we're getting says it's huge – 4,000 curies? Some radiographer with ten millicuries of cobalt is not our source. And it's a strong gamma emitter, so we can eliminate many of the medical licensees. That cuts our list way down – maybe fifty sites. Knoxville will have those checked in two days, and that should confirm whether it came from here or not."

"I'm sending an alert system-wide. We'll be doing the same thing everywhere until we find it. This is going to be one huge cluster-fuck."

She was right. Neal was still in the EOC when she got back and told him Nashville was on it, and that the Louisville Field Office was lead and responding.

"So is everyone else, it seems. This is going to get out of control in ways our exercises never planned. Everyone wants in on the action. They've been training and preparing for years and now here it is. NNSA is putting its AMS planes up. FRMAC is sending a Consequence Management Response Team. The Kentucky National Guard is mobilizing its Civil Support Teams. The local DOE RAP team and our HMRU are on their way. FEMA Regional is setting up a command post. Shit, I expect someone from the International Atomic Energy Agency to show up on the next flight from Vienna. The good news is that the Lexington ASAC is on his way to take command at the scene. I'm wondering if all these assets and lines of communications are adding too much complexity to the situation. All these other agencies scrambling to be part of the action. We're gonna end up calling this the Con-fusion Center!"

2.03   NATIONAL NUCLEAR SECURITY ADMINISTRATION, WASHINGTON, DC

When, eighteen minutes earlier, the Level 3 Alert had flashed on her screen, Veronica had gone through three distinct reactions in a fraction of a second. The first was surprise – she hadn't seen this particular screen since her training had finished seven months earlier. That led to the second – disbelief. It had to be a drill, some test to make sure the Sunday evening Watch Team at the Forrestal Operations Center at DOE headquarters in Washington wasn't watching 60 Minutes instead of their monitors. The third was action, rejecting the drill notion and recognizing that this was real and only two levels away from "bend over, put your head between your legs, and kiss your ass goodbye," as the joke about protecting yourself from a nuclear bomb went.

Veronica's protocol in such an event was to re-send the alert to the appropriate personnel even though they had no doubt received the original one just fractions of a second after she had on their secure Government Emergency Telephone System phones. Her version included the schedule, login and password instructions for the inevitable Secure Video Tele-Conference that would take place in minutes with most participants using their GETS phones to call in from wherever they happened to be.

Within the DOE, representatives from across the National Nuclear Security Administration would participate. Liaisons from across the DHS, DoD, and other Federal agencies would also be participating. But none of this would happen until Veronica set it up. And she did.

The SVTC started right on schedule and the NNSA Emergency Response Officer called everyone to order from his console in the EOC. He first summarized the situation, then polled the participants for their status.

"RAP. Let's start with you."

While a DOE asset, the RAP program was regional in organization, allowing the fastest response regardless of the location of any incident. The Region Two RAP coordinator, working out of the DOE facilities in Oak Ridge, would be responsible for responding to this incident.

"Our team has been alerted. The incident scene is a tweener, just on the edge of car or helicopter as the fastest mode, and we'll drive it. The team will be on-site around 2 AM, best guess right now."

"OK," the Supervisor acknowledged. "AMS, how about you?"

"We're ramping up the aircraft now. Fixed wing will get there from Andrews in less than an hour from takeoff, so less than two hours before they're on scene. They're flying high and fast, looking for any spread on the ground or in the air. Helicopters should arrive thirty or forty minutes after and take measurements from about 150 feet. They'll be able to pinpoint any radiation source."

"FRMAC, you're up."

"We're standing by until we get the request to deploy. Either from the locals or from RAP or AMS. Right now, it's a traffic accident with complications and there's no indication that we need a local center on site. We have a Consequence Management Team on standby in case they're needed."

"NEST?"

"On our way- first team will arrive in less than 4 hours. For now, recommend you get some type of isotope identifier on it, and get a long count. Either a local CST or our closest RAP team need to send along the spectra to us ASAP."

The remaining DOE assets had no immediate roles to play, and reported so. The FBI and DHS liaisons briefly summarized their status, and then it was the Department of Defense's turn.

"The Kentucky National Guard is mobilizing their Civil Support Team. They can provide additional monitoring and measurement resources, and assist in site security. They'll be under the direction of the Governor, and he'll likely turn them over to the Kentucky State Police command on-site."

With everyone reporting in, the Operations Director closed the meeting with a last directive.

"Everyone keep me informed. It's after 2200 now. Let's reconvene at 0600 and get updates. For now, get the closest CST or RAP to put an isotope identifier on it —and share the spectral data with the incoming DOE NEST Team and everyone else."

2.04 GRAINGER RESIDENCE, FRENCHTOWN, MT

Long before the news crews arrived and started their frenzied coverage of the events on I-75, before the Fusion Center started monitoring the State Police activity, even before the traffic accident itself, Tag Grainger knew it would happen. He didn't know the details, but he knew it would be big news. He'd planned it that way.

When his phone rang, he recognized the Caller ID and answered with a terse, "What?"

The driver of the slightly-damaged Toyota pick-up, still in his seat by the side of the road near Lexington, Kentucky, watching the receding white van, said, "It's done. They're running. Police have been notified and descriptions provided. Next contact will be tomorrow."

Tag hung up without a word. He had Muslim terrorists on the FBI radar. *His* terrorists, as he now thought of them after all these months of planning.

***

Theodore Allen Grainger, Tag for short, had met his terrorists for the first time just four months previously, on what started out as just another cold, quiet Saturday in Frenchtown, Montana, home of 882 people in addition to Tag. Tag was the founder and still the leader of the White Aryan Resistance, WAR, a neo-Nazi hate group dedicated to the eviction, and even the extermination, of Jews, blacks, and other non-Caucasian, non-Christian people from the United States.

Saturday morning was his time to get his silver hair cut short, almost shaved, and then drive to the U.S. Veterans Center in Missoula to visit his wife, Marion. The visits always tired Tag. Not that it required any great physical effort. Even at seventy-three, Tag was still fit, unmistakably a former Marine, starched and pressed and rigid in posture and temperament. He could easily drive the twenty-five minutes to the nursing home, and the walk, pushing Marion's wheelchair around the grounds, wasn't especially strenuous, either. No, it was an emotional weariness that settled over him after each visit. His wife of fifty-two years unaware of who he was, his two daughters married and gone, now a very infrequent plane ride away, no other family, many friends dead and gone. The visits reminded him of the precious little time he had left, and how far he remained from his goals.

Saturday afternoons after the visits were a time for quiet reflection at home, one of the few times Tag allowed himself to think back instead of plan forward. The thinking back was good, though. It helped him remember why he was planning forward the rest of the time, what he was planning and working for - a future more like the past.

Their house had been built in the fifties, and he and Marion had lived there for forty-four years while he worked at his job, showing up each day and giving his best. They'd raised their daughters, paid their taxes, voted in every election, sat on the PTA, went to church each Sunday and every Christian holiday. They'd done what they were supposed to. And here he was, his pension a joke after the company closed, Social Security just enough to buy food and gas, his beloved wife in a state nursing home.

On that particular Saturday in February, he'd closed the front door behind him as he returned from his visit to see Marion, flipping the dead-bolt behind him out of habit. He'd taken two steps before he saw the man sitting in his favorite chair across the room, and he stopped.

The man had risen, smiling, appearing unthreatening. But just being in the house, a stranger, uninvited, able to get past the dead bolt, was an implied threat, and Tag took threats seriously. He hadn't reacted to the stranger, hadn't said anything, just stood his ground and watched him.

"Good day, Mr. Grainger," the man had said with a slight accent that Tag couldn't place. "I apologize for entering uninvited, but it seemed more discrete to wait indoors, rather than on the street where others might wonder who I am and what I am doing here."

Might, indeed, Tag had thought. *You'd stand out pretty well in these parts.* But still he had said nothing, watching and waiting.

"My friends and I would just like a moment of your time," the man had continued, and on cue two men had stepped into Tag's view, one from the hall to the bedrooms on Tag's left, and the other from the dining room behind the stranger on the right. "Please, sit down so we may talk comfortably."

Tag hadn't moved, except to nervously finger the ornate western-style belt buckle he always wore.

"Please, Mr. Grainger. I assure you we mean you no harm. I have been asked by my employer to speak to you on a matter of utmost urgency. A matter that you will find most interesting, and even rewarding."

I wonder why it takes three large young men to offer a reward to an old one, Tag had thought. *What have I done to piss off the A-rabs? At least I hope they're A-rabs, and not kikes.*

When Tag didn't respond, the leader had nodded to the man to Tag's left, and he had strode forward. As he'd reached for Tag's left arm, apparently to guide him to a seat, Tag had jerked his right hand away from his buckle, the hidden dagger with its t-shaped handle now in his fist, the blade extending between his fingers like he was making an obscene gesture, and punched the man in his chest.

The two-inch blade was long enough to pierce his left ventricle, and the man had dropped dead without a sound. Tag had rushed at the stranger, hoping to take out the apparent leader before the other man could react. The stranger had stepped back, unperturbed, giving the other man enough time to reach Tag and tackle him.

Tag had swung the dagger as they had fallen into the Parson's table in front of the large window at the front of the room, and stabbing the man in his left shoulder blade, the dagger deflecting off the scapula and causing a nasty, but non-lethal gash. The man had landed on top of Tag, driving the air out of his lungs and leaving him unable to resist as the two strangers had turned him onto his stomach and secured his hands behind his back using plastic cable ties. Leaving Tag face-down on the floor, the wounded man had stripped his jacket and shirt, revealing the damage the dagger had caused.

"You'll need stitches," the leader had told him. "Go clean it in the bath while I get the kit."

The wounded man had left without a word, and from the floor, Tag could see the leader had picked up a large, leather messenger case from behind the chair he'd occupied earlier. Lying there, his head near the window, Tag hadn't been able to see what they were doing behind him. He'd struggled to swivel his body to get a better view, and the leader had put his foot on the middle of Tag's back, holding him down.

"Just stay still, Mr. Grainger. You have caused an unnecessary inconvenience, and I must see to my men before we can continue our talk. Or start it, actually, as I've noticed your reluctance to speak."

Tag had continued his silence, this time wondering what the *kit* was, why they'd come prepared to deal with wounds, and why they would consider what would normally require a mortician and a hospital visit an inconvenience. He had found no solace in the answers he could imagine.

He could hear and feel the wounded man return, sensing the shuffling and movement as they had attended to the casualties. After several minutes, they had lifted Tag by his bound arms and had set him roughly on the couch. The body was gone, to the kitchen, Tag had guessed, where blood would be easier to clean. The stain on his rug would be much more difficult.

The leader had then sat back down in the chair while the wounded man still stood within quick reach of Tag. If he hadn't stabbed the man himself, he wouldn't have known he was injured.

"You are not a trusting man, I see. My mistake. I should have been more diligent. I now owe a great debt to Sayed's family. But that does not change my instructions. I am here to request that you accompany me to my employer's home for some consultations. Consultations that I assure you will be of the utmost interest to you. And, as I previously noted, quite rewarding.

"You have provoked me greatly, and yet I have not retaliated in any way, nor shown you any discourtesy except to bind your hands to prevent further mistakes. That should tell you several things. First, that you are not in any danger. And second, that my mission is more important than the life of my friend. Now, will you do me the courtesy of some discussion so that we might resolve this impasse?"

"Who is your employer," Tag had asked.

The leader had stared at Tag for a moment before responding. "Very good, Mr. Grainger. You are right to conclude that my identity is of no consequence. My employer, on the other hand, is of great consequence. But at the moment, that is all I am at liberty to tell you about him. As I said, my specific instructions were to request that you accompany me to my employer's home for these consultations. As an indication of good faith, and to prove that we are not here to coerce you in any way, I have $10,000 in cash for you, an incentive to come with me, and it is yours whether you agree to come or not."

From the messenger bag, the stranger had taken several bound stacks of currency and had handed them to the wounded man. He in turn, had removed the paper straps and had fanned the bills in each stack so that Tag could see their denominations, and had then set them on the couch next to Tag.

"I am also to tell you that this gift is petty. The consultations could result in a donation to your cause a thousand times this amount."

1,000 times 10,000 equals 10 million. Tag was good with arithmetic. He was also good with human nature and with conspiracy, and he understood that the only meaningful conversation would now take place with the mysterious employer.

"All right," he'd said. "Where do you want the body sent?"

The leader, whose name Tag still didn't know and didn't care to, had said, "You can handle this? Without, uh, repercussions?"

"Yes. Where do you want it sent?"

"One moment, please," he'd said, opening his own cell phone and pressing two buttons to autodial a number. After some conversation in Arabic, he had asked Tag, "How is it that you can do this without official documents?"

"I can't," Tag had answered. "I'll need your friend's full name and his passport or driver's license so I can have a copy made. He will arrive at whatever funeral home you designate with complete records of his unfortunate death from natural causes."

"One more moment, please," the stranger had said, continuing his telephone conversation. After several exchanges, he had taken a pen and notebook from his pocket and made a note, tearing it from the pad and handing it to Tag.

Without looking at the note, Tag had asked, "Where am I going and for how long?"

"We are going south. It will be quite warm and my employer has extended the invitation for the weekend. You will be back home Monday."

"Are we traveling by plane?"

"Yes. My employer's private jet is waiting for us at Johnson-Bell field."

Tag had nodded and turned to show his hands, still bound by the cable tie. The stranger had nodded to his wounded associate who had picked up Tag's belt buckle dagger and cut the ties, returning the dagger to Tag. Tag turned away and walked to his bedroom to pack. When he had gotten there, he'd closed the door and dialed a number on his anonymous cell phone.

"Josef," he'd said when the phone was answered, "I have some disposal work for you. The trash is in the kitchen. It needs to be cleaned up and packaged properly. Shipping instructions will be on the counter. Send me the bill, and you don't need to economize on this one."

After disconnecting, Tag had dialed another number.

"Marcus, I am going away for the weekend, leaving in twenty minutes. It would be nice to have some company. … Yes, the airport, general aviation. … Good."

Tag had taken a well-used, soft-sided leather satchel from the closet shelf and opened it. He rarely used it for air travel anymore, given the security checks at commercial airports. But general aviation, he knew, had very lax security, and he'd foreseen no problem getting the bag through.

He'd lifted the false bottom and checked to see that his passport and six gold krugerrands were there, safe for any emergency, and to satisfy anyone searching that they had discovered his cache. Then he'd untucked the lining on one of the vertical sides and slid all $10,000 into a pocket sewn there, tucking the lining back under the edge, secured by Velcro. In a duplicate pocket on the other side he'd hid his Glock 26, the sub-compact 9mm he preferred. He hadn't included any additional ammunition. He knew if he ever needed more than ten rounds, it was unlikely he would be alive to use them.

His toiletries kit and several changes of clothes went in, and he'd closed the case, and sat down to wait. He'd said twenty minutes, and twenty minutes it would be.

***

The corporate jet had been aloft for only a few minutes when Tag's cell phone rang. He'd pressed the "Send" button and listened.

"According to the tail number and FAA records, the plane belongs to a so-called energy development consultancy in Houston called Amar Energy. It's privately held, and the owner is Saudi royal family, Ibrahim al Hasan. I'll upload the file."

Tag had disconnected without ever saying a word. The stranger had stared at him, and Tag had stared back, saying, "Wrong number." Then he'd gone back to his phone and read the file.

2.05   AL HASAN RESIDENCE, HOUSTON, TX

In his expansive office in a mansion in the River Oaks section of Houston, Ibrahim al Hasan and his two closest counselors watched the news coverage of the accident on the Fox News Channel. He liked Fox for its more aggressive and iconoclastic style, better serving his mood and his need for more information, even if much of that information was speculation designed more to scare people than to inform them.

After all, scaring Americans was his passion.

His business, like all the other members of the Saudi royal family, was oil and everything associated with finding, drilling, extracting, refining, transporting, and selling it. Ibrahim was a cousin, quite distant but still in the lineage, and his current occupation was Commercial Attaché at the Houston Consulate of the Saudi Arabian Embassy – a diplomat. In that role, he was unremarkable, a dedicated member of the consulate staff who did his job without fanfare, without drawing attention to himself by either achievement or deficiency.

His preoccupation with scaring Americans was the result of the events of September 11, 2001, and that was where he chose to demonstrate his charisma and leadership. In addition to the business that made him rich and the occupation that made him immune, he was the head of the emergent al Qaeda in North America, AQNA to the Federal, state and local law enforcement authorities who had come to recognize the reality of this new al Qaeda affiliate, and who hunted the still-unknown leadership relentlessly.

The few words that were exchanged between the three men watching the sixty-four inch television were all reverent, appreciation that the two martyrs had been able to partially release the weapon, and that they had caused additional mayhem with the shoot-out and the dead bystanders. They wished their brothers well in paradise, with their many virgins.

Ibrahim felt the counselors were sincere in their opinions, and he appreciated their devotion. In his head, he would have strangled both would-be bombers with his bare hands. And he hoped that all their virgins were at least sixty-years-old and ugly.

An accident was not part of the plan, and Ibrahim had no tolerance for anything unplanned. Dead bystanders were all well and good, but a truck accident and dead terrorists and a thwarted mission all made his army look like a joke, reinforcing the image that they were disorganized, foolish rabble, not a highly-trained and skilled military force.

At least the WAR people had gotten away cleanly, he knew, and the two dead imbeciles would focus the investigation where he wanted it to go – Islamic terrorists. Their identification didn't matter – that was part of the plan. There would be no way to track their identity back to Ibrahim, but having it happen five days early gave the authorities a head start. A head start in the wrong direction, as planned, but the more time they had, the more likely they were to discover their error and correct it.

Those authorities would spare no expense to find the source of the cesium and any tracks to where it had gone. The negligence of the two dead martyrs meant that one of the four targets for his suicide bombs was now safe – he didn't know nor care which one – and the increased vigilance that would result from the incident might just cost him another target. But it would not be possible now to stop all three. There was not enough time. If they stopped even one, he would be surprised.

These problems were all bad, and not part of his plan, but they were tolerable problems, deviations to be expected and to be overcome. No, his anger was reserved for his biggest problem – the new al Qaeda leadership who were now alerted to his plan, and how he would deal with them. Since

9-11, the Americans had disrupted the central command and communications structure of al Qaeda, and independent action on his part was encouraged, but this mission went far beyond anything they would have expected that he could pull off. That he could do this alone, without their knowledge, or their money, or any other assistance from them, made him all the more powerful. And there were some who wouldn't like that.

But he wasn't doing it alone. He had some unlikely allies. He was sure that his resourcefulness in developing this alliance would be the key to his success. Back home, that resourcefulness would be interpreted as dangerous at best, and traitorous at worst.

Ibrahim lowered the volume as the newscaster began repeating himself for lack of anything new to say.

"Well, my brothers, what do you think?"

"They served Allah well and ..."

"No no no! Enough about our new martyrs. What do you think we should do now? How will this affect our plan?"

"Ah, yes. That. The plan was always to have the events traced back to our cause, so this shouldn't change anything."

Ibrahim nodded and looked to the other man. "And you, Ismail, what is your opinion?"

"I do not like this, Ibrahim. As I have said all along, involving these infidels is too risky. They are not to be trusted. Once they know that it is we who gave them the cesium, they will turn on us. We are their enemy, they are ours."

"We cannot do this without them, Ismail. We do not have enough people. Already every Muslim is a suspect. We are being watched too closely. No, these WAR men are invisible to the authorities. They will be able to go unnoticed where we cannot. Their soldiers are ignorant. Only their leadership knows the source of the cesium, and they understand the benefits of cooperation in this one action. 'The enemy of my enemy is my friend.'"

"I know that, Ibrahim, but how will you explain it to the Sheik? I doubt that he will share your confidence in this alliance."

"I will explain nothing! The Sheik has failed the mission that Osama conceived and executed with the attacks on New York and Washington. No one has ever accomplished such glory for our cause. I will tell the greybeards in their caves that we are using these infidels to destroy themselves. I will tell them that these WAR fools cannot see beyond their next election, let alone beyond their own pitiful lives. I will tell them that these ignorant heathens make perfect cannon fodder for the coming thousand-year caliphate.

"And I will show them that their time is done. There will be no more hiding in caves. It is our time."

2.06   HOME PAGE OF WWW.THEREALVOICEOFAMERICA.ORG

Mission Statement - The Real Voice of America

"A country divided cannot stand." Abraham Lincoln spoke those words as he set to impose his will and his authority on the Confederate States under the guise of freeing slaves. Freeing slaves had little to do with the Civil War. Lincoln didn't actually proclaim them free until almost two years after the start of the Civil War, when it served his political and military goals. No, like all wars, the Civil War was economic — one side wanted something the other had and didn't want to give it up.

Lincoln was wrong. About a lot of things, but here I mean about a country divided. We are living proof that a country divided can stand. We have stood for over 200 years, the most powerful country the world has ever known. And we are a divided country, more so now than ever.

I'll make this simple to grasp. There are two Americas, a clean America and a dirty America. Clean America is about loving and fearing the one true God, it is about loving your neighbor and doing unto them as you would have them do unto you, it is about the freedom to earn an honest living and keep the rewards of that labor, it is about the right to protect yourself and your family from anyone who would encroach on your well-being, it is about raising your family with the values you hold dear, and about protecting them from the evils of those who don't share those values.

Dirty America, on the other hand, is run by the Zionist Occupation Government that we find has slithered into power on the wave of those who feel they have the right to your money to pay for their drugs and their abortions, and even their food and rent and cars. Yes, this ZOG empire has spread everywhere in our national corpus, like a cancer. Its tentacles reaching out from the birthplace of Christ and grasping for every bit of money and power it touches, corrupting the spirit of that most holy place. And yet it is nowhere, hiding among us like a demon, pretending to love God and mankind, always waiting for the ideal moment to strike and grab just a little bit more of our precious way of life.

I say a country corrupted cannot stand, and Dirty America is a beacon of corruption. A beacon that shines south, guiding foreigners across our borders and into our country to steal and rape and murder. A beacon that shines west, to the yellow countries, offering them our wealth in return for cheap trinkets. A beacon that shines east, to the Arabs, encouraging war and murder in the name of their obscene religion.

The beacon does not shine north, for that is where Clean Americans are gathering, here in the heartland of Real America, and we will not be lured by the foul corruption of Dirty America.

Come and join us. We welcome Clean Americans to Clean America. Together, we can shape a country like the founding fathers of the original America had in mind, before the corruption of ZOG. A country free of drugs and crime, where you are allowed to carry the gun that will keep it that way. A country where an honest day's labor will earn you an honest day's pay, and allow you keep it. A country where abortions are unnecessary because of the values we have instilled in our children. A country where we all speak the same language, where we all worship God and his only son, Jesus Christ, and where we stand together against those who would take these precious gifts from us. Who are right now taking those from us.

Come and join us here in Idaho. Minnesota. Montana. North Dakota. South Dakota. Utah. Wyoming. With your commitment and your energy we can shape the future of Clean America.

2.07 FBI FIELD OFFICE, LOUISVILLE, KY

In the lobby of the Federal Building in downtown Louisville, the directory hanging on the wall between the two elevators reveals a wide assortment of government tenants, from the IRS to U.S. Customs, and even the FBI. According to the directory, there are no tenants on the fifth floor - it is not listed, the levels jumping from four to six. On the elevator, there is no button for the fifth floor. Access is only available from the FBI's dedicated fourth floor space, and only after passing the scrutiny of the FBI's field office security and administrative gatekeepers. This causes much frustration for the permanent staff of the Joint Terrorism Task Force, adding time and steps to get to their offices on that invisible fifth floor.

Inside the fourth-floor lobby, a large number of unfamiliar faces were lined up for verification and, if necessary, escort to the JTTF. Mostly middle-aged men and a few women in all manner of business-casual dress, carrying briefcases or classified courier-approved satchels. A solemn atmosphere, like it was a rainy-day funeral, permeated the group, and there was little bantering or even conversation among old friends and acquaintances meeting up after extended separations. The two on-duty administrative assistants, stressed by this sudden influx of visitors, were processing them and trying to make a deadline that had been set for a meeting only five minutes away. One by one, identifications were established, clearances confirmed, and the visitors approved for access.

There were already nineteen people in the room, and it was only twenty-four minutes since the SVTC notification had been broadcast to the pre-selected list of contacts to respond to a terrorist WMD event, and even more specifically, the subset of people for a radiological weapon. The secure conference room was designed to accommodate forty people at a large, U-shaped conference table so everyone could interact and also have a clear view of the front of the room. The chairs quickly filled, and more would be joining by the secure video system including FBI Headquarters, the National Counter-Terrorism Center, the CIA, and representatives from the President's National Security Staff.

The FBI contingent included the Louisville Special Agent in Charge, Erland Angell "Buck" Buchanan, his ASAC, the JTTF liaison, the assorted JTTF WMD Coordinators, the Hazardous Materials Response Unit Team Leader, and the Special Agent Bomb Technician Leader. Several others would be tele-conferencing in, including the Knoxville Field Office, the Frankfort and Nashville Fusion Centers, and the Lexington FBI Office. It might be a joint task force, but the FBI was clearly running the joint.

The long wall of the conference room had two large, flat-panel monitors that had twelve separate windows open, each tiled in a three-across, two-high checkerboard. Eight displayed people sitting at conference room tables, and four were blank screens waiting for their occupants.

There was a new face in the room, a young lawyer from the U.S. Attorney's Office in Louisville recently assigned to the task force. Everyone looked at him when he said, speaking across the room a bit too loudly, "Can we get started? If people aren't here by now, that's their tough luck."

"In a moment, Bruce," Buchanan answered without even looking to see who'd made the comment. At six-and-a-half feet tall and about 250 pounds, Buchanan did not need eye contact to intimidate, but he could do that when necessary. Instead, he continued his conversation with his ASAC, ending his directions by simply saying, "Watch the lawyer. Toss him if he keeps it up."

At exactly 7:20, Buchanan asked everyone to take their seats. He started the meeting by briefing everyone on the current situation, which didn't take long as they knew virtually nothing at that point except they had a probable terrorism-related threat. The goal of this first meeting was to start everyone addressing it using the same script.

On his screen, he had a list of all the participants who'd been notified. Next to that was a list of everyone who'd logged in, and he could see that four people were missing.

"We're going once around the room quickly with each of you identifying yourself and your agency. Please enter this into the keyboard at your seat and the screen in front of you will display that for everyone. But before we do that, it looks like we're missing four people. Stefanie Levine, my ASAC, has three of them on the line from secure cell phones and she'll enter the information so you can see their names on her screen. Seems we're missing a Dr. Bellotta from DHS."

He said it as if he expected that if anyone would screw up, it would be DHS. Before he could say more, Ted Banks spoke up via the video system.

"Buck, it's Ted. I just spoke to Bellotta and he's on his way in. Seems to be having traffic problems but he should be at his SVTC facility within six minutes. I've briefed him on what we know and told him to get to the facility rather than try to conference in by cell phone."

"You know this guy, Ted?"

"Not personally. He's a WMD rad-nuke expert recommended to me by Mitch Wiley over at Oak Ridge. You may remember Mitch from our field office days. Retired three years back. Bellotta will be coming down here after the SVTC to work with my agents doing the canvass of the radioactive materials licensees."

"Yeah, OK. Let's not get ahead of ourselves. Fill us in on that when we get to it. We'll start and Stefanie will bring Bellotta on line when he gets there."

Buchanan provided a summary of the situation that took less than a minute as there was very little to summarize beyond what they'd all heard on the news.

"OK people, here's what we've got. I'll want your comments and any additional information, but let me get through my list then we'll open it up.

"First, we have a 2002 white Ford E150 cargo van registered to a Patrice Abi Nader in Illinois, Illinois plate number 520-5303. We're researching its history now – who bought it, when, where, insurance carrier, lender, and so on.

"Next – the terrorists. Both dead. There was a near accident at Exit 129 off I-75 and the cargo van fled the scene. It crashed after a brief chase, and one of the terrorists, still unidentified, was killed, crushed by the loose container in the back. The other, the same Patrice Abi Nader, fled the scene on foot after shooting and killing two police officers and eleven civilians, and wounding six others. He then went on a rampage through the neighborhood of Moon Lake Estates, killing six more civilians, wounding three. He was shot dead by a KSP marksman. The shooter was using an AK-47, and we're tracing it as I speak.

"During the investigation of the crime scene, radiation, lots of radiation, was discovered emanating from the van. Initial probes indicate very high radiation levels concentrated in a beam. At least one officer has been hospitalized for observation.

"Let's see. Anything else? Oh, yes, a cell phone and a video camera were recovered at the scene and they are being traced now, as well. That's everything we know at the moment."

He asked if anyone had additional information and got nothing except descriptions of the steps that were being taken to gather information. One of these, a questionable interpretation of the options available under the Patriot Act, brought an objection from the new lawyer, Bruce, and several of the other attendees stated their own objections to his objections, or to the others' objections to his objections, and the meeting threatened to devolve into chaos. Buchanan slammed his hand on the desk and got immediate quiet.

"All right, some valid points. We're going to take a five-minute break and get our thoughts together. OK?"

"No, not OK," Bruce said, pushing well past the point everyone else knew not to cross. "These are valid issues and I don't need to get my thoughts together about them. We can't go off half-cocked, trampling on people's rights and expect to have any legal justification. Fruit of the poisoned tree. Any prosecution will be compromised."

"Nevertheless, Bruce, we're taking a break. Stefanie has Mr. Bellotta on the video and I'm going to bring him up to speed," Buchanan ended the discussion. Then he turned to his ASAC and quietly said, "Take care of this."

Bruce was expounding his opinions to a couple of other members when the ASAC asked if she could have a minute and led him by the elbow to an unoccupied corner.

"I understand your position and appreciate your candor, and you can be sure we'll take everyone's rights into proper consideration, but it's premature to be worrying about prosecution. Right now we've got to do investigation, and to do that effectively everyone here has to be on the same page, so why don't we table this discussion for the moment?"

"You mean bury it. No, it's not ..."

He didn't get the chance to say what he thought it wasn't.

"Bruce," Stephanie said with a little more vigor, "take it up with your boss some other time. Not here, not now. If you persist, you can take it up with him immediately. I'll have you escorted out of my field office and directly there. Am I clear on this?"

None of his law school classes nor either of his previous prosecutorial jobs had covered this particular situation, but Bruce was a quick study and understood that a SVTC under the auspices of the Joint Terrorism Task Force might not be the appropriate forum to debate Constitutional rights.

Things went smoothly and quickly after that, and the meeting wrapped up with the agreement to hold periodic SVTC's until the incident was closed.

2.08   INTERSTATE 75, 15 MILES NORTH OF CINCINNATI, OH

Hadi struggled to remain calm as he watched the news on the television at the Ruby Tuesday restaurant. He was about halfway home to Detroit when he'd stopped for fuel and dinner, and he thought his dining choice fortuitous as they had a television tuned to CNN and he was seeing the report of the accident and shoot-out in Kentucky. Sajid and Rasul had left before him, and their routes were the same for the first 400 miles or so. But Hadi was driving the Buick and had passed them before the accident and missed the live events.

The video alternated between scenes of chaos at the accident site, interviews of various response personnel, and analysis by commentators in the newsroom. It didn't take long for him to get the picture – Sajid and Rasul had crashed after being chased. Both were dead. The talk was of a major dirty bomb attack being averted. The truck and its contents were still on their side, but recovery crews were on the scene and no radioactive material had been released.

He didn't know Sajid and Rasul, having met them only to turn over the keys to the number one van, but their deaths saddened him, and he wasn't sure why. As a devout Salafi Muslim, he rejoiced in their death, and in their martyrdom. At the same time, born and raised in Detroit, he was disturbed by the mass murders these men committed following the accident, as they were not part of *jihad*. An ex-soldier, he was familiar with violent death, and felt saddened for the innocent victims.

With the radiation scare the news was reporting, they must have opened the container before the crash, as their contingency plan required. *Release the weapon before all else* was the prime imperative. If the container was on its side and open, then there was a good chance the cesium would be released despite the recovery efforts. It was in a fragile glass jar, designed to shatter easily, and cushioned in the shield cavity. It wouldn't take much disturbance to break it, and Hadi wasn't convinced that it hadn't already broken and the authorities were covering up the extent of the danger.

He finished his hamburger, fries and Coke and paid the bill. On his way back to the Buick, he thought about how much worse it would be when all the other bombs went off. Today would be a holiday compared to the fear, chaos and damage they would cause. America would topple, and Allah would reign, they had told him. He was not convinced.

Brenda Byrne was asleep in the back seat. Well, not the seat, Wilson McAllister thought, but the back seat area. They had folded up the seats on the trip east from California two days ago and put in an inflatable mattress they'd bought at a Target store along the way. They had decided to do that when it was clear that making love on the narrow rear seat of the crew cab was best left to teenagers.

The trip east had been their get acquainted time, having met for the first time when McAllister had driven the truck down from his home in Stockton to pick her up. He'd told his wife he would be away on business at the home office in Delaware for the week.

He picked Brenda up at the pre-arranged location, the Yucaipa Valley Inn near her home in Calimesa. Even with the assurances from her local WAR leader that McAllister was a good and true "WARrior", Brenda had been reluctant to show a strange man where she lived. Some of the men she trained and worked with in WAR were not anyone she would let near her in the real world.

They had been crowded together for over fourteen straight hours and were on their second rest break of that trip east, at a rest stop west of Albuquerque, when he'd raised the nerve to kiss her before they got back into the truck after eating dinner. She had been very close to him at the time, and the physical contact momentarily overcame his uncertainty, and he just did it. Thinking back now, he realized that the physical contact had been intentional by her, and he was glad she had opened the door that little bit.

At that moment, the trip had become the adventure of his forty-seven-year lifetime. An adventure he had not foreseen nor would have ever predicted. They'd told him he'd be picking up a woman as his teammate, but given the women of WAR in Stockton, he'd expected a tattooed biker chick, not a classy and intelligent divorced woman ten years his junior, or so he guessed. He felt like James Bond, maybe on the senior tour of secret agents, but a secret agent with the beautiful woman just the same.

The radio was on with the volume down to let Brenda sleep, but the word 'terrorist' seemed to jump out of the speaker right into his ear, and he turned it up to hear a report about some shoot-out in Kentucky that had left dozens dead. The report was sketchy, but it seemed that Arab terrorists had arrived in middle America, and he wondered why they would choose Kentucky to attack. *This*, he thought, *is the reason I'm on this mission.* Every day they moved closer to the goal – a revolution in America that would put people like him and Brenda in charge and rid the country of the disease of multi-culturalism.

The Tea Party movement was like the appetizer before the banquet, and WAR was the main course, in his mind. Sure, most of the soldiers he worked with were barely literate thugs, but there was a core of good, solid middle-class Americans ready to assume responsibility for cleansing the country. And the others, the thugs, were the soldiers necessary to do the dirty work that would be required. Wilson knew he could make the plans and give the orders and review the results, but he also knew it wouldn't be him hanging the niggers and Jews and others from trees and lampposts and makeshift gallows, it wouldn't be him standing in line at the firing squads with a rifle, and it wouldn't be him going house to house to root out the trash that would need to be disposed. Soldiers were a good thing.

It was Brenda's turn to drive, and McAllister pulled in at the next rest stop, a simple parking area with one building housing some toilets and vending machines. The change in motion woke her and smiled at him and said, "Hi, Sugar. My turn?"

They both got out to stretch before settling in for another three hours, and took the time for a long and, for McAllister at least, stimulating embrace. They had one rest period to go before arriving in LA, and he wondered how he would be able to continue their relationship after the delivery.

"Anything happen while I was asleep?"

"No. it was quiet. Except for you snoring."

"Snoring! I don't snore!"

McAllister smiled and looked at her. "Just kidding. I was probably still breathing heavy."

"Yeah, you old men have trouble keeping up with us young girls."

"That's the truth. There was something on the radio about a terrorist attack in Kentucky. Couple of A-rabs with automatic weapons shot up some little community there and killed a bunch of families."

"What? Tell me what happened."

"I don't know. The news was very sketchy. Just that two men with automatic weapons shot up some cars and broke into homes and killed twenty people or so in some little Kentucky town."

"Twenty people? Jesus! Can you imagine that? Sitting at home, watching TV or having dinner, and a couple of these Muslim jerks come busting in and shoot everyone? Did they say anything else?"

"That was it. I'll turn on the radio and see if there's more."

"Something's got to be done about this," she continued. "We ought to round up every Muslim in the country and boot them. Screw the Arabs. We've got plenty of oil in Alaska and offshore. It's about time the government turned us loose to go get it. Then see how important those rag-heads are when the price drops to twenty bucks a barrel or something."

This was a side of Brenda that McAllister hadn't seen, and he was surprised and a little envious of her passion. His own allegiance to the goals of WAR came from a belief that other races were inferior, that science had proven that, and if the United States of America didn't acknowledge that soon and do something about it, it would be too late.

"Well, it's not going to happen as long as we keep electing those assholes in Washington," he said. "Republicans, Democrats, doesn't matter one little bit. They're all just politicians out for their own money and power. The time is coming when we've got to take it all back and run this country like our Founding Fathers intended. 'Tree of liberty' and 'blood of patriots'. Just like Jefferson said."

They rode in silence for the rest of Brenda's shift, and made love at the next scheduled rest stop like it would be their last chance.

2.10 INTERSTATE 75, 19 MILES NORTH OF LEXINGTON, KY

By the time the official call had come through around 7 PM, Jerry Holloway was already at his office in the Y-12 Nuclear Weapons Plant in Oak Ridge, anticipating the call up from the news reports and packing up his gear. His RAP team operated on an N +4 protocol, meaning they had to be packed and on their way to any incident within four hours of notification.

When they arrived sometime past midnight, state and local police and emergency vehicles lined the road, many with their strobes of blue, red, yellow, and white lights still flashing, giving the scene a carnival atmosphere. The variety of uniforms heightened the effect, with firemen in turnout gear hanging partially attached, soldiers in camouflage, police in everything from trooper browns to SWAT black, medical techs in white, and civilians in suits and business casual and work clothes.

They were diverted off the interstate to the Joint Operations Center set up in an industrial building about 2,000 feet east of the overturned van. As they drove in, Jerry could see dozens of vehicles, from private cars to large wreckers to a couple of busses painted in military camouflage colors. Another trooper challenged them, the third since leaving the Interstate, and then directed them to park on the west side of the lot.

The team waited at their vans while Pete Fair, their team leader, went inside the JOC to get instructions. One of the other technicians had his PRD, a small, handheld radiation detector, out and powered up and said to no one in particular, "six m-r here," letting everyone know they were in a radiation field that was six millirems per hour, about 150 times the normal background level for the area.

"Here's what we know," Fair told the team when he returned. "The truck is a panel van, and inside is a standard 55-gallon drum with the lid off. It's lying on the body of one of the terrorists and in a pool of liquid, they think it's oil. They used a robot to try to see inside the drum, but the radiation levels are causing interference with the digital camera and the images are severely distorted and unusable, so they don't know what's in there. The reading on the side of the drum is about five times normal background, about twenty micro-R, so there's a lot of shielding in there and we can get close as long as we stay out of the beam.

"Jerry – get your gear set up and start your reading. As soon as you have a spectrum, let me know what we're dealing with.

"Art – get your hi-volume air sampler ready and take it over to the hazmat crew just over there." He pointed to I-75 a little southwest of their position. "They'll put it on their robot and we'll grab a two-minute sample at the wreck and read it back here.

"Howard – set up your counting equipment and someone will be bringing you some soil and liquid samples to read. Right now they don't know if anything is leaking or not. The rest of you, get your equipment set up. Let's go find some photons."

Thirty minutes later, they had found all the photons they needed to understand the situation. The air and soil samples were all negative, so there was no leak of radioactive material, yet. The isotope identifier had quickly produced an almost perfect cesium-137 spectrum, telling them they had a very pure radiation source. The problem, as Pete explained to the lead FBI agent, Richard Owescar during the briefing, was that the cesium was almost certainly in a chloride form – a highly soluble and dispersible salt. Their instruments hadn't indicated this, they simply knew that it was the form of almost all industrial cesium. And with the estimate of between 3,600 and 4,100 curies that Jerry had calculated, industrial cesium was the only possible kind.

"The cesium chloride," Fair told them, "is typically contained in a sealed stainless steel capsule. Actually two capsules, one inside the other, for additional safety. The possibility of breaking one during handling is very low, almost impossible. You need some cutting or grinding tools to do that. These sources will give off enough radiation to kill you in a matter of minutes. Because of that, it's almost certain that the cesium is still in the original capsule. The facilities and technology necessary to open the sources are fairly sophisticated, and it's unlikely any terrorist would have it readily available."

"Last thing before I open this up to discussion," Agent Owescar said. "We got a flexible-stalk webcam into the drum and out of the main radiation beam, and got some pictures. Here's what it looks like."

He typed something into one of the computer keyboards and the flat panel monitor on the wall came on. A grainy, black and white video showed the inside of the drum. The camera continued to move closer, and they could see the cavity and something inside it. Whatever it was, it was flat on top and filled most of the cavity, leaving very little space between it and the walls of the shield.

"It's not a sealed source," Pat Fair immediately said, "although it might be some sort of holder for one or more sources. They'd have to be stacked because that hole is a pretty small diameter. I would guess it's the top of a metal can, and the sources are inside it. See the wire coming out of the top? That's likely a bale to use to extract the cesium container. It probably came loose from the plug when it tipped over. Normally you would pull out the plug and the container would come with it."

"The question is," Agent Owescar said, leaning forward, "how are we going to put this genie back in the bottle?"

MONDAY, JUNE 21

2.11   FBI FIELD OFFICE, KNOXVILLE, TN

The flight on the DEA-confiscated, twin-engine Beechcraft that had been waiting at Andrews was comfortable enough. Cal had even gotten a few moments of sleep, following the rule from his military service – sleep whenever you can because you never know when you'll get another chance.

At the Knoxville Airport, a car and agent were waiting to shuttle him to the FBI Field Office. By the time they got there, it was nearly 1 AM. Based on what he learned from the agent escorting him, he was not surprised to find the offices lit up and bustling with activity. Anyone awake in the residences across the street would have been justifiably concerned about why the entire Knoxville FBI seemed to be on duty.

From the pictures and trophies in his office, Cal learned that Ted Banks was an ex-college football star at the University of South Carolina and drafted by the Atlanta Falcons, although there didn't seem to be any mementos of playing. In his early fifties, he still looked the part – tall, trim, and confident.

"You know this guy," Banks asked after they had settled in with coffee files. Banks was briefing Cal on their initial assessment of the radioactive materials licensees most likely to have significant cesium inventories, and the first one that they were going to inspect.

"We've met, and usually under some adversarial condition. Some of my early consulting was nuclear safety and security work, and I've done independent audits there. Pastor was fine on the safety, but not because he followed procedures, just because he was careful. His idea of security was always 'Why bother? Who's gonna steal this stuff?' He's a very smart man. Smart enough to think he knows better than everyone else and can make up his own rules."

"So you're familiar with his business? And his facility?"

"I've been there several times. Once when it was discovered he had about 20% more radioisotope inventory than he was licensed for. We spent several weeks going through his inventory and documentation and procedures. I then wrote up a set of recommendations for reorganizing his operation and reporting. That cost him a lot of time and money, and I expect he doesn't have good feelings about me."

Banks sat for a moment with his hands cupped over his nose and mouth and his eyes closed. Then they popped open and his hands dropped to the table. "Good. I want you to accompany my team there. You know him and his operation, and he knows you know your business and his. He'll be less inclined to argue and more inclined to cooperate. OK, let's get going. You'll accompany Agents Spellman and Phillips. Enjoy your reunion."

2.12   PASTOR TECHNOLOGY, INC., OAK RIDGE, TN

Waking was not a problem for Kenneth Pastor, Sr. He did it easily and repeatedly. Falling back to sleep, on the other hand, was. So when the first ring of the phone woke him at 3:16 in the morning, he was instantly irritated. 3:16 in Oak Ridge, Tennessee meant 12:16 AM in California, and his first thought was that Ken Jr. was back in some kind of trouble. He debated not answering, but when he looked at the caller ID on the handset, he saw an 865 area code. That was local.

After a terse and guttural answer, someone asked for him, and he said, clearing his voice, "This is Kenneth Pastor. Who the hell is calling me at three in the morning?"

"Sorry to disturb you, Mr. Pastor, this is Special Agent Spellman of the Federal Bureau of Investigation. I need to meet with you right away."

"What's wrong? Is it my son? What's he done?"

"Sir, I don't know anything about your son. This has to do with your business, and as I said, I need to meet with you right away."

"My business? What's wrong with my business? There haven't been any alarms."

"Mr. Pastor, sir, this is better discussed in person. Can you meet me right away?"

"Well, I suppose so. Where? At my office? It will take me some time to get dressed and get there."

"Please hurry. I'm parked in your driveway and I'll drive us there. We can talk on the way."

"Now hold on. I'm not coming outside and getting in a car with some stranger who claims to be an FBI agent based on some phone call in the middle of the night. I'll need some proof, some ID or something."

"I'll be glad to show you my credentials, Mr. Pastor. Why don't you hang up, dial 411 and ask for the Knoxville office of the FBI. Tell the agent there that Agent Leroy Spellman is here and you want confirmation. When you're ready, turn on the porch lights and I'll come to the door and show you my ID. Is that OK?"

Bewildered and alarmed at the same time, Pastor did as instructed. Whoever answered his call confirmed Spellman's request for an immediate meeting, and the ID checked out through the window in his front door. His wife, as alarmed as he was, jabbered nervously the whole time he was getting ready and he was almost relieved to get into the agent's car and get away from her incessant and unanswerable questions.

Getting in the back of the big Ford with Cal, Pastor was surprised to see the familiar face.

"I know you. You're that guy the Feds sent to crap all over my records back in '98." Turning to the agents in front, Pastor continued, "What the hell is he doing here? He's not FBI."

"He's here at our request," Spellman answered, "to assist in our investigation."

"Nice to see you again, too, Kenneth," Cal said. Pastor ignored him.

"What investigation? What's this about my business," he demanded. "And why couldn't it wait until a civilized hour?"

The driver started for Pastor's office without any questions or consultation on locations or routes.

"Did you see the news this evening, sir," Agent Spellman asked.

"No, I don't watch TV news. Haven't watched it since Walter Cronkite went off the air in 1981. Bunch of damned entertainment clowns nowadays."

"Well, sir, there's been an incident. Our agents and the State Police in Kentucky have captured some terrorists and a large amount of cesium. We're trying to locate the source of the material, and you are one of the closest licensees authorized to have that much. We'd like to look inside your offices and see if anything is missing. When were you last there?"

"Friday night. I left at about five as usual. It can't be mine. Like I said, I have alarms and security. Wait a minute. How much are we talking about?"

"The RAP team on site estimates between 3,500 and 4,500 curies."

"3,500 or 4,500 curies? Which is it? Hell, don't they have any good instruments? Isn't that what my taxes are supposed to be buying? I could tell the difference with an old Geiger counter."

"Sir, I'm sure they have very good instruments. My information is that they cannot get close enough yet to the actual source to get an accurate reading for their calculations. I take it that you have at least that much cesium in inventory presently."

"I have 100 times that much in inventory, as you call it. It's my business, son. I make irradiators. But I can assure you, my facility is secure and nothing is missing."

"When was the last time you did an audit, sir?"

"That would have been in February. Regular audit by the Tennessee Department of Environment and Conservation. Yes sir, everything was in order."

Pastor knew that was an exaggeration. There had actually been three findings regarding violations of his own and Tennessee procedures, but none of these had anything to do with how much cesium he had. By that time, they had arrived at the Pastor Technology building and he led them inside, disarming the alarm with a flourish to show them his security. He then took them on a tour, pointing out anything that related to radioactive materials storage and handling.

"See," he said when he was done. "Everything's in order."

"Could we see the cesium, sir? Just to be sure it's there."

"See it! Hell, no, you can't see it. It'd kill you dead. But it's right there, in those lead pigs in the hot cells, just like I said."

"How do you know that on a day-to-day basis? You must have material coming and going regularly."

"Damn right, we do. Every arriving shipment goes into the number one cell over there for verification. We check the isotope and quantity and compare that to the manifest. Then we give it a control number and enter it into our computer. We print out the control sheets you see in the racks in front of the hot cells. That sheet follows the material as it moves through our processes in the different cells so we know what's in each cell at any time. When it leaves here, the sheet is completed and I sign off on it. On every single one. No mistakes here, son. We're careful."

"And the audit in February, how did you verify for the state that everything was here that was supposed to be?"

"We measure the radiation from each source, verify the isotope using our sodium iodide crystal and calculate how many curies are there. Then we match that against the age and the half-life of the isotope to account for decay. If those two numbers match, then it's all there. Simple."

Agent Spellman turned to Cal and asked, "What do you think?"

"We need to see inside the lead shields to verify the sources are there. And then we need to check their integrity and the radiation level to be sure they haven't been tampered with or switched," Cal answered, remembering Pastor's creative inventory techniques.

Spellman turned to Pastor. "Then let's get started, shall we?"

"Get started? On what? You want to do an audit? There's a couple of hundred pigs in these hot cells. It'd take me a week to isolate each one and measure the contents. I don't have that kind of time." Pointing at Cal, he added, "He's just got a grudge against me. Damn near put me out of business last time he showed up. You'll have to trust my inventory records. They're in the office. I'll show them to you."

Cal's patience with Pastor wore thin. "I've got no grudge against you, Mr. Pastor. I was just doing my job, and if you had been doing yours, we never would have had to intervene. We're going to go through the drill again and open every container you have and verify its contents. You and your staff can do it while Agent Spellman and I watch, or he can get a court order and some Oak Ridge techs and we'll do it ourselves."

"Either way," Spellman said, "we start now, and no one is going to be doing anything else in this building until we're done."

"All right, all right. My people will be in at eight and we'll show you that everything is where it should be. We'll be doing this fast, so make sure you're ready."

"That's fine," Spellman said. "In the meantime, I'll have a team here in an hour and Dr. Bellotta can show us how to get it done. That way we'll get three hours of work in before your staff gets here and maybe we can wrap this up quickly."

"What is so important that it can't wait until my people get here, for Christ's sake? You're not going to find anything here that is going to help. Why don't you go chase these terrorists instead of bothering me?"

"Mr. Pastor, we don't have time to debate this. You of all people should understand the potential for disaster here. That is enough cesium to kill a lot of innocent people. And to shut down a major interstate highway. The economic costs of it getting loose are staggering. We've got to safely contain it, and we don't yet know what we're containing. We can't get a good look at the material where it is, so we need to know where it came from, and then maybe we'll get some clues on how to handle it."

"Oh, all right. I'll phone my Operations Manager and have him get a crew in here now. In the meantime I'll start opening the pigs myself. This is going to be a waste of time, and you can bet I'll be talking to my Congressman tomorrow. This is God damn outrageous."

After making the call, Pastor went to the number one cell on the far left and powered up the inside lights and the manipulators. He took a stack of papers out of the metal rack attached to the front wall and started leafing through them.

"Cesium, you say? OK, we'll start with 3407. It says here it has a 2,200 curie source that's twelve years old. That means there's maybe 1,700 curies left, taking into account the half-life of cesium. Let's open her up and see."

Pastor took a control box hanging from a cable at the left side of the hot cell and used it to activate the internal crane that serviced all the hot cells from inside. He lowered the small hook and deftly guided it under the lifting bail on the lead cap of the pig. Once he was certain he had the bail in his hook, he raised it, lifting the lead plug and exposing the contents.

"See there? That's the top of the stainless steel source. It's in a little basket to keep it upright so we can grab a hold of it easily. Told you. Nothing missing. Let's look at another one, shall we? This might not take as long as I thought."

"Wait," Cal said. "Please run it through the multi-channel analyzer and verify that there is in fact 1,700 curies of cesium in it."

"That is a double-encapsulated stainless-steel source, Bellotta. Of course the cesium is in there. It would take you ten or fifteen minutes with a high-speed cutter to get into it safely. And then you would have to get the packed powder into some other container, seal it, put the empty stainless-steel capsule back in the lead pig and put the lid back on. Then put your new container into some shield to move it. Why would anyone bother? You want the damn cesium you just take the source. Better yet, take the whole pig and then you're safe while you're moving it around."

"Kenneth, we're going by the book here," Cal said. "We will check each and every source against your inventory. And, I'm going to have a team come here and review your inventory records and be sure they are in order and that you've accounted for every picocurie of material that has come through here. I've done it before, so it's no mystery to me. We should get started and maybe get done in the next couple of days."

With a dramatic sigh, Pastor went to the manipulator and used his right-hand to grip the controls and to maneuver the slave end inside the hot cell to clamp onto the top of the capsule.

"I put it into the box you see in the corner. That has a shielded sodium iodide detector connected to our multi-channel analyzer in the instrument control room. We go there, and you'll see a spectrum for cesium."

"Stop," Cal said when Pastor had the capsule just above the lead container.

"What for," Pastor asked.

"That source. It looks like it has a flat bottom, not hemispherical like it should be."

Pastor looked at the source gripped between the fingers of the manipulator. "I'll be damned. What the hell is that?"

He twisted and rotated his wrist in the manipulator handle to swing the source up and point the bottom toward the viewing window, and they all could plainly see the empty, hollow tube.

Agent Spellman reacted quickly. "Stop right there. Don't touch anything else. All right, we're out of here, now."

In the office, Pastor recovered from his shock and wanted control back.

"Damn, son, I've got to get back in there and see what's missing. I've got a business to run. There are people waiting for those sources. You can come with me if you want and see what's missing."

"Mr. Pastor, this building is now a crime scene. No one goes anywhere in here without my approval. I've got a forensic team on their way now, and I expect you'll have your building back by the end of the day or tomorrow at the latest. Now we're leaving the building and waiting outside."

While they waited, Spellman called his supervisor and reported that they had found the source of the missing cesium.

"Why the hell would they do that," Pastor asked of no one in particular. "That's a lot of work when you could just pick up the whole shield and be gone in five minutes. Hell, that's hours of work."

"They're making weapons, Kenneth," Cal explained. "Sealed sources are inherently leak proof, making them useless if you want to build a dirty bomb. And if they're going to remove the cesium anyway, what better place to do it than here? You've got all the facilities and equipment to do the job. They couldn't easily duplicate that. So they opened them here and put the cesium in something they can easily break. Ceramic, clay, or glass, most likely. Your cesium is in a jar someplace."

"Agent Spellman," Cal added, looking at the agent on the phone, "let them know it's fragile. They don't want to be banging it around."

2.13   W. Roosevelt Street, Phoenix, AZ

"Fuck! There's no answer." Lou Dressler slammed the butt of his hand into the dashboard to emphasize his outburst.

"You sure you dialed right?"

"*It's a goddam speed dial,* for Christ's sake. One fucking button. Yes, I dialed right."

Dressler was really angry with the other half of his team, Cliff Bergeson, who was currently driving the final leg of their thirty-eight hour trip to Phoenix. It was supposed to have been a thirty-six hour trip, but Bergeson had pulled into a rest stop near Tucumcari, New Mexico when he'd gotten too tired to drive the last two hours of his three-hour shift at 5 AM Sunday morning. He hadn't bothered to wake Dressler, asleep in the back seat of their crew-cab Ford pick-up, and so they'd lost two hours while Bergeson had grabbed some unscheduled shuteye.

The driving rules had been simple and exact and were to be followed precisely – two, three-hour driving shifts and then a two-hour break to eat and rest. Stay at the speed limit. Keep a low profile and avoid any notice. Dial three when they left Pastor, four when they arrived at their destination, and five if there were any delays or emergencies. And if for any reason things went wrong, shut up until a lawyer was sent to defend them.

When Dressler had awakened around 6:30 and found them stopped, he wouldn't dial five. He was too pissed at Bergeson to do it for him, and Bergeson was too embarrassed and scared to do it himself. An impasse, resolved by putting it off, knowing they could dial it at any time in the next twenty or so hours, any time before they got too close to Phoenix. After a while, it got easy not to call, so they hadn't.

"What are we going to do," Bergeson asked.

"We're gonna dial five like you should have when you fucked up. Pull over. I'll drive, you call."

"Why don't you just call?"

"*Because I didn't fuck up.* You did. I'm not taking shit because you don't have the brains of a fucking toad. Now pull the fuck over and call."

Bergeson checked his mirror saw little traffic behind him on I-17, put on his turn signal and pulled to the shoulder, then putting on his hazard blinkers. In silence, they switched, Dressler tossing the phone to Bergeson without a word.

"Let's wait here while I call."

"No. We're too obvious here. A cop might come along and think we're broke down or something. Then we'll be on the record somewhere. I'm going. You just call."

Bergeson dialed five and the call was answered before the second ring. "What's the problem," a male voice asked.

"We're just north of Phoenix and there was no answer when I dialed four."

"You're late."

"Yes, we had some delays earlier."

"Where are you now? Exactly."

"Wait a minute. OK. We're passing mile marker 199. That puts us five miles north of I-10."

"Here's the new address to enter into your GPS. 301 West Roosevelt Street. Someone will meet you there."

The line went dead, and Bergeson said, "That wasn't too bad. We've got the address and someone will be meeting us. See? No biggie."

"No biggie! Jesus, Cliff, you just don't get it. This is not an adventure. We're not on a fucking vacation. *This is a mission!* How long have we been fucking around play-acting like we're really gonna rid America of kikes and niggers and beaners and rag-heads? Six years? And now we have an actual mission. We're doing something besides running around in the woods pretending to fight.

"You think we're gonna find all those foreign assholes in the woods waiting for us to sneak up on them and slit their throats? Shit no. They're in the cities. And where are we going with whatever the hell we've got in back? A city, you idiot. I don't know what is back there, but if they tell me it'll kill a bunch of niggers and Jews, then I'm all over it. You understand? We've got to do this right. When we get there, just shut the fuck up and I'll do any talking that needs doing."

The address at the end of W. Roosevelt St. was a fenced-in lot with several corrugated metal buildings, ranging in size from a two-car garage to a small airplane hangar. Junk metal in all forms, from car skeletons to old pipe and steel plates, littered the yard, leaving some paths for vehicles to navigate. The sun had been up almost an hour, but at 6:17 AM, there was little activity.

Dressler drove inside the open gate and stopped, unsure what to do next. Then he heard a loud whistle and saw a man waving them to come ahead and turn right. He followed the man as he walked through the yard and stopped at one of the buildings with two roll-up doors. He opened the left-hand one and signaled Dressler to drive inside, and then pointed to the left and had him park nose-in against the metal wall.

Dressler and Bergeson got out of the truck and went to the rear end as the man closed the door and came over to them. "What happened," he asked.

As instructed, Bergeson shut up and let Dressler answer.

"Nothing special, we just got behind and didn't want to speed to catch up. Figured it was more important to arrive a little late than to get a speeding ticket."

"So there were no incidents? Just traffic?"

"Yeah, that's right."

"You shoulda called earlier. You don't show up and we don't hear from you and we start to worry a little bit."

"Yeah, I know. We just lost track of how far behind we were. Anyway, no harm done, right? We're here and everything is fine. Now what?"

"Now nothin'. Gimme the keys, get your gear and I'll take you to the bus station and you go home and you shut up. Say nothin' to anyone, not even your squad members. You've already fucked up pretty good. Don't make it worse by blabbin' about the trip. Got that?"

Both men nodded, fully intending to keep quiet, and absolutely certain not to.

2.14 NATIONAL COUNTER-TERRORISM CENTER, McLEAN, VA

**Official Use Only
Law Enforcement Sensitive
Do Not Distribute Outside of
FBI /NCTC/DHS Approved Channels**

National Counter-Terrorism Center/U.S. Department of Homeland Security/U.S Department of Justice Joint Report

Subject: Organized Cross-Border Drug Cartels, Domestic Hate Groups,-and International Terrorism: A Threat Nexus Assessment DHS/DOJ 14507A

Since well before 9-11, many Americans have continued to believe that the only significant terrorist threat to American safety and security is from radical Muslim terrorist cells and foreign al-Qaeda-like organizations primarily directed and controlled from within foreign territories to include Pakistan, Yemen, Iran, Afghanistan, and others. While international terrorism remains the most significant and continuing threat to the United States' safety and security, there is also a real and growing threat to America from homegrown hate groups. There are presently more than 1,000 of these so-called hate groups, with several dozen of them presently under the constant surveillance of the FBI.

These groups are dangerous not simply because they exist, but because their ideology is growing, spreading, and becoming in some cases intertwined with elements of the predominant Muslim Salafi wing of international terrorism. This presents a particular threat to our nation.

Over the past decade, this nexus of common objectives between domestic hate groups and radicalized Salafi terrorist organizations has become apparent. Some of the common objectives that permit these disparate communities to find areas of mutual interest include a shared hatred of Israel and the Jewish people, a moral code that supports the use of extreme violence, the need to demonstrate their respective ideals of religious and moral purity, and a fundamental objection to a pluralistic society associated with democratic institutions and individual self-determination that they perceive as inherently evil and socially destructive.

The link between homegrown domestic hate groups, cross-border drug cartels, and international Muslim terrorist organizations has emerged over the past several years. This nexus between the domestic hate groups, internal terrorist organizations, and the drug cartels has been confirmed by the NCTC and Intelligence Community, and is of grave concern to law enforcement, homeland security, and national defense agencies. The "Los Zetas" cartel provides an excellent case-example of the continuing and growing threat we face from these extremely violent, highly organized Mexico-based groups, and the disturbing nexus to both domestic hate groups and international terrorism.

In testimony before a congressional committee, the U.S. Secretary of Homeland Security said, "We have for some time been thinking ahead about what would happen if, say, al Qaeda were to unite with the Zetas, one of the drug cartels."

This was in response to a question pertaining to the potential use by terrorists of a Mexico-based drug-trafficking organization to smuggle explosives or components into the United States. There have been reports over the past several years that, along with conventional weapons and explosives, there have been attempts to acquire and transport weapons of mass destruction and their components into the U.S. via drug corridors used by the Mexican cartels.

[For more detailed information concerning the confirmed nexus between Los Zetas and international terrorism, see Top Secret NCTC Report # 3456-C11.]

Much of the collaboration between these groups began with co-mingling among inmates in various U.S. and Mexican prisons and penitentiaries. While "Skinheads" and white supremacy groups and various drug cartels carve out and protect their respective space and operations in these prison war zones, they often find ways to co-exist and indeed provide one another with aid and assistance against authority figures and law enforcement forces they consider a mutual enemy. Some, like the Mexican Mafia and the Aryan Brotherhood, have created well organized hierarchical organizations in most of our maximum security prisons. Underneath these large umbrella organizations within our prison population, as well as within the ex-convict populations in our inner cities and larger suburban neighborhoods, reside thousands of satellite groups, affiliated organizations, and loosely connected gangs and tribal-based criminal organizations that continue to mature into more capable threats to national security.

[For more detailed information regarding prison gang organizations, see Secret NoForn FBI Bulletin TVT 678-CC08141.]

 **"DIRTY BOMB" HITS WALL STREET**

APPROXIMATELY $900 BILLION IN MARKET VALUE IS GONE AFTER PANIC OVER POSSIBLE TERRORIST ATTACKS

NEW YORK (CNNMoney.com) -- Stocks skidded today, with the Dow slumping over 600 points in one of the largest single-day point losses ever. Revelations of the theft of an unknown quantity of radioactive cesium by suspected Arab terrorists, and the recovery of nearly 4,000 curies of the material after a chase and shoot-out in Kentucky, led to the massive overnight sell-off.

The day's loss knocked out almost a trillion dollars in market value, according to a drop in the Dow Jones Wilshire 5000, the broadest measure of the stock market.

The Dow Jones industrial average (INDU) lost 674.68, making it the sixth largest point loss ever. However the 6.4% decline does not rank among the top 20 percentage declines.

Part Three – 96 Hours

Monday, June 21

3.01 AL HASAN RESIDENCE, HOUSTON, TX

Ismail asked, "And what are you telling the Sheik?"

He sat in front of the ornate desk in an upholstered guest chair, with Ibrahim in his leather executive chair behind the desk, his position of authority. No comfortable talks in front of the television like yesterday. This meeting was for serious business, and Ibrahim made sure Ismail understood that. The desk was clear, the flat screen computer monitor retracted into its slot, the keyboard in the drawer. The papers from Ibrahim's preparatory work, his research and his thoughts and his plans, had all been cross-cut shredded into perfect squares, each a physical match for the tens of thousands of others, all too tiny to contain recognizable forms that could be reconstructed into a complete text, the detritus of the raw materials he'd accumulated for the plan he was now transmitting to Ismail to initiate.

The Sheik that Ismail referred to was Saif al-Adel, a top al Qaeda strategic planner and interim leader after bin Laden's assassination.

"I am sending an emissary. I have written our manifesto and he will carry it personally to the Sheik," Ibrahim said.

"An emissary? Who can you trust with such a mission? The Sheik will not accept just anyone who says he speaks for you."

"Do not be concerned. It will move by diplomatic pouch to Riyadh to be entrusted to Atiyah Abdul Rahman, and then on to the Embassy of Yemen in Islamabad. He is a certified diplomatic member of the Yemeni government, and he has an open path to the Sheik."

"Rahman? He is very well-known to the Americans and others. Won't that call attention to our communication? What if he is intercepted and the document captured? It would be better to keep this at a lower level, I should think."

"You are correct, but Rahman has the trust of the Sheik and the others. They will know the document is valid if he delivers it. And we have no time to spare for delays that a lower level courier might encounter. You will carry this to our friend at the embassy in Washington."

"And what are you telling the Sheik?"

"Here. You may read it before I seal it," Ibrahim said as he handed him the document, hand-written in Arabic on a single sheet of standard printer paper with no identifying markings of any kind, not even a signature.

The manifesto, written with the appropriate al Qaeda rhetoric, flowed with a delicate balance of self-righteousness, Koranic quotations, and bloody martyrdom. It was everything a fanatical follower of bin Laden would hope for.

When he finished, Ismail handed the paper back to Ibrahim and said, "You have told the Sheik everything. You have even discussed our alliance with WAR. Is that wise? What do you think he will do?"

As he answered, Ibrahim folded the paper into thirds to put in a standard envelope, this one made of Tyvek with an adhesive seal that could not be opened without obvious damage.

"He can do nothing. By the time our emissary can travel to Peshawar and then on to the Durba Khel, it will be Thursday night, their time. Too late. It is a fait accompli, and the Sheik can only accept it and praise Allah for our success at striking the Great Satan."

Ibrahim stripped the protective tape from the envelope and sealed it and then swiveled in his chair to drop the scrap into the brass trash can behind him. As he did that, he placed the envelope on his lap and switched it for an identical one that he'd been secreting there, which he then handed across the desk to Ismail. This second envelope contained an identical piece of paper, and it too was hand-written in Arabic. The message, however, was different than the document Ismail had seen. This version was not quite so candid, and had no mention of WAR or the target locations. Ibrahim saw no benefit in sharing, nor in letting Ismail know that he was controlling the information flow for his own reasons.

The meeting was well under way when Special-Agent-In-Charge Buck Buchanan finally lost his legendary temper. Agent Leroy Spellman had pushed him over the edge midway through his report on the Pastor Tech investigation.

"40,000 curies missing? So far? Someone please tell me that a curie is like the Iranian Rial, and I need 40,000 of them to buy a Big Mac."

Spellman scrutinized the room, searching for someone to answer the question, to deflect the heat away. No one there said a word, and finally Cal Bellotta, conferenced in from the field office in Knoxville, offered his opinion.

"Sorry, but it's not going to be that easy," he said, drawing a scowl at the camera from Buchanan. "Let's say it was money. You wouldn't be Bill Gates, but you'd be driving the big Mercedes.

"Here's the deal. In 1987 in a small city in Brazil called Goiana, some locals found what they thought was scrap metal and while taking it apart to sell as scrap, they opened it. Inside they found a glowing blue powder that turned out to be about 1,400 curies of cesium chloride, the same stuff we're talking about. These unfortunate people and their children and friends screwed around with it for two weeks before enough of them got sick from the radiation poisoning to arouse some interest. In the end, four of them died, twenty-eight were injured with everything from severe burns to amputations, and there were over 200 documented cases of radiation poisoning. Tens of thousands of frightened citizens presented psycho-somatic physical symptoms of radiation poisoning, wreaking havoc on the medical facilities in the region, and significantly disrupting the economic viability of the entire area for years following the accident.

"To clean it all up, the authorities excavated six inches of topsoil and threw away stuff that totaled over 120,000 cubic feet of radioactive waste. It cost over $20 million in 1987 dollars, twice that in today's. And that was some third-world backwater. Drop that in southern Manhattan and you're talking hundreds of millions of dollars. Extrapolate it out. So far, we're missing, what, thirty times that much and still counting? Thirty times hundreds of millions? That's billions if my math is correct.

"So, no, you can forget the Big Mac. This could be a line item in the national debt."

The silence after his speech actually encouraged Cal. He thought everyone was taking the investigation seriously, but as a criminal investigation, not as a potential catastrophe. That hadn't really registered with the straight law enforcement types. He could tell it was registering now.

By the time they'd gotten to Cal's bombshell, Buck had already been updated on the status at the incident scene and the follow-up investigations of the various clues found there. That seemed to be under control and they would be uprighting the van and removing the drum in the morning. With any luck, the scene would be cleared by the end of the day and some of the incessant public pressure and news coverage would be relieved.

Now it was Owescar's turn to update the search for the missing cesium.

"Here's what we have. First, there is the Pastor scene. Agent Spellman already briefed us on that. We've gathered enough trace evidence for it to be useless – there's no way we'll be able to tell what came from where. We might as well have had a Shriner's convention in there. We've also swept the building and we'll examine everything, including the sink and toilet traps, to see if there's anything, but we're not real hopeful.

"We have the security video from the building next door, but all that gives us is a timeline for the beginning of the theft, and the make, model, and year of the car used by the person opening the building for the terrorists. That car is the same model as the one owned by Pastor himself. He didn't know about the security camera so he might have gotten careless. We're looking hard at him, but so far nothing interesting. He's had a few license violations, well, more than a few actually, but nothing of this magnitude. We'll be digging to see if there are any problems with his records.

"We're also compiling a list of everyone who had access to Pastor's building. There is a security system and it was properly deactivated with no tampering, so no alarm occurred. Someone with knowledge of the building and system let them in.

"Which leads us to the thieves. Unless this was totally an inside job, they had to have run substantial surveillance on the Pastor facility, and they had to have trained for the cesium handling. We're looking at every security camera in a one-mile radius and every hotel, motel, gas station, bed & breakfast, campground, et cetera in a thirty-mile radius. We'll be canvassing restaurants in the area to see where they ate. And we're looking into the remote manipulators used to handle the cesium to see if we can find where they trained. There are not too many facilities with that kind of hardware.

"As far as the incident scene goes, we won't have much until we get the truck uprighted and the cesium safely removed. We do have the dead shooter. His ID shows him as Patrice Abi Nader, a Moroccan student at the University of Illinois in Springfield. The school says he enrolled last year but has been inactive there for the last seven months. We're canvassing the campus for any information – residence, friends, whatever. He has no police record and doesn't show up on any watch lists. The State Department tells us his student visa is technically valid although he is not attending classes.

"We have the truck itself, and it was bought by one Mervat Saad, a second-generation Arab-American from Atlanta. We are checking to see if he matches the dead terrorist in the van, but we won't know for sure until we've removed the drum and the body. In the meantime, we're canvassing Saad's home and history.

"What's strange here is that these are good ID's – there was no attempt at subterfuge. It's almost as if these guys wanted to be ID'd. And maybe they did. Or maybe they didn't want to take a chance that a false ID would set off alarms in some routine check.

"As far as the truck goes, Saad bought it off Craigslist three months ago. Paid cash, registered and insured it. Again, no subterfuge. Our crime scene and forensics teams will be sweeping it for trace evidence once we've removed the drum and body. By the way, the liquid that was in the drum is standard lubricating oil. It is being analyzed, but we're not likely to find anything there.

"We did recover a video camera from the truck, presumably intended to record whatever they'd planned. There was no video on it. We're tracing it as well.

"The weapons were Kalashnikov AK 47 Type 58A, manufactured in North Korea. There are no serial numbers. Ballistics will be compared to the records and we'll see if anything turns up. Our experts are particularly interested in this North Korea origin. Weapons coming out of North Korea have been shipped to nations hostile to the United States, and their origin might help identify the responsible government.

"And finally, we have the drum itself. Right now we only have an approximate drawing based on the x-rays, but we'll get the exact design once we've got it in the lab. Lead is a toxic substance so you need a license to melt and pour it. We'll be canvassing all the licensed lead pourers and see if we can find where it was made. If it was homemade, that will be harder to track. We'll look at lead sales, but the quantities are small enough that there might not be any records.

"Gentlemen, and lady, that's what we have at the moment."

Buck was silent for a moment, and then summarized.

"Could have been a three-word report – we've got shit. Not your fault, Richard, but we're stuck with forensics, and I don't see that getting us anywhere very quickly in this case. If these terrorists divided the cesium equally, which seems to make sense, then we've got between six and ten other loads out there somewhere. And probably more, but we won't know that until the inventory is done at Pastor and we've checked other licensees for missing material.

"We need leads. First, alert all law enforcement and emergency responders of the circumstances and likely extrapolations. They need to enhance their radiation detection protocols and dirty bomb indications and get them read by everyone. Everyone. Including patrol officers and rent-a-cops. I got a heads up that the DNDO is notifying all state and local rad detection units so they are all on full alert. We need an All-Points Bulletin on heavy-duty, unmarked cargo vans, middle-eastern drivers, single-drum loads. Work with Public Affairs to get sanitized information out over the media. Just identify the drivers as young men, twenty to thirty-five years old. Let people assume the middle-eastern part. Do not hint at the number of these trucks that might be running around, just play up the need to ID these guys. Let's also get these two identities out into the media. Maybe someone will remember something or we'll get some links.

"We've got the spectral analysts at NSA reviewing their own records based on a whole new set of keywords and phrases. I want law enforcement everywhere to lean hard on all sources. Maybe the weapons angle will turn up something.

"What else? Anybody?"

Cal spoke up through the computer speakers. "I would suggest we all work with the Bureau's WMD Directorate at Headquarters and all the local WMD Coordinators, and make sure they engage the Quantico people, and through them coordinate with the Joint Analysis Center at DNDO. That will get the word out to all Federal, state and local law enforcement nationwide. We need to deploy all available gamma detection systems, pagers, vehicle monitors and static systems. And make sure everyone has fresh batteries in their radiation monitors. Also, lower the action threshold. Someone gets a reading, they report it and investigate. Take nothing for granted, there's no such thing as a false positive until we've recovered all of this stuff.

"Every truck inspection station needs to have its monitors running. If these guys are in vans, that won't find them, but if any are in big rigs, we could. In short, every radiation monitor in the country had better be turned on and facing outwards. And any time a needle jumps, we need to know it."

"One last thing," Buchanan said without acknowledging that Cal had even spoken. "We've clamped an absolute blackout on the amount of material missing. The DOE RAP team from Oak Ridge is doing a curie-counting inventory at Pastor. Pastor himself is in protective custody and incommunicado. Do not tell anyone how much there is out there. When you're asked, play down the number but emphasize the danger and the need for everyone to be on the lookout. That's it, back to work."

Eileen Daler had said nothing during the meeting, and she said nothing now. She was wondering which of her family she should be tactfully telling to take a vacation in some quiet, rural setting far, far away.

3.03   KENNETH PASTOR JR.'S CAR, OAKLAND, CA

The caller ID on his cell phone said 'Bill Edgerton' and Kenny considered ignoring the call. Edgerton was his local WAR contact and the closest thing Kenny had to a friend in California. He didn't want to answer because there was no way it could be good news. Edgerton wasn't going to call him to tell him everything was fine. Kenny answered anyway – he couldn't avoid him for long and he needed to get the conversation out of the way before getting home. Patsy, his wife, would be curious if he talked to Edgerton in front of her, and she didn't need to know about his plans for them, and how they were funded. Not yet.

"Hey, Bill. What's up?"

"Where are you?"

"On my way home. I'll be there in five minutes."

"The big boss wants to meet with you like right now. There's been a complication with the shipment and he needs your advice."

Their conversations were always circumspect, knowing the vulnerabilities of cell phone transmissions to monitoring. Kenny couldn't imagine anyone monitoring him, but he wasn't so sure of the WAR people, and even these references to bosses and shipments were a little obvious for his liking. He knew there would be no escaping the meeting, though. 'Complication' could mean anything, right up to and including an FBI officer standing beside Edgerton, coercing the call to trap Kenny. He was suspicious – what complication could he uncomplicate?

"I don't know anything about any shipment. Why does he want to meet with me?"

"It's not the shipment. It's the cargo. And you're our expert on the cargo. I'll meet you in your parking lot. I'm there now, near the Wayne Avenue entrance."

The cargo. What could have gone wrong? So many things, he knew. And even a little 'gone wrong' with that cargo could be a disaster for anyone nearby. He called Patsy.

"I'm gonna be late. I've got to go meet with Bill. It's about that job he's got for me down south."

"Why now," she asked. "Dinner will be ready soon, and I've got to put Ginelle to bed. Can't it wait?"

"No, he said now. Someone from the company is here and has some spare time and wants to meet. I've got to do it, honey. I can't keep driving vegetables around. It's a great opportunity. I shouldn't be too late."

He'd told Patsy that there was a job opportunity for him with a competitor of Pastor Tech. It was supposedly a new company in Southern California doing both commercial and Homeland Security work who wanted his knowledge and experience and contacts from Pastor. His involvement had to be kept secret, he'd explained, because he'd signed the standard non-compete agreement with Pastor, and because his criminal record would cause security clearance problems for the company.

When he got to the lot, Bill was waiting there in his idea of an innocuous car - an orange Dodge Ram pick-up jacked-up about fourteen inches higher than standard. He jumped out and jogged to Kenny's Mustang and got in, saying, "You drive. I'll tell you where to go."

As soon as he'd pulled out of the parking lot and turned right as Bill directed, Kenny asked, "What happened?"

"One of the shipments had a traffic accident. It's been all over the news. You didn't hear it?"

"No. I went to the garage and worked on my car after work, and I was just on my way home when you called. One of the shipments? How many were there? And what happened? Is there a spill?"

"We only know what's on the news, and all they're saying is there's an accident involving radioactivity. They've called in some rap group, whatever that is, and the boss wants to know what will happen now so we can decide how to handle it."

"It's a RAP Team, government radiological experts. They're technicians, not cops, but it won't take long to trace the stuff back to Pastor. There's gonna be a lot of heat, and some of it will be coming my way. Shit. We've got to be sure I'm covered, or else I've got to split."

"That's the other thing. The boss wants to review your role and figure out how to keep it secret no matter what."

"Where are we meeting?"

"At a crack house in Richmond."

"A crack house? No way. I get caught there and I'm violated. I'll be right back in Solano."

"Relax, we've got that covered. The crack house really isn't one. It just looks like it. There's no drugs, just our guys. It's a safe house we keep for meetings like this or when one of us has to disappear for a while."

Kenny didn't like any of this – not an accident, not a meeting, not anything. He'd counted on more time once he'd returned to California, time to establish his alibi beyond doubt.

"Where did it happen," he asked Bill.

"Someplace in Kentucky. Lexington, I think. Why?"

"Lexington? Shit, that's only a couple of hours from Oak Ridge. They'll be at Pastor first thing, maybe already. Did they catch the driver?"

"Driver*s*. No, they're both dead. And they're not our guys, so it can't be traced back."

Our guys? None of you are my guys, Kenny thought. "Whose guys are they," he asked.

Instead of answering, Bill asked his own question. "What does Patsy know about all this?"

"Patsy? Nothing. I haven't told her a thing. And she doesn't know about the money, either."

"Good. Let's keep it that way so she isn't in danger."

"Danger? What danger?"

"Just from the cops if they come asking questions. If she doesn't know anything, she can't lie and get caught or anything."

Kenny wasn't sure he liked that answer, either. Patsy wasn't part of this, and he wanted it kept that way.

They were somewhere in South Richmond or Eastshore – Kenny wasn't familiar with the neighborhood – when Bill pointed to a liquor store and told him to pull in and park.

"This doesn't look like much of a safe house," Kenny said after they parked around back.

"It isn't," Bill answered. "We wait here. Someone is meeting us to lead us there. I don't even know where this place is."

After a pause, Bill said, "What is this cargo? The news said there was radiation. Is it some kind of nuclear bomb?"

"You mean they haven't told you?"

"They don't tell anyone any more than they need to. So, what is it?"

"It's not a nuclear bomb. You need fissile material for that – uranium or plutonium. I don't really know, either. I just showed them how to get into my father's plant and what to do when they did. I don't know what they took, or what they're going to do with it, and I don't want to."

"What do you think they'll they do with it?"

"Your guess is as good as mine. They'll spread it somewhere, I guess. In a water supply or food or most likely a dirty bomb they'll blow up somewhere."

"Jesus. How many people will die?"

"Not as many as you'd think. Anyone in the blast radius of the explosion, and maybe somebody nearby who gets a heavy dose of radiation. Mostly it's an economic and psychological weapon. It'll panic people and wherever it goes off, the area will have to be evacuated and cleaned up. If I had to guess, it'll be some ZOG target – someone's business or maybe a government office. How long do we have to wait? I don't like this place. We're the only white people here."

"Not long. Lemme see your wallet."

"What for?"

"I'm supposed to put this card in it. They said to do it myself to make sure it doesn't get lost. It's an emergency phone number."

Kenny's look was skeptical, but he handed over his wallet, just the same.

"That's my ride coming now," Bill said, and put Kenny's wallet in one pocket and took the silenced 9mm pistol out of the other.

"Your ride? What about the …" Kenny stopped talking when he saw he gun.

"Listen, Kenny, I'll make sure Patsy and Ginelle are taken care of. I'm sorry it had to be like this. Well, not as sorry as I was before you told me about this dirty bomb shit, but still, I kinda liked you and your family."

He shot Kenny three times in the chest and got out to go home, leaving behind what looked like a drug deal gone bad.

TUESDAY, JUNE 22

3.04   CNN NEWS HEADQUARTERS, ATLANTA, GA

 **GOVERNMENT EVACUATION PLANNED**

CRITICAL PERSONNEL AND FUNCTIONS TO BE MOVED TO SECURE LOCATIONS

Washington (CNNPolitics.com) -- The Secretary of Homeland Security and the Director of the FBI held a joint meeting this morning behind closed doors with key White House and Congressional leadership. Rumors are rampant that the three branches of government might be close to initiating unprecedented continuity of government protocols, to ensure the continued operation of the Federal Government in the event of any WMD attacks on the nation's political epicenter. Under these protocols, critical government personnel and functions are moved to secure locations scattered in undisclosed locations, presumably outside of the Washington DC metropolitan area.

3.05   MILE HIGH METALS, DENVER, CO

The second-gear synchronizer was worn, and Billy Bates wasn't much of a double-clutcher, so the downshift into second to negotiate the final incline up to Mile High Metals got a laugh from his co-driver, Justin Anderson. Billy wasn't happy about that and simply said "Fuck you" as he drove the forty-foot self-loading trailer into the large, paved yard surrounding the airplane-hangar-sized metal recycle facility.

They had left the terminal at Psalter Freight before dawn to get an early start and make the first pickup before the workday began. No sense having a bunch of people watching them load a small but very heavy container into a drum of chemicals.

There were no doors on the building, just an opening wide enough for two trucks to pass comfortably and high enough that the trailer passed under with plenty of room to spare. Inside, the building was a huge open area with a concrete floor and concrete walls rising eight feet above it. Steel-framed corrugated metal walls and roof sat atop the concrete tub, creating a covered space that could accommodate a high-school football game, including the stands for the fans. Punts would have been a problem, though, with the web of trusses holding the roof up creating few openings for something to fly through in a straight line.

The building was empty except for a single pickup truck in the far corner, and that was where he headed, arcing his path so he could back the trailer close enough to the pickup for the extendable crane built into the trailer to lift what they had been told was a 1,500 pound load. He and Anderson both got out and went to the back of the trailer, opening its doors and swinging the two hinged trusses that opened just like the doors, but stopped ninety degrees later, creating the rails for the internal crane to ride out on to get directly above the drum in the back of the pickup. Once positioned, they removed the drum lid and, reaching into the oil in the drum, found the lifting bail and hooked it to the crane. From there, it was a simple but slightly messy job to transfer the lead pig and its contents to a waiting drum in their trailer, one of three centered among another seventy-nine identical drums, all properly labeled as containing methyl ethyl ketone peroxide, a class 5.2 organic peroxide oxidizing agent, to discourage any close inspection. Seventy-six of the drums actually did contain MEKP, and now one contained approximately 4,000 curies of cesium.

3.06   LAWSON MCGHEE LIBRARY, KNOXVILLE, TN

When he added it up in his head, Cal figured he'd been in planes or boats or cars getting from one point to another nine different times for a total of fifteen or sixteen hours in the past few days. A lot of short, tiring trips. He matched that against the eleven hours sleep over the same time, also usually in short spurts, and figured he had every reason to be tired and grouchy. He needed someplace to go where he could think, actually close his eyes and try to assemble everything he'd seen and heard over those days. Then he could frame it within his own broader knowledge and experience and try to figure out what was going to happen. And if he could do that with any accuracy, maybe he and others could figure out where and when it would happen and do something about it.

That was his job – analyzing threats, specifically terrorist threats involving radiological weapons – and developing scenarios so those threats could be neutralized. The difference here was that his job was usually theoretical, reviewing the intelligence gathered at the DHS Office of Operations Co-ordination, planning for what might happen based on that intel, and then developing scenarios and training exercises for those on the prevention and enforcement side of homeland security. His specialty was "Thunderbolts," tabletop exercises he created in response to real threats in order to challenge the thinking of high-level staff, senior leaders in the White House, DNI, DHS, FBI, DOD, NCTC, and others to consider scenarios that were outside their comfort zone, to get them to recognize that their opponents were cunning, adaptive, and very creative. This was his first involvement in what was actually happening, not what might happen, and it was a whole different set of pressures.

The Lawson McGhee Library was a three-block walk from the Knoxville Field Office, and Cal decided to work there on his analysis and report, with a triple-shot cappuccino and a muted cell phone. The Starbucks across the street from the library provided the cappuccino, and Cal set his phones to vibrate, hoping they didn't vibrate him back to the real world while he tried to visualize a made-up one where the good guys found the bombs and caught the bad guys.

Reviewing what he knew from the events and investigations of the last few days didn't take long because there wasn't much known. He knew there was a lot of cesium chloride missing, as much as 60,000 curies, it now appeared, stolen over a weekend from Pastor Technology. And maybe more, if anyone else was found to be missing inventory. He knew that the thieves had taken the time and risk to remove it from its sealed capsules, which meant they had a significant level of sophistication and training, and a need for it to be in a dispersible form and container, but no facilities to do the work. He knew that there were two dead terrorists of Middle Eastern descent who had about 4,000 of those curies in their possession when they died. He knew one of their names and the fact that it didn't appear anywhere on the intelligence community or law enforcement radar, not even foreign services, which was very troubling. And he knew that the shit was about to hit the fan. His goal was to find out which fan.

In the quiet of the secluded corner of the library, he was able to make some quick and easy predictions. The first was that the cesium would be used in suicide bombs. He gave that one a 90+ percent confidence factor. Suicide bombs were the default vehicle for terrorists, well ahead of improvised explosive devices, IED's, except in war zones like Afghanistan and Iraq. Suicide bombs were easier to assemble and deliver, and provided better control. Once an IED was built and placed, risk of discovery multiplied and the concentration of victims varied. A suicide bomb was a smart bomb – it could go where the target was at that moment and take evasive action when required.

His next guess was also pretty obvious – divide 60,000 by 4,000 and you get fifteen bombs, give or take one or two. It was improbable that the terrorists had taken the time to carefully measure the curie content as they divided the lethal powder. They most likely just filled each of their containers, whatever they were, to the brim. Since the containers would almost certainly be the same size and shape, then each would contain 4,000 curies, give or take 20% to account for different radioactive decay in different sealed sources.

Because the material was a chloride powder, it would be very susceptible to moisture, so the containers would need to be well-sealed and easily breakable, a non-porous material, glass or fragile plastic. Glass was better because it shattered uniformly. The size and shape of the jar would be similar to the explosives so the suicide belt could be made without special pockets that could be confused in the chaos of getting ready to kill yourself. So, smaller than two inches diameter and less than six inches tall. He knew that the responders on I-75 would likely have the container and cesium back in the FBI lab by the end of the day, so he didn't consider the container design any further – he would know it soon enough.

That ended the easy part of the analysis. The hard part was also the important part – where and when. He smiled at the thought that flicked through his mind – *If I were a terrorist, where would I go to die?* Other than the terrorists themselves, there were very few people more qualified than Cal to answer that.

I would make a political statement, was the first conclusion. That meant Washington, DC. The possible targets there were almost innumerable. Would I try to set off fifteen bombs in DC? No, of course not. Radiological dispersal devices, RDD's, were not weapons of mass destruction. The most dangerous part of an RDD detonation was being close enough to the blast to get killed or injured by the explosion itself, and the bomber was the only certain victim. The cesium was there to terrify, to turn a small area into a no-man's land where the fear of radiation would far outweigh the relatively small risk of injury or death from the radioactive material. No, RDD's were weapons of mass denial, isolating an area from possible human habitation and costing huge amounts of money and resources to clean up.

That itself further limited the possible targets. The bomber would want crowds, an area where as many victims as possible would be injured or killed by the explosion and contaminated by the cesium. Where crowds gathered, that specific place was by definition important to society, and the need to restore it for use would assure that the money and time would be spent to clean it up, and the inconvenience caused would be a constant reminder of the terrorist's power. RDD's were economic bombs, putting some critical place out of business and costing heavily to get it back.

The target would need great symbolic value, something to further spread the fear that the terrorist could strike any location, anywhere, any time. The bus terminal in Harrisburg, Pennsylvania, though crowded occasionally, was not a likely target, whereas the State Capital Building there would be.

And the site would need to be hard to restore. Buildings would need to be demolished, roads torn up, critical pieces of property and structures put out of commission at great cost and effort. Even within these limited parameters, there was a wealth of possible targets in Washington alone. Many more than could be adequately covered by the available resources for patrol, detection and prevention.

But Washington was only one possible target, and as everyone knew from the 9-11 plane crashes, it wasn't necessarily the top one. So he was back to his original thought – if I were a terrorist with 60,000 curies of cesium, where would I apply it for maximum effect in achieving my ultimate goals? What fourteen or fifteen or sixteen places would further my cause? In addition to a political symbol, what other targets would I want to hit? Financial, obviously. Lower Manhattan, just like 9-11. But that's been done, so what other financial targets had similar allure to a terrorist? Ft. Knox and the gold reserve? Clearly too heavily guarded. Federal mints and Reserve Banks? A possibility, but these were usually built like a prison and would easily withstand the force of a man-carried suicide bomb. Something commercial, then. More accessible, more costly to restore. So, look to the junior financial capitals in the country – Chicago, Houston, Charlotte, San Francisco, Boston. One or more of those cities were on the list, he was certain.

He scribbled notes as he went through his mental *what would I do* exercise, and almost three hours later, he had his list, and a good idea on how to narrow it down.

3.07   FBI FIELD OFFICE, LOUISVILLE, KY

"All right, everyone, let's get started."

Buck Buchanan called the Tuesday evening SVTC to order. Once again, he had a packed house – seventeen in person, four conference rooms by video, and three by secure cell phone.

"We'll stay with the format we've established. Stefanie, my ASAC – well, I guess you all know that by now – will summarize today's news and then we'll add any that you might have, and then we'll set marching orders for tomorrow. Stefanie?"

"At the I-75 scene, the van was successfully uprighted today and the drum containing the cesium was transferred to a secure shipping container and is on its way to the FBI labs for examination. Investigation of the truck is ongoing.

"With the drum removed, we were able to recover the body of the second terrorist. As expected, he is the owner of the van, a Mervat Saad. We've been interviewing friends, family, associates, anyone who might have bumped up against these two. The results are contained in the reports that you were given on arrival, so I won't go into details. The interesting point is that neither were incognito nor took any steps to conceal their identity, and neither has yet shown up on any watch list, foreign or domestic.

"The cesium. Pastor Technology was identified yesterday as the source of the cesium and right now we're estimating the loss at 60,000 Curies. That appears to be everything missing from Pastor, and no other losses have been reported. Audits at other licensees will continue until we're sure that's everything. If the material was divided equally, we have maybe fourteen more loads so far to find and recover.

"The cell phone was examined and is a generic, prepaid phone with no service contract. No entries in the call log and it seems to be new and unused. Nothing new on the weapons and little likelihood they'll provide any useful leads.

"We have one new situation that we're investigating closely. Kenny Pastor, Jr., the son of the owner of Pastor Tech, was murdered yesterday, apparently part of a drug deal gone bad. He was a convicted drug dealer and recently paroled in California, where he had lived for the past two years, and where he died. He is estranged from the family and hasn't seen his father in over two years, so it seems a coincidence. However, none of us really believe in coincidence in a matter like this, so the circumstances are being looked at very carefully.

"Forensics at the Pastor building turned up a cigarette butt in one of the hot cells. It was a Morven Gold, a popular Middle-Eastern brand made in Pakistan by Phillip Morris and available here. It will be tested for DNA and matched against our two dead terrorists.

"That was it as of an hour ago. Any questions?"

No one had any – they had all been briefed on the events as they had transpired – and Buck moved to other events.

"We've got Special Agent Wolfson out of the Springfield, Illinois Field Office on the video. Please bring us up to date on the shooter – Patrice Abi Nader."

On the video, Wolfson seemed nervous, uncomfortable with talking to a computer screen that had dozens of listeners, most of them several pay grades above his. His presentation was quick and to the point – they had virtually nothing for the last seven months. He'd moved out of the small studio apartment he was renting and disappeared. No credit card trail, no new address or utility connections or driver's license changes, nothing at all on the grid. He'd had no real friends at school, so there was no one to miss him and no one to point the investigation in any useful direction. They were looking back at his life in Morocco before coming to the U.S. Wolfson's nervousness might have been related to the total lack of substantive information he'd been able to provide.

Agent Bellecks from the Atlanta Field Office had a lot more on the other dead terrorist, Mervat Saad. He had a family and friends and a history in the Atlanta suburb of Eastpoint where his father was a life-long civil engineer with Parsons Corporation. His family and friends had been interviewed and each and every one denied that there was a radical thought anywhere in Mervat's history. His mosque was moderate and there were no ties to any radical group, known or suspected. No one on any law enforcement watch list had ever been a member. In short, Mervat was a typical American twenty-something who happened to be Muslim.

"We've got his computer and personal papers," Bellecks went on to report. "The computer disk drive seems to have been wiped and it's been sent to Quantico for in-depth evaluation. Speculation here is that he got radicalized and recruited over the Internet, but we're thinking that only because we have no other leads. This family is absolutely clean, and if they're some kind of long-term sleeper cell, well, they deserve an Oscar for the performance. Hell, my mother looks more dangerous than these people."

"Parsons does nuclear construction," Cal Bellotta interjected from the SVTC facility in Knoxville. "Does the father have any ties there? Any history with Pastor?"

"We haven't looked. I didn't see that possible link. We'll check that out."

Buchanan was annoyed by the answer, due in part to Bellecks' oversight, but more because it was Bellotta's insight.

"You do that," he muttered at the computer screen, not even trying to hide his sarcasm. "See if we can't get some kind of answer before one of Mervat's buddies blows one of these things up."

Cal's report had been distributed earlier in the day, so all of the participants had a chance to review it. With updates completed and little progress to report, Buck expected everyone would jump on Cal's speculations as if they were a Warren Buffet stock market prediction. He personally gave the report the same credence as he would the ramblings of a Sunday-morning news show host – it sounded good and would keep the audience enthralled, but it had no investigative value. That, he thought, was the problem with most DHS product – it played well to a political and policy audience, but it wouldn't solve anything. And that audience in this investigation was becoming larger and louder than the law enforcement one. So it was with some trepidation that he turned the meeting over to Cal to summarize his report and answer questions.

"Here are the highlights, then," Cal started. "These are summarized on the first page and I'll go through them quickly.

"First, there will likely be between two and five simultaneous dirty bomb attacks using suicide bombers in the coming days or, at most, two weeks. I arrived at that number by estimating the 60,000 Curies had been relatively equally divided for maximum distribution, and that the terrorists will want to explode three to five bombs simultaneously to show their strength and capabilities. In addition to the inherent terror of the dirty bomb itself, simultaneous detonations will demonstrate that they are a highly organized, thoroughly trained and effective para-military unit, and that is one of their primary motivations. This means coordinated attacks. Two is too few for their purposes, and they won't want to expend more than one-third of their inventory, so five is the most we can expect. Since the one bomb we've captured might well have been scheduled to be one of the original three to five coordinated bombs, we may have as few as two after all.

"Next, the remaining bombs will be exploded on some predictable schedule. That is the best way to spread the terror – taking one time or place and making it high-risk. For example, they might choose rush hour on any given day in any major city as the schedule, or they might choose a particular type of target like shopping malls and focus on these. This would make people fear that particular time or place and avoid it, causing chaos far beyond their actual targets without actually doing anything. If everyone stopped going to the local Galleria or changed their commuting habits, that would play havoc with commerce and cost us far beyond the clean-up costs of any single bomb.

"Finally, and hardest to predict - the targets. The terrorists will be looking at symbolic value, immediate economic devastation, maximum casualties, and huge recovery costs. We're talking financial centers, religious sites, large entertainment venues, government buildings, airports, communications centers, and other critical infrastructure. These should be in crowded areas, like lower Manhattan or downtown Chicago. That kind of geography will limit the spread of contamination, but wide dispersal won't be their goal. Shutting down a crossroads of commerce or government or civil society will. We're not going to see contaminated corn or cows.

"When you carry this to its logical conclusion, we've probably eliminated 98% of the geography of the country. The problem is covering the remaining 2%. There are over three million square miles in the continental U.S., so 2% leaves us with over 6,000 square miles. That's bigger than Connecticut. Imagine that entire state as densely populated as suburban DC. Forty consecutive miles of Connecticut Avenue in each direction – north, south, east, and west. Homes, apartments, shopping malls, office buildings, gas stations, one after the other, no breaks, no parks, no fields or forests. Nothing but people and vehicles and the infrastructure that supports them. Then break it up into hundreds of small pieces and scatter them around the country to make it even harder to cover. It's simply not possible to monitor it all with the resources we have.

"We've prepared for this kind of event for years, so we do have a head start on identifying targets and making plans. And with this particular event, we have some known facts. We're trying to correlate these facts with our research and experience and see if we can't make some predictions and come up with a prioritized list of targets where we can concentrate our monitoring. Since we're looking at coordinated attacks, we can identify common factors such as the time of day, the local conditions such as crowds and security and events. For example, rush hour. That meets the criteria for crowds, for maximum chaos, for cost to respond and recover, and to disrupt us by making every commuting day a potential risk. So we look at the different conditions at all of our high-value targets and see when they correlate, when their optimum impact matches the optimum impact at another target. Where these match, we have a nexus, a time of day and set of places ideal for the terrorists' goals.

"What we're doing is matching each target's value with a time of day or set of conditions and then matching these with the others. Where we find, for example, that at 6:30 PM next Tuesday there is a confluence with three or five targets, we can focus resources then and there. This is a huge task, but the computers at the Army's Information Dominance Center have the horsepower and the terrorist rules-based gaming algorithms to do it. We can identify all of these confluences and rank them according to the terrorist goals and methods and then focus our traditional investigative resources there. We know, for instance, that we're looking for cargo vans, for middle-eastern drivers, for heavy steel barrels, for any traces of radiation, etc. It makes the most sense to look for these things in the places they're most likely to be, so we're identifying those places.

"I hope that explains it clearly. We'll need to put the analysis in motion at the IDC and see if we can't narrow the search down a bit and increase our chances. Any questions?"

Buchanan didn't even wait to see if there were others before jumping in.

"This all sounds, uhh, real technical and cutting-edge and all, but how are you going to identify the terrorist's goals or priorities when we don't know who the terrorists are? I mean, if you ran this analysis on McVeigh, you'd get a whole different set of targets than if you ran it on Mullah Omar. Sounds to me like window dressing, looking like we're doing something productive when in fact it's all an educated guess."

"That's a very good question. In fact, it's probably the most relevant question to this whole thing. And the answer is, we can't. We can't know the terrorist's goals and plans, we can only play probabilities. And most of the parameters that go into a terrorist's decision-making are actually quite similar across all kinds of groups, whether they are fundamentalist religious or social radicals or just plain crazy. McVeigh wouldn't have targeted a grain silo in Nebraska any more than Omar. The differences are in the fundamental principles of the group. Earth Firsters are less likely to target the National Cathedral in Washington than Wahabi Muslims. And these same Muslims are less likely to go after the big lumber companies."

"We do have indications, albeit flimsy ones, that this is a Muslim terrorist group. The dead terrorists are both Islamic, and the sole clue from the crime scene is a cigarette butt from a brand popular mostly in the Middle-East. Not much to go on, so we've broadened our search parameters to include all types of targets. No guarantees that we'll be right, but it's the best we've got at this point."

One of the FBI participants added his own, more specific addendum to Cal's answer.

"Would your analysis have identified the Twin Towers as a likely target?"

"Different scenario," Cal answered. "If we had been dealing with an airborne threat, then certainly it would have. Dealing with an RDD, it's less likely except in the context of Lower Manhattan as a general target."

"A follow-up to that. You're running a very sophisticated analysis of the motivations and goals and priorities of these terrorists. Aren't they more likely to make very unsophisticated decisions? Like targets-of-opportunity. *I'm in this town with this RDD, where should I blow it up?*"

"True, but the answer to the 'where should I blow it up' is exactly what we're identifying. We're trying to model the considerations and come to a set of conclusions that narrow our search, downsize the probable choke points, and make better surveillance and detection team decisions. And remember, he isn't acting in a vacuum. He's likely coordinating with other terrorists, so this narrows his choices."

Buchanan interjected at this point, clearly impatient with this topic.

"You think, you don't know. All right, let's have one more question and then let's all get back to finding these guys. Yeah, Marjorie, you have a question?"

"How can we be constantly adjusting our monitoring resources as these identified targets change with time?"

"Again, we can't. Certain locations will jump out as high-value targets and we'll concentrate there. So if we find that Kansas City has some significance, we'll place resources there. But we won't be jumping back and forth between KC and, say Phoenix. Both will get coverage commensurate with the threat."

With that Buchanan stood and started out, signaling the end of the meeting and, in his mind, a return to the real investigation.

3.08   LT. GOVERNOR'S LIMO, IDAHO FALLS, ID

Margaret Hancock had her own Atomic City to inspect. Unlike the FBI efforts in Oak Ridge, hers was symbolic and took about eight seconds as her car passed through it on the way back from the Idaho National Lab. Atomic City, Idaho had a population of twenty-four, several of whom took notice of the black Lincoln Town Car simply because it was the only moving vehicle in the last forty-three minutes. No one knew or cared that the Lieutenant Governor of Idaho was in the back seat, and that they had just witnessed the highest ranking political figure to come to Atomic City in the last eight years.

After the events at Pastor had become known, the Governor had decided it would be beneficial to show all Idahoans that he was out in front of the crisis, and that Idaho's own nuclear industry, concentrated around the former National Reactor Testing Station, now the INL, west of Idaho Falls, was safe and secure. The task of implementing that assurance fell to Margaret. After all, she had nothing better to do.

Margaret had a different opinion. She had a lot to do. Most of it focused on building the political capital she would need in three years to be elected Governor in her own right. Conservative Idaho, with 45% of its population either Mormons or evangelical Protestants, was not inclined towards female leadership. A young-looking and energetic thirty-seven year-old lawyer, she had served very successfully as the State's Attorney before being selected to soften the ticket led by the sixty-two year-old Governor, a man of out-spoken and often ill-conceived ideas.

Margaret's greatest advantage was fund-raising. She was very good at that, focusing most of her efforts on one dedicated, out-of-state benefactor who managed to pour substantial sums into her campaign coffers through a number of perfectly legal means. By Idaho standards, Margaret was very well funded.

Her secret benefactor was on her mind on the drive to the airport in Idaho Falls. He had called after the news of the accident in Kentucky and arranged to meet with her on Sunday to discuss "some new developments" which he said would affect her future. Very cryptic, and very frustrating, as usual. What developments? Affect it how? If it weren't for their relationship and mutual self-interest, she would have had anxieties about him withdrawing his financial support, bankrupting her future plans. But as it stood, she knew he wouldn't do that.

On the trip back from INL, in the quiet and comfort of the Lincoln back seat, she considered her next moves, her case for continued and even expanded support, the other revenue sources that she had grown lazy about tapping. Yes, she had a lot to do. At least until Sunday.

WEDNESDAY, JUNE 23

3.09   U.S. ARMY INFORMATION DOMINANCE CENTER, FT. BELVOIR, VA

Cal was familiar with the output of the Starlight program, having seen and analyzed and used its product many times in developing his Thunderbolt exercises. But this was the first time he'd seen the machine actually do its work, and he was suitably impressed by the presentation.

He sat in what looked like a miniature IMAX theater with seating for an audience of fifty-six curving around the – he couldn't call it a screen because it was more holographic – viewing area that was a twelve-foot cube. Cal had no idea what the technology was, but he'd only seen things like this in science fiction movies. He did think he knew where the seats must have come from – the first-class section of a very expensive airplane – because they were adjustable in almost every direction and had a built in folding table and cup holders.

Walter Lohman was the only other person in the room and he explained the display to Cal as he manipulated it on some wireless control box built into the fold-out table at his seat.

"What you're seeing is a three dimensional representation of all the data points that Starlight has identified based on the input parameters that we gave it, and their possible connections color coded by the magnitude of the connection, starting at a light shade and progressing to the brightest. Red means it's a primary connection, blue is a secondary one, green tertiary, and yellow is tenuous. These will change with time or any other parameter that you want to specify such as location, genre, population, etc. We can rotate it to highlight any particular node …"

At this point, Walter twisted the joystick on the control box and the data points and lines rotated like a planet, centering on one node labeled "110629 E Los Angeles".

"… such as this home baseball game between the Dodgers and the San Francisco Giants. The label tells us the date, 'E' means it's a one-time event, and then the location. If I select it by placing the cursor over it, the full description comes up and then we can query the connected events and see what priority they might have. We can also move through time to see how these nodes and connections change, we can map the nodes to see geographical relations, we can tie the events to other input such as transportation schedules, weather reports, and, of course, any intel coming in from the field or from any of the other agencies. This is real-time updated, which will explain why the colors and connections change. Questions?"

"How the hell do you know what you're looking at?"

Lohman chuckled and said, "It takes some getting used to. But once you get acclimated, you can visually analyze very complex relationships amazingly fast. Our analysts can see things in milliseconds that used to take days to model."

"That's great for your analysts, but how do I get output that I can give to our investigative and preparedness resources that they can actually use?"

"That's tougher. We're limited to words. What Starlight can do is snapshot any moment with whatever parameters are set and give you a prioritized action list. It's an electronic file and the reader can select any item and expand it to get more detailed information. Not as much fun, and takes a lot longer to digest, but short of being here, it's the best we can do."

"So what I need is to identify the relevant snapshots and get the Starlight report electronically?"

"Yes. We've set up so the FBI SIOC and lead field offices can log into the parameter menu and select what they need. Reports will be virtually instantaneous."

"What about backlog? Won't all those requests stack up in some queue?"

Again, Lohman chuckled. "You haven't got enough FBI agents to overload Starlight, so don't worry about that."

Jules Vincenzo crossed his legs, then uncrossed them and tried crossing them the other way, as if the deeply padded and upholstered chair in the reception area of the Deputy Director for Intelligence Collection was somehow uncomfortable. It wasn't, but Jules was. It had taken over six hours of concentrated effort to get there, calls to people whom he barely remembered, cashing in chits they barely remembered. Even then, he hadn't been able to score a meeting with the Director of National Intelligence, settling for someone two levels down the chain of command. And still he had to cool his heels watching some GS-5 administrative nobody type away at her computer.

It looked like his efforts at Georgetown University's School of Foreign Service were finally going to pay off, and he could escape the GS-13 plateau where he felt marooned. Thirty-seven years old, and still a thirteen. *Well, not for long,* he thought.

Jules' career at Georgetown was not the traditional one. Acceptance had been gained not through particularly high SAT scores, but through the very high financial scores his father had made, ostensibly from the olive oil import business in Philadelphia, which had financed the construction of Vincenzo Hall, a classroom and office building at the 36th and P Streets corner of the Georgetown campus, an expensive piece of real estate. As many IRS and DEA investigators had tried in vain to prove, Sal Vincenzo's olives were just a bit too profitable to be legitimate. His was more in the poppy extract level of commerce.

At Georgetown, Jules had majored in relations. Not foreign ones, but useful ones. He'd made it a point to establish a network of contacts that he'd figured would still be valuable long after everyone stopped looking at his college transcript. And now, it seemed he might have been right. Ibrahim al Hasan had been one class ahead at Georgetown, but that didn't stop Jules from making contact with him, and reinforcing it every chance he got. Ibrahim was royal family, and royal family was oil, and oil was what made America great. So the phone call he'd received from Ibrahim that morning asking to meet was a pleasant surprise, but not a total shock. The seed was germinating, and he hoped it would blossom before the day's end.

The door to the office finally opened and two men emerged, smiling and parting after an apparently jovial meeting. One of them Jules had never seen, but the other was Alby Pearson, the Deputy Director, and Jules' pulse ramped up a bit and he tried to swallow to keep his mouth from totally drying up and impairing his normal radio-quality voice.

Pearson turned to Jules and smiled, greeting him by name even though they had never met. Jules' position at the State Department's Office of Education and Cultural Affairs was unlikely to have ever come to his attention. That was about to change.

"Come in, Mr. Vincenzo. Let's see what was so important that Billy Randall at DHS felt I needed to see you ASAP."

"Thank you, sir," Jules answered. "I think you'll find that my information will be a valuable use of your time."

Jules settled into one of the guest chairs in front of the desk and told his story.

"This morning, an old friend from Georgetown stopped by to talk to me. Ibrahim al Hasan," Jules said, even though Ibrahim had asked his name be kept out of the situation. "He's the Commercial Attaché down in Houston for the Saudis. Well, it seems he has come across some interesting information concerning the recent cesium theft, and he felt he should talk to me about it so I could pass it on to the right people. According to Ibrahim, an emissary is right now on his way to Pakistan with a detailed report on the entire terrorist plan, including the targets and schedule."

That clearly got Pearson's attention, and he visibly stiffened, as if ready to leap up and accept some award.

"Right now? Who is this emissary? Where is he? Wait, first of all, where did this Ibrahim get the information? Is it good?"

"Al," Jules replied, assuming a familiarity with the Deputy Director that wasn't warranted, "Ibrahim is Saudi royal family. He's wired into everything of importance in the Middle East community."

"Why come to you? Why didn't he use his own chain-of-command and report this up through the ambassador?

"If he came to *me personally* with this, it's good information. He wouldn't tell me his source, but he staked his reputation on its veracity. Perhaps he thinks there is some complicity within the Saudi diplomatic corps."

"And this emissary, who is he?"

"He's a low-level attaché in the Yemeni embassy."

"A diplomat? From Yemen?"

"Yes. According to Ibrahim, there is some Yemeni connection here, and the emissary is on his way to report to the new al Qaeda leadership itself."

"Wait a moment. I've got to get some others in on this."

Pearson picked up the phone and pressed two buttons and said, "Martha, get Logan and Wernecke in here now."

"OK," Pearson continued to Jules, "where is this emissary, now?"

"He's probably on a flight to Peshawar. According to Ibrahim, he left for Riyadh last night to connect there for Pakistan. He should be arriving about 3 PM Peshawar time."

"Last night! When did Ibrahim tell you this?"

"Oh, about ten this morning when he came by my office."

"This morning? Shit, that was six hours ago. You sat on this information for six hours while this guy got into Pakistani air space?"

"I didn't sit on anything." Jules answered, startled at the sudden turn the conversation had taken. This wasn't in the script he'd imagined as he'd made his calls. "He was already on his way to Saudi Arabia when I talked to Ibrahim. And it took six hours to get through to you. I can't help that."

"Me? Why the hell did you ..." He was interrupted when the door opened and two men entered, *Logan and Wernecke, no doubt,* Jules thought, thankful for the interruption.

Pearson summarized the information for them, emphasizing that it was now six hours stale, and in Pakistan it was almost 2 AM.

"First, run this Ibrahim guy through our terrorist nexus database, and have the NCTC and FBI run him through theirs, too. And get in touch with TSA's Emergency Operations Center and have them check all flights that could directly connect to Pakistan during the last twenty-four hours with a priority on any through Riyadh. Sort and prioritize the passengers by nationality and run the Saudis, hell, run all the Arabs through the database. And forward the list to the NCTC and FBI so they can run them as well. We'll need a team at Peshawar airport to intercept this guy, and we don't have a lot of time to get it set up. Martha," he yelled, bypassing the phone, "get me in to see the DNI now, not five minutes from now. I don't care if he's talking to the President, I need to see him *now.*"

He turned back to Logan and Wernecke and said, "Help Martha get a SVTC set up ASAP. We'll need CIA, DoD, DHS, State ..."

"I'm State," Jules said, but no one acknowledged the sounds he made.

"... FBI, CIA, NCTC, DoD, Energy, particularly the guys at the weapons labs. They'll have to find and neutralize this stuff as soon as we know its whereabouts."

Pearson stopped for a moment, and then continued, "Look, this intel hasn't been vetted and it could all be bullshit. But, thanks to Vincenzo over there, we don't have the time to check it out. We're taking a real chance here grabbing a foreign diplomat in another country, and if we come up empty, we're dead. Understand that? Careers over, national disgrace, the whole ball of wax. But if it's real, we can't let it go. This could be the solution to a potential catastrophe of monumental proportions. We've got to take the risk. Try to get some corroborative data points that help justify what we're about to do. All right, get to it. Martha, am I in?"

"Yes sir. He's expecting you."

"Vincenzo, come with me. And keep your mouth shut unless one of us specifically asks you a question."

Jules started to protest, but stopped when he saw the look on Pearson's face. This was not going at all as he'd expected.

3.11   BBC News Headquarters, London, England

BBC Jewish Defense League Threatens Action Against Arab Terrorists

Calls for defense of American Jews by any means necessary

The Jewish Defense League (JDL) of the United Kingdom, a radical religious-political militant organization whose stated goal is to "protect Jews from anti-Semitism by whatever means necessary" has asserted that it "unequivocally condemns the Arab WMD terrorism attacks upon the United States" and re-stated that it has a "strict no-tolerance policy against terrorism and other felonious acts" and would defend American Jews, Synagogues and Jewish heritage sites. The JDL was classified as a "right-wing terrorist group" by the U.S. Federal Bureau of Investigation (FBI) in 2001. According to the FBI, the JDL has been involved in plotting and executing acts of terrorism within the United States. In response to the JDL statement, the FBI has issued a public warning to the JDL and all other extremist groups that they will be dealt with quickly and severely if they incite or initiate any violence or threats of violence.

3.12   FBI Field Office, Louisville, KY

The early results were in, and Cal could plainly see that Buck Buchanan was not happy. If it had been an election, Buck would have been preparing his concession speech.

"There's got to be ten thousand possibilities here. How the hell am I supposed to cover them all? I told you this was a goddam waste of time. Give me a fucking lead, for crissake, not a goddam scavenger hunt."

"This is just a hardcopy of the first level," Cal explained. "Most of these targets are repetitive locations because this sort is by chronology. Look, the financial district in New York shows up almost every hour during business days. That's a pretty obvious target. But the Mayor's speech only shows up once. We'll do further filtering to get a list of just the high probability targets and the occasional events. We cover the high-probability targets constantly, and add the events as they occur. You'll find this is a manageable list when we run that."

"So when do I get this new list? And how many places am I going to have to cover?"

"You can have it now. All the agents can get it electronically in real-time, so they can add or change parameters and instantly see the current situation. Right now, there are 367 high-priority targets over the next week."

"So what the hell are you showing me this other crap for? Do I need that for anything?"

"No. It's just to give you an idea of the depth of that analysis so you can understand the value of the results."

"Fuck that. Just give me a list. One is as good as another at this point. We've got nothing to go on but computer games, so I might as well use those."

That wasn't exactly the buy-in Cal had been going for, but it would have to do.

"Most of these can be covered by increased local activity and awareness," Cal said. "We need to get the information and directions into the hands of local law enforcement to know what to look for, and to the responders to know what to be prepared for. You'll need to coordinate that, and possibly get additional agents into some of these locations if you don't think there are adequate local resources. For example, you see that Branson, Missouri has a two-day country music festival coming up this weekend. No way they have the resources to find a dirty bomb before it goes off or to respond to it if one does."

"How do the field teams access this?"

"Here," Cal said, handing Buck a USB memory stick. "I've prepared a description of the software and the results that can be expected along with instructions on how to change the parameters. Agents and analysts will need to use their complete ID badge name as the user ID to log on, and their social security number as their password. Take a look and then get this out to everyone. DNDO and NNSA are distributing some additional equipment and response teams to the high-priority target areas on this list."

"I'd feel a lot better if I had an actual clue."

"You've got plenty of them. Cargo vans, driver profiles, radiation signatures. This is just to tell you where to follow them."

3.13 Enrico Fermi Nuclear Power Plant, Monroe, MI

As always, Hadi arrived for work at 3:30 PM. That gave him thirty minutes to review the day-shift activity, and for the requisite shift change briefing by the commander. He stopped at the gun locker and checked out his Glock, ran through the inspection to make sure he had a loaded magazine and an empty chamber, and holstered the weapon on his uniform's equipment belt, snapping the safety strap so it was secure. From there, he went to the Command Room to review the day shift reports and wait for Captain Bridges to brief him.

"Hey, Lieutenant," the older, overweight sergeant monitoring the video display screens greeted him. "Coffee's hot, but it's really bad today. I think Jarvis must have left it on and boiled off the coffee and then brewed a new pot without cleaning it. I mean, it's toxic."

"Thanks, Sergeant. I think Jarvis does that on purpose. The graveyard shift isn't his favorite."

The Wackenhut security staff at the Enrico Fermi Nuclear Generating Station maintained a military-style discipline, including using rank to address each other. As the Two-Shift Commander, Lieutenant Martin Washington, Hadi's birth name, was accorded the title.

Hadi grabbed the metal clipboard from its hook on the wall and took it with him to the shift commander's office, settling into the guest chair until he formally took command and would use the desk. As usual, the reports were routine, not even an animal intrusion on one of the perimeter alarms. As Hadi closed the cover, Captain Bridges entered the office, and Hadi stood as a sign of respect, not exactly coming to attention, but standing until Bridges took his seat behind the desk.

"Afternoon, Lieutenant. Nothing in there of any interest," he said with an offhand wave at the clipboard. "I do have one piece of news, although it's more in the realm of gossip than news. It's about the cesium theft down in Tennessee."

Hadi stiffened, wondering how anything to do with the theft could be of interest to the security of the plant. A nuclear power plant was probably the worst possible target for a dirty bomb. They were secure and isolated enough to contain the dispersal of radioactive material. And if there was any place equipped and ready to deal quickly and effectively with a radioactive materials spill, it was a nuclear power plant.

"You know the calibration lab here uses one of the Pastor automated units to calibrate our instruments? Well, it turns out that's where the cesium was stolen from, and Pastor's kid is some kind of person of interest to the FBI. He worked for his old man and did maintenance on our calibrator, so he's in our security records. That was before your time here. Anyway, he was murdered on Monday out in California, and we got a routine call asking about his record, anything unusual in it, any contacts he might still have here, you know, the whole fill-the-file-questions routine. Nothing there, of course, but we go through the motions."

Hadi didn't relax. His immediate concern that the investigation was coming his way had been unfounded, but the news that Pastor's son might be connected and he was now dead, murdered, caused a whole new set of concerns. Who was this guy? Was he involved in the theft? Who killed him, and why? Did he know something?

"Hey, Marty," the Captain said, using Hadi's familiar birth name, "you all right? You sort of went off there."

"No, I'm fine. Trying to think how that could be of any concern to us," Hadi said.

"Well, it isn't. Just routine. I'm heading out. You have a good shift. Enjoy the coffee." The last sentiment was accompanied by a knowing grin, and Hadi smiled back, his thoughts still churning over the news.

It couldn't be a coincidence, he thought. Not on the day after the theft. He must have had some knowledge and been a threat. Maybe he tried to blackmail someone. More likely, he was under suspicion and someone was afraid he would talk. But that meant the FBI was onto something. Someone who planned and carried out the theft was afraid. And if he was afraid, shouldn't I be afraid? If Pastor's son was expendable, aren't I?

The more he considered this development, the angrier he got, but it ebbed as anxiety took hold. Hearing just the television news all week and not knowing what was really happening caused him to imagine a lot of scenarios that always ended with him in handcuffs. He had no co-conspirators to contact, no support group to talk to, not even a leader to report to. Hadi was alone, involved in something he hadn't wanted.

He'd participated in the theft only under duress, when two strangers had shown up at his apartment with recordings of the phone call to Qaeda al-Jihad, one of the al Qaeda affiliates in Afghanistan, and a grainy video of his meeting in Afghanistan. Before he'd become Hadi, even before he'd changed his name to Mohammad Saleem Riskiq, he'd been Staff Sergeant Martin Washington, U.S. Marines. Two tours of duty in Afghanistan, highly respected, highly decorated. And a traitor.

Watching what was happening there over his two years as part of a Specified Target Team, Hadi had begun to question his mission, both in Afghanistan and in life. The STT was a six-man hunter-killer squad with a list of by-name targets to neutralize. His STT of three Marines and three Afghan Army Commandos had murdered civilians on the flimsiest of evidence, evidence that wouldn't even get an indictment back home. And they'd enjoyed it, joking and taking gruesome photos for souvenirs.

As a hunter-killer, Hadi had access to information about possible terrorist cells and he'd used that, making contact with one of them at great personal risk. He wanted revenge for what he believed were the innocent dead, and gave up his team to get it. It was a simple matter. They gave him a cell phone, and when his team was to set up their next mission, he simply called a number and told someone when and where. And then he went to the infirmary. His whole team had been ambushed, and Hadi had become a terrorist.

His fear of exposure, the threats to his family, and the appeal to his religious beliefs had overcome his doubts about taking *jihad* to innocent civilians. Now he wanted to put it behind him, to forget it and hope that the perpetrators forgot about him. An unlikely event, he knew.

The phone rang, snapping him out of his reverie. He listened as the sergeant dealt with some minor issue, and when he hung up, Hadi put on his hat and said, "I'm going to walk the perimeter. Call me if anything comes up."

"Walk it? That's almost two miles. Why don't you take the Jeep?"

"Feel like a walk, that's all."

Hadi walked south across the parking lot to Enrico Fermi Drive and turned left, toward the beach. The plant was located on the western shore of Lake

Erie, less than thirty miles south of Detroit. The Pastor news shook him. The bombs hadn't even been used yet, and already the plan seemed to be falling apart—traffic accidents, murdered conspirators, and who knew what else. Hadi didn't know what the plan was beyond his role, but if some of the participants were being silenced, then clearly there were problems. Did they consider him a problem? Whoever *they* were. From their perspective, they shouldn't. He was isolated and didn't know the identities of anyone, not even the others involved in the theft.

From his perspective, Hadi knew they should consider him a problem. He had all the information that was needed to thwart the plan. As the trucks had been loaded at Pastor, Hadi had recorded the license plate number and the company names and information painted on the logos on the doors. He didn't know exactly why he did that, he just figured the information might be useful someday.

Maybe someday had arrived. If Hadi had thought to record the information, maybe the others behind the theft had thought that he might. Maybe they were targeting him right now. He was safe at the plant, but as soon as he left, he was an easy target.

As he walked, working it out in his head, Hadi thought about how he could protect himself. Dying at the hands of his own people would not make him a martyr, and he would have no guarantee of automatic entry into *Jannah*, paradise. In fact, being responsible for the deaths of many Muslims in Afghanistan, he would likely be barred. If they were targeting him, he would never be safe. He was on his own, and he needed to be ready. *Jihad* would have to wait until he'd secured his own safety.

Looking east, Hadi realized the solution was right across the lake – Canada. A thirty-mile drive to Detroit and then across the Ambassador Bridge connecting Detroit to Windsor, Ontario. From there, he could go anywhere in Canada. He instantly liked the idea. He could disappear, and as long as he kept a low profile and didn't attend a mosque, al Qaeda wouldn't be able to find him. He would need money. He had almost $16,000 in his Scottrade account, and over $24,000 in his 401K at work. That would be plenty, he thought, to get him settled somewhere else as someone else.

His immediate problem was surviving long enough to get the money and prepare to disappear. He would have to be on guard every minute now. And he would need a weapon. His Glock would be perfect, but all the guns were kept at the plant and were accounted for at the end of each shift. But he had a personal weapon, a 9 mm Beretta, hidden in his apartment. Smuggling that into Canada would be a risk, but one he would have to take.

He decided to move to a motel temporarily and stay away from his apartment until he could sort things out. He would close his 401K and Scottrade accounts and work with cash, avoiding any credit card trail.

Turning back to the plant, he had a plan. He knew plans always went awry, but he was trained for that. He wondered how well-trained his adversary would be.

THURSDAY, JUNE 24

3.14   ISLAMABAD INTERNATIONAL AIRPORT, PAKISTAN

The CIA field agent watched the debarking passengers from a seat at the gate, looking like the other people waiting to board the return flight to Riyadh. He also watched the two ISI agents he'd managed to pick out of the crowd, one a waiting passenger like himself, but a bit too observant, and the other working a cart selling drinks and snacks, and not doing a very good job of it. The Pakistani Directorate of Inter-Services Intelligence ran as professional an operation as any in the world, the CIA and Mossad excepted, he believed. Picking out the two operatives so easily meant they were intended to be seen, and there were at least two more who weren't. He wasn't worried, though. Today, they were working together.

Picking out the Yemeni attaché was easy – Atiyah Abdul Rahman was well known to international law enforcement for his suspected association with al Qaeda in the Arabian Peninsula. He looked worse for wear after the sixteen-hour flight including stops in Damman and Dubai. According to their information, he'd been directed to deliver the envelope himself, so he wouldn't be ending his journey at the Yemeni consulate in Islamabad, he'd just be getting outfitted for another.

When Rahman had passed, the CIA agent got up and trailed behind, watching carefully for any interaction with anyone else, especially anyone not from the plane he'd arrived on. It was possible that he'd given the document to someone else on the plane, but everyone agreed it would be more likely that he would pass through immigration and customs with the document and claim diplomatic privilege for it if he was stopped.

As expected, he went straight to the far aisle in the immigration area, the aisle marked "Crew & Diplomatic Personnel Only." The other passengers peeled off to go to their selected aisle and the agent and one other person, no doubt a previously unidentified ISI agent, were the only two to follow the Yemeni. The immigration officer, another ISI agent, asked for Rahman's papers and examined the diplomatic passport.

"What is your business here in Pakistan," he asked him, speaking in Urdu, the official if not dominant language of Pakistan.

"I am here for meetings at my consulate, and I am being met by someone from there."

"Where will you be staying? And for how long?"

"The consulate has made arrangements for my accommodations, and I don't know where. I will be returning sometime this weekend, depending on my meeting schedule here."

"Are you carrying a diplomatic pouch, either with you or in your luggage?"

"Yes, I have some official papers for my consulate."

"With you?"

"Yes. In my briefcase."

"Very good," the agent said, stamping the passport with an entry visa. "Please pick up your checked luggage and go to the customs station number nine. They will clear you for entry."

***

Chad Mellon watched Rahman while he picked up his single bag and proceeded to customs station nine, as directed. Mellon was in an office just off the customs area, watching the video monitor with Lt. Colonel Javed Parvez Riaz, the senior ISI agent in charge of this mission. He and Chad were well acquainted, having worked closely together before, Chad representing the CIA in Pakistan.

"Now things will get interesting," Riaz said in English.

"Yes, they will," Chad replied in Urdu, a little game they played whenever they were talking privately.

***

"Your briefcase, please," the customs agent asked Rahman. "Open it for me."

He did as directed and watched as the agent inspected each file and magazine and pocket and item. When he held up a plain, C6-sized European-format Tyvek envelope, Rahman stiffened.

"What is this," the agent asked.

"Diplomatic papers," he answered. "They are privileged."

"Ah, privileged," the agent replied, nodding his head. Rahman, fluent in Urdu but not fully aware of the tones of sarcasm in that language, missed it. "Why are there no markings on the envelope indicating this privilege?"

"I am an accredited diplomat of the Republic of Yemen, and I am traveling on my diplomatic passport on official business. That is sufficient to grant me free passage without any markings or other identification under the Vienna Convention. Now, please, do not delay me any longer. I have someone from the Consulate waiting for me."

"Yes, yes. I see. Someone waiting. Have you been re-assigned to the Consulate here? And have you any papers formalizing that assignment?"

"No, of course not. I am assigned to the Embassy in Riyadh. And as I said, I am traveling on official business."

"So Saudi Arabia is your host country. And you enjoy these privileges there. I see. Very good. But you see, those privileges are not valid here in Pakistan, are they? Here, you are just another businessman traveling to our country to conduct your affairs. You have not been accredited by your embassy here, and I see no documents granting any special status for this official business you have. You might as well be on vacation. So I guess I will ask you one more time, what is this," again holding the unmarked envelope.

"I must protest this treatment. I demand to see your superior immediately. Otherwise, I will report this through official channels and there will be consequences."

"Yes, my superior. And consequences, you say? Please wait here, and I will get him."

The agent turned and started to walk away, still holding the envelope.

"Wait," Rahman called. "Leave the envelope. That is a privileged diplomatic communication and must remain with me."

The agent turned and looked at the envelope and replied, "Yes, I understand. But you see, there are no markings as such. And if I am to bother my superior over a simple unmarked envelope, he will want to see it before accommodating your request to meet him. Do not worry, I will not steal your privileged document."

The agent turned and left, ignoring Rahman's protests.

***

Chad and Javed watched as the ISI document expert examined the envelope, first with his naked eye, and then through what looked like a jeweler's loupe.

"Yes yes. It is a standard C6 Tyvek, adhesive-sealed business envelope made in the U.S. Perhaps an unusual size there, but still, quite common. I, of course, do not have this same one. We don't import such common products. Ours are all made by the Pakistan Paper Products Company in Karachi. They the same size, you see, but the interior printing is quite different. On the outside, ours have this thin blue border around the sealing flap. If your man has paid close attention, he will see the difference."

"Now that we know what it is, can we get this envelope," Javed asked him.

"Oh, of course we can get it, but it would have to be flown here from some location where they use U.S. paper products. We checked with the U.S. Embassy in Karachi and the consulate, and we have samples of every envelope they have in stock. None of them match."

"We can't keep him here long enough to get an exact match," Javed said. "Can you open this one without damage? Possibly from the seam on the end?"

"Oh, we can try, but I doubt it. They will bend and stretch, but it will also tear in a jagged pattern if enough pressure is applied. The adhesive is not soluble in water, and any solvent we use would also affect the Tyvek. We can try to cut it and reseal it, but you see here? These seams are machine made and they emboss the plastic. We can't cut into them to separate the two sides, there will be some tearing where the ridges are. Again, a subtle change, but one someone who examined the envelope would be sure to notice. It is better, in my opinion, to have them wonder if the envelope is original or not than to give them something damaged."

"Chad, what do you think?"

"We have to go with your man's recommendation. I don't see any options. Let's just do it. The longer we delay, the more suspicious he will become and the more likely he is to examine the envelope. Open it, make two copies, put it in the new envelope and give it back to him. Oh, can you take photos of it before it's opened so we can reconstruct any evidence of wear. And also be sure there are no hidden markings that identify it."

The process took just under four minutes, and Javed, in civilian clothes, assumed the role of the customs supervisor. With the phony customs inspector, he took the envelope back to the impatient Yemeni.

"I am sorry for the delay," he said, "but you must understand that we cannot be too careful these days. I've phoned my superiors and they in turn have checked with our Ministry of Foreign Affairs and we have been instructed to allow you to proceed. Do you need any assistance in expediting your mission? A ride to your consulate, perhaps?"

"No," Rahman replied, "I have someone waiting to meet me. I'll just take my document and be on my way."

"Very good, sir. I hope your mission is successful and if there is any need for assistance, please contact me anytime. Here is my card."

***

Back in the office, Chad and Javed watched the video monitor as Rahman cleared the customs area and entered the terminal. By then, most of the other passengers were gone, and the crowd had thinned appreciably. He walked toward the terminal exit and past the waiting taxis and busses to the passenger pick-up area. The camera view changed twice and picked him up outside the terminal. The airport was located in a secure military zone and heavily guarded, including barriers to control pedestrian and vehicle flow. Rahman paused near the exit and then approached a plain black Toyota Premio. The driver opened the window and spoke to him. After replying, Rahman opened the back seat and threw his suitcase in and then got into the front passenger seat and the car drove away.

"That was not an official vehicle from the consulate," Javed said. "It had civilian license plates."

"Yes, I noticed that as well. You will track them, of course," Chad said.

"Yes, of course."

Neither noticed the tiny light moving rapidly 18,000 feet overhead, just a slight discoloration in the sky, though they both knew it must be there.

3.15   FBI HEADQUARTERS/SIOC, WASHINGTON, DC

The document had landed on the Attorney General's desk at 6:18 AM, where he had been impatiently awaiting it after learning the day before of the operation in Pakistan and the possibility of capturing a road map to the dirty bombs. Twenty-eight minutes later, Carson Nevins found himself in the secure conference room in the SIOC with half-a-dozen NCTC and FBI counterterrorism analysts poring over its translated contents, debating back and forth just who would get what information. His job was to carry the opinions and decisions of the Department of Justice about the document to the meeting and see that they were fully understood and adhered to.

The job of this ad hoc team was to distill the information into a series of tear-sheets, individual reports, all on the same subject, but each sanitized for the specific recipients, from top intel and law enforcement leaders and specialists down to the Fusion Centers and local law enforcement. The goal was to share the information for the most desired results—the early identification and capture of the terrorists and their dirty bombs—while respecting the legal separation between the intelligence communities and law enforcement. There was some tension in the room as they tried to give everyone the most information they could use, in a form they would best understand and implement. In his impatience to get this information out, Carson found himself wanting to give everyone more information than was legally advisable, and he had to force himself to draw lines that were not necessarily where he would have liked them to be.

At the highest level, senior law enforcement and intel personnel would get the actual document, annotated with explanations of the significance of each new piece of information gleaned from the largely doctrinal language, designed more to glorify the events as the will of Allah than to describe them in any rational way.

Carson's bullet points for the annotation at this level noted that there were in fact sixteen bombs originally, meaning fifteen were still out there. The schedule was vague, only referencing what could best be translated as an 'inaugural incident' that would happen on some undefined 'auspicious occasion', but the Arabic phrasing had religious connotations that needed explanation in one of the myriad of annotations. It also went on to say that the bombs would be used to "celebrate the holiest time for the Five Pillars" and that "the sons of Ali ibn Abu Talib" would "emanate the Fifth Caliphate" and raise the "Great Mosque of Sana'a" to its glory.

When the scholars of the Islamic religion who had been poring over the document in an adjacent conference room provided their interpretation, Carson filled in the blanks. The obvious choice for the inaugural incident would be the start of Ramadan, just fifteen days away. The theory was that the bombs would be used over the course of the month of Ramadan as this was an especially important time for Shahada, Salam, and Sawm, three of the Five Pillars of Islam. Ali ibn Abu Talib, Carson learned, was the son-in-law of the Prophet Muhammad and the Caliph or Imam, depending on if you were Sunni or Shia, who brought Islam to the area now known as Yemen, the home of the Great Mosque of Sana'a.

Carson's annotations for the top level tear sheet made it clear—next month was the time and al Qaeda of the Arabian Peninsula, based in Yemen, were the perpetrators. At the bottom level, the Fusion Centers were advised only to be on the lookout for more, similar weapons in the hands of Islamic terrorists.

3.16 VETERANS ADMINISTRATION HOSPITAL, MISSOULA, MT

At 4 in the afternoon on a beautiful, sunny day, overhead the blue was an advertisement for Big Sky Country. Just another summer day in Missoula, Montana. A grand day for a surprise visit to his wife, Tag thought, even though she would have no idea what day it was, or that it was a surprise, or even who it was who pushed her wheelchair around the paths on the grounds of the facility.

The decision to make the half-hour drive and visit was a surprise to Tag as well. He'd wanted to be alone on this day, the eve of the dawn of a new age. But as the day progressed he'd found his frustration and anxiety growing. He'd checked and double-checked the status of his men and vehicles, making sure everything was well-hidden from the coming shit storm. He watched the slow progress of his clandestine plan on the map displaying the location of his little surprise, using the GPS tracker on the vehicle. It was imperative that it reach its destination on time, before tomorrow's events closed the country down like Russia under Stalin.

He'd watched the 24/7 news channels, flipping from one to the other, looking for any hint that something was amiss in one of the target cities. He even checked the traffic conditions to see if anything unusual was causing a traffic jam. Only al Hasan had any communication with the bombers, so Tag had no way of knowing their operational status until the actual event.

Finally, he had to get out of the house, and what better company than Marion? He could tell her everything with the certainty that she would make no judgments, offer no opinions, and certainly never tell another person what was going to happen.

"Those ragheads are gonna get a surprise, honey. I can guarantee that. They come to me with their money and their big plans and think I'm just some stupid hick who fell off the turnip truck. They think I'm gonna let them blow their dirty bombs up wherever *they* want. They think their money gives them the right to dictate to me? No way. They can have the rest of America to spread their filth – hell, it's already filthy – but they're not gonna spread it where good, honest Americans are still in charge, like Minnesota. Old al Ass-on didn't see that coming. ZOG may have the coasts, they may have the big cities, but they don't own the rest of us yet, and no A-rab is going to tell me what to do about it.

"When we press the button, honey, ZOG is gonna be pissed. Their precious multi-cultural experiments will be ruined, and they're gonna go broke trying to clean up the mess. All those foreigners and losers will be screaming for the government to save them. They'll probably expect ZOG to bring soap and water and wash them off themselves. Meanwhile, the good people of America will be safe and secure.

"You see, I fooled those bozos. All that stuff they had planted in the heartland of this great country? Well, I moved it. Yes, ma'am, I moved it. How do you like that? They said one bomb in Washington was enough, and the airport, for Christ's sake. They said it would scare the people and cost the government billions to clean up. Well, this isn't about scaring the scum of Zionist-occupied DC, it's about shutting it down. And when the three bombs I sent there go off, it will be a ghost town.

"Yes, honey, the prophecy is coming true. Soon we'll have a land of the free and a home of the brave again. Maybe not as big as it used to be, but big enough for all of us who believe in it."

3.17   SILVER DOLLAR DINER, GILLETTE, WY

Officer Lloyd Elkins crossed the parking lot of the Silver Dollar Diner, using a toothpick to get the remnants of the steak sandwich from between his teeth. As he passed the white cargo van with Washington state license plates, his brand new pager device started chirping. Startled, Lloyd jammed the toothpick under his gums. "Shit," he cursed, momentarily forgetting the friendly chirping from his equipment belt. But it caught his attention again and he tried to remember what it meant and what to do about it. Since the device was supposed to detect radiation, he thought the first thing he should do was to move away from the van.

The chirping slowed and then stopped as he moved to his patrol cruiser, six cars away. This was only the second day he'd worn the pager, and he'd already forgotten most of his minimal training. The thirty-one patrol officers of Gillette had each been given one, purchased by a semi-retired movie star with a horse ranch outside of town who likely thought himself a prime target for terrorists based on his previous action films where he'd defeated many of them. Gillette now had more radiation detection equipment per capita than any city in America.

Not sure what to do, Lloyd got into his cruiser and radioed headquarters, forgetting his radio protocol in the excitement.

"Janine," he said into the microphone to the surprised dispatcher, "it's Lloyd. Let me speak to Henry, quick."

"You OK, Lloyd? You need backup or something?"

"No, just get Henry. And hurry."

After very few seconds, nothing in the Gillette Police Department's offices in City Hall being very far from anything else, Henry Burke got on the radio.

"What the hell is going on, Lloyd?"

"Sarge, my pager thing went off! I'm out at the Silver Dollar Diner and I investigated a white cargo van with Washington plates and the pager started beeping. I've got it under surveillance, but you need to get some more boys out here pronto."

"Is it beeping now?"

"No, it stopped when I went to my car."

"Alright, Lloyd. You stay put and call Janine if anything changes. I'm on my way."

"Am I gonna die?"

"No, Lloyd. Those things are set to go off at the first sign of radiation. You probably got as much radiation as a tooth x-ray."

Henry had no idea if that was true, but he figured he'd better keep Lloyd calm.

"Where's the book on these pager things," he asked Janine. She reached into the file cabinet next to her desk and handed him one of the thirty-one user's manuals that were filed there instead of being in the hands of the users, where they might do some good.

Henry leafed through the manual until he found the part on the alarms and quickly read the instructions. Noting that if the beeping had stopped, there was no danger, he felt satisfied with his direction to Lloyd.

"Janine, get out a general alert. All cars to close on the diner. No sirens. Have them hold a quarter mile back until I get there. Shit, who do we call about this?"

Janine opened her phone directory and scanned the pages.

"Here it is, the Wyoming Office of Homeland Security in Cheyenne."

"OK. Get them on the phone and let them know what we've got and then call me on my cell phone. Keep this off the radio. I don't want those assholes from KSWY to find out about this until we've got it controlled."

Janine was still leafing through her manual and stopped to read something.

"It says here that the State Police are supposed to respond to any radiation incident involving transportation. If it's in a van, that's transportation, right?"

"Of course. Call Captain Willis and let him know. Have him meet me at the east side parking lot at the WalMart. And get the fire department to send their HazMat team there, as well. No lights or sirens from anyone. Oh, shit, I almost forgot. Get a hold of Chief Artelson and fill him in. Got it?"

"Homeland Security – Willis – WalMart – HazMat – Artelson – stealth. Got it."

With that, Burke was out the door.

***

When a man emerged from the diner and went to the van, everyone was ready. At Burke's direction, a patrolman in civilian clothes had let the air out of one of the rear tires and then stationed himself between two cars and waited. His job was to casually stroll by and point out the flat tire in case the driver didn't notice it. They wanted to apprehend the driver outside the truck and immediately immobilize him to prevent any remote detonation of a bomb.

While the patrolman engaged the driver, a fifty-something man, balding and overweight, in a discussion about the flat tire and local gas stations who could come out and fix it, several state troopers moved into position. Another patrolman in civilian clothes inside the diner hustled all the patrons through the kitchen and out the back door.

Watching the scene through binoculars from the WalMart lot, Les Willis said, "He sure don't look like a terrorist to me. Something's wrong here, Henry. You sure those pagers are working right?"

"How would I know," Henry answered, watching the same scene through his own binoculars. "I've had the damn things for two days. For all I know, Lloyd was hearing things."

At that moment, they saw the van driver reach into his pocket, and all hell broke loose.

3.18   CNN News Headquarters, Atlanta, GA

 POLICE CHIEFS ISSUE NEW TERRORIST "PROFILING" GUIDELINES

MUSLIM GROUPS TARGETED FOR "NON-RELIGIOUS" ASSESSMENT

ATLANTA (CNNNational.com) -- The International Association of Chiefs of Police today issued new set of guidelines to help all U.S. and Canadian police and law enforcement organizations to more effectively identify possible radical Muslims across North America and to hold them for interrogation. Spokesperson Emily Blount of the American Civil Liberties Union denounced the guidelines as "profiling ethnic and religious groups for unconstitutional search and seizure." A Bloomberg Poll of 21 constitutional scholars found that 18 of them believe the so-called Muslim Profile and Detention Laws are constitutional in light of the unabated and ongoing WMD terrorist attacks on America.

3.19   FBI Field Office, Louisville, KY

The Thursday SVTC was about thirty minutes away when Buck called Cal to his office. Cal had just sat down when Buck dropped a two-inch-thick file on his desk from as high as he could reach and still be sitting. It landed with a substantial thump.

"That's the results of your clues. There are hundreds of false alarms pouring in, mostly from places we've alerted based on your computer games. All we're doing is causing panic. Shit, the police shot some poor delivery driver in Gillette, Wyoming. He was on his way to the local hospital with some medical isotopes and someone's radiation detector went off and they panicked when he reached for his cell phone."

Cal ignored the file. "Sooner or later, one of those false alarms will turn out to be the real thing and someone's vigilance will save a lot of lives and a lot of trouble. It's all we've got for the moment."

"It's shit, and you know it. We've got no intel from any agency. We've got no leads from the two dead guys or anywhere else. We're no closer to finding that cesium than we were four days ago."

"I can't manufacture leads. All I can do is point you in the right direction and tell you what to look for. Here's what I do know – you need someone to encourage every one of these false alarms. Let the police in Gillette and everywhere else know that it's better to follow up on a false lead than it is to miss a real one. Congratulate them, don't blame them. Did the driver die?"

"No, he was wounded along with a local cop. Friendly fire, because the driver was unarmed and harmless."

"Tell them they did good. Send the driver a commendation or something, but make sure no one gets timid because of the possibility of another mistake."

"I can't be encouraging hot-dogging by local cops. All we'll get is more innocent victims, and one of them is bound to be dead."

"A lot of people are likely to be dead before this is over, Buck. They killed nineteen people in Kentucky already."

"That's what you've got to offer? I'm supposed to tell everyone that more people will die? And some by mistake?"

"Unless you want to lie to them, yes."

FRIDAY, JUNE 25

3.20 SYBRIUM CONTAINER SOLUTIONS, BREEZEWOOD, PA

"What three special drums? Says here you got seventy-nine drums of MEKP. Don't say shit about nuthin' else." The forklift operator handed the manifest back to Justin Anderson and said, "Back 'er in number four so's we're close to the cage and we'll offload."

The cage was a locked area of the Sybrium warehouse, secured for the hazardous chemicals they used to make fiberglass tanks for petroleum products and other liquids. The MEKP was the catalyst that cross-linked the polyester resins and hardened into the final stiff, strong, and light material.

"All I know is we made three extra stops and picked up some extra containers of some kind, and they're in the drums I marked on the manifest. See? Here, here, and here."

"Like I said, I don't know nuthin' about that. You back in and I'll get the dock foreman. Maybe he knows."

The forklift operator was waiting with another man after Billy got the rig positioned. Justin got out to talk to them.

"Yes yes yes," the foreman said, glancing around. "Pull those three and put them in the other cage. I'll take care of them. You just forget about them. They're for a special project. Nothing to worry about."

I wasn't worried, the operator thought and went about doing as he was told.

3.21 CONSULATE OF THE KINGDOM OF SAUDI ARABIA, HOUSTON, TX

Not surprisingly, the call had come first thing that morning. Ibrahim's secretary informed him that there would be a meeting with the Consul General at 4 PM, and he was to make himself available at that time. The timing was fortuitous. He had planned to be somewhere public, anyplace where his movements during the day would be documented. When 5 PM arrived, he would be safe, secure, and totally unconnected to the events he knew were about to take place. A meeting with the Consul General after a day on the Consulate grounds would remove him from immediate connection with the bombs.

He could guess the agenda of the meeting with almost absolute certainty. Rahman had delivered the manifesto and the U.S. authorities no doubt had a copy. The meeting would be connected to that. After all, it was his information that had caused those events, and Vincenzo would certainly have given up his name when questioned. It would be his opportunity to establish his innocence, and to reinforce his cooperation with the U.S. authorities. All as he had planned and prepared.

They met in the Consul General's private conference room on the second floor, and Ibrahim was satisfied to see that the FBI ASAC – Houston was there personally, an acknowledgment of the importance of the information he'd provided. Having never met the man, Ibrahim feigned ignorance of his identity before they were introduced, and curiosity once they were.

"The FBI? Why would the FBI want to talk to me?" He looked to the Consul General and asked, "Isn't this a bit irregular?"

The Consul nodded and replied. "This is a voluntary meeting, Ibrahim. These men have come to us with some disturbing information about the recent cesium theft, and we have agreed to assist their investigation in any way we can. This comes directly from the Ambassador, and of course, that means from the King himself. So I ask that you please cooperate fully and answer their questions and disregard any diplomatic immunity considerations that you enjoy. So, let us be seated, please."

Ibrahim could speak diplomat as well as anyone, and understood this was a warning that he "enjoyed" that immunity at the discretion of the Ambassador, and that it could and would be withdrawn at any time they wished.

"Very good, sir," he replied, and sat. "What can I do for you, gentlemen?"

"Well, sir," the SAC began. "We believe that you might have sources that can lead us to the perpetrators of the cesium theft, and we're here to enlist your cooperation in the investigation."

"Why would you believe that? Do you think that the Saudi government had something to do with this heinous threat to your country? We are allies in the war on terrorism, not adversaries."

"Nothing like that. We appreciate the cooperation and the support of your government. No, we think you might have personal sources that you could tap to help us."

"Personal sources? I can assure you that I do not know of any terrorists except those my country has incarcerated."

"Do you know a Jules Vincenzo at the Department of State?"

"Vaguely. We went to college together at Georgetown. He was a year behind me, I believe."

"Well, sir, he has named you as his source in identifying someone we believe is a simple courier carrying some documents germane to the theft. This courier was a Yemeni diplomat assigned to the embassy in Riyadh, and he has disappeared in Pakistan. We would like to verify your meeting with Mr. Vincenzo and its subject."

"I see. Mr Vincenzo named me? Why would he do that? I barely know the man."

"Mr. Hasan, there is no doubt that the meeting took place. We have Mr. Vincenzo's testimony and the visitor log to his State Department office and the security camera footage showing your entry at 10:12 AM on Wednesday. So, please, if you don't mind, we do not have time for cat and mouse games."

"All right, you are correct. I did meet with Mr. Vincenzo. And the subject was some information I had learned that might have relevance to this cesium theft. You understand that I am in a very sensitive position here, and cooperation with your law enforcement authorities could have dramatic consequences for my government. However, we are allies in this war on terrorism, so I felt it important that the information be provided to you as quickly as possible."

"Why Mr. Vincenzo? Why not go through your Embassy?"

Ibrahim turned to the Consul General and engaged all the sincerity that he could affect. "This information came from personal sources that I would rather remain confidential, and I did not want to implicate my Embassy in any way. Additionally, such a path would have taken more time than I thought was available. This courier that I had learned of was already en route, and any delay would have risked his escape. I went to Vincenzo to distance myself from the entire matter in order to protect my Embassy. As I said, I barely know the man, and I asked that he keep my identity confidential. Clearly, he did not do that."

"I would like to know the names of your personal sources, please," the ASAC said.

"I'm sorry, but I cannot provide that information. Violating the trust of that source would simply assure that I never learn any information in the future. Information that might be of use to you and to my government. And this source will have his own source and before long word of my betrayal would spread, and I would be isolated from any flow of information. Not only would I no longer be able to help the U.S. government, but I would be putting my own work and possibly my life and the lives of my family in jeopardy."

"Mr. Hasan, these are perilous times for all of us. This threat is unprecedented and our response will be commensurate with the gravity and nature of it. It is critical that we know the perpetrators and find the cesium, and that we capture and punish all those responsible. If you can help us, we would obviously be in your debt. And the U.S. government always pays its debts."

"I understand your position, but I must reiterate that I cannot reveal any sources that I might have for the reasons I've already stated." Turning to his superior at the Consulate, Ibrahim continued, "Consul, I believe that we should discuss this further privately and then we can schedule another meeting with these gentlemen when we are clear on all of its implications."

Before the Consul could respond, there was a light knocking at the door and an assistant entered and handed a note to the Consul General. A look of grave consternation crossed his face and he handed the note to the FBI ASAC.

Ibrahim knew what it must say, and rightly guessed that the meeting was over.

Part Four – The Bombs

FRIDAY, JUNE 25

4.01   THE CHICAGO MERCANTILE EXCHANGE, CHICAGO, IL

Twin Towers, Mahdi thought as he parked the van directly in front of 20 South Wacker Drive in Chicago. *How fitting*. These towers would not fall, he knew, but they would stand abandoned, a monument to the power of Allah, a gravestone marking the death of America.

It was rush hour, and traffic was thick on the southbound lanes. His illegal parking would attract attention before too long, but he knew Dhakir only needed moments to load the vest and put it on. Mahdi got out before he started so he would not be exposed to the radiation and crossed Madison Street and planted himself under the portico of the Civic Opera House, an ideal vantage point to video the carnage and chaos soon to be visited upon the intersection of Madison and Wacker and the main entrance to the north tower of the Chicago Mercantile Exchange Center.

***

Patrolman Edgar Watts watched the van park as he walked down Madison and toward Wacker. *A delivery*, he figured. One of the many financial houses inside the CME Center needing to get some documents somewhere before close of business. He'd give the driver as long as it took him to cross both the north and southbound lanes of Wacker and get to the vehicle and if he wasn't back, he'd write a parking ticket.

But the driver didn't go into the Merc, as the CME was known. He crossed Madison going north and went to the Opera House. Watts picked up his pace, now determined to ticket the van. As he crossed Wacker and approached it from the left rear, two things registered. First, it had Michigan tags, so it wasn't a local delivery van. And second, it was rocking, something moving around inside.

He walked toward the driver's door and the van stopped moving. So did Watts. Then two things happened almost simultaneously; he heard a loud clunk from inside, as if someone had dropped something heavy, and his recently issued radiation pager, strapped to his big black belt, suddenly vibrated and made an audible alarm. He'd been briefed every day since Tuesday, along with every other cop in every other location across the country, to be alert to this scenario – radiation, possibly a white van, and two young men, probably Middle-Eastern.

***

Mahdi watched the curious policeman from behind the concrete post that supported the roof of the portico. *Hurry, Dhakir*, he prayed. Mahdi had no weapon, nothing to incriminate him if he was swept up in the post-bombing confusion. All he could do was video the action, and he lifted the camera to his eye and began to record everything.

***

Watts drew his Glock and rushed to the driver's door. There was no one in the passenger compartment. He flung open the door and saw a surprised man crouching in the cargo area, struggling to put on a cumbersome vest. A vest similar to the ones Watts had seen many times in news reports, and most recently in his briefings. Watts' radiation pager was now on a constant alarm, indicating very high radiation levels. Without hesitation, without warning, without any remorse, Watts put three 9 mm bullets into the terrorist's head. Then he went tracking down the driver.

***

Mahdi lost sight of the policeman behind the van. Then he heard the shots. There was no explosion, nothing. Just *bangbangbang*. He lowered his camera and turned north, walking quickly up Wacker and entering the Opera House at mid-block, just as they'd planned in case something went wrong. Inside, he turned left, heading back toward the Madison Street entrance, the plan being to let pursuit overtake and pass him while he headed back toward the Merc and then escaped up Madison and across the Chicago River.

Dhakir was dead, he knew, and he made a decision – he would not try to escape. Sajid had not tried to escape when they'd been chased down by the police. He had martyred himself gloriously, killing many before dying for Allah. Mahdi decided he would do the same, he would detonate the weapon. He would be welcomed to paradise by Allah himself. At Madison Street, he turned left instead of right and walked to the back of the van, opening the rear cargo doors and reaching for the detonator on the vest tangled in Dharkir's dead body.

***

Watts ran into the Opera House, following his glimpse of the driver before he'd entered the building, and looked both ways. Even with only a few people in the lobby, he could not see his fugitive. *Shit*, he thought, *I don't have time for this.* Their briefings had been thorough, covering not only the description of the suspects and vehicle, but also of the weapon and the potential for disaster, detonated or not. The I-75 event was fresh in everyone's mind, including the overexposure to the policeman stationed near the crashed van before the cesium was discovered. Watts knew his job was to clear the area. The terrorist would have to wait for another day.

He ran back out the Wacker Drive entrance, keying his shoulder mike as he went.

"Patrolman Watts. 22845. I've got a 10-79 at Wacker and Madison. Repeat, a 10-79. My PRD is alarming. Radioactive material involved."

As he cleared the Opera House portico, he again had a clear view of the van and saw the man across the street approaching the back doors. The traffic light was against him and there were rush hour pedestrians stacked up at the crosswalk, blocking his progress and a clear shot at the terrorist. His gun still in his right hand, Watts shoved his way through and ran into the traffic, frantically signaling cars and trucks and dodging them when they slowed or swerved. He was still in Madison Street traffic when he saw the doors open and he knew his time was up. Forgetting traffic, forgetting pedestrians, forgetting everything but center mass on the back of the terrorist, he planted his feet, left foot in front, took his two-handed target-range posture, and put a three-round grouping into it.

The man collapsed, his arms dragging out of the van as he sank to the street. Watts lowered his own arms and, still holding the Glock in both hands, looked left at the taxi whose bumper was just touching his left leg. He almost laughed at the expression on the driver's face.

Fida drove the van northbound along Aviation Circle. Traffic was jammed as always, especially on a Friday afternoon when many people were escaping Washington, either back to their home constituencies, or away to somewhere cool, away from the heat and humidity of Washington in the summer, or home after a week of lobbying. Or, as Fida thought of it, bribing or stealing or planning conquest, all the things they do in America's capital city as a matter of course. Fida was born and raised in Lebanon and came to the U.S. at about the same time he started shaving, landing with his family at this very airport fourteen years earlier after transiting from Toronto. That trip had no good memories for him.

As he edged closer, he kept up a running description of their location and the outside activity to Jalal, waiting in back to load and don his vest. The information allowed Jalal to stay hidden from view and therefore not arouse suspicion from the omnipresent security by climbing from the front seat into the back. When they were close, he would open the package and load the vest, and when they were there, he would make his break for the main entrance to the original terminal, now the "A" terminal. Once inside, he would immediately detonate the bomb, killing any passengers unfortunate enough to be close to him, and symbolically attacking the America's air transportation at its heart – the capital of the country.

"We are almost there. Get ready." Fida told Jalal. And then, after several minutes of no forward movement, he muttered "Shit." Traffic had stopped and a policeman was in an animated discussion with a driver four cars ahead of them. He turned to check Jalal's progress and saw that he had loaded his explosives and was loading the cesium jars.

"We're stopped, and there is a policeman just ahead. You may have to get out here and run to the terminal."

From what he could see, Fida guessed the car had stalled, maybe overheated, and the cop and driver were arguing over what to do. Time was passing, and by now Jalal had received a fatal dose of radiation and it would only be a matter of minutes before symptoms would weaken him and jeopardize the mission. The brake lights on the SUV in front of them went off, and for a brief moment he thought they would move. Instead, the driver got out and came to the rear, opened the hatch and started to remove luggage for his female passenger.

"You'll have to go from here," Fida said. "We aren't going to move very soon. Go out through the back. *Allahu Akbar*."

Jalal tried to open the rear door but it only swung a few degrees, creating only an eight-inch opening before hitting the front grill of the car that had inched up to close behind them. The vest, packed with explosives and the cesium, was too wide for the opening.

"I can't get out," Jalal shouted. "The car behind has the door blocked."

"Wait, I'll pull forward," Fida said.

But when he tried, the driver of the SUV was too close, and he was boxed in. He nudged the man slightly with his bumper trying to gain inches, and he turned toward them, slamming his hand on the van's hood and yelling at Fida, shaking his fist. They were attracting attention and Jalal was panicking, as if his flight to paradise was leaving without him.

"Come up front," Fida said. "Use the passenger door."

Once again, the vest was too bulky and Jalal too big. He managed to get his shoulders and arms through the opening between the seats, but he couldn't force his way further forward.

"I'm stuck. The vest caught on the seat. Push me back."

The activity had caught the attention of the SUV driver, and he moved his face closer to the van's windshield, trying to see what was happening. He must have figured out what the vest was because he pushed the woman, shouting at her to run, and started yelling for the policeman.

The traffic cop turned their way and then started running toward them. The SUV driver ran away, following the woman. Other people, catching the signs of panic, began running themselves.

"Jalal," Fida said with calm conviction. "We are discovered. Detonate the weapon."

"I can't," Jalal yelled, fully panicked and thrashing, stuck between the seats.

Fida spoke again, this time with force and authority. "Jalal! Detonate the weapon."

His thrashing stopped and he seemed to deflate. "I can't," he sobbed. "I can't reach the detonator. It is under my left side."

As a cargo truck designed for hauling, there were few luxuries in the van, and a center console was one of those that had been left out. Jalal was suspended between the seats, stuck in the opening as it narrowed from the top of the backrest down to the seat cushion itself. Fida leaned forward for a better view under Jalal and saw the detonator dangling on its wire just inches above the floor.

"I see it, my brother," he said. "We go to paradise together."

The policeman was hammering on the passenger window, and getting no attention from Fida, drawing his pistol.

Fida reached down and grasped the detonator, and whispered *"Allahu Akbar,"* and pressed the button.

4.03   EPCOT CENTER, ORLANDO, FL

Growing up in Southern California had been a circus of entertainment for Jimmy Strobel, not too different from the entertainment at Disney World in Orlando, where he waited to start. Tall and blond and thin, he'd surfed and skateboarded and roller-bladed and scuba-dived and bungee-jumped and all the other things that the State of California shows in its travel brochures. And now, at twenty-seven years old, he marveled that his youthful experience on a dirt bike, trying out motocross racing, was his ticket to paradise. He would literally ride his Yamaha WR 250R to martyrdom as Ubaid, the Faithful One.

They'd arrived early and parked the van very close to the main entrance and spent some time doing one last tour, confirming their plan before having lunch at the Restaurant Marrakesh, another omen Ubaid appreciated. The real Marrakech, capital of Morocco, symbolized for him and his brothers the invasion of foreign influence into the Caliphate, the Ottoman Empire of Islam dismantled by Kemal Ataturk on March 3, 1924, to the dismay of true believers. The Fifth Caliphate was their goal, the last Caliphate, and today's blow against the Great Satan, the land where Jimmy had grown up, would long be remembered as the beginning of the new glory of Islam.

After lunch, they'd ridden away on the Yamaha to wait for the appointed time, leaving the van close to the entrance. The afternoon had gone very slowly, with nothing to do but wait. They'd stayed in the hotel room, the Do Not Disturb sign in place, and watched television, read the Quran, did their prayers, careful to avoid the unexpected by not letting the world get near to them in these final hours. There was little talking – they'd said it all before many times. Now was the time for solemn reflection, for individual anticipation.

Though they'd only met days before when they were assigned as a team at Pastor, Ubaid knew that Tawfiq envied him, that he wished to be the martyr instead of the witness, that he wished for the assured entry into paradise, the only guaranteed path there. Paradise was only a possibility for Muslims, and until the appointed hour of death, one could not know if his sins would be, not forgiven, but *accepted*, and he too might gain eternal life, awaiting the Day of Resurrection. But dying as a martyr was a guaranteed ticket, the only guarantee, and Ubaid and all of his brothers in the *jihad* were eager to purchase theirs with their lives. together with the lives of infidels. And the thing that separated him from Tawfiq was the ability to keep his balance on two wheels at a high speed over difficult terrain. *Allahu Akbar*.

Yesterday they had reconnoitered that terrain, and Ubaid had his route engraved in his head. To his delight, the Disney architects had laid out a field of ramps for his use – the metal sculpture garden, rectangular marble and steel trapezoids of various sizes and angles. Several were ideal for his plan to get the bike airborne as high as he could for the moment of detonation. To be floating above the crowds, as if the launch was actually his departure for paradise, symbolically rising in the air as he punched his ticket.

The motorcycle ride was not intended for show—it was necessitated by security. Physical security at Epcot individually inspected each and every guest, and there was no way to get his vest past that. And barriers prevented getting the van into place, physically inside Epcot for the spectacle, and nearer to the hoped-for crowds for casualties. So a motorcycle was selected to race through before security could react, and to detonate directly in front of Spaceship Earth, the geodesic globe that symbolized Epcot. And Ubaid would appear as orbiting it, very briefly.

***

From his position under the dome, more or less behind the support stanchion at the left front, Tawfiq was closer than safety dictated, ready to get the most dramatic video recording possible. The chance of dying in the explosion didn't bother him. He'd decided that would make him a martyr, even if he wasn't carrying the bomb. There was a kernel of doubt, though, enough that he had subconsciously selected a spot that was shielded from what would be the worst of the blast wave and shrapnel.

He knew he was the prototypical terrorist profile – an MWC, a Muslim with a camera. But everyone around him was a something with a camera, and no one paid him any heed. He heard the sound of the raspy two-stroke engine before he saw Ubaid. When he did see him, he was weaving in and out of screaming tourists, causing waves of movement as people saw him and became aware of the danger and darted away. Then he saw the security guards, three of them, on foot and hopelessly behind.

He watched Ubaid line up on the sculpture he'd selected the previous day.

He watched him slow slightly as he approached it.

He watched him twist the accelerator wide open and jerk the front wheel off the ground and onto his launch platform.

He watched the motorcycle surge forward and up.

He watched it rise in the air, stopping just inches above the top of the trapezoid, and hang there.

He watched Ubaid spread his arms and push the button.

He watched the bright flash that replaced Ubaid and the bike.

Then, temporarily blinded, he turned away, trying to hold the video camera on the same scene.

Looking back, he watched as eighty-three people died. And he saw the many wounded and radiated tourists who would soon consider the dead the fortunate ones.

4.04   The Chicago Mercantile Exchange, Chicago, IL

Fifty feet away, Watts thought. *I'm OK for the moment.*

Since the incident in Kentucky, local law enforcement across the country, and especially in urban areas, had been drilled in the consequences of a dirty bomb similar to the one found. If they found the cesium before it was dispersed, the mantra was ten inches for ten minutes and your dead. Ten feet for ten hours and you're probably dead. Ten yards for 100 days and you're maybe dead.

In order to drill the concept of *time – distance – shielding* for protection against over-exposure to radiation into the heads of potential responders, the NNSA had created an index-sized card that taught the mantra, complete with little stick-figure drawings. Get away from the cesium as fast as you can; get away as far as you can; put something big and heavy between you and it. Two inches of concrete would cut the exposure in half, no matter how close the cesium was. The cards had been distributed in areas considered high-value targets, and the numbers drummed into their heads daily.

Watts was still standing in the left hand lane of three westbound lanes of West Madison Street. The gunshots had stopped everyone in their tracks and he knew that would last only fractions of a second before panic set in. He had to act before that happened, so when it did happen, people ran away from the van and not toward it.

"Everyone listen to me," he screamed. "There is a nuclear device in that white van. Get as far away ..."

That was as far as he got before recognition set in and people started running away like they were propelled by some unseen anti-gravitational force centered on the van. And the screaming started, drowning out any hope of further communications.

Into his mike this time, he shouted, "Watts 22845. 10-57. Shots fired. Wacker and Madison. I have two terrorists down and a huge radiation reading on my PRD. *I need backup now!*"

He could barely hear the response, but it was clear he'd been acknowledged and help was being sent. He ran to the entrance of the Merc where some people were still exiting and others stood inside, confused.

"There is a nuclear device in that white van. I need everyone to move away. Exit the building at the rear and go down Madison until you're across the river." As an afterthought, he added, "And then keep going."

He saw the security guard at the desk start to move in that direction and shouted at him, "Hey, security. I need your help."

The guard turned and looked anxious and uncertain. Watts decided to firm up his resolve and raised his Glock, pointing it at the guard.

"Now. Get over here or I swear to Christ I'll shoot you dead."

The guard, a tall, mid-forties man looking like an athlete gone plump, believed him and came jogging over.

"You need to implement your building evacuation procedures. Get everyone out the back and moving west. Stand behind that pillar," he said, pointing to a two-foot square support near the door to the lobby that he hoped was solid concrete, "and make sure no one goes out the front. The pillar will shield you from the radiation so you'll be safe. Got that? Repeat it back to me."

Satisfied that at least the process was started, Watts ran out the front door and turned left, entering the Opera House by the nearest Madison Street door. The lobby was less crowded, and he started herding people north, away from Madison Street, shouting the same warnings he'd used at the Merc, and exiting them at The Civic Theater entrance at Washington Boulevard. There was no security guard or receptionist at the desk, so he found a fire alarm and broke the glass with his Glock and pulled the lever.

He then went outside and back toward the van to try to direct people away. The concrete pillars supporting the portico provided a good vantage point – he could see the van and the Merc clearly if he stuck his head out briefly, and he could stay protected the remainder of the time. He was trying to figure out how to divert traffic when he heard the first sirens and saw the lights approaching on Madison. The perimeter, he decided, would be Washington on the north, Adams on the south, and Wells on the east. At least until someone who knew more than him came and reorganized it. That covered a twenty-two-block area, maybe 700 feet from the van in those directions, with the river closing off the western approach at about 400 or 500 feet. As a foot patrolman, he knew his distances.

And then the accident happened. Watts saw it happening in slow motion, but he was powerless to prevent it. The southbound car on Wacker sped up to beat the light, oblivious to the on-coming police car on Madison. The police car, already slowing to stop at the intersection, skidded to a halt in the southbound lanes of Wacker. It would have been a near-miss if the southbound driver hadn't panicked and swerved right onto Madison, going too fast and skidding out of control. Trying to recover, the driver swerved back left, jumping the curb in the center of the divided Wacker Street and sliding sideways into the two-foot retaining wall.

As accidents go, it wasn't a bad one, but it left the occupants of the southbound car disabled only forty feet from the van. Even that wouldn't have been so bad if the occupants had stayed in the car and waited for help, but they didn't. When the woman passenger saw the man on the ground behind the van, her reaction was that the accident had somehow hurt him, and she rushed to his aid. And the driver rushed after her.

"No!" Watts screamed as he dashed from behind the pillar. "Get back."

The two good Samaritans saw a crazed policeman with a drawn pistol bearing down on them and froze a few feet from the dead terrorist. Watts grabbed the woman and started dragging her away, back toward the disabled car. She struggled to stop him, pleading to let her tend to the poor injured man. Her husband grabbed Watts, pulling him away from the woman and back toward the van. All the while, each was shouting their own exclamations, and no one heard the other. The two policemen fresh on the scene ran to their comrade's aid, and five people struggled in a 460,000 millirem/hour radiation field, and only one of them knew it.

Watts let go of the woman and got his other arm free from the man and stepped back, bringing his pistol up to point in the man's face, getting his full attention.

"That way," he shouted at the now quiet couple, jerking his head to the left toward their car. "Move!"

As they did, he quickly explained to the other police that the radioactive material was in the van and they were all in danger. That added some urgency and everyone was across Wacker to the other side very quickly.

Later, after more backup arrived and they were able to set up the incident perimeter as Watts suggested, his radiation pager would show that the scuffle cost him twelve rem of exposure, two and a half times the maximum yearly dose allowed for a professional radiation worker. Added to the nine he'd already received dealing with the terrorists, Watts' white blood cell count would drop significantly for a while, and his risk of cancer would rise by 1%.

4.05   Ronald Reagan International Airport, Washington, DC

Airport Fire Chief David Kalbaugh was the initial responder to arrive on the scene, running to the explosion from his office in Terminal A. His electronic dosimeter had started alarming in his upstairs office before he even left it, so he knew he was dealing with some kind of radiological disaster. And since the explosion hadn't flattened the building, he knew it wasn't an IND – Improvised Nuclear Device, a homemade atomic bomb. A Radiation Dispersal Device, a dirty bomb, was the obvious conclusion.

The Ronald Reagan DCA Airport Fire Department was well-equipped for any disaster, including this one, and they were well-trained and knew what to expect. In this case, Kalbaugh knew that the dead and injured would be the result of the explosive, not any radiation because dirty bombs were weapons of mass denial, designed to cause economic and emotional disaster rather than mass casualties. Exercising standard precautions would protect most everyone from lethal radiation poisoning.

He took the stairs, the instinctive reaction of a professional firefighter, and as he neared the lobby, his dosimeter continued to sound. The initial alarm was set low – ten millirem per hour – to provide an early alert to any radiation and to define the perimeter of the incident scene. The ten millirem-per-hour boundary was the point where access to the scene would be controlled with no one entering who didn't have specific emergency responsibilities. The thought finally registered and he realized the boundary included his office. That shouldn't be possible with a dirty bomb. He was over 100 feet of air and concrete and steel from the explosion that he could now see was in front of the terminal. Ten millirem-per-hour at his office meant a lot of radiation at the epicenter. Then he remembered the number – 4,000 curies.

Shit, he thought, *a lot of people are going to die ugly.*

He stopped for a moment and quickly surveyed the scene through the shattered glass doors and windows. Using his belt-mounted radio to raise the communications office, he gave a quick rundown of what he knew and what he wanted.

"An RDD has been detonated on the frontage road at Terminal A. Foam 331 and 345 approach from the north and hold at Terminal B entrance. Foam 326 and 336 approach from the west and hold at the fork at Aviation Circle and the frontage road. Medic, rescue, and MCU hold at that same point. Medic to set up triage. Hazmat to both points to establish the perimeter and set up decon tents. I'll meet you at the Aviation Circle and frontage road intersection. Make sure my gear is on one of the vehicles. Patch me through to Chief Stein."

Herschel Stein commanded the Airport Police.

"Hersh, we've got a dirty bomb detonation at Terminal A. I need you to close access and egress to the airport on the west at Aviation Circle and on the north at Terminal C. No one out or in until we know the extent of the contamination. Call the tower and shut down incoming and outgoing flights. Have the planes on the ground muster away from gates one through twenty-two. We're going to need help so get on the horn to Arlington and send out the alert. I've got a shitload of radiation here, so we're going to need everyone."

By the time Kalbaugh got to the muster point, the first EMT vehicle had arrived and the two techs were out and staring at the smoke and devastation. He gave them some direction.

"Tyvek suits, hoods, half-face respirators. Make sure your dosimeters are set. Watch the levels and listen to the alarms. There will be some really bad hot spots. Move."

As the other men and equipment arrived, he made sure the same orders were issued. The Tyvek suits were lightweight, tear-resistant plastic designed to keep contamination on the outside, and Kalbaugh specified the smaller respirators that covered just the mouth and nose in order to maximize his responders' vision and to minimize the panic victims might experience being treated by some alien-looking being with a huge glass face.

The dosimeters were set to alarm at the EPA-mandated exposure levels to balance responder safety with their task of rescue: one rem for normal emergency response activities, ten rem for fire-fighting and saving property, and twenty-five rem for life-saving activities, equivalent to about 104 years of normal background radiation.

As responders arrived and suited-up, they were assigned to three-man teams – two firemen with a stretcher or gurney and one emergency medical tech with his bag of gear. The procedure was to triage in-place, directing ambulatory victims to decon and medical treatment tents, and categorizing the others for priority in evacuation and treatment. Just as in the hospital, plastic wristbands were used to identify the victim, but not for their name, only their chances of survival.

Like most disaster scenes, this one was chaotic, with the cars jammed together providing additional obstacles. Some were still running, abandoned without being turned off, and a few still had drivers trying to maneuver to get out. The responders paused long enough at these to take the keys and direct the occupants to the decon and triage tents.

Because of the extraordinary amount of cesium that might have been released – most dirty-bomb scenarios speculated on less than a hundredth of that – and the vagaries of explosive-induced dispersion among the physical interference of the cars, Kalbaugh knew there would be some areas of critically high radiation levels, especially in and around the van. The dosimeters also had dose rate alarms to warn the responders if they were in one of these areas, and alerting them to get out. There was nothing his men could do for the victims there. They were already dead whether they'd stopped breathing or not.

***

Congressman Evan Winslow, R-Oklahoma, blinked uncontrollably, looking at the ceiling, and hearing only a strong buzzing in his head. Beside him, Gloria Randall, one of his young aides, lay still, no longer bleeding from the wound in her left thigh where the oversized rear-view mirror from a shuttle bus had slashed her femoral artery after shattering a window. She didn't have enough blood left for her heart to pump.

His death a few hours later in the Mass Casualty Trailer would be a shock to the Congressman's wife. The fact that he was traveling somewhere other than where he'd told her he was going, on a mission different from the fact-finding trip he'd explained to her, with an attractive younger woman, wasn't such a shock. She had mixed feelings about the tragedy.

***

Brenda Simon, fourteen-months-old, faced out the hole where the rear window of her father's Chrysler Sebring used to be. Her car seat had absorbed the shock wave, but not before it had killed both her parents in the front seats, facing a bent and blackened white van, three cars ahead of them. NNSA experts later estimated she'd absorbed over 190 rem before she was found and evacuated, and she would become a living medical test lab for the rest of her short life.

***

William Lloyd sat in the Pontiac G5 he'd just rented, covered in a thousand glass pieces, bleeding from a hundred small cuts, barely conscious and without a thought in his head. He didn't know how long he sat there, the question never occurred to him. Time was no more relevant than the weather back home in Boston where he would have been except for the visit to DC where he'd planned to spend the weekend with his fiancée at her apartment in the Adams-Morgan neighborhood.

He didn't hear the sirens as the airport emergency crews spun up their equipment and rushed to their staging areas. He didn't see the emergency workers flooding the area in their protective gear, searching out survivors, applying first-aid and loading victims on gurneys for evacuation to the inflatable medical tent that had been set up 120 feet away from him. He didn't hear the screams of the injured or the shouts of the workers or the loudspeaker instructions to evacuate to the tent for triage and decontamination. He didn't even feel the tiny cuts, or the blood oozing down his face and neck and hands.

When, after seventy-four minutes that he didn't know or care had passed, an emergency worker found him still at the wheel of the Pontiac, he didn't register him as a rescuer, just as some force that caused him to move his arms and legs through guiding hands, to get out of the car and walk with strange legs that didn't really seem to work all that well. It was only in the tent when they were stripping his clothes and cleaning his wounds and washing his head and hands to remove any residual cesium and dressing him a hospital gown that he became aware. And then only briefly before he passed out. It would be Saturday night, twenty-seven hours later, before his fiancée tracked him down at Inova Alexandria Hospital, one of the designated WMD treatment facilities in the DC area, and he remembered nothing before waking up to seeing her by his bedside.

***

Sami Zardooz shuffled forward two short steps as the line moved. He was in Terminal C along with several hundred other dazed, frightened, and confused travelers. They had been directed to the north end of the terminal complex where they were being processed and released. Most had nowhere to go and no way to get there, having been at the airport to leave on a now-cancelled flight or arriving to be met by now unavailable friends or family members. So for the most part they mingled around the terminal, waiting for someone in authority to organize their transportation out of there.

When Sami reached the front of the line, he was confronted first by a technician in a white suit, hood and a face mask. The fact that he wasn't similarly outfitted caused Sami some concern for his well-being. The tech slowly swept what looked like a vacuum cleaner upholstery tool over him, except that it was made of a silver metal and the part that would normally suck up the dirt was covered in what looked like aluminum foil. It was connected by a cable to a small instrument the tech held in his other hand, listening to a series of clicks that increased and decreased in tempo as he moved the device. Sami could see a needle on a dial on top of the instrument jump up and down, again causing him concern for his well-being. When he had swept Sami from head to toe, he said what sounded like "less than a thousand – you're good to go" and waved him on by.

That got him to an airport policeman who asked for his identification and got Sami's Iranian passport. He examined the passport and compared the picture to Sami. Satisfied they matched, he handed the passport to another policeman, policewoman, actually, and she laid it, with his name and picture visible, on what looked like an oversized, weird microscope and took a picture of it and Sami at the same time, like the Department of Motor Vehicles had for his driver's license.

While she was doing that, the first policeman asked, "What was your business here today?"

"I was flying to New York for a few days and then home."

"Home as in Iran?"

"Yes. I'm a student at George Washington University and school is over for the semester. I spend the summer with my family."

"OK. I want you to go with this officer," he said as he waved a uniformed TSA officer over to their table. "We have some more questions for you. Shouldn't take long."

"What questions," Sami asked, nervous and angry at the same time. "Why aren't you asking these other people more questions? Where are you taking me?"

The TSA cop, his right hand resting loosely on his gun holster said, "It's just standard procedure, sir. Nothing to be concerned about. We're trying to get everyone processed and out of here as quickly as possible. It's for your own safety."

"My safety? What are you talking about? We've just been bombed. What do you want from me? I'm just ..."

"Calm down, sir," the officer said, waving his left hand in a calming motion while his right one took a firmer grip on the handle of his pistol. "Just come with me and we'll have you out of here in no time."

"No, I'm not going with you. They said I was fine. I want ..."

By now, two more TSA police had joined the group, surrounding him, and Sami was turning his head rapidly as he talked, trying to keep all of them in sight.

"SIR! Calm down, now. We're just going over there to that tent to ask you a couple more questions. There is nothing to be concerned about. Please cooperate or we'll have to cuff you."

Sami grew more agitated, his body starting to rotate with his head. The first officer nodded and the other two grabbed him, one on each side, and pulled him in the direction of the tent.

"Someone help me," Sami called growing more frantic, but no one moved.

4.06   Epcot Center, Orlando, FL, Friday

AnnM0994 omg sum guy on a motorcycle just blew up. he jumped his bike into the air and exploded. omg!

AnnM0994 omg omg dead people all over. omg mr stiles is there. & becca. they're all dead.

MacTheMan12 we heard it. we're @ the electric umbrela. where r u?

AnnM0994 at spaceship w/ karen & ellen. phone doesn't connect. we're gonna hide.

SarahJane0727 ARE U OK?   WHAT HAPPENED?

billwoo ur full of shit. quit fuckin round.

SexyBecca someone help me i cant feel my legs

MacTheMan12 where r u becca?

ProfBergman There's been a bomb explosion at the Epcot entrance. Many dead and injured. Send ambulances. I'm going to help my students. PLEASE RETWEET.

DaveGeek111 ann i tried to call u. cell towers r crashed. text works.

SarahJane0727 ANN I M CALLING UR PARENTS TO TELL THEM. ARE U OK?

MacTheMan12 where r u becca?

E_Matthews2012 becca is in the sculpture garden toward u. she isn't moving. i think they're all dead.

MacTheMan12 i m going to get her. mike's w/ me.

Vanessa.Klein i'm bleeding oh god someone help me

DaveGeek111 wait man the guard here says theres radiation all their alarms are going off.

ProfBergman Everyone cover your face with a wet cloth and get away fast. Meet at Showcase Plaza by the lake.

SarahJane0727 GET OUT OF THERE ALL OF U.

MacTheMan12 i can't find becca. where is she?

4.07   THE MALL OF AMERICA, MINNEAPOLIS/ST. PAUL, MN

There was a sale at Macy's on women's and children's summer clothes, attracting mothers and families to the store at the southeast corner of the Mall of America, the largest enclosed mall in the U.S., second only to the West Edmonton Mall in Canada in physical size. But second to no one in shoppers, with over forty million passing through each year.

There was a concert in the Great Room of the Nickelodeon Universe, the largest indoor amusement park in America, and families were gathered around to hear the children's chorus sing all their favorite traditional songs. The Great Room was outside the Macy's entrance, attracting more people to that corner, the sheer size of the crowd seeming to tip the whole mall in that direction as if it was floating.

The sixteen screens at the *Theatres at Mall of America* were all operating, showing the latest movies in different venues, some with moving seats for realistic chase scenes, some with beer and wine for getting as uninhibited as the action in the story. All located at the South entrance to the mall, near Macy's.

At the moment dirty bombs were going off in Washington and Orlando, and two terrorists were dying in Chicago, thwarted in their mission, there were 36,482 people in the mall. About a quarter of them were within the intended blast radius of the bomb vest.

At that moment in The Mall of America, all those people were going about their lives, oblivious to the events, to their danger, shopping or working or just having fun.

And at that moment in The Mall of America, nothing happened.

Their bomb was in the FBI radiation forensics lab instead of on Mervat Saad, standing with the crowds in front of Macy's, waiting to martyr himself.

Their cesium was safely in a storage container instead of contaminating a million square feet of some of the most densely populated floor space in America.

Nothing happened at The Mall of America, and no one realized it.

Part Five – The Reaction

F R I D A Y , J U N E 2 5

5.01   CNN News Headquarters, Atlanta, GA

 **President Condemns Attacks and Warns Terrorists**

Congress unanimously supports the president's comments

ATLANTA (CNNNational.com) -- In a nationally televised speech, the President today condemned the unprecedented series of WMD terrorist attacks upon the United States. "These despicable acts of mayhem and murder will not go unpunished. To the terrorists, their allies and others who have aided in these heinous acts of terror and destruction, I promise you, your days are numbered. Every resource of the United States is now focused on you, and you will not escape justice."

Both houses of Congress unanimously supported the President's comments and promised emergency funding appropriations for the expansion of surveillance and suppression capabilities.

5.02   Ambassador Bridge, Detroit, MI

Fucking banks, Hadi murmured to himself. Ready to take your money with no questions asked, but when you want it back there's always another piece of paper to sign or a delay while some other office somewhere processes its own paper. And now this – a fucking traffic jam. Hadi was caught in Detroit rush hour, and it seemed like everyone in Michigan was going to Canada for the weekend. And maybe everyone from Ohio, too. He was already tired and jumpy when he'd started the trip, and it was ten times worse, now.

Trying to get his 401K cashed out had proven to be more difficult than he'd thought. First, he'd had to go to the bank on Thursday and sign all kinds of documents acknowledging that he was taking his money out early and there would be taxes and penalties if he didn't use it for an IRS-approved reason. He'd lied and said he was going to college and there were more papers and questions about when and where and he found himself making up more lies that could be easily refuted. He'd worried all Thursday and then Friday morning and then Friday afternoon that he wouldn't get the money. Finally, at 2:30, the bank had called and said they had his check, and he'd said no check, he wanted cash. That resulted in more papers to sign and notifications to the authorities about a transaction involving more than $10,000, and he was sure he was screwed and that at any moment someone from the Treasury Department would show up and start questioning him and the whole thing would fall apart. Or that some sniper somewhere would put a bullet in his head and he'd never even realize he was dead, he just would be.

It had been a difficult two days.

Everything had seemed to go wrong. First, he'd had to alter any possible routine, driving different routes everywhere and going to his apartment only after careful surveillance. Then, he had to find a place to hide the gun and the almost $40,000 in cash to smuggle across the border. The gun was in the space his sunroof retracted into and he'd repaired the headliner as well as he could, but the fabric looked all wrong to him and he hoped no one would notice.

He'd thought the money would be bigger than the three inch stack of one-hundred dollar bills that he was literally sitting on, and he'd tried to find another clever place to hide it. He'd had his security guards run a search of his Nissan Xterra as a training exercise, telling them there was a device hidden on or in the car they had to find. This had also solved another problem that he had considered – some kind of tracking device on his car that would let the assassin find him anytime. In the end, they'd found nothing and had given him no ideas about hiding places, so he just stuffed the bills into the springs under his seat and hoped for the best. By then the delays had precluded anything fancier, anyway.

So here he was, running six hours behind schedule, sitting on $40,000 in cash, a loaded gun over his head, and with more clothes than one person on a short visit to Canada would need. That alone would probably attract some border guard's attention.

And now, stuck in a traffic jam at the Ambassador Bridge. It had been a *really* difficult two days, and it showed no signs of improvement anytime soon.

The checkpoint was finally within view, but that caused Hadi even more stress as he could see armed, uniformed law enforcement officers questioning people and examining documents. It was so strange, the hunter-killer of Kabul more scared than he'd ever been, even facing a heavily-armed and highly-motivated enemy. Then things got even worse.

There were nine lanes of cars lined up for clearance to enter Canada, and Hadi was six cars from the checkpoint when shouting and movement two lanes to his left erupted. Canadian border police, weapons drawn, were converging on—*oh shit*, Hadi thought—a white cargo van. People in the nearest cars were getting out and running, while others ducked below the window level.

It couldn't be, Hadi thought. *No way they were taking the cesium into Canada*. Of course the authorities wouldn't know that. Maybe the people in the van were middle-Eastern and had acted suspicious. But this seemed like an overreaction. There had to be twenty cops surrounding the van, but not too close. They were urging people out of their cars and sending them back up the line, causing more panic. The wave of people reached his car and he was forced to go with them or attract the attention of the cops.

When the crowd thickened to the point that it became totally congested and stopped, people ducked behind whatever vehicle they were near and peeked over doors and hoods and trunks.

"What's going on," Hadi asked someone near him.

The guy shrugged, but then someone else said, "It's another dirty bomb. They're trying to blow up the border."

The last part didn't make a lot of sense, but Hadi had stopped rational thought at the words 'another dirty bomb'.

"What do you mean, another dirty bomb," he asked the stranger.

"It's all over the news. Dirty bombs are going off all over the country. It's that cesium stuff the Arabs stole. They're blowing up America. And now, Canada, I guess."

SHIT! It's too late, Hadi thought. His information was now history, his get-out-of-jail-free card now useless. All he had was $40,000 and the need to disappear. Would they close the border? Even if they didn't, where would he go?

While he crouched with the others, trying to figure out what he would do now, loudspeakers suddenly crackled on, and a voice said, "Attention, everyone. That was a false alarm. Everything is safe. Please return immediately to your vehicles and proceed through the checkpoint. I repeat, that was a false alarm and everyone should immediately return to their vehicles."

Some people slowly stood, uncertain, like maybe this was a trap. Others followed, and soon some started toward their cars and trucks. Hadi was amongst the first, feeling certain there was no bomb threat, just a huge personal one. As the crowd moved, it seemed to speed up, like now the rush was to get into the cars, instead of away from them. Impatience showed as some people were slower to return, and abandoned cars temporarily blocked the lanes, and horns started honking, drivers yelling at each other to get a move on.

When Hadi finally reached the checkpoint and handed his passport to the border guard, he realized he had just been given a blessing from Allah. Everyone passing through the checkpoint was nervous and scared, not just him. The border guards themselves were nervous and scared and were rushing cars through like a toll booth instead of a security check point.

And suddenly, Hadi was in Canada, and he didn't know which way to turn.

5.03   REAGAN INTERNATIONAL AIRPORT, ARLINGTON, VA

The same twin-Beech that had brought Cal to Knoxville and then to Louisville had been waiting at the airport to take him back to DC when the summons came. He began to think of it as his personal plane. The summons had come twenty-three minutes after the bomb had exploded outside Terminal A at Reagan Airport, the same terminal Cal could see from his window as the pilot took him on a quick air tour of the devastation. That was made possible by the total lack of other air traffic as inbound flights were diverted and outbound ones cancelled.

The scene was what Cal had tried to recreate over and over again in his disaster exercises and plans, and from this unique vantage point, he could see just how naïve he'd been in many regards. The question that flitted through his mind was – *How can I possibly simulate this? How do I demonstrate utter chaos?*

The scene was like a huge and very strange carnival. Red, blue, yellow, and white lights flashed everywhere in some bizarre syncopation. Lines of headlights and taillights snaked in every direction where there was pavement, and many where there wasn't, none of them moving. Every imaginable emergency vehicle was parked somewhere. Planes were lined up as far away from ground zero as possible, pointing in every direction. Crowds gathered at the perimeters, milling around like they were the ingredients in some simmering soup pot. To add to his disorientation, the only sound was the muffled roar of the planes turbo-prop engines.

This was not going to fit on a table top.

***

Even by middle-of-the-night standards, traffic was almost non-existent and the two-mile ride to the Old Executive Office Building took just minutes. Except for the rare private car or taxi, Cal saw only military and police and emergency vehicles along the way.

He was met by two men in suits, somber in clothing and expression, asking politely that Cal accompany them, passing through metal and explosives detectors to an office with a sign that read "Senior Director for Homeland Preparedness – National Security Council." This was as high as Cal had ever been in the Washington food chain, but he was too tired and overwhelmed to even notice.

He was ushered past several admin types, busy at computers, and into a large office with the man Cal expected was the National Security Staff's Director for National Preparedness, sitting behind a large and ornate desk, and two others seated in front. His escorts withdrew and the Director came around to introduce himself and the others. Cal promptly forgot their names.

"Dr. Bellotta," the director began after they were all seated. "I've been asked to talk to you about your report on the cesium theft and what seems to be an almost prescient prediction of the events that have taken place today. I'd appreciate it, sir, if you would take us through your investigation and the analysis that led to your conclusions."

Not entirely sure what this was all about – after all, this was covered in detail in his report to DHS – Cal walked them through everything once again.

"And as far as prescience goes," Cal said after the review, "it has nothing to do with my conclusions. They're simply the result of my understanding of these weapons and the mindset and goals of those fanatics who would use them."

"That's all well and good to say, but why were you the only one to reach these fairly specific ones?"

Cal thought this line of questioning to be more appropriate to a suspect, but answered as best he could.

"I can't speak to other analyses. I was on the scene and saw first-hand how these particular terrorists worked and I put that together with my experience and education and tried to think like them. This is a very sophisticated group, and that actually helps because they are more likely to act in a rational and carefully-planned manner. If we know their starting point, cesium in breakable containers, and their goals, figuring out what comes in-between is easier."

"Let me ask you this. You've recommended some pretty unorthodox actions, specifically the training helicopters at Ft. Rucker. What was that all about?"

That question sounded almost accusatory and now Cal *was* feeling like a suspect.

"Excuse my candor, Director, but governments function on procedure and protocol. There are rules and chains of command and everything has its place. No one looks at what is available and thinks about how it could best be applied to current circumstances. They think 'what is the procedure for this?' Well, in this case, there is no procedure, at least not one that effectively responds to the specific circumstances. The commander at Ft. Rucker would no more think of using his training helicopters and pilots and students for a real mission than the Special Forces would consider traffic control duty. That's not what they're there for.

"Someone like me, not really bound by organizational or experiential restrictions, can better see the whole picture and how parts might be moved around to react. Actually, that's my job. I try to look to the whole community of assets and resources at our disposal, and it occurred to me that we have these aircraft and pilots, and they could be a way to stretch our capabilities.

"Here's another example. The government has been buying radiation monitoring equipment since World War Two. It never gets thrown away, just stored away. There are warehouses full of instruments that, while not up to today's standards of wireless communications and computerized data analysis, will nevertheless respond when hit by a gamma ray. Let's get some of these out, bench-test them, supply plenty of fresh batteries and some quick tailgate training, put them in the hands of targeted law enforcement and National Guard and even military personnel and show them how to detect radiation. As a control against mistakes, super glue the knobs in place so no one can change the settings. Paint a red stripe with nail polish at the action threshold. It doesn't take a lot of training to turn these people into useful contributors to our overall search. Putting them in all those helicopters, and also on every street corner in targeted cities, will turn something up sooner or later, or at least help to channel the adversaries."

No one spoke for a few moments, and finally the Director said, "Well, I guess the President was right about this. Dr. Bellotta, I recognize that while DHS is your funding client you have been effectively op-conned to the FBI's

WMD Directorate during this operation, and that will stay in place. I'm providing you with some additional authority that might help you cut through obstacles as you attempt to move your so-called atypical concepts into implementable solutions.

"While you were en route here, the commanding general at Ft. Rucker responded exactly as you said he would. 'Hell, no,' were his exact words, I believe, and he went on to lecture us on liability concerns, posse comitatas, logistics and readiness concerns, and every other risk-adverse and protocol-bound thing he could think of. In the end, a call from the President to the Joint Chiefs got them released, but not without a lot of grumbling.

"I have here a White House National Security Staff identification card in your name and a letter from the President instructing all Federal agency officials, and requesting state and local government officials, and hell any American citizen you come in contact with, to give you every cooperation and to offer you the resources and assets you request."

Cal, a little shell-shocked by this unexpected turn, quickly read the letter and thanked the Director, commenting that he wasn't sure exactly what he could do, but he would try. As his escorts came in, the Director said, "That's all we ask. Well, actually there is one more question that I have. Calogero Taddeo? Exactly what kind of name is that?"

5.04   GRAINGER RESIDENCE, FRENCHTOWN, MT

The expected call came at 4:22 PM, Mountain Standard Time. Twenty-two minutes after the 5 o'clock bomb in Chicago and the 6 o'clock bombs in Orlando and Washington. Twenty-two minutes was well inside the limit Tag had set in his head. That was good.

"I can't talk very long. Things here are going crazy, as you can imagine," Margaret Hancock, Lieutenant Governor of Idaho, told Tag when he answered. "We're about to convene a continuity of operations meeting with the Governor and senior officials. I just wanted to check with you first because I don't know what will happen, and I may not be able to talk again for some time."

"I don't think that should be a problem. My sources on this tell me that it's over for now. You might want to raise your profile by volunteering to be the public face in Idaho while all the other officials scurry underground."

There was a pause at Margaret's end.

"What sources? How can you be wired into this? No one knows what's happening. How do you?"

"It's not important, Margaret. I have sources everywhere, and nothing will rebound on you, so don't give it another thought."

Another pause, and then, "All right, I won't. Do you have any message you want out there? After all, if I am to be the public face here, I ought to have something to say."

"It is obvious that this is linked to the cesium theft and the accident in Kentucky. That will be confirmed very quickly. The perpetrators are Muslim terrorists, that is also certain, although not publically known at the moment. I think you ought to get ahead of the curve on laying blame where it belongs, with clear references to the root cause of Muslim extremism – Israel. I know you need to tread gently there, but some inferences will go a long way with our people."

"Yes, that needs artful phrasing. I'll give it some thought."

"Bring the threat home to your constituents. The nuclear lab is there. Tie it into what's going on in Tennessee. Put a little fear of God into them. And then let them know that God, through you and other leaders like you, is watching over them and you'll make sure they're protected."

"How can I promise that?"

"Because I told you. I've never misled you, and I won't this time. We will be posting some new information on the web site soon. That will contain some talking points. Also, check your secure pages there frequently in case there is new information or something we need to discuss. We should meet Sunday to plan how to take best advantage of this, and prepare for any future incidents so you can be leading the response, both in Idaho and nationally."

"Future incidents? There will be more? How do you know that? Do you know when and where?"

"Relax, Margaret. Four bombs have been discovered so far. My sources indicate that there was enough cesium stolen to make sixteen of them, so it stands to reason that there will be more."

"Uncle Theodore," she said, using his proper name as she did whenever she wanted to command his full attention, "what are these sources of yours? Why hasn't Washington released that information? If lives are in jeopardy from twelve more bombs, it is my duty to announce that and give people a chance to protect themselves."

"Washington is afraid, as they always are. They hope to find the twelve bombs and capture them before there is any further panic. It is in our best interests to let them proceed. If they do find the bombs and prevent any further incidents, we have lost nothing. Muslim extremism will still be blamed.

If they do not, and if, God forbid, another bomb explodes, the Washington government will look ineffective, and our cause will benefit."

"You still haven't told me who these sources of yours are. I'm reluctant to base my statements on unknown operators with unvetted intel."

"I'll fill you in as much as I can on Sunday. After services, in the office at your church, as usual. And Margaret, get out in front on this. I assure you that you won't regret it."

5.05   FBI FIELD OFFICE, LOUISVILLE, KY

"Goddamit everyone, shut the fuck up!"

Buck Buchanan was standing, and even for him, the outburst was savage. And it worked. Mouths closed, speakers muted, heads turned. A number of those heads were rarely spoken to in that manner; a couple of them, never. They outranked Buck in their various agencies, and even in his, but they all, without a mutter of protest, obeyed instantly. What had a moment earlier been the most tumultuous SVTC any of them had ever attended became as quiet as a eulogy.

In addition to his normal 7 PM packed house, Buck had the SAC's from Chicago and Tampa and Richmond on his video screens, the Fusion Centers from Tallahassee and Springfield and Richmond and DC, FBI reps from the Foreign Terrorist Tracking Task Force and the WMD Directorate and more. Attendance had to be some kind of record, and Buck wondered if they'd reached critical mass and were about to explode. That was when he'd shouted.

He slowly scrutinized everyone in the room, and then turned and stared into the video camera. He wanted every participant to feel like he had singled them out specifically for the rebuke. People who were standing took their seats. People already seated folded their hands on the table or desk in front of them. Everyone looked to Buck, whether in person or electronically.

"That's better," he said. "This meeting will remain orderly. I will dismiss or disconnect anyone who I think threatens that order. If you want to speak and you're in the room with me, raise your goddam hand. If you're on video, click the little icon on your screen that says 'communicate'. If you're on a secure cell phone, press the pound key. Stefanie has everyone on her control screen and she will recognize you in order at the appropriate moment. Everyone got that? Good. Now let's proceed.

"I'm dispensing with the review of last night's SVTC. I'm sure everyone agrees that we have an entirely new situation, and the on-going investigation of the Scott County incident is now simply the starting point for a whole new and significantly more urgent action, if that's possible. Copies of the status reports are available for download at the conclusion of this meeting for anyone who doesn't already have them.

"First, I want to hear from each of the SAC's to give a rundown of what happened in their jurisdiction and the current situation. Then I want the same from each of the Fusion Centers. Then I will entertain questions and comments. Orderly, professional questions and comments.

"We're going to start with Kevin Kraus in Chicago. Kevin, go ahead, please."

Kevin related the facts that had been established so far, and they were quite close to what everyone had heard on the 24/7 news channels and their secure alerts already. The only additional information he could add was that the buildings within the 8-square-block evacuation zone were for the most part cleared. Area hospitals were overrun with panicked people demanding attention and describing a range of symptoms that included every known and imagined condition of each and every part of the human body. The dead terrorists were, as he put it, 'cooking' in a multi-thousand rem radiation field and would be charcoal by the time the robot could get the cesium source into a shield. Replacing it in the terrorist's container was not possible as it was in the vest, still partially on one of the bodies, and it would have to be cut off and placed in a larger container. There was no way they were going to try to remove the glass vial stuck in a canvas pouch with mechanical arms. The risk of breakage was just too great.

As they could not approach the van until the source was secured, the only additional information was the license plate, and it was registered in Michigan to a Faisal Sameer, and that was all he knew at the moment.

The SAC's from Tampa and Richmond followed, with Reagan National Airport technically in Virginia. Their reports detailed the extent of the devastation, and the current body count was "over fifty" at Reagan Airport and "around eighty" at Epcot, but both took care to point out that these were very early estimates and the numbers were bound to go up. Maybe way up. The Virginia SAC confirmed that one congressman was among the casualties, and the Tampa SAC reported that they had one terrorist on the loose and were trying to button up the Orlando area "tighter than a bull's ass in fly season." He didn't mean it as a joke, and no one took it that way.

"Fusion Centers," Buck called. "Let's hear what you have to add."

Their answer was short and direct – nothing. Buck sensed the change in atmosphere with the lack of information or direction and moved quickly to quell it.

"All right, because this is my SVTC, I'm going to issue some directions here, even though I don't have the authority to do that outside of my region. If anyone disagrees with them, for Christ's sake, speak up. The same if anyone has anything to add. We all need to be working from the same script, so let's agree on it now. Based on the amount of missing cesium and our best guess at the distribution, it looks like we've got as many as twelve more of these things out there, and so far we're batting .500 on finding them, if you count Chicago as a success. And I do. We can't count on more traffic accidents to saves our asses. We need detection and we need more diligence and observation like we saw in Chicago, and we need to find these bastards before any more are detonated. For all we know, the fuse is already lit on any or all of those twelve, so we've got to move fast.

"First, I want all field offices to update your lists of the top RDD targets in your region, especially in any of the UASI-designated cities," he said, referring to the sixty-four cities that had been designated as part of the Urban Areas Security Initiative, cities determined to be high-risk targets and given additional funding for anti-terrorist activities and equipment. "You will also need to examine what we know about these terrorists and their methods so far and come up with your criteria for selecting those targets so we can establish some standard method for risk assessment. We need to deploy our manpower where it is likely to do the most good, so the criteria and the targets will need to be vetted through all of us and then we'll have to figure out which of those targets to focus on without endangering other sites. Part of your analysis might include any speculation on where the Kentucky device was heading, and why you think that.

"Next, give me some idea of the resources you'll need to protect those targets. We're gonna get stretched mighty thin before this is over, so let's get a jump on what we need.

"Then, we need every bit of information ever developed on the seven dead guys. Somewhere there is a connection, and if the information on the first two is any indication, it's not gonna be easy to tease out. I don't need to remind you that we are gonna come under some pretty intense pressure to get on with the retribution part of the investigation / attribution / retribution formula for dealing with terrorist organizations and the countries that host them. But we need to get it right or retribution serves the purposes of the real perps and earns us even more enmity in the Muslim world."

At that point, Stefanie tapped Buck's arm and pointed to his computer screen. A brief flash of annoyance shaped his face before he acknowledged Cal Bellotta.

"NEST, FRMAC and AMS will certainly be deployed over all major cities and we need to make sure it happens right now," Cal advised, referring to the Nuclear Emergency Support Team, the Federal Radiation Monitoring and Assessment Center, and the Aerial Monitoring System. "The cesium is a strong gamma-emitter and easily detected if it's outside the shields. They might make a mistake and open one of the containers or transfer it to another one and we could get lucky. Our detection resources are going to be stretched very thin by this, especially if we want the detectors in the air. I've been in contact with DoD and the helicopter training facility at Ft. Rucker. They have nearly one thousand choppers there for training, and trained pilots to fly them. They'll be at our disposal, along with a bunch of radiation monitors that were stockpiled. They'll be getting everything set up a Ft. Rucker, and you'll need to include that in your resource inventory."

Buck smiled and responded. "Exactly what I was asking for. Ideas. Let's figure out what other resources we've got and get them moving. Anybody else?"

Later, Buck would regret that last question because the answer became 'everybody else' and even with Stefanie controlling the electronic communications, things became disorderly quickly. This was mostly due to some pretty unrealistic and even offensive suggestions, ranging from traffic controls that would effectively make all U.S. streets and highways into parking lots to what someone called "no-fault shoot-to-kill" orders and absolution for the police if confronted with a suspected terrorist. Someone even suggested the registration and licensing of all Muslims, and it actually got discussed as a viable option. At that point, Buck closed the meeting and Stefanie shut down the communications links.

5.06   THE MEDICAL DISTRICT, CHICAGO, IL

In Chicago, the area south of the Eisenhower Expressway and east of Historic Route 66 is known as The Medical District. With good reason. The 560-acre area site includes four massive hospitals that provide almost 2,000 beds and the same number of doctors and residents to treat the patients filling them. By 7 PM Friday night, there wasn't an available parking space, bed, chair, or even a place to stand. Or a doctor or nurse who wasn't overwhelmed with urgent, and often hysterical, demands.

Gabrielle Penton, an emergency room nurse at the Stroger/Cook County Hospital, imagined this is what it must look like in time of war or a great catastrophe – except for the lack of the real wounds, blood, screams, and death that were nowhere to be found in the hospital that night. The injuries they did encounter were uniformly the result of a fall or a fight, both typically the result of trying to get away from the radiation and to the head of the emergency room line. When Gabby had become a nurse, she'd learned that her parents had inadvertently named her after an anti-seizure medicine, gabapentin, and the thought crossed her mind that she might need some before the night was over, for herself.

South Winchester Avenue, a one-way loop that provided hospital access, was literally a parking lot from the emergency room entrance back to Ogden Ave, with abandoned cars completely blocking the road. If you weren't on foot, you weren't getting to the hospital. This presented a real problem for the actual injuries and illnesses, and ambulances were being diverted to the other hospitals as far away as Cicero, seven city miles to the west.

The crowd had overflowed the emergency room, and Gabby and the other nurses were performing triage on the sidewalk, trying to separate the possibly exposed from the merely panicked, while still identifying genuine broken bones and heart attacks and the other, real reasons for a trip to the ER. From what she could tell, radiation exposure must cause every known human medical condition – she had heard them all described authoritatively. Rashes, headaches, cramps, blindness, and pains of every description. One woman gave her a blow-by-blow description of the cell mitosis going on in the cancer that she could feel growing in her brain as a result of her wandering down Madison Street several hours earlier.

Gabby and the other nurses and doctors had quickly developed their own form of triage – a simple set of questions. Where did you start your journey past the radiation source? When? Where did you go? What was your route? How long did it take? Those people who had passed within fifty feet of the van went inside the ER. Anyone who was further than that but within 200 feet stayed for further questions. Otherwise, they were sent home. That last option was greatly complicated by the lack of any vehicle access or egress route, and most of these people sat in their cars or milled about or tried to create new routes across the lawn and planting areas.

5.07 LOS ANGELES INTERNATIONAL AIRPORT, CA

World Way, Sky Way, and Center Way were blockaded at the east and north ends, and every vehicle trying to enter Los Angeles International Airport was being stopped and searched. Special attention was paid to any that had the capacity to carry two people and a 1,500 pound drum. Heavy-duty cargo vans, like the one Luis Herrera and Daniel Ortiz were driving, might as well have been labeled "al Qaeda Shuttle."

Luis and Daniel had not heard the news and were unaware of the reason for the monumental traffic jam. They just knew they were going to be very late for their scheduled delivery of several cases of wine and liquor to The Encounter Restaurant in the Theme Building in the middle of the Center Way loop. And when a National Guardsman, carrying some odd device, and the two SWAT-uniformed policemen carrying easily identifiable automatic weapons, approached their van slowly, aiming at the two deliverymen through the windshield, they panicked, Daniel being an illegal and all.

The Guardsman, a member of the 9th WMD Civil Support Team assigned to provide radiation detection capabilities to the police at the airport, looked like a soldier to Daniel, and he thought that if the Army was after him, he must be in serious trouble.

Luis was driving, and he and Daniel both had their hands raised. The police were over a car length away, and moving very slowly towards them. The seconds dragged into what seemed to Daniel to be hours, and the guns grew more menacing, acquiring a savage aspect, like they were living things, irrational beasts, preparing to attack. When the Guardsman held up his right hand, holding a tube connected to a cable that ran to the device in his left hand, Daniel took that as the preparatory signal for the onslaught and scrambled to escape between the seats into the cargo area, hoping to jump out the back door and run all the way to Mexico. He didn't make it as far as the seat back.

Both police opened fire in three-round bursts, just as they'd been trained to do, and Daniel and Luis died within seconds. So did Richard Chadwick, the driver of the car behind the van. One of the rounds made it through the sheet metal of the rear doors with enough force to shatter Richard's windshield and hit him in the throat, severing his carotid artery, and he bled to death in moments while his wife screamed in the passenger seat.

What had moments before been an inconvenient and frustrating traffic problem became, in an instant, riotous. People, already chafing from the delay and anxious over news of the earlier attacks, scrambled from their cars and ran. Police and Guardsmen converged on the van, weapons and instruments ready, causing even more panic and confusion. In the van, they found two dead Hispanic men and several cases of liquor.

**

Back in Joplin, Missouri, Richard Chadwick's sister ordered her husband and their three children away from the TV to sit down to a family dinner, determined to maintain some normalcy for the sake of the kids. She wouldn't learn about her brother's death until the next day, but she mentioned him and all of their extended family in her before-dinner prayer, just as she did every evening. She put a little extra into her prayer that night, feeling her country could use it.

SATURDAY, JUNE 26

5.08   AL HASAN RESIDENCE, HOUSTON, TX

It had been a late night, and Ibrahim was in a deep sleep when the encrypted cell phone on the table next to his bed started vibrating. The initially subdued ringing escalated as he didn't answer, and his dreams evolved to incorporate the new stimulus. His wife, herself awakened, elbowed him, and that was too much for his subconscious to assimilate and he immediately awoke.

He was not startled by the unusual hour. With his homeland nine hours ahead, he often got such calls. As he calibrated his conscious mind to where he was and what was happening, the satisfaction of the previous day, when everything had gone nearly according to plan, put a brief smile on his face. The interview with the Americans, where he had successfully, he thought, allayed any concerns about his involvement and reinforced his commitment as a trusted ally. He had no doubt that he was still on their watch list, and probably under surveillance, but they would see nothing, hear nothing, and eventually give up.

The bombs going off while the FBI interviewed him was almost too good, a piece of luck he hadn't planned. But it had brought an instant urgency to the conversation, and Ibrahim had been able to play his role, reluctantly giving up a phony "source" who the authorities would have problems tracking because he existed only on paper, and even then with a very light footprint, intentionally prepared by Ibrahim and ending in Sana'a in Yemen, with the official entry in their immigration records.

"Hello," he said in a clear voice that might have been awake for hours, not seconds.

"Ibrahim, it is I."

Ibrahim recognized Ismail's voice instantly even though he spoke in a hushed whisper and the encryption on both phones distorted the sound ever so slightly. Ismail continued without waiting for an acknowledgement.

"They are coming for me. They are here now."

"Who is there? Be clear Ismail. What is happening?"

"Mabahith. They know I delivered the document. There is not much time. I will not be able to resist for long. They may be coming for you even now. You must run."

"Ismail, answer me this - when is your day of birth?"

Ibrahim's odd question was actually a simple code they had worked out to validate communications when one of them might be under duress.

"The day we met, *sayyd.*"

"Thank you my friend. *Allahu Akbar.*"

Ibrahim disconnected the cell phone and touched his wife's shoulder gently.

"Taja, we must go. Quickly and quietly. Get the children dressed. Do not turn on any lights and stay away from the windows. Wait in the kitchen and I will join you momentarily. We will not be coming back."

This was also a situation Ibrahim had prepared for. Taja, his wife of eighteen years, knew of Ibrahim's secret life and approved. They were ready to flee at any time, small bags of essentials including phony documentation, cash and gold coins, some extra clothes, and necessary toiletries and medicines always packed and ready. She quickly dressed in the light of streetlamps through the windows.

Ibrahim pressed an autodial button on the cell phone and Tariq, his bodyguard, asleep in the small gatehouse, answered immediately. His instructions from Ibrahim were short, but he knew what to do and awakened his wife to prepare for flight.

Ibrahim dressed and went to a closet door in his office on the first floor and opened it, revealing a bank of video monitors showing his property and the streets around it from every possible angle. There was no movement, no cars parked anywhere in sight, nothing the least bit suspicious. That did not lower Ibrahim's anxiety.

Of all the agencies that might be chasing him, Mabahith worried Ibrahim the most, even more than Mossad or the U.S. authorities. They were ruthless Saudi secret police, accountable only to the King, and able to threaten Ibrahim and his family in ways that the Mossad would have paid dearly to use. In their custody, Ismail had no chance to resist. They wouldn't stop at torturing him to get what they wanted. They would bring in family and torture them in front of Ismail until he surrendered and told them everything.

How did Mabahith know? Who had betrayed them? Was it their courier to Yemen? He didn't know what he was carrying, and his contact was only to be with Rahman. Was it Rahman? Something had gone terribly wrong, and Ibrahim didn't have the time to figure out what.

His family, Tariq, and Tariq's wife were all in the kitchen when he arrived. Ibrahim took Tariq aside and whispered, "It is Mabahith. There is no sign of movement or surveillance. You will drive. We must get to the beach house and the yacht. Is everything ready?"

"Yes. The Escalade will leave from the garage as a decoy and drive to the airport and park there. The backup team will follow us and stay back to provide cover. It is over 60 miles, *sayyd*. If Mabahith wants you, they will surely have many opportunities before we are safe."

"Yes, I know. We will call ahead and have the crew bring the yacht to Tiki Island. Just get us there and we will be fine."

They waited in the dark kitchen until they heard the garage door open and Ibrahim's Escalade drive quickly away, the door closing behind it. Then they followed Tariq to the basement and out the concealed door there, into a narrow tunnel that led sixty feet to the garage of their neighbor, a house owned by a shadow corporation that Ibrahim controlled, and was leased long-term to a wealthy Arab needing a home in the Houston area. The Chrysler Town & Country Touring Van parked in the garage belonged to the same corporation and was clean of any tracking or listening devices.

Six people crowded into the van, with Ibrahim's son and daughter, both in their teens, in the rear seats. Tariq started the engine and said, "Everyone please fasten your seat belts. OK. We go."

The garage door opened, without lights and very little sound, with a click of the remote, and the van crept quietly out without headlights, turning left onto Inverness Drive after checking both ways on the quiet residential street. Turning right on Willowrick, a main north-south street that would take them to the Southwest Freeway and then I-45 to Galveston and seeing no signs of any pursuit, not even their back-up car, Tariq was relieved and turned on the headlights. Their elaborate escape plans and precautions seemed to work as planned.

Tariq could not see his back-up support car because it was driving with no lights, counting on the streetlamps for its only illumination. They had picked up the van as soon as it turned onto Willowrick and followed several blocks behind. The two men inside watched it approach Westheimer Road when suddenly a large SUV, dark and ominous, shot from the Encore Bank parking lot on the left, its lights coming on only when it reached the street on a collision course with the van.

The driver slammed the accelerator to the floor and his Ford Crown Victoria Police Interceptor surged forward, lights still off, a stealth vehicle intent on doing some damage.

***

Tariq almost felt the lights of the SUV, they were so close when they came on, and he did feel the thump as it tried to force him off the road. Operating on reflex alone, he jerked the steering wheel to the right into the Exxon station at the corner, then jerked it again left to avoid the gas pumps, and then right as he slid onto Westheimer Road, heading west, away from his destination.

***

The back-up car driver saw the van bumped by the swerving SUV as it tried to run it off the road. Fortunately, the van was able to cut across a gas station at the corner and speed off down Westheimer. The SUV took too long to recover and slid sideways as its driver tried to make the right hand turn. Seeing the opportunity, the Crown Vic's driver continued to accelerate without his lights.

It hit the SUV broadside at about 50 miles per hour, crushing both passenger side doors and pushing it about twenty feet to the curb next to the Wells Fargo Bank. The airbags in the Crown Vic deployed with a deafening bang, and Ibrahim's two bodyguards, stunned by the impact of the crash and the explosion of the airbags, wavered on the edge of unconsciousness. It took them several minutes to recover, and then they groped to release their seat belts and get out of the car before the others, or fire, or both, killed them.

Weapons drawn, they limped and stumbled around the wreck, watching for any movement from the SUV. They reached the driver's side and found the men there unconscious. Without hesitation, they shot them both. They didn't bother with the others, who even in the reduced light were obviously dead. A quick check of their wallets revealed they were Saudi nationals, and both men knew that meant Mabahith.

"Let's get their wallets. Then burn it," one of the bodyguards said. And they did, after removing the Crown Vic's license plates and using a can of gasoline from the trunk to get things going fast. Then they walked away, the lead bodyguard autodialing his cell phone.

***

Ibrahim answered on the first ring.

"What happened?"

"There were four. Mabahith. They are all dead. We have their ID's. The car is destroyed and we cannot follow you."

"Contact me when you are safe. *Allahu Akbar.*"

Ibrahim turned to Tariq. "We are alone. Get us there safely."

5.09   BBC News Headquarters, London, England

B B C   NATO Reacts To Possible European Threats

Mutual Assistance Protocols Invoked and Restrictions Implemented

NATO has initiated several Mutual Assistance Protocols in the wake of the U.S. WMD bombings and what it calls "credible intelligence" that suggests the attacks could spread to major European cities and targets. AWACS surveillance planes are presently in the air over Europe and the Americas and no-fly zones initiated over member's capital cities and critical infrastructure hubs and financial centers. New restrictions on commercial air traffic are being implemented, including military escorts of commercial flights. Delays and diversions are expected to become the norm.

5.10   Epcot Center, Orlando, FL

It was as eerie a scene as Sean Maloney remembered ever witnessing, and in his twenty-three years with the Bureau, he had witnessed some doozies. He catalogued this one in his head as *The Evil Pillsbury Doughboy On Wheels.*

The early-morning gloom provided the perfect backdrop for the hazmat technician in full protective gear, including his white, fully-enclosed protective suit and air tank, on a Segway x2 off-road model with two large cargo cases, one above each wheel. The left-side case contained thirty heavy-duty zip-lock evidence bags, each numbered and containing a bean-bag with the same number. The right one was empty for the moment. A digital radiation meter had been cable-tied to the handlebar so he could see the ambient radiation level and the bright-red LED alarm, warning him if the radiation got too intense.

Maloney was in charge of the crime-scene investigation at Epcot, and in the pre-dawn hours, they were going to collect the best evidence they could conceive – cameras and cell phones. Almost everyone at Epcot had one, and there were eighty-three dead bodies scattered around the Sculpture Garden. It was possible that any one of them had a picture of the escaped terrorist.

They were working on theory. No one had seen a second terrorist, but in the other three cases there had been two, so it was a safe assumption that there had been two at Epcot. In every other case, both terrorists had died, but again it was a safe assumption that hadn't been planned. The Chicago and

Washington attacks had been discovered before the intended detonation, and both terrorists died before carrying out the complete plan, and the third team had never even made it to their target. Only at Epcot had the attack seemingly gone as planned, and there was no cargo van found, so it was likely there was a terrorist on the loose in central Florida, and Maloney's job was to find him.

The hazmat technician was a member of the FBI's Hazardous Materials Response Unit. He had twenty minutes to find and collect as many cameras and phones as possible, and then another tech would take over, minimizing the radiation exposure to any one person. The Sculpture Garden had been sectioned into grids and search patterns prepared based on the location of the bodies that had been mapped during the night as volunteers, mostly firemen and emergency medical techs, moved quickly through the area searching for survivors and marking the location of the victims. The blast had blown out most of the lights in the area, so they'd had to use flashlights until portable lighting could be set up.

The decision to use the HMRU techs to do the collection instead of robots was the result of urgency and science. They needed every camera possible as fast as possible, and searching with robots would be slow and clumsy and might miss some. The force of the blast had scattered the cesium over a wide, irregular area as the blast wave encountered buildings and trees or skimmed over open walkways and parking areas. There were hot spots where the airborne cesium hit an obstacle and slowed sufficiently to fall to the ground, and there were relatively cold areas where the explosive wind had swept the ground clean. There wasn't yet a detailed map of these hot and cold spots, only a general idea that the ambient radiation level was about seven rem per hour in the kill-zone of the blast. Based on that, the HMRU team leader had settled on twenty minutes as the maximum safe stay time.

The Segway was supposed to make those twenty minutes as productive as possible. It's ease-of-use and cargo-carrying capability would allow the tech to collect more items than traveling on foot lugging the load. And even the six inches of ground clearance would help with his total dose to his feet. The plastic bags and bean-bags would allow him to collect a camera quickly and leave behind a marker to identify the location of the camera and link it to a body when it was eventually identified. Put a camera in the numbered bag, seal it, drop the numbered bean-bag, and move to the next victim.

When the job was done, Maloney hoped to have a thorough visual record of the crime scene before, during, and even after the explosion. Somewhere in that record was a terrorist, and Maloney's next task would be to figure out who. The motorcyclist had to have come from somewhere, and in all likelihood there had been a cargo van that had been recorded on the surveillance cameras in the parking areas. With luck, they would catch some interaction between the terrorists as the cesium was transferred out of the shield and into the suicide vest. Then it would be a matter of cataloguing every picture and video, assembling a record of his progress into Epcot, and picking the best shots for the facial recognition software. And again with luck, he would be in the record somewhere and they would have a name. With a name, they would have somewhere to start and a history to uncover. With a history there would be a trail, and with a trail, there would be a capture. There was no way Maloney and his colleagues were going to let this guy get away.

5.11   FBI FIELD OFFICE, LOUISVILLE, KY

Saturday morning, Buck Buchanan sat at his desk looking rested and alert and ready for anything. He was alert, anyway, fresh from a shower and change of clothes in the Louisville Field Office fitness center. Rested and ready were a bit of wishful thinking. What little sleep he'd gotten was on the couch in his office, and after following the reports from Orlando and DC and Chicago through the night, he was not ready for anything else to happen.

He got something anyway, and it was finally something good.

He was reviewing the Urban Area Security Initiative list of sixty-four urban regions in the country that were designated as the top priority for Home-land Security funding, and the sites that would receive the most attention in assigning resources for detection and interdiction of the terrorist's cesium. Knoxville wasn't on the list. An oversight that he felt had come home to roost now that Oak Ridge had become a focus in the only WMD attacks ever in America. Well, maybe that was unfair, he thought. No one had attacked Oak Ridge – almost the reverse when you thought about it, with Pastor being used as the weapon to attack others. His phone interrupted that train of thought.

"Orlando just called. They found the van in a Wal-Mart parking lot on East Osceola Parkway in Kissimmee, Florida. White, heavy-duty, same description as the others. They're taking it to Tampa, but the preliminary search turned up nothing. An empty shielded container like the Kentucky one was all they found. No radiation, no papers, nothing. It's registered to a James Strobel of Encinitas, California. Bets are that pieces of him are scattered all over Epcot."

Buck thanked the caller and turned his attention to his own investigation. The van would be a dead-end, he thought, just like the Kentucky one. And Strobel would be, too. This group was unique – they didn't seem to care about concealing their identities, and that meant the identities themselves had to be dead-ends. The only way an identity was a dead-end was if it had no connection to anyone else in the group, and if the owner had no information that could be gleaned under interrogation. The only guarantee of that was to preclude interrogation, and that meant they all expected to die rather than be captured. *We'll need to be very good if we find the one that got away*, he thought. Incapacitate him before he has a chance to die, by his own hand or forcing the hand of his captors – suicide by law enforcement.

The phone rang again. *Busy Saturday*, Buck thought as he answered, and he was right.

"al Jezeera just announced they'll be broadcasting a video of the Epcot bombing at 5 PM their time," his ASAC told him. "That's 10 AM here. Everybody will be in the main conference room in fifteen minutes to watch."

"What video?"

"They say it was shot by the second terrorist, and they are confirming it came from AQAP. Looks like we've got an attribution winner. I'm thinking if I'm in Sana'a I'd better get out before the retribution."

"All right. I'll watch it in the small conference room. Come up and bring Adams, Ericson, and Spellman."

Adams and Ericson were Knoxville's SABT, the Special Agent Bomb Technician, and its WMD Coordinator. Spellman was the lead on the Pastor theft investigation. All of them would have a special interest in the video of the one that got away.

5.12   AL JEZEERA BROADCAST, DOHA, QATAR

Good evening. This is Ahmed Zartoori in Doha for al Jezeera with an exclusive video of the so-called dirty bomb attack yesterday on the U.S amusement park Disney World. The video comes to us from verified sources in the Arabian Peninsula. To date, no group has taken responsibility for the attack. We'll get to the video in just one moment.

The attack was one of three attempted yesterday, and speculation is that a fourth was aborted by a traffic mishap one week ago that left twenty-one people dead, including the two occupants of the van carrying what was apparently the fourth dirty bomb. The others were killed during the subsequent chase and killing of those occupants.

The bombs were targeted at downtown Chicago, Reagan International Airport in Washington, DC, and Disney World in Florida. The Chicago bomb was not detonated due to the quick actions of a local police officer, Edgar Watts, who spotted the suspects preparing the device and killed them both. The Washington device was detonated prematurely, according to U.S. authorities, and the damage limited. The airport remains closed while authorities collect evidence and conduct the clean-up.

Now we'll go to the Disney bombing video. It is short, just one minute and forty-seven seconds, and it does contain graphic images. It starts with the view of the Disney park entrance. As you can hear and then see ... now, a motorcyclist enters the park at a high rate of speed, scattering vacationers as he weaves past the obstacles in his path and aims for the area known as the Sculpture Garden and ... now, see how uses one of those steel and stone decorations to launch his motorcycle high into the air ... right there.

He detonates the bomb and he is immediately engulfed in smoke and debris. The videographer taking this film clip is apparently struck by something and falls ... right there. After a moment, he, or she, we don't know which, struggles to his feet and takes a slow panoramic shot of the damage. You can see the lifeless bodies of the dead and unconscious victims, and see some wounded moving about, trying to recover and escape.

The authorities arrive almost immediately and start to check on the wounded until ... right now, when apparently one of them is alerted to high radiation levels and they begin an immediate evacuation. It is at this point, ... now, that the video stops. We presume that the videographer was forced to exit the area along with the others.

Reaction to the events has been prompt from leaders and officials around the world. A rare Saturday session was called at the United Nations and a resolution condemning the action passed almost unanimously, with only North Korea and Iran abstaining. In Islamabad and other Arab cities, there were demonstrations despite official crackdowns, and here we can see several hundred people dancing and chanting as an American flag is burned and trampled.

We'll have other reactions to this event right after this short break.

5.13   DEPARTMENT OF HOMELAND SECURITY, WASHINGTON, DC

Cal stared at the computer screen in his office at the Department of Homeland Security and tried to make sense of what he was seeing. Ibrahim al Hasan had been under surveillance ever since the report of the Yemeni courier three days earlier, and had been interviewed at his office in Houston just the previous day. There had been no indication that he was anything other than what he said he was, a Saudi diplomat with some good sources who had reported a valuable piece of intelligence. His cars were tagged, and one had left during the night and was now in the daily parking garage at Houston's George Bush Intercontinental Airport. The agents shadowing the car reported that after parking nothing had happened. No one had entered or exited it, and it hadn't moved. Agents had finally knocked on the tinted window and found one Saudi national, asleep in the driver's seat.

No one else had come or gone from the house since al Hasan had returned the previous evening after his interview was cut short when the bombs were detonated. And yet ...

There were four dead Saudi nationals not one mile from his home, identified only because the Houston Fire Department had quickly responded to a car fire and the police were able to get fingerprint identification of all four. They were low-level employees of the Saudi government without any diplomatic protections.

Also involved in the accident was a Ford Crown Victoria registered to a leasing company and leased to what turned out to be a fictitious company in Houston.

And now, agents had gone to the al Hasan residence and there was no answer at the door. They exercised their discretion and broke in and found the house empty, but apparently not abandoned as all of the accoutrements of normal life like toothbrushes and medicines were still in place.

The first thought was foul play. Had someone kidnapped the family and servants in retaliation for al Hasan's reporting of the Yemeni courier? And if so, how did they do it under the surveillance of the FBI? And how did four dead Saudis fit in? Were they bodyguards trying to rescue al Hasan, or were they the kidnappers? Or ...

Ibrahim was running. That was Cal's conclusion. But from whom? And why? Oh, and where?

The reports coming from the local authorities did nothing to clear up the situation, and there was nothing in the larger intel or law enforcement community that seemed connected. What Cal did know, as he went to the office of the DHS Under-Secretary who was his point of contact at the agency, was that al Hasan was missing and they had a situation.

"Oh, Christ," was Glenn Farr's conclusion. "If the Saudis are involved, we've got a mess. They're our allies, for crissake. They just finished briefing us, and they allowed us access to their protected personnel. Including this al Hasan person. No way the President is going to hold them liable. They're too important."

"I didn't say it was the Saudi government. Just that there are too many connections here to ignore. Rahman is assigned to the Saudi Embassy in Sana'a, al Hasan is a Saudi diplomat, the dead guys in Houston are all Saudi, and so are several of the bombers. We've got to be prepared for the possibility that this operation is being run out of Saudi Arabia and this Yemen connection is a diversion."

5.14 U. S. Army Garrison Ft. Rucker, Dale County, AL

It would have been hard to find a more morose group of technical professionals. About thirty people, some radiation safety techs from the DOE lab in Aiken, SC, and the rest helicopter maintenance personnel, worked at long folding tables like some high-tech sweat shop. The only animation occurred when someone from the rad tech group yelled at a maintenance tech, or vice versa.

Stacked at one end were about a hundred new but somewhat obsolete hand-held radiation detectors flown in earlier in the day from the Savannah River Lab along with the techs. While quite sensitive, they remained unopened and unused for all these years after the initial acceptance testing found they required new batteries after four hours of use while the purchase specs had specified twelve.

At the other end were stacks of cage-like metal crates the size and shape of a toaster oven. The instruments, along with hundreds of others scheduled to be arriving from DOE warehouses across the country, were being pressed into service along with the 500 or so of the TH-67 training helicopters at Ft. Rucker's Army Aviation Center of Excellence. The instruments had been quickly checked in the DOE calibration facility and flown to Ft. Rucker to be set up by the rad techs, and installed in the metal cages and attached to the outside of the co-pilot's door on the helicopters by the maintenance techs. Neither group was happy about the assignment, and the heat inside the maintenance hangar just aggravated the tension.

The training helicopters and pilots, some of them still students who would serve as co-pilots, were pressed into service as the airborne platform for these battery-eating radiation detectors that normally were held in someone's hand. The pilots and co-pilots were provided with a narrow, mission-focused understanding of why they needed to fly low and slow, and to hover if any detection, no matter how small, was identified by the installed gamma detection device. They were all provided with a short technical set of guidelines on a single laminated typewritten sheet that gave clear instruction on how to proceed with any positive reading.

"Fuck," one of the maintenance techs yelled when the GM tube on one of the instruments slipped out of its too-loose clamp and banged on the floor. "I thought you guys were high-tech. A clamp too fucking complicated for you?"

A rad tech yelled back, "If you guys could read, we wouldn't have to be down here doing this shit. I gotta paint red stripes on these so you know when you got a problem? Maybe we should draw you stick figures so you'll know what to do."

The Rockets' Red Glare   157

"And glue these things shut," another yelled, "just so you won't monkey with the settings and miss the fucking bomb going off under you."

"Finding the fucking bomb won't be the problem," the maintenance tech shouted. "Your piece-of-shit instruments will probably crash one of us. You guys have any idea how precise the electronics in these birds are? The electro-magnetic radiation from these things is going to throw the air-worthiness off. I can't believe they're putting these things in without re-certification."

"You telling me that these things can be brought down by four D-cells? Does the Taliban know that? Maybe they'll start using flashlights instead of RPG's."

An Army sergeant said, "Will you guys shut the fuck up? It's bad enough we're here on Saturday instead of at the beach."

She was one of only a few women in the building. Most of the female pi-lots of child-bearing age and inclination had declined the assignment, fearing any radiation exposure that could affect an embryo that could be growing, unnoted, at that very moment.

"Just try to remember why we're here," she continued. "Some fucking ragheads are running around with weapons of mass destruction, and it's our job to find them. Do your fucking job."

5.15 U.S. Army Information Dominance Center, Ft. Belvoir, VA

Ray Nassiri took a deep breath and mumbled to himself, his head bobbing ever so slightly as he prayed for patience and humility. As a devout Muslim, he knew that prayers would bring him the serenity he needed for the next thirty minutes. Those minutes would determine the success or failure of his mis-sion, one that he had worked on without deviation since the cesium theft had been discovered, and all night the previous night, after the bomb explosions in Orlando and Washington and the attempt in Chicago. A mission that put everything he'd worked for at risk.

Ray was aware that he wasn't liked. He knew his manner alienated people. He didn't need Dr. Phil to tell him that. But it was *his* manner, and try as he might to suppress it, someone would say something stupid and his ego would burst out, and his imperious reaction would offend. The problem was that his Stanford-Binet intelligence quotient was 156, at the very top of the 99th percentile, and well above any of his peers. So he thought pretty much any-thing they said contradictory to his opinion was stupid. Comparatively, at least.

Add a life of affluence and entitlement, and the result was no patience and little tact. He was the current incarnation of his grandfather and his father, privileged men who had enjoyed the power and prestige of being at the side of Mohammad Revi Shah Palavi until 1979 when the Grand Ayatollah Sayyed Ruhollah Mostafavi Moosavi Khomeini led the Islamic revolution in Iran and sent them all into exile. Ray was even named after the Shah, Revi Heider Nassiri.

So the prayer, while fervent, was no guarantee of success. He was meeting his boss, the Chief Information Officer at the Army's Information Dominance Center in Ft. Belvoir, Virginia, and he planned to present an unpopular conclusion, one that would make him even more suspect, that would isolate him further as the sole Muslim in the group. His birth in Canada and his naturalized U.S. citizenship created even more suspicion, though everyone would deny it. They simply didn't like nor fully trust him.

Margery, the fierce gatekeeper who protected the boss from distraction, and who was particularly fierce on a Saturday after the first-ever WMD attack on the United States, told him it was okay to go in, although her expression said otherwise. One last deep breath, one last prayer, and he stood, picked up his leather portfolio, and walked in, a smile sculpted to his face.

Chuck Melli was seated at his desk, already impatient.

"Well, Ray, what do you have that's so important at this particular moment? I'm a little busy, as I'm sure you can understand."

"Well, sir, I've been reviewing our intel on AQNA and doing some, umm, creative analysis using a new algorithm I wrote for the Starlight visualization tool and the intelligence network fusion software program. I've come up with a pretty irrefutable conclusion about the cesium theft."

"You know who's responsible?"

"No, sir. I know who is not responsible. Al Qaeda in North America."

"Ray, we've got seven dead terrorists, all except one middle-eastern men between eighteen and thirty. And the one is a Muslim convert. We've got standard-issue suicide bombs vests, the hallmark of Islamic terrorists. If not AQNA, then it's one of their proxies."

"It's a lot more complicated than that, sir, and I can provide some crucial information along with statistical confidence levels that lead to several unexpected possibilities. Our initial assumption that we were facing AQNA has been challenged by my most recent correlation modeling. Everything points towards the homegrown American hate group known as WAR."

"You're telling that you tweaked the computer to put this on some neo-Nazi skinheads who can't tie their shoes without diagrams?"

Ray tried to control his anger even while his body posture broadcast his desire to leap across the desk and choke Melli.

"I do not tweak computers, data, or algorithms. I have applied a proven set of analytical methods, along with our most sophisticated visualization tool, in order to establish connections. I have combed through literally millions of disparate facts and judgments contained in our electronic libraries. And I have dispassionately analyzed the output and reached conclusions."

"All right Ray – my bad," Chuck said, realizing it would speed things up if he just smiled and agreed. "How about quickly presenting your assessment of why you think WAR is bombing its own country, and give me some idea of the assessed confidence levels you and our $100 million IDC system are spitting out."

"There are simply too many statistical correlations to dismiss," Ray said with renewed confidence. "I was able to glean an extraordinary number of correlated traffic network hits from NSA intercepts from known members of WAR's regional battalions and traffic patterns pointing to and from the source of the cesium in eastern Tennessee."

Ray paused before showing Melli map print-outs from his analysis. "There are numerous and statistically significant focal point links between this group and these traffic patterns that occur precisely during the time you would expect surrounding the cesium theft. I can make this all very clear to you if you can provide me with one hour of your time down in the Starlight."

Trying hard to avoid a confrontation, but wanting to make clear his annoyance, Chuck looked through the maps and data and then responded to Ray's assessment in a carefully constructed manner.

"You've Nadered your analysis," he said, referring to Ralph Nader, the consumer activist often accused of using only the facts, some of them very questionable, that supported his own conclusions.

His tone was much sharper than his words, and Ray struggled to stay calm.

"You've reached a conclusion and twisted the data to support it," Melli continued. "I'm not taking this upstairs. We're already stretched beyond belief by this, and we don't have the resources to go chasing off after a bunch of retarded gun nuts in Montana. Those guys can barely fill their gas tanks, let alone build a sophisticated dirty bomb. Now, drop this and get back to real work. I want you backstopping the analysis of this event. Check everyone's work and make sure they haven't missed something."

"Backstop everyone's work?" Ray sounded like he'd been asked to muck out the stable at his father's farm, and his nature took the opportunity to break loose. "I don't check other people's work. They check mine, although I don't know why you bother with that. I don't miss things. And I don't twist data. My algorithm is orders of magnitude beyond what those others are doing. My conclusions are sound. You ignore them at your own peril."

Ray's boss fumed. "What is that, Ray? A threat? Don't push me today. You're already on thin ice around here. Now drop this WAR bull and get on with your new assignment."

Ray started to speak, but his boss held his hand up, showing his palm in the classic "stop" sign. "No more discussion, Ray. Go. Now."

Ray walked out, taking his file with him. And he kept walking. To the elevator, and through the lobby, and out the front door.

5.16   ISLAMIC CENTER OF ORLANDO, ORLANDO, FL

Cars and trucks and motorcycles were parked haphazardly along Ruby Lake Road and 4th Street in Orlando, with many more in the open field and parking lot outside the Islamic Center of Orlando. The mob outside had been a demonstration until someone got the idea to text everyone and turn it into a flash mob to protest the attack on Epcot, just three miles west as the crow flies. Then the crazies came out in force and the demonstration degenerated into a siege.

The Center itself was built like a huge, twenty-foot tall concrete bunker with a gold dome on top and a gold semisphere, a quarter section of a sphere, above the door. Eight tall, narrow windows were on the front and sides, looking like vertical gun slits. The whole thing looked like some architect had foreseen just what was happening at that moment designed it to be defensible.

Inside, dozens of Muslim worshippers, gathered there and trapped by sheer bad luck, cowered behind the locked doors as rocks and bottles and cans bounced off the tempered glass of the windows. No police were evident although they had been called several times. When one particularly well-placed stone shattered one of the windows, the Imam decided it was time to act. Against the pleas of the others, he opened the door and stepped outside and put his life in Allah's hands.

The mob closest to the door saw him emerge, and in the split-second of silence that followed their surprise, he spoke in a clear, commanding voice.

"My brothers, thank you! And may God bless you and grant you a long and joyous life."

Those nearest continued to listen, curious what this man had to say in the face of their hostility. Behind them, the crowd continued to chant and throw debris.

"I am saddened and distressed," the Imam continued, "by this attack on America and our freedom and way of life. All of us, Christians and Jews and Muslims, must join together to right this wrong, to find and punish the …"

He never finished the sentence. The gunshot parted the crowd as people screamed and tried to push their way out, to get as far as possible from the leather-jacketed and bearded man holding what looked like an old-fashioned six-shooter. The man stared at the body of the Imam for a moment before holstering the gun and walking away, saying "fuck him" to no one in particular.

5.17   THE GROVE HOTEL, BOISE, ID

Margaret's staff didn't know what had happened in the closed Continuity of Government meeting Friday evening – they just knew a different Margaret came out than went in. Everyone was pressed into service at a time of crisis when they wanted to be home with loved ones. Two junior staffers quit rather than pull the all-nighter they foresaw when she outlined her plans.

First, a press conference was called. Given the press's focus on the bombings, a lot of individual calls to news outlets and Internet bloggers were made to assure a good turnout. The conference would be held at The Grove, arguably Boise's grandest hotel, and lunch was to be served as an added motivation to attend. With the short notice, this was expensive, and some on the staff wondered where the money was coming from. It wasn't in her office budget, so it had to be private.

The topic was to be nuclear security, and the dais would be shared with the Board of Directors of Clean Energy Idaho, an advocacy group promoting nuclear power in Idaho. A controversial topic the day after radioactive dirty bombs had been detonated on U.S. soil. She was counting on that to attract attention. That and a sumptuous buffet.

Much staff time was spent rousting the necessary CEI members and resources to help develop talking points and positions in light of the events. Many of these were less than enthusiastic about her timing, but enough were cooperative to make it work.

At 1:30, she called the conference to order. Plates were still being removed and coffee and drink refills poured, but it quieted quickly when she vigorously tapped her water glass with her spoon and moved to the podium. Without a preamble, she rolled right into the red meat that would be their dessert.

"Yesterday, like December 7, 1941, is a day that will live in infamy. Like then, a cowardly foreign group, enabled and motivated by fossil energy interests, launched a sneak attack on U.S. soil. Like then, our brave and selfless defenders, surprised and overwhelmed, fought back valiantly. Yesterday, our alert law enforcement officers thwarted one attack completely, and forced a second to act prematurely, reducing the damage inflicted. Only one attack, one of four planned, succeeded.

"And like 1941, and like 9-11 too, our enemies will find that payback is a bitch!

"Today, we call on Federal, state, and local governments to act. To put in place the laws necessary to prevent future attacks. To wean our great country from any dependence on foreign oil. To punish any who would try to impose their oppressive, rights-restricting, and un-godly way of life on our great nation, its independent states, and patriotic citizens!

"Let's talk some specifics, and then we'll open this up for questions.

"First, we want to make it clear – yesterday's attack had no connection to nuclear power. None. The stolen radioactive material was intended for medical purposes, and no one here would advocate prohibitions on cancer treatment and other medical procedures.

"And while no one here today would wish this catastrophe on any others, we are a little removed from the consequences, perhaps a little less motivated to react. But what if one of those vans had stopped at the corner of State and 8th? The Capital Building, the Legislative offices, yes even the *high school* would today be radioactive wastelands.

"We are not immune. Chicago and Washington are not the only attractive targets for these terrorists. React as if it had been your loved ones who had been injured or contaminated or, God forbid, one of the casualties. React with the anger of personal vengeance.

"Clean, safe, and secure nuclear power is one of the primary deterrents to terrorism. Without the money and protection afforded by wealthy, undemocratic, and corrupt Arab oil producing states, global terrorism would wither and die. Energy independence is the solution that neutralizes oil-supported terrorism. Clean nuclear energy, along with homegrown gas, oil and coal are all part of this solution.

"Finally, we must recognize the root cause of terrorism and neutralize it. Muslim extremism is the symptom, and we will cure that. But the cause, the sickness that produces that symptom, is much more insidious, much more difficult to cure. It has been infecting international relations for generations, and it is time to put a stop to it once and for all. A Middle-East solution, a final Middle-East solution, must be developed and implemented. With or without the sanction of other countries.

"Now we'll take questions."

There were plenty.

5.18   HOTEL KRISTOFF, MARACAIBO, VENEZUELA

In the eighteen plus hours of escape, Ibrahim got to know his family a little better, and he was not at all sure he was pleased with the knowledge. The drive to Tiki Island had been one of constant danger and stress. His daughter cried most of the way, and his son withdrew, adopting a sullen, aggrieved attitude that he would maintain the entire trip, speaking to no one and seemingly resentful of the inconvenience of fleeing for his life. Only Taja remained true to herself, or at least Ibrahim's perception of herself. Clearly his perceptions of his children had been incomplete and he was learning about them. But Taja remained as always, respectful and submissive, inquiring only about his well-being and shushing the children in favor of some calm for his sake.

On the yacht for seven hours, hugging the coastline to avoid notice by overhead surveillance, the immediacy of the threat had lessened while the stress and anxiety remained. Laila, his daughter, whined the entire trip, especially when he had confiscated all the cell phones and thrown them overboard, something he realized he should have done back in Houston. The boat motion had upset his son's stomach and he continued to retch long after he had vomited all its contents overboard. Again Taja did what she could to maintain calm, and Tariq and his wife kept their distance.

In Playa Laura Villar, just over the border in Mexico, they had found two taxis for the thirty-mile ride to Matamoros. Ibrahim had ordered the boy to ride with Tariq and his wife and had gotten a withering look in return, the first emotion besides gloom that he had evidenced since leaving.

The last leg of the trip, a seven-hour flight to Maracaibo, Venezuela on a chartered business jet, had at least offered some comforts—food, comfortable seating, a stewardess to serve them. Everyone was so tired by then that they took little advantage of it and slept most of the flight.

And finally, the Hotel Kristoff, where they had arranged rooms while in flight using the false passports and ID that Ibrahim kept in his escape kit. While the clerk checked them in and the bellman loaded the meager baggage on the cart, Ibrahim spoke to Tariq.

"We will get some sleep tonight and provisions tomorrow. Taja and your wife will shop for clothes and essentials. You will need to locate several anonymous cellular telephones for my use, and weapons for you and I both. Call Maliki at the Consulate to find some local contact to assist you. And then we will need additional security, at least two more guards at all times.

"And thank you, my brother, for what you have done today. I will not forget."

Part Six – The Chase

S U N D A Y ,   J U N E   2 7

6.01   NATIONAL COUNTER-TERRORISM CENTER, McLEAN, VA

It's time to clean this up with extra-strength TIDE, Matt Bowman thought to himself. It was his personal, and not very good, joke as the Chief Technology Officer for the Terrorist Identities Datamart Environment – TIDE. In his database at the National Counter-Terrorism Center in McLean, Virginia, he currently had individual identities and associated information on over 600,000 people worldwide who had at one time or another studied, planned, or committed terrorist acts, or raised money or recruited members or provided support for terrorist organizations, or whose name and history had somehow got mixed up with someone who had done any of these things. This last group was an on-going public-relations nightmare every time some innocent person got denied access to a flight, and he was constantly winnowing the list. In the last year 30,000 names had been removed, but 52,000 got added, so the list continued to grow.

He'd received several excellent photos from the cameras and phones of the victims of the Epcot attack, and they had been analyzed by 3DFR, his latest three-dimensional facial recognition software. This new version allowed him to turn regular, two-dimensional photos into virtual 3D by projecting a grid onto the face and extrapolating from specific points to create a high resolution 3D model. With this software, he could get near-fingerprint accuracy of an individual's identity even when the subjects used disguises or grew facial hair. The ratios of distances between specific facial features, and the distance to a specific central point provided a set of twelve very distinct numbers, the facial equivalent of the whorls and loops and arches of a fingerprint. It would take his computer network less than two hours to provide a list, sorted by probability, of possible identities.

One hour and fifty-one minutes later, he had the list. Two-hundred and thirty-six names – fewer than he'd expected but not an unusual number given the stringent restrictions. The surprise was that the highest confidence factor was only 83%. Usually they stopped considering candidates below 90%. The inescapable conclusion was that this guy wasn't in the TIDE database. Matt decided to broaden his search.

In addition to TIDE, the NCTC had access to an even larger database of photos and names, but without the additional information that correlated them to any terrorist connection. Surveillance photos, mug shots, passport and immigration pictures, news reports, and many other sources, some not well sanctioned. These were also constantly changing and therefore not as well indexed and integrated into the 3DFR, so an analysis would take a lot longer and the results would be less definitive. He started the search and specified hourly downloads of any hits at the 90% confidence factor or above.

Seven hours later he had his result – a 99% level hit on an immigration photo almost two years old on a student visa belonging to one Bander Ashoor. Matt patted his flat-screen monitor like a pet. *Good computer*, he thought.

6.02   CNN NEWS HEADQUARTERS, ATLANTA, GA

 **WESTBORO BAPTIST CHURCH DEMONSTRATES AT EPCOT**

VICTIM'S FAMILIES MOURN WHILE WESTBORO CONGREGATION CELEBRATES

ATLANTA (CNNLocal.com) -- Members of the infamous Westboro Baptist Church today demonstrated in Orlando, thanking God for the dead and wounded following the Friday terrorist attacks with dirty bombs. Removed from the Epcot Center parking lot by Disney security, the members gathered at the entrance road and displayed signs that read "Pray For More Dead Fag Lovers" and "God Hates Cartoon Fags Too". Fred Phelps, pastor of the tiny congregation, issued a proclamation claiming the bombing was God's punishment of America and promised to follow-up soon with a "roster of the damned" – the names of the victims of these unprecedented attacks by suspected foreign Arab Salafi terrorists.

6.03   I-495, Exit 15A, Largo, MD

At the same moment Matt Bowman was patting his computer. Bander was at the IHOP off of Interstate 495, just eighteen miles east of NCTC and Bowman. Bander had no idea that NCTC was even there, or that his immigration photo had just become the most important computer file in the war on terror.

He was tired, having driven almost 900 miles in fourteen hours, and sleeping just seven in his Subaru Outback's cargo area at various rest stops along the way home to Worcester, Massachusetts from Kissimmee, Florida. He had no souvenirs from his trip to Orlando, his video camera having been crushed by the tire iron and left in pieces in the trash receptacle in Georgia after he'd downloaded the video to his anonymous cell phone and transmitted it to the Internet FTP site he'd been given. It had then received the same treatment near Jacksonville. The only trace of his visit to Florida would likely be grains of sand that clung to the fibers in his floor mats.

The tilapia was tasteless and the hollandaise needed lemon, but Bander hardly noticed. It was food, and it was necessary to keep him moving. He had classes tomorrow, and he'd already missed enough of them to jeopardize his high class rank at the UMASS Medical School.

***

After Matt Bowman clicked *Send*, the picture started on its electronic trip that ended three minutes and four stops later at the office of the Director of National Intelligence. To get any higher in the organization chart, it would have to go to The White House, which it did after several more minutes.

The DNI also forwarded the information to the FBI Director and the Secretary of Homeland Security who brought several other high-ranking DHS personnel into the loop. A SVTC was scheduled for 7 PM, twenty-eight minutes away. The FBI and the NCTC were already working on locating Bander Ashoor. They wanted him under pervasive surveillance, in a net so tight they would know if he changed his underwear.

The DNI knew, correctly, that DHS and the FBI would want Ashoor picked up and questioned vigorously. He didn't. He wanted Ashoor on the move, doing what he'd been instructed to do, because those instructions would inevitably lead to the instructor. His staff was preparing for the SVTC by preparing a plan and rationale for surveillance, and his job would be to convince the President that this was the best course of action.

***

The Director of the FBI was only minutes behind the DNI in his evaluation of the new circumstances and the preparation for his role in the SVTC.

Ashoor was the only link in the human chain of terror that had, for the first time in history, employed weapons of mass destruction in and against the United States. Ashoor needed to be confined so tightly that sensory deprivation would be an improvement, and questioned so vigorously that everything he knew would be discovered and investigated. The process had already begun and Ashoor's life was being deconstructed at that very moment. If he had a cell phone with an active GPS, they would find him in minutes. Other methods might take longer, but they would find him.

He understood that the DNI and his staff would want Ashoor on an invisible leash, and his job would be to convince the President that any leash could be slipped, and Ashoor was too important to risk losing. His staff was preparing for the SVTC by preparing a plan and rationale for capture and interrogation.

6.04   Church of Jesus Christ of the Latter Day Saints, Boise, ID

Tag was already in the pastor's office of the Morman church meetinghouse when Margaret arrived. She hadn't seen him in the congregation, but they'd used the church for most of their clandestine meetings, and she'd never seen him arrive or leave. She appreciated his discretion as any association with him would cause her re-election problems, even in the militia-friendly lands of Idaho.

After their warm greeting, Margaret got right to her point, almost a cross-examination, which she was very good at.

"Alright, Uncle Theodore, what do you know about these incidents? And how do you know it?"

"I'll tell you what you need to know. How I know it is my business, Margaret. There are twelve more dirty bombs. The Feds might stop a few, but they won't be able to stop them all. Muslim extremists from Yemen are responsible, and as soon as the government confirms this, they'll retaliate. When that happens, all hell will break loose."

Margaret interrupted. "When that happens, everyone will get behind the administration. How will that help us?"

"If you'll let me finish, I'll tell you. Yeah, they'll be popular for a while, but then there'll be questions about how these terrorists managed to pull this off, and there'll be demands for tighter security and destruction of these terrorists. And we don't give a damn about this administration, anyway. We're not going to change the whole country. We're not even going to try. We're just going to protect ourselves and our way of life.

"Your job, Margaret, is to get out in front of this movement and be a leader. Use the information I'll feed you to lead the movement. You need to open channels now to right-minded leaders in the other six Mid-America States. Your objective is a seven-state compact, the Mid-America Compact including Idaho, of course, Utah, Montana, Wyoming, North and South Dakota and Minnesota. These states will pledge to assist one another to fight the war on terrorism on a regional basis."

"Assist how? We don't have the intelligence resources and law enforcement manpower to fight terrorism. The States have always played a supporting role, providing local manpower, developing local information."

"That has to change. The compact states will agree to share information and resources and coordinate investigation and enforcement activities. Eventually, there should be a standardization of laws, starting with anti-terrorism laws. State law enforcement agencies should be permitted to operate cross-border. Regional leadership, political and administrative, should evolve."

"That's not going to happen. States are not going to cede their territorial integrity."

"Maybe not today with the indigenous population, but there is going to be a mass migration in this country over the next few years. There are currently just over thirteen million people in these states, and already they are 40% or more hardline conservatives and another 20% moderate conservatives. An influx of just three million people will tilt the balance, Margaret. A majority of the voters will support our vision. State boundaries will be less important to these new residents, and before long they will develop a regional patriotism to rival national patriotism. In effect, we will have created an autonomous region within the United States."

"And you, Margaret, are the leader who will give birth to this new, what shall we call it? This oasis of good and right, this new land of the free and home of the brave."

Margaret was stunned silent. Governor of Idaho was one thing, but the leader of the new world in America? That was a challenge worthy of her, and she smiled ever so slightly.

6.05   BELLOTTA RESIDENCE, KENT ISLAND, MD

Cal and Claire worked in their kitchen overlooking the Chesapeake Bay, sipping the Viognier white wine from a local winery owned by Cal's friend, Mark Cascia. On the stove, Claire had chicken simmering in her spicy red curry while Cal chopped some onions and tomatoes to add to the lettuce mix for their salad. After spending a long Saturday night in DC, he'd caught a ride to the Naval Academy that afternoon and picked up his boat that had been left there since the first SVTC. It was his first break since the cesium theft, and with Friday's bombings, he didn't expect to be home again for some time.

He'd spent Saturday and most of Sunday reviewing the available intelligence as it came in and trying to fit it to what he knew or suspected about the thieves and their motives and plans. A meeting with the Under-Secretary of National Protection & Programs and his staff the night before hadn't gone well, with everyone's nerves frayed and tensions high. Cal didn't help the mood with his several comments and questions about the assumptions that everyone had made and conclusions that they drew from them, namely that they were dealing with an Islami-fascist organization operating in the U.S. without any footprint. While all the available evidence pointed that way, Cal found it hard to believe that there had been no hints of an operation of this magnitude, and he didn't hesitate to point this out whenever it seemed appropriate. Devil's advocate was in his job description.

The doorbell rang and Claire said, "Would you get that? I'm stirring."

Cal opened the front door to a tall, clean-cut young man in a suit. *Jehovah's Witnesses* was his first thought, and he mentally prepared his polite no-thank-you speech. But without any preamble, the man asked, "Dr. Calogero Bellotta?"

His first fleeting thought was, *how does Jehovah's Witnesses know my name?* Before it even finished, he knew the answer – this wasn't a spiritual visit. The next question was *who calls me Calogero besides Claire when she's mad at me?* He didn't know the answer to that one, and simply said, "Yes. I'm Cal Bellotta. What can I do for you?"

The man reached into his inside jacket pocket, causing Cal a moment's reflexive reaction to a possible threat, but the man just brought out his wallet and opened it, showing Cal a government ID from the Army's Information Dominance Center, and handing him a business card that labeled him a Senior Analyst.

"I'm Ray Nassiri. I know this must be an intrusion, but I have something very important that you must see. Do you have somewhere private that we could talk?"

More thoughts flashed through Cal's mind. *Intrusion? That doesn't even begin to describe an unannounced visit to my home on a Sunday afternoon after the bedlam of the last few days. And why here? The IDC is in Virginia and it would have been much easier to meet in DC.*

"Whoa. Slow down. Ray, you said? What do you have that's so important that you drive out here on a Sunday afternoon and interrupt my dinner?"

"I know who has the cesium. And I know where it is."

Cal realized that was probably the only thing Ray could have said at that moment to get his full attention. So he was a little skeptical.

"All right. That's good. But why are you out here telling me? Why aren't you telling your chain of command back at IDC?"

"I already told them, and they don't believe me." Ray sounded aggrieved, his own expression and tone showing disbelief, and Cal guessed he wasn't used to being ignored. "They're so entrenched in their current Muslim terrorist scenarios that they won't consider other possibilities. According to the report on your meeting last night, you have some skepticism, and as far as I can find out in what little time I've had to research it, you may be the only one who does."

"My meeting last night? You've seen a report on that already?"

"Of course. We have virtual instant access to all activities related to homeland security. And you made it clear that there are some discrepancies in the current analysis. I have the information that will clear those up. So, as I asked before, do you have someplace private we can talk?"

"Yeah," Cal said, stretching the word into a three-second sound effect as he considered this news and the curry simmering in the kitchen. Claire, too, would be simmering soon, but if this guy had real information, and a Senior Analyst at the Information Dominance Center likely did, then Cal had to hear it. "Come in. Have a seat over here," he said, pointing to a couch in the living room. "I'll just let my wife know to hold dinner."

"Who was that," Claire asked when he returned to the kitchen.

"Not was, is. Someone from Fort Belvoir and he needs to speak to me right away. Can you keep things warm for a bit while I hear him out?"

She gave him a look that told him she knew 'a bit' was likely to stretch into Monday. "Take him to your office," she said with a sigh. "See if he wants some curry and wine and I'll bring it to you there."

Cal's first-floor office in the back corner of the house was designed for work, not show, and was furnished with several file cabinets and a large "L" shaped desk. Two upholstered chairs and a small side table that had migrated from the living room during a redecoration several years earlier provided the only conference facilities, and Cal had Ray sitting in one while he took the other.

The offer of curry and wine was met with an offhand "no thank you, I don't use alcohol" response, reinforcing Cal's first impression that the man came from privilege and was unaware of his slightly patronizing attitude. He hoped he wasn't some foreign-service dilettante with a crazy conspiracy theory.

"Look, this is pretty complicated stuff," Ray said as he opened his briefcase and pulled out a laptop computer. "You'll just have to take my word for it that the computers at IDC can do this, and I can write the code that will let them."

Cal didn't take offense at the almost backhanded condescension, replying, "I am very familiar with IDC's capabilities and I work with Stan Amos frequently," naming the Deputy Director. "But before we get into the details, why not just tell me? Who has it and where is it?"

Ray hesitated, and then answered, "Because until you see the evidence, you're not going to believe me."

"Try me," Cal said, holding his stare at Ray until he nodded.

"OK. The White Aryan Resistance has the cesium, and the containers were taken to Boston, Denver, Detroit, Houston, Kansas City, Las Vegas, Los Angeles, New York, Philadelphia, Phoenix, San Francisco, and Seattle."

Cal took note of the alphabetical listing of the cities before responding, "WAR? Jesus, no wonder your boss didn't believe you. They simply aren't that sophisticated. And how do you explain the suicide bombers? None of them are WAR. Are you suggesting some alliance between WAR and Muslim terrorists? That's really far-fetched."

"Now that is exactly why I said you needed to see the evidence first." Ray's response was a little agitated. "You've already developed a sub-conscious bias against my analysis and conclusions and everything will now be tainted by that. You won't be able to make an honest appraisal and reach an unbiased conclusion."

"Ray, here's a thought for you. You've just made a pretty uncharitable judgment about my intelligence and objectivity that has no basis. If you've approached your boss the same way, then I understand how he might be disinclined to listen to your opinion. You'll certainly get further with me if you drop the pretension and explain what you know and how you know it. You might be surprised to find that I am bright and open-minded."

As if she had been waiting for just the right time to break the tension, Claire appeared with a tray with two bowls of curry, some flatbread, water for Ray, and wine for Cal. Ray seemed flustered, and visibly breathed deep, evolving a calmer demeanor. Claire winked at Cal as she left the room.

"OK, Ray. Give it to me."

Ray hesitated, and then began. "I started with the only four facts that we have – the cesium theft from Pastor; the accident on I-75; three suicide bombs in three different locations; and a group of previously unknown terrorists responsible for them. Everything else is speculation at this point, including the claims of this being the work of Islamic terrorists. All we have to support that is the ethnicity of seven of the eight suicide bombers and an unvetted video on al Jezeera. None of the seven have any known ties or sympathies with Muslim fundamentalists or *jihad*. And we certainly can't be trusting al Jezeera.

"We can make some *assumptions* from these facts. First, the remaining cesium has been divided into a number of other weapons, probably twelve as you will see from my analysis. Next, these remaining twelve weapons are scattered around the country, the same as the four that we know of so far. And, the method of transportation is similar to or the same as the four known vehicles. Having different containers and vehicles makes no sense. That gives our computers a number of valid points to evaluate to look for patterns.

"Using these facts and logical assumptions, I wrote some algorithms to look at the resulting visible evidence that would be left by twelve trucks moving to and from Eastern Tennessee. The problem is that the trail is lost in the mass of unrelated data, and I needed to filter that out. Now here is where my assumptions start to get less tenable, but they are reasonable, just the same.

"The drivers need portable money. That means cash or bank cards, either credit or debit. If they are using cash, then tracking them becomes orders of magnitude more difficult, so I decided to start with the easier analysis – credit cards. I can go into great detail here, but that might be better done at IDC where the computers will give a powerful visual representation of the analysis.

"Here's the bottom line. I was able to discover the source of the credit cards used, get their numbers, trace their transactions, map the routes, and in some cases, match them to an individual. In all of those cases, the individual has WAR connections. Here is what the result looks like."

Ray opened his laptop, which was either very fast to boot up, or had been in a sleep mode as the screen came to life instantly. It showed a simple outline map of the continental U.S. with the states drawn, but no other information such as roads or cities, and all of it in black and white.

"This is a time-accelerated depiction of the relevant credit card transactions. The first set of routes starts three days before the cesium theft, depicting the time span necessary to get everything in place before the theft. There is then a second group starting early Saturday morning of the Pastor theft and ends Monday night, eastern standard time. This is the deployment of the weapons after loading at Pastor."

Ray clicked the 'enter' key, and a single white dot appeared in western Washington state, nearly in the Pacific Ocean. A digital clock and calendar identified the date and time as just after noon on Wednesday, three days before the theft. Quickly, a second dot appeared in northwestern California, then another in southwestern California. Another dot appeared in someplace labeled La Grande, Oregon and was connected by a thin white line to the first dot in Washington. More dots popped up in Nevada, Arizona, Texas and then quickly all around the Mid-west and East Coast states. Lines connected more and more dots, and it became apparent that they would all converge on eastern Tennessee. When they did, everything except the clock and calendar went static, with no movement.

Then, as the clock passed 8 AM Saturday morning, a new dot, this one red and labeled Vienna, Illinois, appeared west of the convergence of the inbound tracks. Just as before, more red dots appeared, connected by red lines, but this time moving away, back along the same routes as the incoming white tracks. By Monday evening, all the return paths were complete, and all ended near one of the original starting points.

Cal sat back in his chair and thought about what he'd seen. Of course, given fifteen minutes with Adobe Illustrator, he could have created an identical presentation. And Ray Nassiri had the power of IDC's Starlight computers to make something even more convincing, if he chose.

The relevant question was, where did the dots come from? If they came from a reliable trace of credit cards in the hands of terrorists, then this was a remarkable piece of work and just the thing they needed to get the investigation on-track. If, on the other hand, Ray had consciously or sub-consciously programmed the computer to select these particular dots out of what must have been millions of credit card transactions over the period in question, then he was mistaken at best, and a willing participant in a plan to divert the investigation at worst.

"Look, Ray, that's very impressive, but if it was that easy to track the terrorists' credit card use, the FBI would already have this information and we'd have this whole thing wrapped up."

Ray made a sound that might have been "ha" but it came out as more of a grunt as he flopped back in his own chair.

"Easy? This was hardly *easy*. It took Starlight seventeen hours to analyze the data and come up with this. Do you know what seventeen hours of data crunching on that computer could do? In seventeen hours, that computer could scan every book ever published in any language, translate them to English, and tell you how many time the word 'it' appeared."

"We both know Starlight's capabilities," Cal said. "And you know that the amount of time the data is crunched isn't relevant. It's what data was crunched and how the crunching was done. What was the computer told to look for? What connections did it make from the various inputs? What data did it have to look at in the first place?"

Ray sat up and started to say something, but stopped and took one deep breath. "I'm not going to convince you with this little animation, am I? No, of course not. You'll have to come to the IDC with me and see the actual analysis for yourself."

"Good idea," Cal said. "We can do it first thing in the morning."

"No, I meant now."

"Now? Look, Ray, your analysis is interesting, but I'm not traipsing into DC tonight. I'll meet you at IDC in the morning and we can see it then."

"That's not possible. I won't be able to get computer time in the morning. It has to be at night when the third shift is on duty."

"I'll talk to Stan Amos and get us time in the morning. I'm sure he'll accommodate me."

"You don't understand. This analysis is off the books. My supervisor specifically told me to drop it. I can only get computer time when Richard Savidge is the shift supervisor on duty. He and I are friends and he signs himself on and lets me do my work without anyone knowing. So, it has to be now."

Cal could hear Claire working in the kitchen, probably already knowing somewhere in her mind that he would not be at home tonight. Cal put his hands on his knees, ready to push himself up, looked down and mumbled "damn," and got up.

6.06   HOTEL KRISTOFF, MARACAIBO, VENEZUELA

Laila was locked in her bedroom on the sixth floor, the top floor, of the Hotel Kristoff. She was locked from the inside to keep her father and everyone else out. Eighteen hours of boats and cars and planes and then being stuck here where the stores weren't even open on Sunday so she didn't have any nice clothes and her father being even more mysterious than usual and taking away her cell phone had turned the normally cheerful 16-year-old into a tempest of hormones and attitude and privilege. If she hadn't locked herself in, her father might well have done it from the outside just to get some relief.

She needed the privacy so she could indulge the only activity that had kept her from jumping overboard and letting the sharks eat her - texting her secret boyfriend back in Houston. Alain was the 18-year-old son of a French diplomat and two grades ahead of her at The British School. Her father would never approve of him because of his age and nationality, so they'd kept their romance a secret. He'd even given her a secret cell phone so she could talk and text without her father knowing. Good thing, too, now her father had taken hers away, saying that no one could know where they were. Alain was not just anyone, and she had no secrets from him.

"832-579-9422 im in maracaibo. sorry i took so long. daddy watching. miss u."

"832-291-1190 maracaibo? why? u ok? miss u 2."

"832-579-9422 daddy dragged us here. hes got some problem."

"832-291-1190 when r u coming home?"

"832-579-9422 don't kno. daddy is all weird + secret. whats going on?"

"832-291-1190 nothing. every1 1ders where you and farid are."

"832-579-9422 god I hate this. i miss u."

"832-291-1190 me 2. maybe i'll come there."

"832-579-9422 really? that would b cool."

"832-291-1190 yeah. maybe this weekend. parents r away."

"832-579-9422 cool! hotel kristoff."

Laila disconnected and smiled. *Maybe Maracaibo won't be so bad, after all.*

MONDAY, JUNE 28

6.07   U.S. ARMY INFORMATION DOMINANCE CENTER, FT. BELVOIR, VA

Crossing the Bay Bridge on a Sunday night, in the summer, going towards DC, was always an adventure, a test of patience for the slow traffic and the daredevil driving. The Bay Bridge was the choke point for all the DC and Baltimore area residents returning from Rehoboth, Fenwick Island, Ocean City, or any of the Atlantic resorts of Maryland and Delaware, after a weekend of too much sun and too much fun.

Ray drove his Lexus coupe cautiously, which Cal appreciated in the crowd of tired and frustrated drivers. Ray had offered to bring Cal back after the presentation, but Cal knew he would just have to turn around and come back into DC, so he packed for a few days, not really knowing where he would be spending the next few nights. Neither man spoke, Ray intent on his driving and Cal not wanting to distract him and happy for the time to consider what he'd seen and the implications if it turned out to be accurate.

WAR? When did they get this sophisticated? Cal's knowledge of WAR was more limited, their never having been a WMD threat before. Well, that wasn't strictly true, as many FBI families from Oklahoma City would vouch. But even that had been a crude device, crudely placed, and didn't require the kind of preparedness and response plans that were Cal's specialty. And since the Southern Poverty Law Center successfully sued them in 1990 and won a $12.5 million settlement, their funding had disappeared and with it, much of their credible threat.

Even so, Cal was aware that they were a growing menace, and if they were involved, then they had found new money. What he couldn't understand, and the single most significant fact arguing against their involvement, was the participation of Muslim suicide bombers. How did they pull that off? WAR's normal tactics involved threats and bullying and many-on-one violence, so maybe these Muslim "terrorists" were unwilling participants. Cal couldn't believe that, given the apparent enthusiasm of the terrorist in Kentucky who so eagerly killed all those innocent civilians and police.

The next most likely way was deception. If not unwilling, then maybe unwitting. Could WAR have created some phony terrorist group and recruited these kids under a false banner of *jihad*? With the anonymity of the Internet and its value as a lure for the disaffected, that seemed to be the more likely method.

There was one final, very remote possibility – WAR had allied with an existing terrorist group like AQNA and were working toward some common goal. The problem there was that the goals of each organization included the destruction of the other. Still, stranger things had happened in the world of international terrorism.

The sixty-five mile drive to Ft. Belvoir took Ray ninety minutes, including the time passing through security. The IDC was in the Nolan Building on the north end of the base, and at 9:30 on a quiet Sunday night there was ample parking.

"We're early," Ray said, "so we'll have to wait in my office until ten when Richard comes on duty."

They passed through building security and took the elevator to the second floor where Ray had what looked to be one of not many private offices. Cal figured his work required both quiet and security. Ray had a coffee machine that used the little pods of coffee to brew single cups, and he made some for both of them.

While it was brewing, Cal asked, "Who is this Richard guy we're waiting for?"

"He's the deputy supervisor on the third shift, and about the only guy here who is willing to support my work. It's odd, because he's Jewish, and you'd think he'd be the last person to trust me."

"I don't get that," Cal said. "You work in one of the most secure installations in the country, and you've clearly been vetted every which way. Why wouldn't your associates trust you?"

"It's not trust, exactly. It's more that they resent me. And since the terrorist in Kentucky killed all those civilians, it's gotten worse. It's just their biases, I don't take it personally."

Their biases, and Ray's predilection for arrogance, Cal thought. After sipping their coffee until the 10 o'clock shift change, Ray led Cal to the elevator to go to the 4th floor location of the IDC computer terminals.

Ray called up his program from one of the terminals, and the first set of graphics were forming on the screen while Ray was explaining to Cal that this was a map and analysis of credit card thefts in the weeks preceding the cesium theft. They were filtered and prioritized by criteria Ray had set that would make them candidates for the cesium transportation. As Ray was explaining some of these and how he'd arrived at them, the door burst open and someone that Cal didn't recognize came in, a short, intense and clearly pissed off guy with an I'm-in-charge expression barged in, followed by Ray's friend, Richard.

"What the hell is going on here, Nassiri," the man almost shouted. "What are you doing, and who authorized it?"

Ray was standing now, stiff and tense.

"I am reviewing some of my analysis for Dr. Bellotta from DHS. He's involved in the RDD investigation and wanted to see what I've developed."

"Oh, shit, Nassiri. Not more of your crazy WAR theories. Didn't Mr. Melli tell you to drop that? Computer access here is limited and very valuable. We've got analysts backed up waiting to get time, and you're wasting it on some half-assed theory that no one believes in!"

"These 'half-assed theories' are well beyond *your* comprehension and I don't expect you to understand or appreciate their significance. And this time was legitimately reserved, so I'll thank you to let us proceed."

"Forget it. I'm in charge here and the computer was reserved for a totally different use. So pack it up and get out. I'll be reporting this to Mr. Melli in the morning."

"Something new has come up that takes precedence and Richard willingly ceded his computer time to me. DHS wants to assess this analysis, and Dr. Bellotta traveled a long way on a Sunday night to see it."

"This is nothing new. And if DHS wants to know what we're doing, then they should be going through channels just like everyone else. Shut this down and go home. Let someone with a real need in here to work."

Cal had sat and watched the battle of wills. The new person was clearly some higher level manager, but probably not in Ray's chain of command given his willingness to argue. Whoever this new guy was, he was trying to exercise his authority for no apparent reason other than he had it. And Ray was not used to being bossed around, so he'd pushed back. It was nearly a stalemate, but Cal figured in the end the officious little manager would win.

"One moment, if I might," Cal interrupted. "I would like to see Mr. Nassiri's entire analysis. We're here, and it doesn't look like there is a line at the moment to get to the computer, so why not just let us finish and then we'll get out of your way."

"I don't know who you are or how you do things over at DHS, but that's not how we do things here. Computer access is granted on a priority basis, it is scheduled in advance, and proper authorization is required. Nassiri has no authorization for his fairy-tale, and until he does, I'm shutting it down."

"I'll tell you what. Why don't I authorize it?" Cal took out his wallet and handed the man his brand new White House National Security Staff ID card and the letter on White House stationary from the President of the United States himself requiring full and immediate cooperation. "If you'll just call the White House switchboard – you have their number, I presume – and ask for the Director of National Preparedness and use my name, they'll put you right through to him and I'm sure he'll be glad to verify my authority."

The White House authority got his attention. Holding the card and letter in two hands like he was afraid to drop them, he glanced back and forth between them and Cal until he made a decision.

"That won't be necessary. You may proceed for the allotted time. And in the future, Nassiri, if you're going to divert computer time, at least have the courtesy to advise me first. Dr. Bellotta, I would like to make a copy of this letter for my superiors, if questioned about this unorthodox decision on my part."

With that the man wheeled and left, firing a scathing look at Savidge, who shrugged his shoulders at Ray in a 'sorry but what else could I do' mannerism, and left, following just as he had when they'd arrived.

"Wow," Cal said as they sat back down. "Who was that?"

"He's the facility administrative manager. Just some stupid little man with a little bit of power that he abuses at every opportunity. Let's get back to my analysis so we can finish before my time runs out."

"As I was saying, the starting point is the theft at Pastor. We know the thieves divided the cesium into at least four separate loads, and, as you'll see, the number is actually sixteen, including the four we know about. Handling the cesium is very dangerous and difficult, so they likely made sixteen identical containers and filled each one using the facilities at Pastor.

"So we have a starting point, and we can assume that sixteen vehicles left Tennessee in a specific time span for various and unknown locations across the country. We know three of the locations from the bomb attacks, and we can surmise their routes from the start and end points. There are many requirements for transporting the cesium this way – vehicles, shielded containers, drivers, and, of course, money. The FBI is examining the vehicle, container, and driver leads, so I decided to concentrate on the money.

"Travel expenses would include first, fuel. Then we have food, either restaurants or grocery stores, tolls, and finally rest stops such as motels. The only certainty is fuel as they could have packed provisions for the entire trip and slept in their vehicles. And tolls would almost certainly be paid in cash as they would not use credit or wireless billing services such as EZPass.

"The money would be untraceable – cash or phony or stolen bank cards, either credit or debit. If it was cash, then I had no way of tracking it so I focused on bank cards."

Ray went on to describe how he'd analyzed credit card thefts preceding the Pastor theft and, using a series of assumptions that were each perfectly valid by themselves, but the margin for error compounded as more were piled on. The analysis was illustrated by the constantly changing display of the Starlight computer. Credit card thefts were pinpointed, and charges using those stolen cards shown like tens of thousands of points of light suspended in space on a 3D representation of the United States. Many of these blinked off as Ray's assumptions and analysis eliminated them from consideration, and new lines were drawn connecting events and text flashed as captions to graphics that came and went. It was all very mind-boggling, and Cal could see how someone might reject it as cherry-picking information to support a predetermined conclusion.

"I narrowed the credit card use down to one theft in Dallas," Ray continued to explain. "The theft was from a legitimate ATM equipped with a 'skimmer' to capture the card number and PIN. The thief got almost 200 credit and debit card numbers along with PIN's. He has been identified, and his identity is significant to my conclusions, because he also has links to WAR.

"Many were recovered unused, and this got the list down to 120. Eighty-three of those had been used one time only and for gas. This correlated very well with my calculations that showed a uniform distribution of the containers throughout the country using the average vehicle gas mileage of these types of van would result in between seventy-seven and eighty-seven gas fillings. So it would appear that after a single use, the cards were disposed so no trail would be created. Very clever.

"I plotted all the gas purchases from these cards and added the other travel related purchases and then developed possible routes given the typical distance between fillings. I got fifty-three possibilities, including the twelve that I showed you going to and returning from Tennessee."

Ray paused and the screen held static showing fifty-three white lines.

"The trick here was to assume a round-trip. The vans would have to come from somewhere, and it would be foolish to buy them all in the same locale. That would be easy for law enforcement to spot. And the drivers would also have to come from somewhere. And go home when they were done, so it seems likely that they would be bought locally and used for a round-trip. Using the purchases and the schedule that is required surrounding the theft itself, we get this."

Ray sat back in triumph as the giant display recreated a much more elaborate version of the time-phased route plotting that Cal had seen on Ray's laptop. It was all very impressive, and possibly even valid, except for one thing.

"OK, say I buy into all of your assumptions. This tells me where the cesium went, although there is no guarantee that it is still there, but how did you make the leap to WAR?"

"That's where it starts to get a little, ummm, empirical."

Starts to get, Cal thought. Aristotle would be turning over in his grave if Ray thought everything so far was governed by the scientific method. Even so, Cal thought that Ray had some strong evidence of where the cesium had gone, no matter how he'd arrived at it.

"Of course you know the government surveils a lot of known or suspected threats, tens of thousands of people here in the U.S. alone. Credit cards, driver's licenses, utility bills, phone calls, and all the other signatures of their lives that are created by just living in U.S. society. In many cases, there is active surveillance as well. So we have a lot of data that places them in time and space. I took the location and time on the route map and compared it to all of the data we have on all these subjects to see if we get any matches. And, of course, we did. Hundreds, in fact. Way more than are relevant. But most of these were one-time matches, and only four actually tracked our routes in any way.

"Now this isn't perfect because in all cases we don't have a person match for every stop on the route. In other words, the person in question didn't do something that we would pick up at every stop, so there are gaps. Let's look at the Seattle route. That's the longest and therefore has the most points of observation."

The computer map erased all the routes except the Washington to Tennessee and return one, and zoomed in so it took up the whole screen.

"We have seven stops at approximately 335 mile intervals. That correlates well with the range of these vans. Each stop uses a different credit card from the stolen cards to buy gas, an average of 19.47 gallons, again correlating well with the expected gas mileage of this type of van. At one of these stops we also have a personal credit card purchase made in the gift shop. And at four other points along the round-trip routes we have cell phone calls made from one phone at the approximate time we would expect the van to be within the range of the cell tower that picked up the signal. All five of these transactions can be traced to a man named William Morse from Parma, Idaho. He has WAR ties and was arrested at a rally-turned-riot in Portland, Oregon two years ago. That was the incident that got him on our radar as he publically threatened the President during his interrogation. And, he bought and registered a used Ford F-250 pick-up two weeks before the theft.

"Each of the other three hits are similar—a personal credit card or cell phone use traced back to a subject with WAR ties, and in two cases, the recent purchase of a used pick-up truck. That confirms 25% of the transported cesium as being in the possession of WAR operatives."

"Confirms is a pretty strong description," Cal said. "All you really know is that four people with some tenuous connection to WAR were traveling at that time. Statistically, that's meaningless. Hundreds of thousands of people, probably millions, were traveling over that time period, and many of them had to be on these routes. I'll bet you could come up with similar evidence for any group of people, say members of the Elks fraternal order. And, they were driving pickup trucks, not vans. How do you explain that?"

"You're right. This is a low probability with just this evidence. There are two additional facts supporting my conclusion. First, no other terror organization has a similar result, and I've checked them all. Not one hit along any of the routes. And second, I searched the whereabouts of all known WAR operatives and eight of them dropped off the grid over the time period in question. No cell phone use, no credit card use, no visual reports, nothing. And here is the home location of each, including the four we identified."

The computer screen blinked to show the twelve projected cesium locations in bright red dots, and smaller white dots appeared near seven of them with several having two white dots.

"My conclusion is that twelve teams of two WAR operatives bought trucks in their home area, drove to Tennessee, picked up the cesium, drove back to some storage location near their homes, and then left it there, either until it is to be used, or for some other team to pick it up and move it along. And I believe the pickup trucks were used to avoid connection with the suicide bombers so any search would overlook them. That's what I have."

Not bad, Cal thought. Nothing to go to court with, but better than anyone else had done. It might pay to dig into this.

6.08   BBC NEWS HEADQUARTERS, LONDON, ENGLAND

BBC NORWEGIAN NAVY STEPS UP NORTH SEA PRESENCE

ACTION TO INCREASE SECURITY FOR ITS OIL RIGS

Norway today increased security around its North Atlantic Oil extraction and processing rigs, deploying its naval forces and ground troops to protect essential infrastructure and seaways from unspecified threats. With the price of oil skyrocketing, officials are worried that the platforms have become targets for groups seeking to expand the recent WMD attacks in the U.S. to other high-value, European targets.

6.09   I-84N, EXIT 2, STURBRIDGE, MA

The drive from Maryland was unpleasant, even with the rest stop in New Jersey to avoid New York City rush hour. Bander's mood lightened as the traffic grew thin in rural Connecticut and Massachusetts, and he had time to reflect on his role in history. That was how he saw it – he had a major role in making history, in striking the first real blow that would bring about the Fifth Caliphate. The World Trade Center didn't count towards that goal in his mind. It was a lesson, a shocking lesson for him and his brethren in the *jihad* that even when two major office buildings in the heart of the biggest city in America were collapsed, a few years later things had not just returned to normal, they had worsened if you were a true Muslim.

America hadn't fallen, maybe just tripped a little. When it got its balance back, the reaction was painful. Money and technology drove his cause into caves and handwritten communications. But just as 9-11 hadn't toppled America, America hadn't killed true Islam. And now it was time to strike, to show the world the truth and power of The Prophet.

The portable signs started two miles south of Exit 2 off of I-84 near Sturbridge, Massachusetts. The first one simply read, in flashing yellow light bulbs, *Detour. All traffic exit at Rt. 131*. It woke Bander out of the light trance that nearly thirty hours on the road had caused.

His first thought, his natural reaction, was that it was a police checkpoint, that they had somehow identified him and were waiting. He quickly rejected that thought. There was nothing to connect him – he'd never been part of any Muslim organization or attended any radical mosque, he'd never traveled to any training camps, and there was no record of him in Florida. He'd paid cash for everything, and their rooms had been rented by someone else under phony names. He'd left his cell phone off and in his car in Kissimmee and hadn't made or received any calls since. He'd only turned the phone back on when he crossed the New York border, supporting the story he'd gone to the city for the weekend.

At the exit, another sign straddled the road, assuring all cars followed the instruction. Bander could see portable lights and some construction vehicles at an overpass about a quarter mile ahead. Massachusetts had developed something of a reputation for failing infrastructure in recent years, and news reports of concrete falling off overpasses were not uncommon. He figured this was another case. His bad luck – only twenty-five miles from home. At least he was close and somewhat familiar with the area.

The exit ramp split at the end, and another portable sign told him to re-enter I-84 by proceeding straight across Rt. 131 and onto the northbound entrance ramp. *Yeah*, he thought, *an overpass problem and a simple off-and-on detour around it*. A policeman was directing the non-existent traffic at the intersection and after a momentary panic, Bander wondered who the cop had pissed off to get such lousy duty. With no cross traffic in sight, he was waving Bander through the stop sign.

Bander never saw the car that hit him. He felt the impact; he knew his car had been hit hard at the rear and spun wildly before coming to a stop in the grassy median on the other side of Rt. 131; he saw the policeman running towards the car, and then everything stopped.

6.10   FBI Field Office, Louisville, KY

In Louisville, traffic on I-40 West was almost non-existent at 4:52 AM, and Buck Buchanan made it to the office in record time. He was speeding, with good reason. The call that had gotten him out of bed thirty-eight minutes before had simply said, *we found them*. Buck didn't need an explanation.

They met in Buck's smaller conference room – Buck, his ASAC, the WMD Coordinator, and the two agents leading the Pastor investigation. On the SVTC screen they also had the SIOC in Washington and the shift commander was explaining the find.

"It's a social networking site called Twitter. Users can communicate to others in short, 140-character messages. These messages are called Tweets, and can be searchable or kept private. We got a national security waiver to work with the NSA on this and their Twitter vacuum cleaning efforts got some hits.

"The NSA started by doing a cyber-profile on the Ashoor guy that TIDE identified. With the information we got off his IP address history, we were able to identity a number of his social network sites, names, passwords, etc., including Facebook and Twitter accounts. On this Twitter site, you can have any user name that isn't already being used, but when you sign up for the service and get an account, you need to post your name and provide a valid email address

"The Ashoor link was the key. From what our signals intelligence teams are telling us, he and eight other guys are operating a private social network cell. All of the bombers we've identified so far are there, and we have a reasonable confidence band that unidentified ones are the others on this site. Split your screen and I'll post the list of names and the addresses we've found to go with them. Based on an analysis of the messages, these are the four, two-man teams plus a leader, and their targets. From their chatter, it looks like the Kentucky bomb was heading for The Mall of America.

"The leader seems to be this Hadi. His real name, or maybe I should say legal name, is Mohammad Riskiq. I say legal because he was born Martin Malcolm Washington in Detroit. He still lives in the area, and we have his home and work under surveillance. With any luck, we'll have what's left of this cell rolled up today."

Buck did the obvious arithmetic in his head and said, "Four teams, about four-thousand curies each, that leaves ten or twelve bombs still out there."

"That's right. We're looking to see if there are other cells out there, each discrete, and if they're also using Twitter to organize. There are over hundreds of billions of these Tweet messages so far and they're growing at a rate of like

20 million an hour. NSA has developed a new set of search criteria, and with the national security waiver, we have access to all public and private messages. The Twitter people didn't like it, but their lawyers explained the full potential of the Patriot Act to them and they cooperated.

"It will take several days to search everything, but we're focusing on the same time period as the cell we found, and we will be through that by late tonight. Statistically, we should start getting some leads within hours. We should have these guys, and their targets and schedules, identified by tomorrow and be locating the cesium soon after. We'll concentrate all our detection equipment on the targets and hopefully find them all before they're detonated."

It can't be that simple, Buck thought to himself. A terrorist cell can't be so sophisticated as to identify Pastor as a source of cesium, plan and execute a very complex theft, build suicide bombs with special shields to hide them, move to the target and detonate two of them on U.S. soil despite a massive search, and then be stupid enough to post their real names and addresses on some Internet site. It was like they wanted to be caught, like they wanted public acclaim for their deeds, like they were all planning suicide, not just the four wearing vests. It was like they were disposable, and Buck thought that was exactly the case.

But who was doing the disposing?

6.11 HARRINGTON HOSPITAL, SOUTHBRIDGE, MA

Bander woke to familiar surroundings, just not his familiar surroundings. He instantly recognized the sounds and smells and colors and shapes of a hospital, just not his hospital. He recognized the IV feed and the connections to the various monitors, and the bandages on his arm and head. He'd just never seen these things on himself before. He remembered the accident and knew why he was where he was, he just didn't know where he was.

It was a semi-private room and he was the only occupant. The types and quantity of monitors told him he was in intensive care. That meant the monitors would recognize the change in his respiration and heart rate and someone was now aware he was awake if they were doing their job properly. Out of professional curiosity, and because he was in no pain or distress that he noticed, other than a mild headache, he decided to wait for someone to come to him. It didn't take long.

A male nurse came in, greeted him without warmth and set about checking his IV and dressings.

"What are my injuries," Bander asked.

"The doctor will be here in a few minutes and I'm sure he will explain them," the nurse replied without ever looking at Bander. "Someone will bring you breakfast," he added and then left the room.

Breakfast – that meant the 6:20 indicated on the clock was AM, so he'd been here around four hours. Before breakfast arrived, the doctor hustled in, chart in hand, stethoscope around his neck, and his name, Dr. Goldstein, embroidered on his lab coat. *A Jewish doctor*, Bander thought. *How trite.*

"Well, Mr. Ashoor," he said, making it sound like ass-whore, "you are a fortunate man."

He hustled around the bed, checking the needle in Bander's arm and the tube and pouch feeding solution through it and the monitors above Bander's head. He listened to Bander's heart and lungs and made some notes in the file at the foot of the bed.

"What are my injuries?"

"Well, let's see. Your right elbow has a hairline fracture at the ulna, probably a result of being jammed against the center console of your car. You have a slight concussion from the left side of your head striking the window, and some minor contusions. Nothing too serious. You should be out of here tomorrow or the next day."

With that, he left, saying over his shoulder, "Your breakfast will be here soon, Mr. Ashoor. Ring for the nurse if you need anything and I'll be back this evening to check on you."

***

In an office down the hall, a crowd watched a row of four video monitors and listened to Special Agent Perry O'Donnell play doctor. He was pretty good at it, having been pre-med at the University of Connecticut and done one year at NYU School of Medicine before losing interest and joining the FBI. His loss of interest in medicine coincided with his loss of both parents on September 11, 2001 at the World Trade Center where they were attending a meeting with their securities broker.

Bander's room was rigged for full, 24-hour surveillance, including the bathroom. Not that he could actually get there with the myriad of connections to electronic monitors that effectively immobilized him, and tubes that catheterized him so he wouldn't need to go anyway. But he might get a visitor who would, and they wanted everything on tape. The scenario was set and rehearsed as much as time allowed, and all traces of FBI presence hidden behind closed doors. Again, there was no way of knowing who might be watching Ashoor and come to visit.

The plan was to place him under immediate and constant anxiety, to do and say things that could play on his fears and uncertainty, but to never actually mention terrorism or the bombings. Promises would be made and ignored – breakfast wasn't going to arrive no matter how many people told him it would, and his other meals would be designed to be unpalatable for his cultural background. Questions would be asked that could be construed many ways. Accusations would be leveled that were serious and totally unconnected to Epcot. People would answer his questions with platitudes and evasion. Bander's psychological profile would be quickly assessed by behavioral scientists and the script would provoke a sense of discordant anxiety and confusion. The goal was make him talkative, looking for confirmation and support from others. They had three days to find out something to help break this case before he would be arrested, charged, and interrogated. Or maybe they'd skip the first two and go right to interrogation.

"OK," Supervisory Special Agent Alex Clark said, "send in the cop." Agent Raoul Goodwyn put on his sport coat and headed for Bander's room.

***

"Mr. Ashoor," Goodwyn greeted Bander, pronouncing his name as if he'd been raised in Medina in the Kingdom of Saudi Arabia, just as Bander had, "I'm Detective Holmes of the Massachusetts State Police Detective Unit. I've got a couple of questions for you, if you feel up to it."

"A detective? What are you detecting? Am I being accused of something?"

"No sir, no accusations necessary at this time. I'm the lead detective on the accident you were in last night, and I need to get some information so we can conclude our investigation as quickly as possible and get this matter closed. So, first, what is your immigration status here in the U.S.?"

"Immigration status? I'm here as a student. I study medicine at the University of Massachusetts in Worcester. What does that have to do with the accident?"

"Just routine background information, sir. So you live in Worcester?"

'Yes. I share a house with three other medical students."

"OK. What were you doing on I-84 this morning at 2 AM?"

"I was on my way home. From New York."

"New York City? OK. When was the last time you left the country? Were you returning to the U.S. through New York?"

"No. Why would you think that? I haven't been out of the country since last summer when I visited my family in Saudi Arabia. Why are you asking me this?"

"Just routine, sir. You know how things are now. We have to gather certain background information on any foreign national we're involved with. It's nothing personal, just the world we live in these days. So, what were you doing in New York that put you in Sturbridge at, let's see here, it says 2:07 AM?"

"I was sightseeing and stayed late for dinner and a show. Nothing wrong with that, is there?"

"No, sir. Nothing at all. Which show?"

"It was the Blue Man Group. At the Astor Place Theatre."

"Were you alone?"

"Yes, alone. I don't know anyone in New York."

"Really? No one? In all of New York? OK. You were in Saudi Arabia in the last twelve months, you say. How long were you there?

"Four weeks. What is this all about?"

"Where did you stay? Were you in Medina with your family the whole time?"

"How did you know I was in Medina? I never said that."

"Well, you must have. I've got it written down right here. See?"

Goodwyn showed Bander his note pad with a bunch of barely legible scrawls, one of which might have been Medina.

"I am a medical student. I was involved in a traffic accident after a weekend in New York City. I wasn't drunk or on drugs and I didn't break any laws. What does my trip to see my family have to do with this? What do you want from me?"

"Just routine background information. I'll put a *yes* on that question, OK? Now tell me about New York. Where did you stay?"

"Listen, Detective Holmes, I don't know what is going on here, but I want a lawyer present."

"Wow. A lawyer? Here? Why? Did you do something wrong?"

"No, I did nothing wrong. I just don't like where you're going with these questions and I'd feel more comfortable with a lawyer."

"OK. Do you have a lawyer? What does a Saudi med student need with a lawyer?"

"No, I don't have a lawyer. But I'll call my embassy and I'm sure they'll be happy to recommend one."

"OK. Here, I'll tell you what. I think I can ask some questions that you'll find relevant. Rather than bother your ambassador, why don't I ask a few and you can either answer them or tell me you want a lawyer. No harm. And that way maybe we can wrap this up quickly."

"Will your questions be germane to the accident? Nothing about trips and family and such?"

"I'll try to stay on point, as they say in the corporate world. Not that I'd know anything about the corporate world, but I watch some of those financial shows on TV and pick up a thing or two. So, here we go. Did you see the stop sign at the end of the exit ramp?"

"Yes, I saw the stop sign."

"OK, then why didn't you stop?"

"There was a policeman there directing traffic and he was waving me on through. You should know that from the accident report. He must have filed one."

"Accident report? Yeah, he sure did. Looked it over myself. How fast were you going when you went through the stop sign?"

"I don't know. Maybe thirty miles an hour."

"Thirty, huh. Yeah, that's about what the accident investigators estimated. Did you see the car you hit?"

"I hit? He hit me. I never saw him. What is going on here?"

"Hit you?" Goodwyn glanced down and flipped back through a couple of pages in his notebook and read something. "I guess that technically he did hit you, didn't he?"

"Technically? He ignored the police officer and ran into the side of my car. That's not technically. That's indisputably."

"Indisputably. Good word. I'm gonna use that in my report, if you don't mind. So, why do you suppose he ignored that policeman directing traffic?"

"I don't know. Why don't you ask him? I'd like to hear his answer. He could have killed me."

"Could have, that's for sure. But he didn't, did he?" Goodwyn let his hands fall to his side and cocked his head slightly to the right, like he was intent on listening to something important rather than saying it. "See, the problem I have with asking him is that *he's* dead," Goodwyn lied. "And his wife, well, she'll live but I'm not sure she'll be happy about that. No more walking for her. So what I've got right now is you."

"Dead? Someone died? Allah be merciful. What about the policeman directing traffic? He can tell you what happened."

Just then Goodwyn's cell phone buzzed and he lifted it off his belt and looked at the screen. "I gotta take this," he said. "I'll be back later to finish up. They told me to tell you breakfast would be coming soon."

Goodwyn opened the door and started to step through, but then stopped and looked back at Bander.

"About the cop's report. He says he was in his car the whole time. Didn't see anything until he heard the crash."

He turned and walked out without another word, closing the door behind him.

"What? Wait!"

But it was too late, the door closed and the detective was gone, leaving behind a turbulence of confusion in Bander's head.

He stared at the door, not seeing anything as his mind focused on grasping everything that the detective had said. Someone had died, and the cop on the scene must be blaming it on Bander. *Why would he do that?* He saw what happened. He must have. The accident must have come close to killing him, standing unprotected in the intersection.

Why didn't it kill him? Bander remembered his car spinning, probably right where the cop had been standing. Maybe he did kill him and there was no witness. Maybe they were mad because he'd hit a cop. Maybe they were messing with his head. Maybe there was no cop directing traffic. Maybe he'd been dozing at the wheel after the long drive. Maybe he'd imagined the cop directing traffic. Maybe he imagined the detour. Maybe …

Stop!

Bander seized control of his mind. He'd seen what he'd seen. He knew what he knew. So why would someone else be lying about it?

Maybe they knew about Florida. Maybe this was all an elaborate ruse to confuse him and get information. Maybe they had caught the others and …

Stop it!

That was just stupid. There was no way to connect him to Florida. He'd been over this a hundred times on the long drive home. There was no evidence of him having been south of the accident scene from last night. That was the only event that recorded his location in the last two weeks, since he'd left school for the training and the cesium theft and the Epcot bombing.

Wait!

They would investigate his story now. Someone was dead and he was likely to be accused of vehicular homicide at the least. His New York City explanation would fall apart the first time they went to check on a hotel stay. Then they would start to dig into his whereabouts over the past two weeks and find out UMASS thought he was on compassionate leave to attend a family death and funeral.

He had to think, now. Think about things that hadn't occurred to him before. Things he should have thought about instead of just believing what they'd told him. Think about holes in the plan that were sure to implicate him.

How could anyone know he'd been to Florida? Forensics! They'd take his car apart and find sand or pieces of palm trees or something tiny that only grew in Orlando. Or pictures! Didn't toll booths have cameras? Did they photograph every car? If so, how long did they keep the pictures? What about surveillance cameras? They were everywhere. Disney must use them. They might have taken his picture while he was unconscious and were right now using some super-software that the CIA had to identify him.

It had just been a bluff before, but now he realized that he did need a lawyer. He had no one else to turn to, no other source of advice and guidance. Without a lawyer, the FBI would tear him apart. They would tear him apart and learn nothing because he knew nothing. Not even the real names of the others. He only knew that last summer, on that last trip home, he'd been foolish enough to tell his cousin about the stuff he'd been reading on the Internet, and to listen to his answers and to agree to help the cause when and if he was called upon. It had all seemed important enough at the time. And safe enough when they'd told him what he would be doing.

He needed a lawyer, and his only contact with the world beyond his room was his cell phone. He rang the nurse call button and the same male nurse came back, with the same attitude.

"Yes?" was all he said, looking at Bander without emotion.

"They said I'm supposed to get breakfast. Is someone bringing it to me?"

"I'll check, sir," the nurse said and started to leave.

"Wait. I had a cell phone when I came in. Do you know where it is?"

"Yes, sir. It's in the wardrobe with your clothes and other items. But you're not allowed to use them in Critical Care. They can interfere with the sensitive electronics."

Bander concentrated on being nice. "Look, I'm a medical student at UMass and I work in the hospital there, so I know that's mostly bullshit. No one knows I'm here. I really need to contact the school and let them know where I am. People will be worried about me. Couldn't you just let me try it while you watch the monitors, and if anything goes wrong, I'll turn it off."

"Sorry, sir, but rules are rules. There's a phone on the table right next to you. Just dial nine for an outside line."

"I see. Can you at least get me the phone so I can look up the numbers I have to call?"

"Of course, sir. But if you do use it, it will be confiscated."

"I understand. I won't use it to make any calls."

The nurse got the phone off the shelf in the wardrobe and handed it to Bander and left, saying over his shoulder as he did, "I'll check on your breakfast, sir."

6.12   DEPARTMENT OF HOMELAND SECURITY, WASHINGTON, DC

Again, Ray drove in silence while Cal admired the rush hour traffic in Washington. The drive to his office at DHS was less than twelve miles from Ray's apartment, but it took forty-three minutes. *People do this every day*, Cal thought, glad he wasn't one of them.

At Ray's insistence, Cal had spent the night in his guest bedroom at the Meridian apartments in Alexandria. Clearly Ray wasn't living there on his IDC salary. Cal guessed the rent on the top-floor was at least $3,500, and either Ray had excellent taste or a very good decorator. Ray had money, and Cal guessed it was family money and that might account for his occasional lapses into arrogance and entitlement.

They'd gotten to the apartment around midnight after the review at the IDC and gone right to bed for the night. Cal was up early as usual, and even with what he thought was a head start, Ray was dressed and ready and had prepared a breakfast of feta cheese and tomato omelets with toast made from a bread Cal didn't recognize and strong coffee. *Better than room service*, he thought, glad he'd accepted Ray's invitation, and mentally adjusting his assessment of Ray.

The plan was to take Ray's analysis to Glenn Farr, Cal's boss at DHS, to get past the roadblock at IDC. When they got there, it was too late – IDC had already moved to block the attempt to out-flank them.

"I've already seen it," Glenn said when Cal told him about Ray's analysis. "IDC was on the phone to the deputy director early this morning, complaining long and loud about your late-night show. They sent a copy of the report, complete with a DVD of the alleged transport routes. They included their comments on Mr. Nassiri's methodology and conclusions, and I've got to tell you, we agree with them. This is too far-fetched and the analysis built on too-many questionable assumptions to allocate scarce resources to chase it down."

Ray started to stand, but Cal spoke and Ray stopped mid-rise.

"I really think you should hear him out, Glenn. Yes, it's a stretch to think WAR could pull this off, and yes, there are a lot of assumptions, but it is still the best theory we've got documented. It shows a complete picture, not just a bunch of discrete actions by some mysterious organization that we don't know about."

"What about those discrete actions? According to the IDC comments, the three bombs that went off and the one in the traffic accident don't fit into the maps that Nassiri's program created. So in effect, he's created a new story that ignores the only actual events that we have. His puzzle isn't missing pieces, it's got extra ones that don't fit."

Ray spoke for the first time since being introduced. "That is incorrect. My theory has two separate operations working in parallel. The suicide bombs are a diversion, and of course the two would be isolated to protect the real plan."

"A diversion? From what? Four dirty bombs, all going off more or less at the same time, is a plan, not a diversion. And what is this so-called real plan? You have WAR taking twelve RDD's to cities around the country and detonat-ing them? WAR's objectives are not going to be met by attacking their own country. That would make them pariahs, and they would never achieve their goal of a white, Christian country."

Cal knew that rationally Farr was right – Ray's theory just didn't fit with anything they knew about WAR. And yet, he'd found Ray's research and even his assumptions compelling, and his conclusion about the whereabouts con-vincing.

"Maybe it isn't a WAR operation, at all," he said. "Maybe these guys are free-lancing. It could be that our terrorists are using them because they're white Christians, and therefore less likely to come under suspicion. Your own point is that no one would believe they are the terrorists, so they can move about without risk. Or at least with a lot less risk."

"Sorry, Cal, but we just don't buy it. How are Muslim terrorists going to enlist twenty-four free-lance jackass white supremacists without there being some leak? Someone would have talked, there would be some clues. Look, I appreciate your open-mindedness on this, but let's leave investigation to the investigators, and you get back to analysis and response. OK?"

Cal immediately stood and said, "You're right, Glenn. We'll do just that." He reached out over the desk to shake hands.

Farr hesitated for a second, like he couldn't believe that Cal was giving up that easy, and stood himself, shook hands with Cal, and then turned to do the same with Ray.

"Mr. Nassiri, I really do appreciate your efforts, and thank you for making sure you got the word out to us about this. We will certainly keep this in mind and be watching for anything that might steer us toward your theory."

Ray was still seated, seemingly caught unprepared for the sudden wrap-up. He looked from Cal to Farr and then to the proffered hand, and without a word got up and walked out, ignoring the polite protocol. Cal shrugged his shoulders and followed Ray out.

Ray was well ahead and almost running to the elevators, with Cal trailing behind. By the time Cal caught up, the elevator had arrived and they both got in, joining several others already on their way down. Cal could almost feel the heat coming off Ray and hoped he wouldn't explode in front of a bunch of strangers.

They were alone in the parking garage with Ray repeating his near sprint to his car when he finally did ignite.

"Please get your suitcase and I will be on my way," Ray said when they got to the Lexus.

"No, I think that I will be needing it, and you'll be needing to stop back at your apartment and pack, too."

"What are you talking about? You made a fool of me in there. These people are no better than the IDC. They have made up their minds and they're not going to allow any other possibilities. I'll take care of this myself, thank you."

"Ray, Glenn was right. We need to leave this to the investigators. So pack a bag and we'll go to Louisville and do just that."

"Louisville? What for?"

"The FBI SAC there is the lead investigator on the first bomb. Let's give him something to investigate."

6.13   Harrington Hospital, Southbridge, MA

The fake lawyer arrived promptly at ten, as he had promised, and gave Bander his business card. According to it, Samuel Allen Drury practiced criminal law alone, in Boston, but the embassy had found and recommended him and made the appointment, so Bander felt confident he was competent to represent him. Bander had spent much of the previous day and night thinking about what to tell, and what to hold back. The detective had returned after lunch, the first meal Bander had received despite the promises of breakfast, and Bander had refused to talk to him, informing him that he had been in contact with his embassy and they had advised him to wait for the lawyer they would arrange. The detective wasn't happy about that, pointing out that no charges had been filed, and made some implied threats that served only to harden Bander's resolve to talk to no one until he'd met with the lawyer.

"Well, Mr. Ashoor," Drury said, "you seem to have some problems with the local police. They are not being very cooperative with me and have only provided the accident report from the officer there. Why don't you tell me what happened from the start?"

"Don't we need to sign some papers first? Something formal so you're my attorney and everything is confidential?"

"Certainly we can do that if it makes you more comfortable. I have a standard engagement letter with me. Read it through and sign it if it is satisfactory. My rates are on the second page. Until I know more about your situation and the prosecutor's intent, I won't be able to estimate the total cost. I'll need a retainer to make things official. Let's start with $1,500. Is that acceptable?"

Everything seemed in order to Bander and he signed two copies of the letter, and Drury gave him one for his records. To pay the retainer, he had to use the emergency credit card his father had given him. That would mean his family would know of the trouble as soon as the bank got the transaction, and he was concerned how his father, a pragmatic businessman without political or social opinions as far as Bander knew, would react if the truth were to come out.

Bander told a condensed version of the events of early Monday morning, starting with the construction detour and ending with the detective's questions and revelations. The discrepancy between Bander's story and the police report became the focal point of Drury's questions.

"So, according to what you told Detective Holmes, you attended the 8 PM show at the Astor Place Theatre and then came home. That's about a three-hour drive at that time of night, so you left around 11 PM. And you were driving your own car, correct? We'll need to establish the sequence of events. Did you happen to save your ticket stub? As a souvenir, perhaps?"

"No, I don't have it."

"That's OK, there'll be a credit card charge for the ticket, I presume. That will be good enough. Also, we'll have the records of your stay in New York."

"Why is any of that important," Bander asked. "It has nothing to do with the accident."

"Yes, that's true, but if the police do decide to charge you with some crime other than a minor traffic violation, they'll do a check of your story, and we'll need to be prepared to prove your whereabouts leading up to the accident so we can establish your physical and mental state at the time."

"But it isn't relevant. I was doing nothing illegal, just driving my car on public streets. I wasn't doing drugs. I wasn't drunk. The hospital tests will show that. I'd stopped to rest, so I wasn't tired. I did nothing wrong. Why is it any of their business where I was?"

The lawyer didn't speak for several moments, causing Bander some discomfort. Finally, he asked a question and Bander knew he was in trouble.

"You stopped to rest? On a three-hour trip? Where? And why?"

Bander didn't answer and the silence went on for several more uncomfortable seconds.

"Look, Mr Ashoor, I'm your attorney, and if there is more to this than what you've told the police or me, I need to know it or I won't be able to defend you. I need to know just what led up to this tragic accident."

"It's personal, and it has nothing to do with the accident. I don't see why it's relevant."

"Was it a woman? Are you trying to protect someone?"

"No, no. Nothing like that. I was just away on personal business and I don't see why anyone has to know what I do."

"Mr. Ashoor, as you know, we live in difficult times. This country is under attack and the police and authorities take that very seriously. And, as troubling as it may be, your Saudi citizenship will cause them to look very carefully at everything you say. Now, please, tell me where you were coming from and we can decide how best to handle it."

"I can't."

"Of course you can. I am your attorney and anything you tell me is confidential. That's not optional. I don't get to decide what is confidential and what isn't. If you tell me, I am bound by law and my oath to keep it to myself. So you can tell me anything without concern for its publication."

"What if the police have this room bugged? They could be listening to us right now."

"Good. I hope they are. Anything you say to me is protected client-attorney communications and inadmissible in court by the prosecution. Anything that you tell me will be unusable for them and will actually help you personally. So I ask you again, where were you coming from?"

Bander again didn't answer, and after several seconds, Drury started gathering his papers and packing his briefcase.

"What are you doing," Bander asked.

"I can't help you, Mr. Ashoor. I'm sorry, but you'll have to find another attorney. One who won't be so, um, conscientious."

"All right. All right. I was driving home from Florida. I took two weeks off and went to Florida to rest. The University thinks I've been at a family funeral and if they find out different, I'll be expelled."

"Florida. OK, where in Florida? Do you have records showing your travels? Hotel and restaurant receipts, that sort of thing."

"No, nothing. I don't save those."

"Well then, just tell me where you stayed and I'll subpoena the records and use them."

"I don't remember. Just some motels that I stopped at when I was tired."

"You were in a motel for the better part of two weeks and you don't remember its name?"

"No, I moved around and didn't stay in one place. I don't know, they were just cheap motels."

"Mr. Bander, I simply don't believe you. And if I don't believe you, then the police are certainly not going to. Let me ask you straight out. Were you involved in anything illegal during this two-week vacation?"

"What if I was? It's not relevant to the accident. Can't we just keep it focused on the accident?"

"Yes, if you simply plead guilty to whatever they charge you with, that should end it."

"OK, then, we'll do that. Find out what the charges are and I'll plead guilty."

"If, however, there is this discrepancy between your story and the police officer's, if they are lying about what happened, they're going to wonder why you would plead guilty to false charges. As would I, quite frankly. No, on second thought, I don't think pleading guilty will stop this thing."

"If I was involved in something illegal and I told you, what would you do?"

"I'd defend you, of course."

"No matter what?"

"It's my job. More than that, it's my commitment. I believe in every person's right to a full and vigorous defense, and that's what you'll get from me. And remember, if you tell me what happened and the police are listening, well, we've just put a big hole in their case because they can't use anything you say to me."

So Bander told him, starting with his cousin in Saudi Arabia. For some reason, the lawyer didn't seem surprised.

6.14   CNN NEWS HEADQUARTERS, ATLANTA, GA

 OIL, GOLD PRICES SURGE FOLLOWING DIRTY BOMB ATTACKS

RECORD HIGHS FOR COMMODITIES ON TRADER'S FEARS OF MASSIVE UNREST

NEW YORK (CNNMoney.com) -- Oil prices surged in anticipation of a worsening of relations with Mid-East oil-producing countries following the Kentucky terrorist attack yesterday with West Texas Intermediate jumping almost $5 per barrel over the previous all-time high. Gasoline prices are expected to rise in the coming days and may also exceed all-time highs. Gold moved up sharply by $278 per ounce and the US dollar fell against other currencies to a three-year low against the Euro. In overseas bullion trade, gold soared nearly 11 percent on the London benchmark fixing price.

6.15   ROUTE 93N, CHALLIS, ID

After spending the night with a local WAR official in Idaho City, Tag got an early start home. He was taking the slightly longer Route 93 direction north through the Salmon-Challis and Bitterroot National Forests, completing the eastern loop of his circuit through central Idaho. Saturday he'd come south on Route 12W through the Lolo and Nezperce National Forests, appreciating the concentration of natural beauty like a New Yorker appreciated Broadway. It was in your backyard, but you didn't go there nearly often enough. He still had 350 miles to go, seven plus hours of America the Beautiful, and he welcomed the opportunity to relax and think on the almost empty two-lane road.

The meeting with his niece, Margaret, had gone well, as he'd expected. She was tough and ambitious and right-minded. She just needed an opportunity to break out of her Boise cocoon. Tag had no problem with her being a woman – Marion had long ago rid him of any illusions of male superiority – and he thought it might actually be an advantage as most people wouldn't suspect her WAR affiliation, as loose as it was, and financial backing. She would be better able to navigate the local politics of the states in Tag's dream country – the Christian Covenant of America.

He had no illusions any more. He knew it wouldn't be a true country, that it would always be a part of the United States. The fantasy of *The Turner Diaries* – a violent revolution in the United States culminating in a stolen nuclear bomb vaporizing the Pentagon, the overthrow of the government, and, ultimately, the extermination of all Jews and niggers and all the other inferior races – wasn't going to happen. When he'd founded WAR the book had been their manifesto. It had guided their ideals, gave them something to strive for, an independent country, built on the precepts of the Bible, free of the malignancy of mongrel races and their Godless beliefs

Over the years it became clear that it was just a fantasy. The Zionist Occupation Government in Washington was too clever to openly challenge the rights and power of white America, giving impetus to such a revolution. No, they just chipped away, grabbing a little here, adding a little there, until one day we'll wake up and find ourselves a minority in our own country, find that our job is to support those inferiors with our taxes, find our sons and daughters lured to apostasy by the multi-culturalism that disguised miscegenation as social progress.

Tag's dream now was to turn the tables, to chip away at the ZOG the same way they had done it to him and his followers. And the way to do that was to concentrate their power, to end the dilution caused by the uncontrolled immigration that they encouraged, and by ending the creeping socialism that was destroying our personal freedoms.

And next week it would start. No, not start. They'd started long ago. But move to a new level, move out of the dark, secret meetings and into the light of good people throughout the country. Next week these people would see the threat, up close and personal, they would see the government's helplessness to control what they'd started with their pandering of these mongrels and heathens, and they would hear the battle cry of Margaret and the others. Come to Idaho, the new Land of the Free. Come to Utah, the real Home of the Brave. Come to Montana and Wyoming and North Dakota and South Dakota and Minnesota. Come and start a social and economic revolution to return to the principles that had made this the greatest country ever. Come and be part of the Christian Covenant of America.

Those states, with a population of just over thirteen million and a white, Christian majority already, would be the beacon for three or four or even five million more, lured by the promise of a return to the principles and religion of the real America, creating a regional power that could standardize laws and ensure the exclusion of the disease that infested the country. Eventually an autonomous region, complete with its own militia, ready to protect that way of life even by force of arms. If the overthrow of the government described in *The Turner Diaries* was impossible, so would the converse be true. No one would be able to overthrow new, clean CCA.

His cell phone rang, snapping Tag out of his reverie. The caller ID told him it was Marcus.

"The A-rab is gone," Marcus said with no further explanation.

"Ibby? What do you mean, gone?"

"Just that. Vamoosed. Our sources report he skipped in the middle of the night and no one knows where he is. Took his family."

"Are you sure he's not in custody and spilling the beans?"

"Yes. The Feds are frantic. They questioned him Friday afternoon and Saturday morning he's gone. They figure someone dropped the ball big time and they're gonna look like fools."

"That's good. The questioning must have scared him. Well, let's help that along. Put the diversion plan into effect. Use the southwest contingency. And quickly. We will have very little time."

There was a long pause at the other end. "OK. I'll make the calls," Marcus finally said.

As he hung up, the first traffic light in 200 miles appeared. Salmon, ID, and just in time for lunch at The Junk Yard. That was good. He needed to give this new development some thought.

6.16   FBI FIELD OFFICE, LOUISVILLE, KY

Once again, Ray was the driver. This time it was the Ford Taurus they'd picked up from Hertz at the Louisville International Airport. The Monday SVTC was about to start, and Cal dialed in from his secure cell phone. They were only fifteen or twenty minutes from the Federal Building in Louisville, but Cal didn't want to miss the initial summary of the investigation from Buchanan. Ray was not part of the SVTC, and "guests" were not allowed without proper clearance and approval. Cal decided no mention of Ray's presence was necessary as long as he used his hands-free earpiece to keep the meeting private and didn't say anything of significance himself.

"Let's get started," Buchanan said moments after everyone had arrived or called in. "We've got a lot to cover tonight. First, we have identified all the members of the terrorist cell that pulled off the bombings. There were nine involved. Seven are dead. We have one in custody, and we are searching for the ninth. He is the apparent leader and the primary focus of the investigation at this point. He is a resident of Monroe, Michigan, just south of Detroit, named Martin Malcolm Washington, aka Mohammad Saleem Riskiq, and his terrorist cell name is Hadi. He is a 27-year-old U.S. citizen, born in Detroit. Here's where it gets a little, uhh, weird.

"Washington is an former Marine. A highly decorated, staff-sergeant ex-Marine who did two tours in Afghanistan. He was a member of a covert hunter-killer team searching out Taliban and terminating them. His team was ambushed on a mission one night and all were killed except Washington. He was in the infirmary at the time."

Buchanan paused here, and Cal could imagine him sweeping the room with his eyes, making sure that everyone understood the full implications of that event in light of what they now knew about him.

"He returned home after that incident and finished his enlistment at Camp LeJeune. He moved back to the Detroit area and took a job as a private security guard. He is, or rather was, a Shift Commander at the Fermi Nuclear Power Plant in Monroe. He legally changed his name about a year ago to Mohammad Saleem Riskiq, although his employers still know him as Washington."

Another pause, then Buchanan continued, "He didn't show up for his shift yesterday at 4 PM, and his employers have been unable to reach him. His apartment is vacant, and he appears to have left as there aren't many clothes or personal items or toiletries. His car is gone. We don't know when he disappeared. The last information we have is that he picked up his paycheck Friday, closed his bank accounts and cashed in his 401K. That was all done by 4 PM. He is clearly running and has about $40,000 to do it with. We have a nationwide alert and his passport has been flagged."

"Next big news – we have the second Orlando terrorist in custody. I'm not going into much detail on this because it is still unfolding, but the guy has given us a complete description of the theft, from planning to training to the actual theft and escape. We won't be able to use his statement for prosecution as there are issues with how we obtained it. And before any of you jump to conclusions, there was no water-boarding or any other coercion involved. We don't do that shit. We just weren't supposed to be listening.

"He's a Saudi national here on a valid student visa and is in med school at UMass. Name is Bander Ashoor, and we think his cell name was Tawfiq. He will be held as long as necessary and then deported with the Saudi government getting a full briefing on his participation. Prosecution here is moot.

"Unfortunately, his information doesn't really help us at this point. These cells were completely isolated and he has no knowledge of any of the cesium except his own. He was part of the theft team and did confirm that there were a total of sixteen loads. So, we still have twelve out there."

By that time, Cal and Ray were in the parking lot of the Federal Building, and Cal signaled Ray to stay put. He continued to monitor the SVTC by phone, not wanting to disturb the flow of the briefing by entering late.

"As you will recall from last week, we have reason to suspect that the terrorists are part of al Qaeda in the Arabian Peninsula, specifically run out of Yemen. The document we captured outlining the plan is still being validated. The Yemenis have, quite naturally, denied any involvement, and they have rounded up some of the mid-level AQAP leadership who also deny any knowledge or participation. We had questioned the original source of the information and came up with nothing new. And as you already know, that person, Ibrahim al Hasan, has disappeared. We don't know if he is fleeing or was kidnapped and we're searching intensely.

"I bring this up again as there is no indication as of now that any of these nine terrorists ever visited Yemen, spoke on the phone to anyone there, or in any other way had contact with anyone associated with the AQAP. In short, as of now the AQAP angle is probable but unverified. You have a question, Bert?"

The NSA man spoke up by phone. "We have reviewed all our communications for the three months leading up to the theft and there is absolutely no indication of any unusual traffic in or out of Yemen. If they were responsible, they were in place here well before the event and had no contact back home."

"There is a lot of pressure on us to attribute this thing so we can retaliate." That came from the DoD representative. "If not al Qaeda, then who?"

"It's still too early to say, and if you think you have pressure now, wait until we send a cruise missile to the wrong country," Buchanan answered. "All right, let's move on."

The meeting continued for another thirty-seven minutes with various participants briefing the group on the status of the identification of possible bomb targets, the search for cargo vans, the source of the custom shielded containers, the background of the dead and captured terrorists, and the status of the bombing sites. Nothing was mentioned about Ray's analysis and the decision not to pursue that angle. Cal wasn't surprised and figured the information had never left his boss's office.

As the meeting broke up, Cal asked Buck to meet him in his office.

"When? I've got to leave soon."

"We'll be there in two minutes," Cal answered.

"Where are you?"

"In the parking lot. We didn't want to interrupt."

"We? Who else is there?"

"Someone from IDC. We've got something interesting for you."

When they got to Buck's fifth-floor office, he was fuming. "Leave him outside," he told Cal before he could introduce Ray. "I want to talk to you privately."

Ray looked a little puzzled, but left Buchanan's office to wait in the reception area.

"What the hell are you doing bringing someone into *my* SVTC without getting clearance first?" Buchanan punctuated his snarl with finger pokes that, if he'd actually been touching Cal, would have caused significant bruising. "I ought to arrest you on the spot."

"He wasn't in the SVTC, he was driving the car. I used my earpiece so he heard nothing. And I made sure I didn't say anything of significance."

"Nothing of significance has pretty much always been your contribution. What does this guy bring to the party?"

"He's a senior IDC analyst and he's come up with some interesting results. They're built on a lot of supposition, and the conclusion doesn't fit with what we currently know and suspect, so he was shut down. He came to me because he also worked on my original analysis and thought I might be more receptive. I think you should hear what he has to say. If you don't like it, just lump it in with all the other insignificant contributions I've made."

The last sentence was accompanied by an arm wave that could have been interpreted as an angry exclamation point at the end of the statement.

Buchanan sat down at his desk, leaving Cal standing. "Tell me in one sentence why I should bother."

"He knows who has the cesium and where it is."

Buck sat up and stared at Cal without speaking for several seconds, and the asked, "Knows? He knows, and the IDC shut him down? I don't believe it."

"Like I said, there's a lot of supposition, and he's the only one who would say he *knows*. Suspects would be my word. I think he might be onto something, and we've got damn little to investigate, so what harm will it do to hear him out?"

Again, Buck stared at Cal without speaking for several seconds and then raised his hands up like he was surrendering before slapping them onto the arms of his chair and pushing himself upright. "All right. Bring him in and let's hear his story."

When Cal brought him in, Ray was clearly leery of Buchanan, and seemed defensive when he went through his presentation of the computer analysis, almost patronizing when answering any of Buchanan's questions. *This isn't going well*, Cal thought.

Buchanan's final question was the same one that had proven fatal to the DHS presentation that morning. "How do you explain that none of the four bombs we know about fit your theory? Not one of them shows up on your little map."

Cal decided to answer, hoping to keep Ray from further angering Buchanan.

"Two separate groups. That's the only explanation. We've got an alliance going on here, and that's why we're at a dead end. There were only four suicide bombers, so trying to find the other twelve is futile. We're not finding cargo vans because it's in pickup trucks. We need to broaden our search."

Buck sat leaning forward, his elbows on his desk and his hands folded in front of his mouth, lightly tapping his chin and saying nothing. Ray seemed to start to speak and Cal shook his head, silencing him while Buchanan continued to think. He sat back, slapping his armrests just like he had earlier when he'd made a decision.

"Fuck it," he said. "At least you have some names and places, something concrete to throw agents at. Let's kick some rocks and see what scurries out."

***

It was after midnight before Cal and Ray completed their list of the target cities. The specific destination of each of the trucks transporting the cesium wasn't certain as the last fuel stop in some cases was within range of more than one target city. There had been some animated discussions before they agreed on the list, discussions that Cal invariably won as the terrorist expert in the conversation. Now it was time to act on the list, and Cal wasn't looking forward to the call.

Cal used his secure cell phone both for security reasons, and to be sure the call would get answered in the middle of the night. "Farr, here," was the succinct and immediate response.

"Glenn? It's Cal Bellotta. I've got something here that needs immediate action. We have a list of the twelve suspected targets and an alert has been sent to the SIOC and the DHS Ops Center."

"A list? How did you get that?"

"I'm in Louisville with Buck Buchanan. We're establishing surveillance on the nine suspected delivery teams. Based on their locations and the extrapolations from our mapping, we've projected the cities that we think are targeted."

"Mapping? Do you mean that IDC guy's crazy ideas? I told you to drop that."

"Actually, Glenn, you told me to leave investigation to the investigators and to get back to analysis and response. That's exactly what I'm doing. Buchanan is investigating, and I've analyzed the data and recommending a response. That's why I'm calling you in the middle of the night. We need to get the monitoring resources alerted and deployed."

"Jesus, Bellotta, you're splitting hairs. You know damn well what I meant and you ignored it. I'm not rousting the Coast Guard and TSA and NEST and AMS and whoever else you have in mind on some wild computer game. So let me be completely clear – drop this IDC guy and his crackpot ideas and get back to your real analysis and planning."

"Too late, Glenn. I was assigned to support Buchanan so I had to brief him, and now he's hot on this. He's already set up surveillance on the nine names we have, and he plans to pull them in once we've got them located and we can grab them all at once. This is our best current shot, and DHS and DOE can't be seen to be lagging behind while the FBI is acting."

There was a long pause, and Cal waited, wondering just how angry Farr would be. *This*, Cal thought, *is why I like being a consultant and not someone's employee. Freedom of action.*

"Bellotta," came Farr's reply, "some days you are a bigger pain in the ass than you are worth. This is one of those days. Fax me the list and I'll make the calls, but your name is going to be all over them. If this flops, you'll flop with it."

"Fair enough. Check your machine. I already sent it."

TUESDAY, JUNE 29

6.17 EPCOT CENTER, ORLANDO, FL

By Tuesday, the work was well under way on some of the most trod upon real estate in the country. A meandering barrier, expected to be 6,280 feet in all, had been started at the southeast corner of the parking lot designated for disabled guests, and it wound south along the access road and across the Avenue of the Stars until it met *The Seas With Nemo and Friends* exhibit. From there, it incorporated uncontaminated buildings and attractions to close an 80,000 square foot area that circled all the way back at the disabled parking lot where it had started.

The wall was constructed of twelve-foot high prefabricated concrete barriers, the same ones used to line highways for noise reduction. Footers had been poured for the first support columns, and the entire structure was scheduled to be complete within fifteen days. At least that's what the engineers and project managers from Stone & Webster had promised.

That would coincide with the new entrance and ticketing facility being built on the site of the disabled parking lot, and the expansion of the small access road to accommodate the busses that would be shuttling guests around the western side of the *Nemo* exhibit to the Central Plaza where they would still be able to enjoy 94% of the park's attractions. That's what it promised in the new Official Guide to Epcot that would be rolling off the presses well before the grand re-opening on Monday, July 11th, seventeen days after Jimmy Strobel had martyred himself. Prices had been lowered 6% to reflect the reduced entertainment opportunities.

The new wall would become an attraction in itself, and a "living mural" was promised. It would be painted with memorials by the relatives and friends of the eighty-three people who died in the sculpture garden that day, and the 172 who were injured. Disney would foot the bill for their trip to Epcot and host them in one of its resorts for five nights.

About 270,000 cubic feet of concrete and soil and plants and buildings were to be excavated over the next four months and the debris stored in 234 twenty-foot cargo containers. These would be stacked two-high within the area bounded by the walled-off parking lot, arranged so those containers with the most radioactivity would be in the center, effectively using all the other debris to shield it so the radiation dose rate at the wall would be within EPA and Nuclear Regulatory Commission limits. Lanes would be left between the staggered rows of containers to allow access and to provide room for temporary shielding should any be required to reach the limits required at the perimeter, although the Stone & Webster engineers had calculated that the 11,000,000 pounds of debris would provide adequate shielding to meet or exceed those limits.

The cesium itself would be sealed on or in whatever it had contaminated by multiple layers of a spray-on, flexible silicon material. The first spraying was underway, and additional coats would be applied as buildings were demolished and ground excavated. Continuous air monitors were positioned around the perimeter and would constantly check for any airborne particles. Fixed and portable misters would catch these in a fine vapor and they would quickly settle to the ground and be re-captured.

All in all, the $310 million plan and project was ambitious and impressive, and the Disney executives congratulated themselves on not capitulating to terror. And on maintaining the cash flow, as well.

6.18   St. Paul Meeting Center, St. Paul, MN

The meeting had been hastily arranged, and because of that it had to be held in St. Paul. Otherwise the Governor of Minnesota would have been unable to attend, and Tag had wanted to be sure and have the most populous state in his secret Christian Covenant of America in attendance. Tag had made the arrangements through the conservative, and as yet unannounced, Political Action Committee that he funded with Ibrahim's money, and the executives from all seven states had been invited. Margaret would be representing Idaho, and besides herself, both Dakotas and Montana had sent their lieutenant governors. Wyoming was the only state not represented, and that was for the legitimate reason that the Governor was in the hospital for some routine surgery and the lieutenant governor decided he needed to stay in-state.

The hasty meeting had been billed as a regional conference to share resources and planning in the aftermath of the dirty bomb attacks. With travel and other expenses underwritten, it was easy for the normally invisible lieutenant governors to attend and get a little time in the spotlight.

Margaret was wrapping up her keynote address to an audience of thirty-two, included the executives and whatever staff they had brought, and, of course, the press. Earlier, she'd hosted a private lunch to get some of the preliminaries out of the way and to gently prep all the others for her speech. Her wrap-up was a summation of the entire speech following the "tell them what you're going to say, say it, and tell them what you just said" school of speechifying.

"The threat, the challenge to our way of life, comes from too much pandering to people whose only contribution to our country is their vote, and the lengths that some of our professional politicians in Washington and the, shall we say, urban areas are willing to go to get that vote. Their willingness to sacrifice the things that made this country great and continue to make us the wealthiest and most advanced country ever is intolerable. The values of this country are not for sale for the sake of re-election! The freedoms we enjoy are not sacrificial on the altar of multi-culturalism and socialism!

"And what are these values and freedoms that we must protect or see our way of life shattered by criminals and terrorists with the most heinous of weapons? Immigration, for one. Our borders are wide open, inviting any and all to come on in and bring your dirty bomb with you. Gun control. Those poor people in Kentucky died because they couldn't fight back. The only survivor was the woman who chased the terrorist out of her home with her own gun. Unregistered, I might add.

"And, if I may use the word again, a word that seems to have gone out of favor as our freedoms erode - socialism. Health care is just the latest example of Washington usurping our rights and taking our wealth and giving it to those whose votes they can buy and the bankers and Wall Street thieves who provide the campaign money to get them re-elected.

"We are a country of law. Laws to protect us, the people who made this country great and continue to make us, as Ronald Reagan said, 'a shining city on the hill.' And it is the strict enforcement of these laws that has brought us order. Today that order is threatened by enemies from every direction. But it is most threatened by the enemies right here at home - those who would sacrifice us for their own benefit.

"Thank you."

6.19   Harrington Hospital, Southbridge, MA

It was nearing lunch time when the two strangers entered Bander's hospital room. They both held up official-looking badges and laminated ID cards, but Bander had no chance to examine them.

"Mr. Ashoor, I'm Agent Rice of the U.S. Immigration and Customs Service Enforcement and Removal Operations Branch. This is Agent Hardens. We're here to escort you to Logan Airport where you will be put aboard the next commercial flight to Riyadh. You are being officially deported and your student visa revoked."

"What? You can't do that. I'm injured. I can't go anywhere until my doctor releases me."

"Yes sir, and he has. Now please, get dressed or we will escort you there in your hospital gown."

"My clothes …"

"Are right here, sir," Rice said, handing Bander a wrapped bundle. "Your belongings will be packed up by the university security office and forwarded to whatever address you request."

"I want my lawyer. There is due process. I have rights."

"Excuse me, sir, but that is not correct. You have been lawfully deported from the country and your rights under American law ended then. The only right you have left is to be treated humanely in accordance with international law, and we will do our best to accommodate that."

Bander stared at the men for a moment, and then slowly got up, disconnecting his own monitors and IV. *I'm dead*, he thought. *If they don't kill me, my father will.*

6.20   BBC News Headquarters, London, England

B B C OPEC Calls For Oil Price Freeze

Plans to calm volatile markets extend to non-OPEC producers

OPEC has announced it will hold oil prices stable and called upon non-OPEC oil and gas producing nations, including the United States, to do likewise. Oil prices climbed again today, with the benchmark crude reaching all-time highs. Meanwhile, Americans are hoarding gas and food, causing unprecedented supply challenges at both the gas stations and the grocery stores. Long lines are now the norm and some fear these crowds present attractive targets for terrorists.

6.21   Covenant of Faith and Truth Apostolic Assembly, Goliad, TX

The clean-cut young man with a backpack hiked up the driveway toward the small church. It was hot under the south Texas sun in June, and he paused to take off his John Deere baseball cap and wipe his forehead with what they still called a neckerchief where he came from. He looked around, as if admiring the drab view of the run-down church and small ranch-style house to the right. Seemingly intrigued by something, he walked around the church, examining its architecture like it was Notre Dame de Paris.

Making a complete circle, he walked up to the front door of the house and knocked and a plain, older woman answered.

"I was wonderin' what time services are, ma'am, and if you welcome strangers."

"Why of course we do, young man. We have a twilight reading every day around 8 PM. You're more than welcome. We don't get too many strangers hereabouts, so I'm sure the Reverend would love to meet you and talk scripture."

"That would be grand, ma'am. I'll try to get by tonight or tomorrow. Bless you."

With that he turned and hiked back up the drive, turning right at the end and starting his long walk back to town.

***

Two technicians watched the flat panel display showing a moving graph displaying an almost flat horizontal line. It was the fourth time today that the scene had unfolded, each time accompanied by a young man that they couldn't see, wearing a backpack and wandering around an address gleaned from Ray Nassiri's list of suspected drivers.

Inside the backpack, sensitive radiation monitoring equipment recorded any gamma and neutron radiation and telemetered the results back to the lab where the technicians watched for any trace of the stolen cesium.

"Nothing in Goliad," the technician said. "Four down, one to go."

Part Seven – The Capture

<u>WEDNESDAY, JUNE 30</u>

7.01   FBI FIELD OFFICE, LOUISVILLE, KY

Cal watched the grainy video on one of the two 60-inch high-definition video monitors mounted on the wall in the EOC at the Louisville Field Office. Five monitors in all were active, including three smaller ones, showing five different dark and ominous scenes. The resolution was poor due to the limited light and the limited capabilities of helmet-mounted video cameras. With him were Buck Buchanan and a contingent of six of his agents, and Ray Nassiri. Cal knew that there must be a dozen similar gatherings at various Federal agencies, with everyone watching in the same hushed silence.

Each monitor had a subtitle overlaid at the bottom giving the local time and location, and the identification of the agent wearing the camera that provided the video feed. The two pictures that Cal was most interested in were the two largest, one labeled Goliad, TX and the other Kansas City, MO. These were the two locations where the identities of both members of the two-person team were known, and both were family teams. Cal thought having both team members and family to play off against one another was most likely to yield useful information quickly. The three smaller screens were labeled Boston, MA; Norristown, PA; and Parma, ID.

These seven suspects in their five different locations represented an unknown threat. They had all been under constant surveillance since early that day, and each of their homes, offices, or other property had been clandestinely searched with radiation monitors and, where possible, by covert incursion when no one was around. As far as anyone could tell, there was no cesium at or near any of the identified addresses. As a precaution, HMRU, SABT, NEST, and RAP were on each scene to respond instantly to any trace of radioactive material.

At 3:04 AM Eastern Standard Time, and 1:04 AM Mountain Standard Time, Buchanan asked for each team leader to confirm readiness, and when they all had, he simply said "Go" into his microphone.

7.02 COVENANT OF FAITH AND TRUTH APOSTOLIC ASSEMBLY, GOLIAD, TX

In Goliad, Texas, the FBI SWAT team stood off, out of sight on the main road, probably 500 yards from the church and house. The church was fifty or so yards off the road with a small parking area in front and extending around the left side. The access driveway continued around the right side to the house, another twenty yards away, and that was where they expected to find the Ebbers family, hopefully with all three of them asleep. The Ebbers had been identified as a target because Billy Ray Jr. had made several calls on his cell phone to his mother during the trip to Tennessee and back.

The FBI surveillance team had arrived in the early morning hours the day before and found that there was no concealment near the rural church. The best they could do was park behind an abandoned gas station a quarter of a mile up the main road and watch through binoculars from the roof. Fortunately, the Ebbers' had made the surveillance easy by never leaving the property that day, and rarely even leaving the house.

The entire team had filtered in quietly during the late night hours and set up behind the gas station. There were now seven vehicles arrayed there, two for the FBI's SWAT team, and one each for the HMRU, SABT, NEST and RAP units and their monitoring and containment equipment, and an ambulance. The plan was to move the 14-man SWAT team single file down the access drive and to set up around the house. Three agents would be held back on the drive, watching the empty church and ready for any attempt by the Ebbers to escape. The insertion team was six agents, two for each target in the house, and the remaining five agents would be deployed around the house.

As soon as the agents had their targets in custody, or before if there was any sign of a dirty bomb, the HMRU and SABT would go in first and declare the area safe. NEST and RAP teams were to then enter the buildings and begin their sweep. To Agent Glen Costas, the SWAT team leader and man with the helmet cam, it looked like a simple and virtually foolproof plan. And that had him worried. Foolproof plans, in his experience, almost always encountered foolish mistakes.

Nine minutes before the go time, his SWAT team set off at a jog, single file down the side of the road. At the drive, they turned left and entered the property, moving more cautiously now. At the church, the team split, three circling to the rear entrance and three to the front. The remaining agents set up in their assigned locations until the grounds were completely covered by well-trained and dangerously-armed men and women. They had floor plans of both buildings and knew exactly where they would go once they forcibly entered the house. It was to be a no-warning entry, crashing the front and rear doors simultaneously, shouting identification as FBI agents, and setting off several flash-bangs to disorient anyone in the house.

When Agent Costas said go, they did, and the doors disintegrated under the blow of the battering rams wielded by the agents.

The three bedrooms of the small ranch house were lined up along the north side of the house, one long hallway connecting them with entrances to the living area at one end and the kitchen at the other. Each team tossed a flash-bang into the corridor as they approached it from opposite ends, and shouted FBI identification and orders for everyone to lie down on the floor, hands where they could be seen.

In the front bedroom, Costas and his partner found Billy Ray Sr. sitting up in bed, looking at the bedroom door like it was a spaceship that had just landed. His wife had the covers over her head and was screaming pleas to Jesus Christ to spare her life. Costas watched the two while his partner checked the bathroom and closet. "Clear," he yelled, and Costas relaxed a fraction.

One agent each had peeled off from the entry teams and headed for the middle bedroom, which, as expected, they found empty, echoing the "clear" signal. The rear bedroom was where they expected to find Billy Ray Jr., but all they found was an unmade bed. "Clear," the agent in the room shouted. And added, "There's no one in bedroom three." Costas' nerves ramped up.

"You two, check the basement. You two check the rest of the house. He's here somewhere, and probably armed. Use flash-bangs on the basement before you go down."

Before anyone had a chance to act, Costas heard the unmistakable sound of automatic weapons fire from outside the house, and the foolproof plan exploded.

"Get these two secure," he said to one two-man team. "You two, out the back and flank whoever is shooting. We'll go out the front."

Radio chatter bombarded Costas' headphones.

"He's in the church."

"Agent down. I've got an agent down."

"Benson. Sewickley. Circle around the back and watch the rear entrance."

"I see him. Southwest window." Followed by a barrage of weapons fire that quickly turned the window and wall into kindling.

Everything got quiet after that. Costas deployed his agents around the church while several others moved the two wounded agents back toward the road to meet the ambulance that had started forward when casualties were reported.

"Teams report," Costas ordered, and he got all clears from each still-active two-man team. "OK. Benson, Sewickley, rear entry on my go. James and I will take the front. Use your goggles," he added, indicating night-vision goggles that each wore. Ready? Go!"

Costas stood to rush the front door and before he'd had a chance to take a step, an automatic weapon fired from the small church steeple, and his partner fell. Answering fire perforated the wood siding of the steeple, with many bullets hitting the bell housed there and setting off a staccato clanging, further adding to the noise confusion.

"Agent down," Costas called into his mike. "There is no front entry. Whoever is closest, back-up Benson and Sewickley through the rear."

***

In the living room of the ranch house, face down on the floor with his hands secured behind his back, Billy Ray Sr. mumbled to himself, "Thatta boy, Junior. Shoot and keep on shootin'. Make me proud, son."

Evangeline, his wife, was lying next to him praying for God to spare her son's life.

***

"We're in," Costas heard Benson say over the radio. "No sign of him. We're on the south side, among the pews. Banks and Armstrong are on the north. We can see the steeple entrance, but the door is closed."

"All right. I'll be coming in the front with Satters. When we're in, Banks and Armstrong move to the door and open it."

Pointing to Agent Satters, Costas said, "Let's go," and they rushed the front door. There was no firing this time, and they burst through, taking cover in the small foyer. The door to the steeple was on their left, and they took up covering positions while two agents moved up and flanked the door, one on each side. The door swung out, so one of the agents crouched along the wall behind it, ready to open it on command. He would be hidden by the door once it was open, and he counted on the training of his teammates to not shoot him by mistake.

When everyone was in position, Costas signaled "go" and the agent flung the door open. It was almost as if the door handle was a trigger as bursts of shots followed the door, spraying the church at random. With the flashes, the night-vision goggles became a liability, and they were flung off without the need for orders. The agents could see Billy Ray Jr. sitting on the landing where the staircase turned to wind its way up to the steeple. They returned fire and instantly Junior was dead, seventeen more bullets hitting him to add to the two already there.

7.03   1243 Anderson Ave., Kansas City, MO

SWAT Commander Claude Fellows had no more heard the word "go" in his earpiece and waved his team forward when a light went on in the Wilkins home. He said "hold" into his microphone and his team stopped, seeking cover where possible.

"I have lights and activity in the house," he reported to Buchanan. This entry was already complicated by the presence of two teenage children in the house. In addition to HMRU, SABT, RAP and NEST units, Fellows had a man and woman from the Department of Social Services to see to their welfare after their parents were taken away.

Movement in the house could be anyone, and if it was one of the kids, Fellows wanted to be sure there were no mistakes, no innocents injured.

After almost two minutes of silence, Buchanan asked "Can you tell who it is?"

"No. It's in the kitchen. Maybe someone snacking."

"Where is the kitchen in relation to your entry points?"

"It's between the two back entries. One is the garage and the other a sliding glass door from a deck. We'll have whoever it is between the two rear entry teams."

"All right. Your call when to proceed."

∗∗∗

Darlene Wilkins dropped her glass of warm milk on the kitchen floor and screamed and screamed and wouldn't stop. Milton woke instantly at the sound of the crashes, like a car had rammed their house, and then his wife screaming downstairs. He leapt from the bed and ran down the stairs, stopping midway at the sight of hooded figures in his foyer pointing weapons at him. His first thought was of black helicopters, and he wondered if they'd landed in the elementary school parking lot, just a block away.

The men were shouting at him, and even though he didn't register the words, he knew to raise his hands and be as non-threatening as possible. Behind him he could hear his 14-year-old daughter come out of her room, shouting "Dad? Mom? Where are you? What's happening?"

The light in the hallway above him came on and Milton saw the figures tense and adjust their aim above him, to the top of the stairs.

"Tom. Sally. It's all right. Stay where you are and …"

"Shut up," came the command from one of the hooded figures. "This is the FBI. Anyone upstairs raise your hands above your head and come out where I can see you."

"Daddy, what's happening?"

"Is that Sally Wilkins? This is Agent Claude Fellows of the FBI. We have a warrant to question your mother and father on a matter of national security. No one will be hurt. Just please, you and your brother raise your hands above your heads and come out where I can see you."

"Daddy…"

"Just do as they say, Sally," Milton shouted. "And you, too, Tommy. This is a misunderstanding and everything will be fine."

Darlene finally stopped screaming and he saw her emerge from the kitchen, sobbing, hands behind her back, two more hooded figures pointing more weapons at her.

"Your mother is downstairs," he continued, and Agent Fellows let him go on. "Go ahead now. Raise your hands and come downstairs with me. Don't do anything foolish, these men are armed."

The two teenagers tentatively appeared at the top of the stairs, the girl in a short nightgown and the boy in briefs and a t-shirt. All three followed Fellows' orders and came downstairs with their hands raised. They were led out the front door as another group of figures, these dressed in white suits covering them from head to toe and carrying some devices in their hands, went in. Milton realized that they were looking for the stolen cesium that he had concluded was what he and Darlene had driven to Kansas City. He wondered how they had found them so fast, and then decided buying those souvenirs along the way for the kids had been a mistake.

7.04   26 Gerritt St, Philadelphia PA

The lights went on and Harrison Andrews bolted upright in bed, listening to shouts from hooded men with guns surrounding the bed. He looked over at Pam Mooney, cowering under the sheets, and wondered what the hell was going on. The commands finally got through to him, and he raised his hands.

"You, too, Mooney," one of the figures shouted. "Put your hands where I can see them. Slowly."

Andrews could see her hands. They were clutching the sheet that she had pulled over her head. She let go and raised them, with the sheet still covering her head.

"This is the FBI. Sit up, Mooney."

"What the hell is going on here," Andrews yelled.

"Shut up, whoever you are. This is the FBI and we have a warrant for Ms. Mooney, here. And you'll be going with us. Mooney! Sit up so I can see you."

Pam did a slow sit-up, using her arms to balance her into a sitting position, the sheet dropping from her front, showing her naked from the waist up.

"Now both of you, out of bed. You first, Mooney."

"I can't," she said. "I don't have any clothes on."

"Mooney. Listen to me. I don't care. You will slowly get out of bed and stand next to it or my men will get you out, and you won't like that, I can assure you. Keep your hands where I can see them and get out of bed. You," he said, indicating Andrews, "stay put until I tell you otherwise. Now move, Mooney."

Pam swung her legs to the left side of the bed and stood.

"Cuff her," the agent said, and one of the other agents lowered his weapon and grabbed her right arm, pulling it behind her back and doing the same with her left one. Plastic cuffs were slipped over her hands and tightened around her wrists.

"Now you," he said, pointing to Andrews, who followed Pam's lead and stood naked while FBI agents handcuffed him.

What the hell have I gotten myself into, Andrews thought. *My wife is gonna kill me.*

7.05   Tattoo You Bar & Grill, Parma, ID

Billy Morse had just ordered another shot of Wilson's scotch, the cheap house brand, and mug of beer when two new patrons entered the bar. He watched the strangers with idle curiosity. Parma didn't get a lot of visitors, despite its location near the Snake River and the magnificent surrounding mountain ranges. And the Tattoo You Bar & Grill rarely hosted a strange face, especially at one in the morning. Billy mentally shrugged and lost interest in them as his focus turned to the fresh shot and cold beer set in front of him by Al, the bar's owner and tender.

He finished the shot in one spasm of arm-raising and swallowing, and tapped the bar twice with the empty shot glass, his habit as he enjoyed the flow of the warm and sharp liquid down to his stomach. He'd raised the beer for a swallow when two more strangers entered, arousing his curiosity again. Curiosity turned to suspicion as they headed toward the bar where he sat. Suspicion turned to anger as they crowded in on either side of him.

And finally, anger turned to panic as one of them showed Billy his FBI identification and said, "William Morse, I am Agent Reynolds of the FBI and you are under arrest. Why don't we step outside and I'll tell you your rights. You see those two men in the back? They're with me. And so are the eight other agents outside. We have your car, and you're not going anywhere except with us, so let's do this quietly and not cause a scene, OK?"

Al-the-bartender noticed the activity and approached. Reynolds held up his ID and said, "FBI. Please step back. And please keep your hands where I can see them. Mr. Morse will be leaving with us now." He turned to Billy and continued, "Isn't that right, Mr. Morse?"

For the first time in Al's memory, Billy had nothing to say and got up, one man holding each arm, and left.

"Hey, what about his tab," Al called. "He owes me $23."

The FBI agent stopped and took out a card and handed it to Al. "Call my office tomorrow and they will arrange payment," he lied.

7.06   50 W. Broadway, Boston, MA

The gun was in his hand even before he was awake. It was a Springfield-manufactured Colt 45, the Custom Professional Model 1911A1. When it came to guns, Frank Healy was old-school and preferred the tried and true. He instantly knew the noise that had awoken him was a forced entry into his second-floor apartment in South Boston. The trespassers identified themselves as FBI, and Frank snapped off three shots through the bedroom door to slow them down.

Frank slept fully dressed out of a paranoid concern over exactly what was happening. Whatever he was wearing at bed time was what he was wearing when he awoke the next morning. He'd never had cause to make a middle-of-the-night escape before, but it only took one to make it smart, and he was very happy at that moment to have everything but shoes on. He slipped into the loafers next to the bed and was out the open window onto the fire escape in seconds.

He climbed down the ladder and dropped to the alley, crouching for a moment while he surveyed the area to see where the next threat would come from. He didn't have to wait as two sets of high beams from cars parked at both ends of the alley lit the scene like a night game at Fenway Park. Frank ducked between two dumpsters and fired two shots at the car to his right. One hit one of the headlights and the light intensity dropped slightly.

"Frank Healy," someone shouted over a bullhorn. "This is the FBI. We have you surrounded. Drop your weapon and come out with your hands raised high above your head. You have no chance of escape. Let's not get anyone hurt, including you."

"Fuck you," Frank replied and took another shot at the remaining headlight on the car, and missed.

"You're not doing yourself any good, Healy. At best, you've got nine rounds in the nice Colt 45 you carry, and you've used six of them already. You didn't have time to grab any extra magazines, so you're pretty well screwed. Just drop the gun and come on out."

At that moment, Frank heard a gunshot, deep and loud. It sounded like a 12-gauge shotgun, and before he could process this, something hit the dumpster to his left with a huge bang, actually moving it a little closer to him.

"What the fuck was that," he yelled.

"Just one of the rubber bullets we're going to use to knock your ass to the ground if you don't give it up."

Having nothing better to do, Frank jumped out from behind the dumpster and fired his last three rounds toward the source of the FBI agent's voice. He had no sooner emptied his gun than he was hit twice by what felt like Mike Tyson punches, and his ass was truly on the ground.

7.07   GRAINGER RESIDENCE, FRENCHTOWN, MT

"We've got problems."

These were words that Tag just didn't want to hear. His caller ID had alerted him that Marcus was on the line, and Tag knew he wouldn't be calling to report nothing, so it would be news. And at 5 AM, it had to be bad news. Even though he didn't want to hear them, he'd known those words were coming before they were spoken.

"Go ahead," was all Tag said.

"I just got notified. We lost one, so I checked the others. Looks like four total, maybe five. All expendable."

Conversations were always kept simple, with no direct references, respecting the surveillance capabilities of the government. Tag knew that losing one meant a team had been captured, and that Marcus' check had revealed that three or four more had been as well. This was a massive roll-up of their network that he knew could only be caused by a very high-level betrayal. The fact that they were expendable teams from the original theft and not involved in his cesium diversion to Washington and Houston narrowed the list of traitors down to the original conspirators. And only one of them was positively untrustworthy.

Ibrahim.

"And?"

"I gave the order. Arrivals should start within four hours. Departures shortly after."

The order was the emergency contingency plan that all the teams had. The teams still free would be directed to a safe house in Kalispell, Montana. Travel there was to be absolutely secret – no cell phones, no planes or other monitored transportation, only cash transactions, tell no one they would even be away. They were promised secure communications at their destination to contact loved ones and jobs. What they really would get was the departure, a ride in a small, single-engine plane that would take them over the remotest areas of the Flathead National Forest southeast of the Hungry Horse Reservoir, flying about 9,000 feet above sea level. This would give their naked bodies about a thousand feet of free fall before landing somewhere on Argosy Mountain.

"And the others," Tag asked, meaning the ones in custody.

"Not available at the moment. We'll know when they are."

The WAR network, extensive within most every prison or jail, would provide notification if and when any of the other teams were incarcerated. Assassination squads inside would dispose of any team members that were accessible, but Tag was not confident any of them would be, given the threat the cesium presented. And that was the limit of their available damage control.

At least within his own organization. Ibrahim presented an entirely different problem.

7.08   RIVERSIDE CORRECTIONAL FACILITY, PHILADELPHIA, PA

"Hello, Ms. Mooney. I'm Special Agent Jared Grayson of the FBI. You are being charged with several very serious crimes under the Patriot Act and others, the foremost of which is conspiracy to detonate a weapon of mass destruction in the United States. That crime alone will put you in jail for the rest of your life without the possibility of parole. Now, you have been read your rights. Do you understand them?"

Pam Mooney sat quietly in the small room, an interrogation room, she guessed they would call it, at the Riverside Correctional Facility, the intake center for females in the Philadelphia Prison Center. It wasn't like the ones on TV, no one-way mirror on blank concrete walls. This looked like a small, sparsely-furnished office, a table and several chairs, some patriotic posters on the walls, even a window, although dark curtains eliminated any indication that there was anything outside the room. Maybe there wasn't even a window behind them. She guessed there were cameras recording all of this, but she couldn't figure out where they were.

"I want to see my lawyer," was all she said.

"Fine," the agent answered as he stood to leave. "I'll get you a phone. And while you're at it, get one for your mother. She'll be charged with conspiracy based on all the calls you made to her while you were touring the country with a 4,000 curie dirty bomb. Don't worry about your daughter. Jennifer, right? That's her name? We'll get her into foster care right away.

"And finally, your lover, Mr. Harrison Andrews. Your boss, right? Real estate, right? He's in a room next door getting questioned as we speak. We don't think he's involved, but he is pretty pissed off. I'm guessing his wife won't understand."

"Wait. My mother has nothing to do with this. Leave her alone. She'll take care of Jennifer until all of this is cleared up."

Grayson sat down again and leaned across the table, looking Pam straight in her eyes.

"Ms. Mooney. When all of this is cleared up, you will be going to jail for the rest of your life. Do you understand that? Your mother will do at least several years for conspiracy because she knew what you were up to and did nothing to report it. The Patriot Act is pretty explicit on that, and the punishment pretty severe. I am not speculating – this is fact. We have the complete record of your trip to Tennessee and back. We have the record of all the charges made on the stolen credit cards that you were given, along with your signatures. We have your own personal credit card charges. And most of all,

The Rockets' Red Glare   223

we have the times and locations of each of the several calls you made daily to your mother and daughter. We have people who will ID you and link you to your WAR partner. We have surveillance photos from toll booths and rest stops along the way.

"And we have your partner. He's going to flip on you, you know. Someone always does. The only question is who does it first. They're the ones who get to cut the deal, maybe keep a loved one out of jail and a child at home. So, if you like, I'll get the phone and you can call your lawyer and he can tell you not to cooperate while we get the complete story from your partner."

The agent waved a file as he made the last statement, seeming to indicate that it was a file on Jeff Simmons, the other driver on their mission. She knew Simmons only vaguely, and she was sure he had no loyalty to her and would probably throw her under a bus to save himself. The WAR reference really startled her. She had thought that her involvement with them through an on-again, off-again boyfriend was a secret. Maybe Simmons had already told them something.

Mooney, tears rolling down her face without notice, said, "All right. Get me a lawyer and I'll make a deal. My mother goes free and takes care of my daughter. That's my bottom line, and I want it in writing. I don't care about me, but make sure Simmons gets more charges. He was the leader in this. I just drove. And I had no idea what we were carrying. Maybe he did, but he didn't tell me."

***

In a conference room just down the hall, three agents watched the video feed from Pam Mooney's interrogation. As soon as she finished talking, one of the agents said, "OK, we've got a name. Let's find this Simmons guy. Get the lawyer in there before she changes her mind. Then let's find out where this shit is and get on it."

7.09 LENNOCKS RANCH, BANDERA, TX

Stully Lennocks' gun belt had two holsters – one on each side like Wild Bill Hickok. The right side held his .44/40 Colt Peacemaker, his answer to any rattlesnakes or other varmints that might cross his path, including those on two legs. The left side held his Globalstar GSP1700 satellite phone, his link to his other world when he was riding his quarter horse, Dancer, inspecting some remote part of his 47,000 acre Texas Longhorn cattle ranch. It was just past dawn when it rang. He was in the far northwest corner of the ranch, twelve miles from the ranch house, and thirty-three miles from anything approaching civilization.

"Talk," he said, his standard response to any telephone call.

"I have a job for you. Marcus arrives in San Antonio at two. He'll fill you in."

Click. Stully's favorite kind of phone call. Short, and profitable.

7.10   OLIN CORPORATION PLANT, HENDERSON, NV

The Olin Corporation plant in Henderson, Nevada made chemicals like bleach and chlorine and hydrochloric acid for industrial uses in water treatment, pulp and paper manufacturing, and food processing. Located in a sprawling facility near multiple railroad sidings, with storage tanks of all sizes and uses scattered around, with vast settling ponds and electrical substations and cooling towers, it also made an ideal location for a company pickup truck to sit unnoticed for days or even weeks.

The truck with three steel drums marked "caustic soda" sat in one of many lots just off Avenue G, right where the driver of the Amar Energy mobile repair truck had been told it was. The repair truck was a modified two-ton pickup with steel boxes and cabinets mounted all around the perimeter of the truck bed, and a 3,200 pound jib crane mounted over the rear axle. A pretty standard configuration for an industrial repair vehicle.

While he had paperwork showing he was picking up caustic soda to use as a chemical neutralizer, ostensibly for cleaning up minor spills, any serious review would quickly beg the question, why was a repair truck being used for pick-up and delivery? And why directly from a truck in a parking lot and not though the office and warehouse? The driver had no good answers to any of those questions and was relying on a cursory examination of his task, or, better yet, no examination at all.

It was late afternoon when he parked behind the pickup, shielding it from view from the only occupied building nearby, maybe 200 feet away, and quickly set about maneuvering the jib crane to the center of the three drums on the pickup. Working with practiced movements, he removed the drum lid, attached the crane hook to the hoist chains on the container centered inside the drum, and raised it out. Once he was clear of the drum, he swung the jib crane 180 degrees and lowered the container into one of three steel bins on his truck that had been modified to hold the heavy shields securely in place. He then unhooked the crane and closed the bin. He returned to the pickup and replaced the drum lid, leaving everything the same as he'd found it, minus 4,000 curies of cesium.

The entire operation had taken just nine minutes, and the driver smiled to himself, pleased with a job well done. He had a very tight schedule and hoped the next pick-up in Phoenix would be as smooth.

7.11   CNN News Headquarters, Atlanta, GA

 ### Hedge Funds Seek to Profit From Fear

Wall Street traders prove there is always money to be made

NEW YORK (CNNMoney.com) -- Hedge funds on Wall Street are moving to make billions of dollars in profits on heightened domestic and international fear. The Wall Street Journal reports that the VIX Index and VIX ETFs logged unprecedented gains, as investors were spooked by the initial and follow-on WMD terrorist attack in the United States. Today, the VIX reached an all-time intraday high of 93.47. The VIX, a popular measure of the implied volatility of the S&P 500 index options, often referred to as the *fear index* or the *fear gauge*, roughly measures the expected movement in the S&P 500 index over the next 30-day period, which is then annualized.

7.12   110 Nicholson Ave., Kansas City, MO

In Kansas City, the FBI SWAT and SABT teams approached Maloney's Diesel Repair Service on foot from Nicholson Avenue, just south and west of the suspected location of the cesium. According to their information, it was in a 55-gallon drum in a pick-up truck in the northeast corner of the lot.

An area of almost six square miles had been sealed off and evacuated without much difficulty early that morning. Milton and Darlene Wilkins had quickly given up the location of the truck they'd driven, striking a deal that kept her out of jail on the claim that she knew nothing and was simply accompanying her husband on a business trip. She and the kids were already home, ironically on Anderson Avenue in Scarritt Point, just a mile south of the truck. That residential area was not evacuated as the prevailing winds were running at about seven miles per hour from the south and southwest, the typical weather pattern in the area. This would carry any airborne cesium away from the houses, and the residents had been told to "shelter in place," that is, stay indoors with windows and doors closed. Police patrolled the area to try to enforce compliance.

Following the SWAT team, the four-man RAP team approached. The lead technician carefully watched the display on his radiation survey meter for any indication of increased readings. The others carried a variety of instruments that they would use to check ambient radiation and search for any leakage into the air or onto the truck and surrounding ground.

"I'm getting nothing," he reported through the microphone inside the hood of his protective suit. He continued to the side of the pick-up truck, and watched as the digital/analog display showed no increase in radiation above normal background. "Still nothing."

One of the other team members lowered the tailgate of the pick-up and they helped the tech onto the truck bed. He slowly swept his meter over all three of the 55-gallon drums in the truck and repeated, "Nothing."

One of the RAP team members handed the tech a two-inch circular fabric disk which the technician used to wipe around the locking rings on all three drums. He handed it back to the other tech, who then placed it on a small sliding tray and inserted it into a chamber and waited. After about thirty seconds, he said, "It's clean."

"All right. Let's set up the air monitor and then open them up."

The technician on the truck set a battery-powered air pump on one of the drums and started it up. He set his survey meter next to it where he could watch the readings as he worked. Someone handed him a small canvas bag with assorted hand tools and, using the ratchet and socket provided, he removed the locking ring from the drum they were told had the cesium inside. After checking his meter and seeing no change, he carefully lifted the drum lid about an inch and used a flashlight to see inside. Satisfied that there were no booby traps or broken containers, he fully removed the lid and then used his survey meter to check inside the drum.

"It's empty," he said.

"That can't be right," the team leader said. "Check the other drums."

The tech repeated the procedure with the remaining two drums and found them both full of oil. There were no radiation readings coming off of either of them, and a probe of the drums using a piece of metal pipe they found nearby confirmed that there was only liquid in the drums.

The RAP team leader removed his hood and breathing filter and informed the SWAT Commander, who took out his cell phone. A speed-dialed number was answered on the first ring, and he said, "We've got a problem, but not the one we prepared for."

Bush 43 had set the precedent, and this President would follow it and visit Ground Zero at Reagan International Airport to mourn the dead, exhort the responders, vilify the perpetrators, and promise justice even if it had to be delivered by a cruise missile. Bush's impromptu speech at the World Trade Center site would be a hard act to follow, made harder by waiting five days so it would be safe to give the speech without talking through a respirator to protect the President from inhaling airborne cesium should a breeze come up.

By Monday, contractors had built a 4,358 foot long berm enclosing 6.4 million square feet of roads and sidewalks and parking lots and buildings and ground. The berm consisted of 863 interlocking plastic blocks, 5.05 feet long each, that were filled with water to provide stability and shielding and then sealed together and to the ground with a thick, spray-on sealant, almost like a giant, but very shallow, bathtub. In this case, twenty-one inches shallow. Even so, it would hold three times the 4.8 million gallons of water they planned to spray at high pressure from fire hoses to sweep the ground clean of cesium. In its chloride form, the cesium was very soluble and would easily dissolve in the water.

Within the berm, all outlets such as storm drains had been sealed, and around the perimeter four outlets were provided for the water to flow into plastic-lined pits that collected the run off. Pumps sucked the accumulated water out of these and pushed it into large, vertical steel tanks about three feet in diameter and six feet high. Inside these tanks, 40 cubic feet of tiny ion-exchange resin beads worked their chemical magic and selectively absorbed 99.997% of the cesium and then returned the clean water to the high-pressure pumps so it could be sprayed again, removing more cesium with each recirculation.

The tanks themselves were in even larger, lead-shielded transport containers, called casks. When the resin reached saturation and would absorb no more cesium, these would be closed and carted off to the radioactive waste disposal site in South Carolina, to be replaced by a fresh tank and cask, eight tanks in all if things went according to plans. The restricting factor in the clean-up process was the limited rate of water flow that could be achieved through each resin tank, and factoring in the amount of water that would be pumped and the down time to change resin tanks and do other maintenance, the engineers were projecting twelve days before the area would be clean enough for demolition and restoration. But by Wednesday when the President arrived, some 1.56 million gallons had been processed through the tanks, achieving a decontamination factor of thirty-three. That meant that 1/33 of the cesium was estimated to still be on the ground, or about 120 curies.

The decontamination factor goal was 10,000, and for that to be achieved, large patches of sidewalks and roads and buildings and ground would be demolished and hauled to the waste disposal site, probably eighty truck loads. After that, four-tenths of a curie would be scattered over the millions of square feet, an almost unnoticeable amount that was well within EPA limits.

It was now safe enough inside the berm to satisfy even the Secret Service, and the President would have his chance to express his grief, outrage, and determination at Ground Zero.

7.14   HOTEL KRISTOFF, MARACAIBO, VENEZUELA

Ibrahim had taken three rooms at the Hotel Kristoff, including the 3-bedroom Presidential Suite for himself and his family, and a Junior Suite for his bodyguard and wife. The third room, registered under another name to protect his privacy while working, was a one-room VIP suite. At some significant cost, the hotel had converted the bedroom area to a sitting room and office where Ibrahim could have the privacy to work, and that was where he learned of the betrayal.

CNN International was broadcasting a live event from Kansas City, and Ibrahim struggled with two dilemmas. First, how to get his mind around the thirty-minute time difference between Maracaibo and Kansas City, and second, how the authorities had found the cesium stored there.

The image showed a dilapidated industrial setting, viewed through some long-range telephoto cameras, with men covered from head to toe in white suits, working around a truck. The newscaster was speculating on the reason for the evacuation of the area and the technicians' activities, correctly guessing that it had something to do with the stolen cesium.

Ibrahim watched the activity for several minutes, listening as the commentator tried to fill the air time with words, most of them bringing no clarity to the situation. Then the technicians started removing their hoods and respirators and gather their equipment to leave, apparently failing to find what they were looking for. Disappointed, the commentator wrapped up the broadcast and threw it back to the news station. Ibrahim turned it off, picked up his anonymous cell phone and called his remaining co-conspirator back in Houston.

"Well, my friend, it seems we have been betrayed. What do you know of this?"

"The authorities apparently have looked in five locations for the cesium," Ahmad answered. "Kansas City, Philadelphia, Seattle, Denver, and here in Houston. They found the Philadelphia, Seattle and Houston weapons, but nothing in Denver or Kansas City, as you have seen."

"We have twice been betrayed," Ibrahim said. "Someone has revealed the location of the weapons. And someone has removed at least two of them."

"It can only be the WAR infidels."

"We are certain it was them?"

"Yes, *sayyd*," Ahmad said. "They are the only ones who know besides us."

"What about the two remaining martyrs? Where are they? Could they have told?"

Ahmad answered. "No. They did not know the identities of the drivers, or even their nationality. The team leader knew the destinations, but he is trusted."

"Nevertheless, I want them found and eliminated. We should have done that earlier."

"What are we to do about the other weapons? Should we move them?"

Ibrahim thought for a moment and said, "No. Don't go near them. The authorities might be using these searches as a trick to get us to reveal ourselves. They are no doubt watching the other weapons to see who comes for them. We must focus on the missing one. I want Grainger questioned. Take the plane. Use whatever means are necessary, but find out what he has done."

7.15   FBI FIELD OFFICE, LOUISVILLE, KY

They were back in the secure conference room in the Louisville FBI building – Cal and Ray and Buck plus his team. Another SVTC had been called when it was discovered that two of the cesium containers were empty, and FBI field offices in all of the target areas identified by Ray's program would be on the line. The consensus in Louisville was that if the cesium wasn't in the containers, then it was deployed for detonation and time was running out.

"There's something wrong here," Cal told the group. "If Ray's analysis is correct, then we have two completely separate attacks going on. Yet we're treating them the same. The WAR cesium is in pick-up trucks, and we've been focusing on cargo vans. That's got to change. And why pick-ups? They're totally exposed. Suicide bombs are not WAR's style, and pick-ups wouldn't conceal the preparations, so we're dealing with a different kind of weapon. Maybe not even a bomb. Maybe food or water supplies. Maybe aerial distribution. Maybe the ventilation system of some building. There are just too many possibilities."

"The Seattle device is on its way to the DOE's Pacific Northwest Lab in Richland for examination and should get there by five our time," Buck said. "And the Philadelphia one will get to our lab in four hours or so. We won't know anything until they can open them up and take a look. It will be ten or midnight before we have any information."

"If it is out of the transport containers like in Kansas City," Cal said, "then there's a chance the rad monitors will pick it up. We need everyone on full alert. AMS planes flying and every mobile unit moving."

"Jesus, Bellotta, do you think we're napping or something? Everyone is already on full alert. You can't get any fuller. All we can do is get them looking for white people in pick-up trucks. That should narrow the search down."

Cal didn't respond to Buck's sarcasm because he was right – all of their meager clues had just been vaporized by the discovery of a new weapon configuration and a new transport method to go with their whole new set of suspects. All they had at the moment was ten unknown weapons in ten massive urban target areas. They were back at square one. Even worse, they could hear the clock ticking.

They all sat silent for a few moments, each reflecting on the predicament. Then Cal spoke up.

"Why two weapons? And are there more on the move that we don't know about? I don't get it. What is WAR doing in this, if they are? And how does that change the situation? Islamic terrorists were pretty easy – suicide bombers, one at a time, spread the terror out. But now it looks like multiple bombs. Why? The only reason is to overwhelm our capacity to respond with multiple simultaneous detonations. Make it the Fukushima of dirty bombs – so much damage all at once that the best we can hope for is to contain the disaster. What does that get them?"

"In Japan, it got them a new government," Ray said.

"Of course! A massive disaster with a chaotic and ineffective response brought down the government. With the elections next year, it would mean a sea-change in American politics. And who benefits? Regressives – the whole WAR target audience. We're running around blaming Islami-fascists, bolstering the us-versus-them theme. That's WAR's theme and we're playing right into their hands. Damn, I should have seen this immediately."

"Whoa, slow down, Bellotta," Buck said. "You've just made a huge leap. You're talking about a virtual revolution. Even if you're right, the damage to the country would leave it economically wasted. America would be severely damaged as a world power. What does that get WAR?"

"WAR isn't looking for world domination. They believe that will come naturally through the example of Christianity. They're looking for domestic power. They want to return America to a white, Christian society as an example to the world. They're isolationists to the extreme. What better way than to create a diabolical enemy, an anti-Christ, than to blame it on Muslims. And foreign oil. They want us self-sufficient, so get the government to bomb some innocent Muslim country in a mistaken retribution and hope for another oil embargo. It all just fits."

"Fits what," Buck asked. "Some cartoon version of geopolitics? It ain't that easy to take over the U.S. government. There's another election coming up after this one and another one after that. And no one is electing the Supreme Court. This is a country of law, and that's not going to change because of some terrorist attack, no matter who gets blamed."

"They don't want the whole country any more, Buck. I did some research after Ray came up with his information. Did you ever read *The Turner Diaries*? It is an incredibly vile book about a white, Christian revolution and the massacre of Jews and Blacks. That used to be their bible. But now they've gotten smarter. They don't want the whole country, just a big piece of it. They're trying to get their followers to migrate to the Upper Mid-West, no doubt looking to establish some super-majority and change state laws to their liking. According to Ray's analysis, none of the bombs are going to that region. The closest one would be Denver."

"Once again, this is all just guesswork. Where's some evidence? Some clues? We have two of these devices moved and you jump to a wacko conclusion. Ray's analysis seems to be pretty good so far, but there is nothing in it that is going to convince anyone that when you get high enough in the conspiracy we're not dealing with Islamic terrorists."

"You're right. Ray and I need to get back to IDC and plug this new information into Starlight and see what we come up with. At least some of the cesium is on the move and maybe we can track it. They're probably still using the same batch of credit cards, and we should start looking for transactions from any of them and immediately picking up the user. Try to establish the WAR connection. Come on, Ray. We'll head for the airport and do the SVTC by phone."

Hadi sat in his room in the Blanka House, a small boarding house on 14th Avenue just half a mile east of the campus of the University of British Columbia. Having three days of little else to do but think while he drove the 3,000 mile long route through Canada to get to Vancouver, Hadi had figured out a plan. First, he knew he was living in a cash situation until everything was settled. No credit cards to trace, no hotels with ID requirements, no personal cell phone. He figured the $40,000 would last him over a year, although he had no expectation of having to hide that long. The favorable exchange rate and a modest budget would stretch his cash for as long as possible.

He'd picked the Blanka House as a small, private home run by a retired university professor and his wife. Hadi had told them he was enrolling in UBC in the spring, and while they'd asked for and recorded his Martin Washington ID, he doubted that it would show up on anybody's radar in the university neighborhood, with new faces constantly coming and going. For an additional $400 per month, they included breakfast and dinner, so his subsistence amounted to $900 per month. He needed very little beyond that.

He'd decided to get a lawyer to negotiate a deal, trading his knowledge for his freedom. He'd worked out a plan to justify his role in the cesium theft and make it easier to cut a deal - he was being blackmailed into terrorism. He'd tell them about the events in Afghanistan and about his meeting with the strangers who had recordings of his involvement and threatened to release them unless he helped with the theft. He'd had no idea what they were going to do and was only trying to save himself.

A criminal lawyer, he figured. They would be better informed than an immigration lawyer or some other kind. Other than bringing excessive cash and a gun into Canada unreported, he'd broken no Canadian laws, and he didn't plan on telling anyone about that, anyway. The lawyer was the unknown in the plan. Were they the same as in the U.S., with strict confidentiality? How much of his stake would go as the retainer? And how much would it ultimately cost? He'd spent the morning in the University library, researching all of this and more.

Hadi's requirements for a deal were, he thought, reasonable compared to the value of the information he had. He wasn't trying to make a profit, just get clear of this whole mess and start over again. All he wanted was to disappear, and to do it with a new and legal ID, residence in Canada with a work permit and some plan for citizenship, his legal bills paid, and a modest sum to get him started, say $100,000. The question was whether he had the time and cash to negotiate the deal. The Friday scare at the border reminded him that he'd better get moving or events would neutralize the value of his chips.

Now it was time to stop procrastination-by-research and make the call. Toronto was three hours ahead, so it was already almost 4 PM there. He dialed the number he'd found in his last bit of research — a successful but slightly tarnished criminal lawyer who would be aware of every loophole and probably willing to use them to enhance his reputation once the RDD's were recovered, or detonated.

***

Colin Avery's intercom beeped and he picked up the phone.

"I have a man on the line who won't give me his name but says it is urgent that he talk to you immediately."

It was not unusual for a criminal defense attorney to receive that kind of call, and Colin had gotten his share. Dealing with criminals every day, typically guilty criminals, left him with some tolerance for their paranoia, and a lot of skepticism for their integrity.

"Put him through," Avery told her, and then answered with his standard, "Colin Avery here. How can I help you?"

"I need a criminal lawyer, but first I have some questions."

"All, right, but first I must tell you a couple of things. I understand you won't give your name at this time. That's fine right up until we have a lawyer-client relationship. At that point, I need to know everything about you and your case that I consider relevant. Second, I charge $300 per hour, and I get sixteen hours up front as a retainer. That's $4,800, so you'll need to have the money before I take your case. Do you have that kind of money?"

Colin expected this would be the start of some heartbreaking story and assurances that the money could be gotten very soon if he'd only take the case, and appeals to reduce his rates for this poor, innocent victim of corrupt justice. The negotiation phase of his work. To his surprise, it didn't happen and he suddenly became more interested in his new client.

"The money is no problem," the anonymous caller told him. "I've got cash."

"Legal cash? If your money is the result of the commission of a crime, it will be seized by the authorities and not available to you." *Or me*, Colin thought.

"Yes. My own money. First question, how does lawyer-client privilege work in Canada?"

Colin noted the "in Canada" qualifier and guessed he was talking to a fugitive from the States. Again, something he'd done several times before.

"Just like in the U.S.," Colin answered. "Once I am your attorney-of-record, anything you tell me is privileged and I cannot divulge it."

"What about the public safety exception?"

So, the guy had done his homework. "As you apparently know, our Supreme Court has ruled that in instances where there is an imminent threat of bodily harm to any person or group, privilege can be disregarded. Note that I said 'can be.' The rules are somewhat ambiguous in most cases, and it is left to the discretion of the attorney."

There was silence at the other end, and Colin let it continue, again familiar with his clients' need to think things through. After several moments passed, the caller said, "I don't think there will be any ambiguity here. The threat clearly exists."

"Are you making the threat?"

"No. I'm not involved. Not anymore, anyway. But I have information about it."

"Well, that's easy enough. I can provide the authorities with the threat information and keep you totally uninvolved."

"No. You can't do that. Not just yet, anyway. OK, so what do we need to do to make you my lawyer?"

"You need to come to my office so we can meet and discuss your case and you can pay the retainer."

"No. I can't come there until I'm certain that, uh, things are safe."

Colin noted that a lot of the caller's sentences started with 'no' and figured he would earn his full rate on this case, whatever it was.

"Here's the deal," the caller continued. "I'm a fugitive from the U.S. and I'm here in Canada, and I need an attorney to negotiate with the U.S. authorities to cut a deal for me. Can you do that?"

"Of course. Any deal will depend on whom we're dealing with and the severity of your crime and the value of the information you have to trade. I assume we're talking about you knowing someone higher up in this crime, whatever it is, and you're willing to trade this person for some reduced sentence."

"No, it's nothing like that."

Again, there was a pause, much longer this time.

"OK, so here's the thing," the caller finally said. "You know about the dirty bombs going off in America? Well, I was part of the team that stole the cesium in the first place."

Colin went rigid. This was possibly the greatest prosecutable crime in modern history that didn't include some warlord somewhere committing genocide. It would certainly be the biggest crime any Canadian lawyer ever handled, and it was his. At that moment, the caller could have gotten Colin to pay him to give him the case. Of course, he didn't say that. Instead, he just said "Go on," as calmly as possible.

"I'm not some terrorist. The people who did this have something on me, something big, and I had to help them. Now I think they want me dead. Everyone else involved is dead already, I think, so I need to disappear. I need you to go to the FBI or whoever is after me and cut a deal. Can you do that?"

"Yes, of course. Tell me what you want and what you have to offer."

"I can give them the cesium. Not the actual cesium, but I've got information identifying all the vehicles that were used. With that, they can find the trucks and the cesium and whoever is behind this. I want a new identity, one that is valid here in Canada with a work visa and the possibility of citizenship. I want immunity from both the cesium theft and any dirty bomb explosions and all other crimes. And I want $100,000 seed money to get started again. Oh, and I want them to pay your bills."

"What is this other crime that was used to coerce you into helping to steal the cesium?"

Avery listened to a short and, he was sure, sanitized version of the terrible events that went on in Afghanistan.

"That last one is going to be hard, I expect. You're maybe talking treason. Your Marines are not going to take that lightly. I'm not sure they even can pardon something like that."

"The President can pardon any damn thing he wants. No one even knows there was anything in Afghanistan. And each and every one of those guys was a murderer. I just saved the Marines the trouble of prosecuting them. How many people will die if those cesium bombs go off? How many billions of dollars will it cost? You tell them that I'm giving this up cheap because I'm an American, and I didn't intend to hurt anyone who didn't deserve it. You get through to the President if you have to and you let him know that I want to tell them where it is. I really do. I just need some protection. You tell them that. And you tell them there isn't much time."

"Do you know when the bombs are set to go off?"

"Not exactly, but I've got a good guess."

"All right, I'll take the case and as of this moment, I'm your attorney and everything we've discussed or will discuss is privileged. We can actually get around the Public Safety exception if you don't tell me where and when. I can't tell them if I don't know. You need to come here and we'll get your statement on paper and I'll start making contacts right away."

"No. I'm not coming in. Like you said, you can't tell what you don't know, and right now you don't know who I am or where I am."

"I have to get your statement, and it has to include details that only some-one in on the theft would know. And it has to convince the authorities that you really can deliver the locations. My secretary can take it and type it up for you to read, but you have to do that here."

"I said no. You and your secretary get whatever you need to do this and I'll call you back with instructions. I'm not taking any chances. I'll write it up and sign it and send it to you. You be ready at eight o'clock tomorrow morning. I'll call you then."

Then line went dead, and Colin considered dancing a jig. Instead, he pressed the intercom button and said, "Pauline, come in here and bring your pad. We've got some work to do."

7.17 U.S. Army Information Dominance Center, Ft. Belvoir, VA

The flight to Davison Air Force Base, three miles from Ft. Belvoir, had taken just over two hours in the twin-Beech, all of it spent with Cal and Ray huddled over Ray's laptop as they tried to analyze the new situation and revise Ray's algorithms to accommodate it. Ray uploaded the revised algorithms as they neared the base and Starlight would be well into revising and expanding Ray's previous analysis by the time they got there. Even so, it would be hours before they had any results.

Once they'd arrived at the IDC, they had focused the revised search on the same set of credit cards, but this time changed the nexus to the cities previously identified by Ray as the destination for the cesium, leaving out the three where the cesium had been recovered. The time frame was changed to the period after the initial cesium delivery to those cities. The final change was to look for diesel fuel purchases after learning that the owner of Maloney's, the storage point for the cesium, had disappeared and one of the staff reported that a standard 40-foot tractor-trailer had come by a week earlier and loaded the containers and left.

The results came through just minutes before the scheduled start of the regular evening SVTC, and they were clear, and confusing.

Pamela Hastings, the SAC of the Washington, D.C. Field Office, kicked the meeting off with a report on the search for the cesium bombs identified so far. By now, nine of the drivers had been picked up for interrogation, including the two co-drivers identified by the Philadelphia and Seattle suspects who had been caught in the initial sweep.

"Additionally, I have some more good news," Hastings said. "We've picked up a Gerald G. Jeffers and his twin brother George G. Jeffers in Detroit. They were identified in the initial list of suspects but eluded surveillance until today. Eluded might be too strong a word for these idiots. We found them at the Toy Chest, a Detroit strip joint, running up a tab on another of the stolen credit cards. And yes, their full names are Gerald George and George Gerald Jeffers. They gave up the location of the cesium and teams are on their way to the scene. We should score another recovery very shortly."

"It won't be there," Cal said over the audio system via his secure cell phone.

Hastings's head snapped up at the interruption. "Who is that? And what are you talking about?"

"It's Cal Bellotta from DHS. I'm at the IDC with Ray Nassiri. We've just this minute gotten the results of the new transportation analysis from Starlight. The Detroit cesium has been moved, along with the Kansas City and Denver devices. And we're going to find …"

"Hold on a minute, Bellotta," Hastings said. "What new transportation analysis?"

"Sorry. Ray and I met with Buck Buchanan and his team earlier today and reviewed the new information about the missing cesium. Ray and I took that information to IDC and ran a new search. It's turned up a clear track, although there are some unanticipated complications. In addition to Kansas City, we expect to find missing devices in Denver, and Detroit. It appears they were headed east with the likely destination of Baltimore or Washington."

There was a long silence while everyone absorbed this news.

"Hello," Cal said, thinking he might have been cut off.

"We're here," Hastings answered. "This is an extension of the search you did that turned up the suspects we have? Same reliability?"

"Yes. We just added the new locations and timing. We got a clear track, one-way only with sequential stops in all three cities. The new twist is that they used diesel fuel, so we're dealing with a new mode of transportation."

"The other surprise," Cal continued, "is that there were no identifiable personal transactions. No cell phones, no credit card purchases, nothing. These were much more disciplined drivers, and we have nothing to go on to identify them."

"What about the WAR connection you speculated on in the initial analysis," someone asked. "Did you find anything there?"

"No," Cal answered. "As I said, there were no personal transactions, and no identified WAR operatives have turned up as possibilities – no one dropping off the grid, no sightings. We're at a dead end for the moment."

"The WAR connection was always tenuous," Hastings said. "I still don't believe they are actively involved in this. We've got some very clever and well-financed terrorists who have managed to recruit a bunch of dupes to do their dirty work. You're bound to find crackpot affiliations with the kind of people they would recruit for this."

"I don't agree," Cal responded. "The evidence is clear and close to 100%. This is not some of the drivers, this is all of them."

"Not true," Hastings said. "None of these people have acknowledged any WAR connection or direction. Not even the ones who gave up their partners and the devices. And most of the connections are very loose and we haven't established any WAR connection for these two brothers. And, of course, we have nine middle-eastern terrorists who set off the first round of weapons. The WAR thing is coincidence, and we don't have the resources to spend a lot of effort investigating militias and rednecks."

Cal stepped back from the conversation at that point, unwilling to engage in a debate he couldn't win, certainly not over the phone. The consensus among the law enforcement people in the meeting seemed to agree with Hastings, anyway. Cal did get support from an unexpected source.

"Don't be so quick to discount these guys," Buchanan interjected. "We've looked into the background of the ones we've identified, and they are not all a bunch of ignorant jerks. I'm not totally buying into this WAR theory, either, but we can't ignore it. And if anyone gets a hint of WAR fingerprints on any lead, you should be taking an especially hard look at it."

Not a ringing endorsement, but Cal was willing to take any support he could get.

7.18 CNN News Headquarters, Atlanta, GA

Good evening. This is Laurie Chapin at the news desk and our top story tonight is the apparent recovery of some of the stolen cesium that has been terrifying Americans for the past thirteen days.

Today, State and Federal authorities at five sites around the country evacuated residents and sent teams of white-suited technicians into these areas in search of the missing cesium. At three locations, Philadelphia, Houston, and Seattle, specialized handling and transport equipment was brought in after the technicians made their sweep, indicating they found and removed something. In the other two locations, Kansas City and Denver, the disappointed technicians appeared to have came away empty-handed.

Our sources tell CNN that some cesium was safely recovered, but there is still an unspecified amount out there.

In an exclusive report, CNN was also told by highly-placed sources that the locations were identified by a special team from the Department of Homeland Security and the Army's Information Dominance Center. The team, led by this man, Calogero Bellotta, has been using some new and unspecified techniques to identify the locations of the cesium. We do not know if these techniques involve some new radiation measuring technology or some other method, but they are apparently successful at least half the time.

In other news …

7.19 FBI Radiation Forensics Laboratory, Quantico, VA

In a new building, identified only as R-41, located at the edge of the Quantico site, Dr. Anton Gerlach directed the technician driving the RCTV, the Remotely Controlled Transport Vehicle, used to move highly radioactive material. Cameras were mounted on it and all around the factory floor, as the staff called the large area housing various stations, displayed its position on multiple screens on the technician's displays. Other cameras, mounted on small, tracked robots, could scoot around at his direction to provide virtually any view of the vehicle and its cargo.

Today, or rather tonight, the cargo was a standard 55-gallon drum recently removed from the shipping cask that had brought it to the Radiological Forensics Laboratory from Philadelphia, where it had been found earlier in the day. RadFL had been designed and built by experts hired away from several of the Department of Energy national labs – Sandia in New Mexico, Brookhaven on Long Island, Lawrence Livermore in California – to incorporate the latest and best technology in radiological forensics in a secure and single-purpose facility: examining radiological weapons and the debris left from their use. A sample from any nuclear device could be analyzed and within hours law enforcement would know from what specific reactor in any country in the world the material had originated, and even when it was produced. A cesium sample such as the one they were about to analyze could be broken down, its contaminants analyzed, and its age and origin predicted with amazing accuracy.

Before any of that could be done, each and every device had to be cleared of conventional weapons, the explosives that were there to make the weapon effective. Then their jobs became even harder when the RadFL technicians detected trace organics in the drum, organics not associated with the oil that had been used to hide the device, but with whatever was present to make it go *boom*. That meant delays while they did additional imaging and robotic searches to discover just where it was and what it would do and how it would be made to do it and most importantly, how to make sure it didn't do it.

What they discovered was a fairly sophisticated two-stage weapon, essentially a home-made fireworks mortar and projectile. The first stage was a cardboard cylinder packed with gunpowder meant to launch the payload vertically, like a mortar. The second, the cesium jar and an accelerometer set to start measuring motion with the launch. When the motion stopped, like at the apex of the short flight of the projectile as it transitioned from rising to falling, a circuit closed and the 9-volt battery charged the detonator, and forty-nine grams of semtex encased in a tight paper wrap with the jar, blew the projectile into splinters and spread the cesium into an approximately 60-foot plume, ready for whatever force, wind or gravity, to spread it around its target zone. The triggering mechanism was a cell phone inside the lead shield and connected to a single copper wire ran out the top plug to serve as an antenna because the lead shielded the radiation trying to get out, and the cell signal trying to get in.

Dr. Gerlach's first call was an urgent one to his colleague at the DOE's Pacific Northwest Laboratories where the other captured device was taken for examination. *Leave it in the shipping cask,* were his instructions, where it would be protected from the cell phone call that would detonate it.

His second call was to the SIOC, letting them know they had a problem. And also a very large clue about the date and time of the planned attacks.

7.20 BROOKHOLLOW MARRIOTT COURTYARD HOTEL, HOUSTON, TX

After his meeting with Marcus, the three-hour drive from San Antonio to Houston had been Stully Lennock's time to relax before the business at hand. He loved everything about Texas, even the flat, featureless scrub of the drive to Houston. Now, at the desk in his room at the Brookhollow Marriott

Courtyard, he scanned social networks from his laptop computer, making occasional notes.

Stully and Marcus had never left the airport in San Antonio. Instead, they'd found a quiet conference room in the United Airlines Club Lounge and reviewed the information Stully needed. He knew Tag only called him when the job was difficult and important, both indicators that it was beyond the limited capabilities of his own troops, and that always meant a generous payoff. Even by those standards, this job was a doozy. A foreign national, a diplomat, royalty no less, on the run, whereabouts unknown, and the job to be completed by Saturday. It was a good thing price had not been an object.

Finding lone fugitives was never easy, and often impossible. Finding someone on the run with a family in tow was less challenging, especially with teenagers involved. Short of binding and gagging them, there was no way to keep hormone-addled children undercover. To them, their friends just *had* to know where they were and what they were doing, and they somehow never understood any threat unless it was right there, right now, with no ambiguity. Their friends not knowing everything that was going on was a matter of life and death. Stully chuckled to himself. This time it would be true.

So finding the 16-year-old daughter, Laila, on Facebook and Twitter had not been much of a challenge. Discovering she had a secret boyfriend was a little more difficult, but she was a high-school girl in America surrounded by every manner of Western influence at her co-ed private school, so he reasoned there had to be one. The real problem had been discovering his identity, and when he narrowed it down to one prime suspect, he still wasn't sure he was right. The 18-year-old son of a French diplomat dating the daughter of a Muslim who wore a *hijab*, the traditional head veil, seemed unlikely.

So now it was a matter of getting to Houston as quickly as possible and having a reasonable conversation with the boy. Or an unreasonable one, if that was what it took.

7.21   BLANKA HOUSE, VANCOUVER, BC, CANADA

Hadi sat in the one comfortable chair in his room, watching the news and wondering how they had found the two trucks. He checked his mental list and recalled that they were the first and eleventh trucks, which knowledge did nothing to improve his mood. *They're finding them without me*, he thought.

He booted up the used laptop he'd bought cheap from a student who was upgrading and then loaded his Internet browser and did a search for Calogero Bellotta. He was glad it was an uncommon name and found that almost all of the many hits were about his guy, this Fed with some kind of magic cesium-finding machine.

The background on Bellotta was different than Hadi had expected. He wasn't some physicist who'd maybe invented a new detector, and he wasn't an investigator or even a full-time Fed. He was an ex-military intelligence agent who'd studied terrorists and WMD, and was now a consultant for DHS. His education was a PhD in national security, not nuclear physics.

A profile in something called *The Bay Times* placed his home in Stevensville, Maryland, and on an impulse Hadi looked up his phone number. Letting the impulse carry him along, he dialed it on his anonymous cell phone, not even thinking that it was after 10 PM on the East Coast.

"Hello?" A woman answered, some slight anxiety in her voice.

"Hello," Hadi answered. "I'm sorry to bother you so late, but I need to speak to Calogero Bellotta right away."

"Cal? He's not here at the moment. Can I take a message?"

"No, he won't be able to reach me."

Hadi paused, trying to figure out how to reach Bellotta without leaving any trace of where he was.

"Sorry," he said, breaking the silence. "Actually you can take a message, and if you have some way of reaching him, it is very important that we talk as soon as possible. Please tell him that I left the cigarette in the hot cell at Pastor. He should know what that means. And please tell him to give you a phone number where I can call him right now. I'll call you back in half an hour to get the number. Thanks."

Hadi hung up before she could protest, figuring he didn't want to give her an opportunity to delay. And then he looked at his watch and started pacing the small room.

***

He stood and watched the seconds count down to zero and then dialed Bellotta's phone number. The woman answered and told him a number and said that Bellotta was waiting for the call. Hadi said goodbye and hung up.

He sat in the chair and considered his situation one more time. He wasn't sure what was compelling him to call Bellotta beyond some panic that this guy held the key to Hadi's survival. How was he finding the cesium? Would Hadi's information make a difference? Was it still worth the freedom he was negotiating for?

Shit, he thought, and dialed the number.

***

Cal answered on the first ring. "This is Cal Bellotta. Who am I talking to?"

"You will likely know me as Hadi. Are you alone? Is anyone listening on this line?"

"No," Cal lied, "I'm in my hotel room getting ready for bed. Who are you and how do you know about the cigarette?"

Around him in the conference room at the Information Dominance Center, technicians watched monitors and quietly tapped keys and watched the monitors some more.

"I know about the cigarette because I planted it there. It was a Morven Gold, smoked down to a butt about ¾ of an inch. Does that convince you that I was there, at Pastor, when the cesium was taken?"

"Yes."

"Good. How did you find the cesium in Philadelphia and Seattle today?"

"Listen, Mr. Hadi, I can't tell you anything about that. Why did you call me?"

"I saw you on the news. My lawyer will be contacting the FBI tomorrow to discuss a deal. I know how to find all of the cesium. There are still ten devices you haven't found, and time is running out. I want you in on the discussions with the FBI and whoever else. I'll tell my lawyer to make sure you're included."

The line went dead, and the technician said, "Vancouver, British Columbia. That's as close as I got."

Buck Buchanan, listening on a secure line, said, "Let's make contact with the RCMP and get some teams deployed there. We'll want to move fast when we hear from him again. Bellotta, you and I are going to Vancouver."

THURSDAY, JULY 1

7.22   CNN NEWS HEADQUARTERS, ATLANTA, GA

 **AMERICAN HATE GROUPS COME UNDER SCRUTINY**

MILITIAS AND SKINHEAD GROUPS GROW IN SIZE AND THREAT

ATLANTA (CNNNational.com) -- The Southern Poverty Law Center recommended today that the emerging profile and detention laws directed at radical American Muslims be extended to domestic hate groups. The SLPC reports that there are currently over one thousand domestic hate groups operating across the country, including neo-Nazis, Klansmen, white nationalists, neo-confederates, racist skinheads, black separatists, and border vigilantes. Leaks from the on-going search for the missing cesium have indicated members of these groups may be involved. The FBI has consistently declined to comment on this possibility.

7.23   GRAINGER RESIDENCE, FRENCHTOWN, MT

Tag was awake when the men entered his bedroom at about three in the morning. It was very difficult to sleep breathing bottled air through a face mask. But the alternative was to breathe the 3-quinuclidinyl benzilate being pumped throughout the house via the central air conditioning system. The gas, abbreviated QNB, was a military incapacitating agent, and even in the high concentrations being used, it took several minutes to take effect. So Tag feigned sleep while the intruders practiced stealth and inhaled enough to be effective.

Tag knew that Ibrahim's agents would be sensing warm skin and dry mouth from the QNB, but would probably ignore these as they focused on their target – him. They would be getting drowsy soon, then confused, and finally unconscious. These last two symptoms wouldn't happen before the intruders got Tag out from under the covers and discovered the breathing apparatus and realized they had been ambushed, so he had a silenced pistol in case they reacted badly.

The alert had come several hours earlier when the control tower at Missoula International Airport was notified that a private jet was inbound and would be arriving after normal operating hours. The airport served just ten commercial flights each day, with none crossing sovereign borders, so the "international" appellation was a bit of municipal vanity. Johnson Field was how the locals referred to it.

The night-shift air traffic controllers – there were only three of them working in a rotation – knew that such unusual activity required notification of the airport manager. He, in turn, knew to give Tag an off-the-record call.

Tag had the sheet over his head when the light went on, trying to delay discovery every additional second possible.

"Mr. Grainger," the familiar voice of the same man Ibrahim had previously sent said. "Please get up slowly and show us your empty hands. There are three of us, all armed, in the room, and two more outside in the hall. I am not underestimating you this time. You have no chance, so please follow my directions. Let us not have a repeat of our previous misunderstanding."

When there was no reaction, he nodded to one of the men who carefully removed the sheet covering Tag. When he lifted it off of Tag's head, he saw the breathing apparatus. He stared for a moment, trying to understand. When he did, he gasped audibly and leapt back, as if Tag were contagious. The leader saw and understood and spoke rapidly in Arabic.

"Everyone out! Quickly! It is a trap."

When they tried to move, they looked like weights had been added to their legs and arms. Everything was in slow motion, and got progressively slower. The first to collapse was the one who had uncovered Tag's head, and he was quickly followed by the other four. Only then did Tag move.

He got up and went to the thermostat, shutting down the fan, and then to the basement to secure the gas cylinder. Still carrying his breathing air, he opened the front door and started opening all of the windows, allowing the gas to dissipate, and then turned the fan back on to be sure no pockets remained in the ventilation system. Finally, he went outside before removing his mask. He was joined on the front lawn by three other men.

"Give it a few more minutes. Go ahead and back the van up to the garage. Leave the lights off," Tag told one of the men.

When Tag felt enough time had passed, they all went into the house and began carrying unconscious Arabs through the garage, putting them in the back of the cargo van. Added to the fifteen bodies they'd dropped there earlier, the bears and wolves and scavengers of Argosy Mountain would be well fed this day.

7.24   FBI FIELD OFFICE, BOSTON, MA

It was 2:04 AM when the FBI agent entered the perfectly square and totally empty interrogation room. No furniture, no windows, no pictures or signs, just Frank Healy curled up and asleep on the cold linoleum floor where he'd been since the last interrogation sixty-three minutes earlier. The agent pushed a nice leather desk chair into the room, kicked Healy on the bottom of his foot knowing that without shoes to absorb any of the shock, Healy would be fully awake.

"Hey, Frank. Did I wake you?"

Healy jerked into a sitting position on the floor, and quickly regained his tough-guy demeanor. The agent sat down and opened the file he had put on the seat of the chair.

"Don't get up. I've got a couple of things to go over with you," the agent continued as he scanned some documents. "Let's see, you've been having a run of bad luck lately, haven't you? Wife left you last year, took the kids. You still get visitation, right? No, wait, I see here that was cancelled. Just today, in fact. Guess they won't be seeing you while you're in Lewisburg. That's got to be 400 miles from here. But wait, they were evicted today, so they'll probably be moving back to her mother's in Pittsfield. That'll cut a hundred miles off the trip. Yeah, but that's still too long a drive to expect them to make just for an hour to chat with Dad by telephone through some thick glass window. And the expense! Gas, hotel, meals. Your wife will probably be waiting tables at some greasy spoon so there won't be a lot of cash for the trip.

"Speaking of moms, what's *yours* going to do without that check you send her every month? Social Security isn't gonna cover the rent, you know. Suppose she'll move in with your brother and his wife and kids out in Dedham? They don't really have the space, I see, but maybe the kids can double-up and she can have one of their rooms. Stairs will be tough on her knees. I see that Medicare has been taking care of the orthopedic bills. Hope nothing happens to that.

"Oh jeez, this doesn't look good. Frank Junior busted for selling crack? That's gonna be twelve to fifteen in Danbury. Guess you won't be getting to see him after all. Oh, wait. I'm sorry, that doesn't happen until Saturday. And it looks like they're calling the loan on your bar on Monday. Fucking banks.

"You got anything to say?"

Healy just glared at the agent with undisguised hatred. And then he spit on the floor at the agent's feet and lay back down.

"OK, Frank. I tried. Gave it my best shot. We're cutting you loose."

Without getting up, Healy turned his head to face the agent.

"Yeah, it's out of our hands now. Some guys will be coming to pick you up in about …" the agent glanced at his watch, "… twenty minutes. That's all I know. You're off our books at that point. Questioned and released. 'Sorry, Mrs. Healy, we haven't seen him since he got into that black van with those guys in black hoods.' Good luck, Frank."

With that, the agent stood, dropped the file back on the chair seat, and left, pushing it like a shopping cart out the door.

***

Frank Healy knew they were bluffing. He'd been arrested and questioned and released enough times to know the drill. The good cop was gone, and now some asshole Feeb would come in and play bad cop. Didn't matter to Frank. He'd never squealed before, and he wasn't starting now.

So when the door burst open and three large men entered, carrying automatic weapons and dressed from head to toe in black with only eyes and mouth showing, he was surprised. When they picked him up without a word and threw him against the wall, cracking his forehead in the process and quickly blinding his left eye from the blood flow, he realized he was in new territory as far as bad cops went.

They pulled the plastic cuffs on so tight it cut off circulation to his hands and then two of them dragged him down the hall while the other trailed behind. Every time Frank gained his footing and tried to walk, the man behind kicked his feet out from under him. No one even glanced at them, like they didn't exist. They continued to drag him to a back door and out into a dark parking lot. A black cargo van was parked with its open rear doors facing them. The men threw him in, and one climbed in with him, taking a seat in the lone chair. The other two got into the front cab and drove the van away.

Frank considered this entirely new experience for what he thought must have been hours while they drove in silence. His curiosity finally got the better of him, and he asked, "Where are you taking me?"

The man answered by breaking his leg with the butt of his rifle.

Frank screamed in pain until the man raised the rifle again, and Frank shut up, biting his lip to hold back the sounds.

When the van finally stopped, the two men in front came around and opened the doors. In the pre-dawn light, Frank could make out parallel worn tracks that substituted for a road into some forest. They went through Frank's pockets and removed everything and then dragged Frank out and threw him to the ground. Two stood back while the third, leisurely holding his weapon, said, "Last chance, Frank. Where's the cesium? Who is your partner?"

Frank reverted to form when confronted by a cop and said, "You can't do this to me. I know my rights. You guys are going to an awful lot of trouble to play bad cop. My lawyer will have *you* in jail. Shit, you broke my leg. That's police brutality."

"You mean that leg," the man asked as he swung his weapon up and shot Frank in the knee.

Frank screamed and screamed, trying to hold his knee in place with his hands while he squirmed on the forest floor.

"We're in the Mt. Kearsarge State Forest, Frank. The only living creatures that can hear you will be wanting to eat you as soon as we leave. But you'll be dead by then, so you won't notice. You're a terrorist, Frank. A terrorist with his finger on the trigger of a weapon of mass destruction. We can do any goddam thing we want to you. We are accountable to no one. Do you hear me, Frank? No one. Now, where is the cesium? Who is your partner?"

Frank continued to moan and roll back and forth.

"Frank, listen to me. Answer the questions or we're out of here, without you."

"Jesus Christ, all right. It's in a silver pickup truck at Leeds Demolition on Ellery Street, near the tracks. The drums are covered with a tarp. The other driver is Art Fogarty. He's a Southie, too, that's all I know about him. We never met before the trip, and I haven't seen him since."

"What's he look like?"

"Jesus, I don't know. My size, maybe five-ten. Heavy, going bald and has a bushy moustache. Probably 35 or so. Tattoos on both arms. Dragons or some such shit."

"OK, Frank. That's good stuff. We've got a chopper on the way to check out the truck. If it's like you say, we're done here. Thirty minutes, tops."

"Do something about my leg," Frank shouted. "I'm bleeding to death."

The man nodded and one of the others went to the van and came back with a fishing tackle box. He took out a spray bottle and liberally coated Frank's wound and then placed a very thick pad over. "Hold that," he told Frank and then wrapped the pad tightly in place with a gauze bandage that stuck to itself like Velcro.

The man returned to his previous position and all three just stood there, watching Frank continue to writhe and listening to him moan. Then a cell phone rang and the leader answered and listened.

"Good job, Frank. My guys report they found traces of radiation around the drum, so I guess you weren't lying."

"See? I told …"

That was the last thing Frank said before the leader shot him in the head.

Part Eight – The Search

Ibrahim arose at his customary 6 AM, 6:30 actually with the crazy Maracaibo time, and prepared for an eventful day. He intentionally took his time, anticipating the interrogation of Grainger and the satisfaction that would bring. He only wished he could be there when the old man broke. At the same time, he worried about just what Grainger had done to betray them, and what he would need to do to repair the damage. His concern was that the plan would fail, and revenge for the murder of bin Laden would have to wait, and he would have to orchestrate it from somewhere else, somewhere much less comfortable.

He went to his office suite and ordered *al-Qahwa*, traditional Saudi coffee, from room service. Once it was delivered and he was alone, he dialed the cell phone of Roshan, the leader of the team he'd dispatched to bring in Grainger.

"Shalom," a strange voice answered. "Mah shlomcha?"

Ibrahim knew enough Hebrew to answer. "I am fine, thank you. Who am I speaking to?"

"Ibrahim? Is that you? It's Tag. Sorry, just a little joke on my part. What can I do for you?"

The rage that erupted in Ibrahim's head and the pain in his heart were not evident on his face nor in his voice. He knew instantly that his men were dead, and once again he had underestimated Grainger and his band of infidels.

"I was calling to inquire about our little problem."

"You mean the traitor problem?"

"Yes. I seem to have a similar one. I was hoping that we could salvage the situation, but I guess that is no longer an option."

"You're right there, Ibrahim old boy. The, uhh, situation got a little out of control when you betrayed my men to the authorities. Twenty-four good Americans, dead or in custody. I don't think we're going to salvage that."

That was news to Ibrahim. Grainger's teams had all been killed or captured? How? The news had not mentioned that, nor had his surveillance teams.

"I did not know that. I am sorry for those people, but I had nothing to do with it. As you know, our mutual interest was in their anonymity. My concern is with the packages they had delivered. It seems some have gone missing, and I thought you might know where they could be found."

"Have you got a tracking number on those? No, I suppose not. I'm afraid I won't be able to help you, then."

"You understand that I am a diplomat, and as such I enjoy certain privileges. Among them, immunity from prosecution. What privileges do you have?"

"Well, let's see. I have the privilege of being an American. I have the privilege of being surrounded by other Americans who will do my bidding for the good of the country. And I have the privilege of freedom of movement. Things get moved, Ibby. But don't worry. The packages will reach their optimum destinations. I'll see to that. You watch out for yourself, boy. It's a dangerous world out there."

The phone went dead. And, Ibrahim knew, so did his plan.

8.02   THE BRITISH SCHOOL, HOUSTON, TX

The campus of The British School was large and open, making surveillance difficult while maintaining any stealth. After walking the perimeter, Stully selected the far corner of the running track and athletic field on the northwest corner of the school. His car was parked on Pinon Drive which dead-ended about twenty feet from the track.

Sitting in his car, facing away from the school and aimed for a quick escape, he texted Alain DeLotte using the cell phone number the boy had foolishly posted on Facebook. "Meet me at the corner of the track," it read. "I have important news about Laila." He didn't sign it and a callback to the cell phone would get a message from an unnamed young female asking the caller to leave a message. Stully figured it might be a wait until the boy could find an excuse to leave class, but he underestimated the ingenuity of a hormone-driven high-school boy, and within minutes he saw a tall, thin young man jogging across the soccer field in his rear-view mirror.

The boy slowed as he got closer, looking around and even turning his whole body, briefly walking backwards, scanning the area. Stully got out of his car and walked toward the boy, calling out, "Alain DeLotte?"

The boy's head swung to Stully and he stopped and said, "Yes. Who are you? Is Laila all right?"

Stully pulled out his wallet and opened it like it was some official identification, holding it up with his left hand as he approached, being as non-threatening as possible so the boy wouldn't flee. After having watched his easy gait across the field, Stully doubted he could catch him if he did.

"I'm Paul Hendricks from the State Department. Sorry for the subterfuge, but I needed to talk to you privately without alerting the school. Laila is fine as far as we know," Stully continued as he put his wallet away, as if he was done with it even though there was no chance the boy could have inspected it from that distance. "We received a rather odd message from her mentioning some danger to you and we're investigating quietly. That's why I didn't want to go through school channels."

Stully stopped in front of Alain. "Would you please come with me? We'll only be a few moments and then you can get back to class."

"Come with you where? What do you mean she sent a message about me? Why didn't she call?"

Alain stopped talking when Stully used his left hand to pull his jacket open, revealing the Glock in his shoulder holster, and said, "Just come with me and Laila will be fine. Don't do anything stupid or you and she will both regret it."

Alain considered that for a moment and, summoning his teenage bravado, said, "I'm not going anywhere with you, man. You're not gonna use that on me. I have diplomatic immunity."

Stully didn't say anything, just stared into Alain's eyes. Without moving his gaze from Alain, he reached with his right hand into his jacket and removed the silenced Glock. As he brought it out, he chambered a round using the slide and shot the ground less than half an inch from Alain's right heel.

Alain leaped back. "Fuck, man, are you crazy?"

"Come with me or the next one takes off your toe. No more soccer, excuse me, *football*, for you after that."

"Yeah, OK. You're really fucked, you know that, man? My dad will have you in the Bastille for this."

Stully didn't respond. He just used his left hand to point to his car while he holstered the Glock.

Alain walked the short distance, looking back over his shoulder at Stully every step or two. At the rented car, Stully secured Alain to the grab bar on the door using plastic cable-tie handcuffs. When Stully got behind the wheel, Alain started to protest again. Stully simply put his finger to his lips and said "Shh." The ten-minute trip to Diehl Road passed in silence.

When they got to a mailbox on the right marked 6234, Stully turned left, following a rutted path with some thick woods on his right and an empty field on the left. The path was meant for the overhead cables held up by poles every sixty feet or so. The rental bucked and banged, not designed for this kind of abuse, but Stully wasn't concerned. It wasn't his.

About 200 feet in, the field on the left gave way to woods, and Stully stopped the car, now hardly visible from Diehl Road behind it or the Lost Forest Tennis Club, another 200 feet in front.

"OK, let's talk," Stully said. "But first, I'm gonna empty your pockets."

In them, Stully found key ring with a BMW key, standard door key, and what looked like a key to a locker. He also found a wallet, a cell phone, and some change. He looked through the wallet and checked the cell phone and then turned back to Alain.

"OK, good so far. Now, where is Laila and her family?"

"I don't know, man. We haven't talked since before she left. I just got a quick text from her saying she'd be away for a few days and wouldn't be able to call me. That's why I came so quickly when I got your message."

Stully stared for a moment and then took out the Glock. Alain lost his earlier attitude and pulled away, crowding the door.

"I'm serious, man. I don't know!"

In one motion, Stully flipped the gun and caught it by the barrel, swinging it down like a hammer until the hand grip slammed into Alain's kneecap. Alain screamed in pain.

"Shut up, or I'll do it again, but harder," Stully said as he turned on the Smartphone and went to the call directory. He was telling the truth - there were no calls from the girl.

Next, Stully went to the text message list and scanned down. It seemed like every other one was from "l0v3@l@1n', with the most recent just two hours earlier. He set the phone down and picked up the gun and again hammered Alain's knee. Trying to shut up, Alain's screams were mostly gags and retches.

"Lovealain, I'm guessing. Not the most original nickname, but it sure makes my job easy. Here's the deal, Alain. I don't have any interest in your Laila. My business is with her father, but of course I don't know where he is. That's all I want from you. Where is she?"

Alain was still groaning and gently flexing his knee to see if it worked. After several moments of no answer, Stully picked up the gun again, but before he could use it, Alain whimpered, "Wait. You'll find out anyway. It's in her texts. She's in Venezuela. Maracaibo.

"In the texts, eh? Well, let's just check that."

Stully searched the text messages and scanned the ones from the nickname. Sure enough, she was at the Hotel Kristoff with her family.

"Not too bright of her old man to let her text like this when he's trying to hide."

"He doesn't know about the phone. I gave it to her so they couldn't monitor our calls. Her parents don't approve of me because I'm not Muslim."

Stully scanned through the texts to see if there was anything that would help him.

"Says here that your parents are away this weekend and you're thinking of going to see her. Who are you staying with?"

"Staying with? I'm staying at home with myself. What did you think? I'd have a babysitter?"

"Are your parents home now?"

"No, they're in France all week."

"How do you get to school?"

"Hey, man, who do you think I am? I'm eighteen. I don't need anybody to get me to school. I drive my car."

"What kind of car?"

"It's a red BMW convertible. 320i."

"Nice car. What are your user ID's and passwords for all your social accounts? Facebook, Twitter, all of them."

Stully opened his Samsung tablet and went to each site as Alain told him the access information. At each one, he changed the ID and password to his own. When he was satisfied, he shut down the tablet.

"All right, kid, I'm gonna let you go now. There's plenty of places nearby where you can go and call the cops, but if you do, I'm gonna develop an interest in your little Laila that you're gonna wish never happened. Got that? If you think the police will find me before I'm disappeared, then go ahead and call. But let me tell you, they ain't gonna find me. I'm a pro, kid. I do this for a living. Ten minutes and this car is history and I'm in something else and gone. So, you want to risk little Laila on the cops being better than me, go ahead. It'll give me some sport when I get to Venezuela."

Stully took his SOG Trident folding knife out of his pocket and Alain cringed. But Stully just cut the plastic cuffs and said, "OK, kid. Go. Straight ahead. Don't look back. Have a nice life and I'll give Laila your regards when I see her. You be cool and that's all I'll give her."

Alain fumbled a little with the unfamiliar door handle but got it open and almost fell in his haste to get out. He started down the path at a fast walk, his head twitching as he tried not to look back.

Stully stuck his left hand out his window and put three 9 mm bullets in Alain's back. Using his left hand was just showing off.

8.03   NSA, Ft. Meade, Hanover, MD

Kelly Jerrick looked at the next intercept that popped up on her screen, the next of the list of intercepts that she and hundreds of other Tier 1 analysts toiled over every day. As soon as she opened hers, the next one on the list would get opened by another analyst and so on in a never-ending scroll up the monitors at NSA's underground facility at Fort Meade in Maryland.

At the top, her screen had a button she could push to hear the intercept if it was audio, watch it if it was a video, or read it if it was a document. Below that the minimal details of the intercept were displayed - when it was gathered, the tripwires of words or sources or voiceprints or phone numbers that had led to the flagging for her review, and a transcription of the any audio material. She first listened to the intercept as she was trained, forming her own opinion before reading the background material, and then listening a second time to verify both her first impressions and the background material. Then she made a decision - flash, stash, or trash.

When she saw the tripwires and heard the name, it was an easy decision —flash it up the line to the next tier. She quickly typed her analysis of the intercept and clicked 'send'.

***

William Barnaby watched his much shorter list of intercepts scroll up the monitor. He knew that he was seeing about 20% of the intercepts that came in, further filtered to those in his area of concentration and expertise, the rest having been stashed in the files or trashed as meaningless by the Tier 1 analysts. William was in his last days as a Tier 2 analyst, having the seniority and clearance to move up to Tier 3, and having passed the promotion test with excellent grades.

His focus was on real or suspected activities of al Qaeda of the Arabian Peninsula and its proxies, and the voiceprint attached to the intercept verified to a 97% level of confidence that this was indeed Ibrahim al Hasan talking to an unknown subject about some operation gone wrong, most likely the dirty bomb attacks that they were focusing on very hard. William's daily directives for the last six days had noted al Hasan as a person of extreme interest, so after quickly typing in his analysis and reasoning, his decision was mostly who to send it to at Tier 3, and he chose the Immediate Threat/AQAP desk at Tier 3.

***

The intercept was a total of seventeen minutes old when Tier 3 analyst Mike Cliffords got it. Less than 1% of the intercepts made it to his level, and everyone was taken very seriously. Cliffords quickly confirmed the details and accuracy of the previous analysts. There was no question, this one was actionable at the highest priority, and because the requesting agency on the original tripwire list was the FBI, it went straight to the SIOC in FBI Headquarters, and then onto the assembled representatives of the Bureau's Counter-Terrorism Division.

***

Thirty-nine minutes after Ibrahim had hung up, a SIOC-initiated SVTC began with senior staff from across several FBI divisions, CIA's AQ and South America Desks, the White House National Security Staff, and the NSA's AQAP desk. Ibrahim's apprehension was the topic.

After a seven-minute review of the intercept and the threat posed, the meeting ended. The White House staff quickly prepared a summary for the President with the recommendation of a covert operation to snatch Ibrahim in Venezuela and get him quickly to a secure location within the U.S.

Assuming approval, the CIA went off to plan the operation.

***

The official flight plan for the Petro Canada Gulfstream G450 had them leaving Calgary, Canada at 10 AM that morning for the seven-hour flight to Maracaibo. In fact, it had been wheels up at 1:48 PM from a private airport in Virginia.

The six engineers on board were ostensibly on their way for a long weekend holiday as a reward for the completion of their successful oil-sands project. The logo on the plane read 'Petro Canada, a Suncor Energy Company' and the tail numbers did indeed belong to a Suncor corporate jet, just not this one.

The six men on board were actually employees of Krait Services, an obscure consulting company operating out of offices in Panama. Krait, like one of dozens of other highly specialized CIA-contracted firms, was primarily comprised of ex-special operations people, all with lots of real-world experience around the globe. Most people who encountered Krait thought it must have been started by someone with that last name. In fact, it was named after one of the ten most poisonous snakes in the world, and the one that had the unique distinction of an almost painless bite. Many people who died from a Krait bite never knew they had been bitten. That was the informal corporate mantra - they won't even know we were there.

While they were in the air, local CIA assets in Venezuela had converged on Maracaibo. The hotels in the area had been discretely probed and Ibrahim was found to have two rooms on the top floor of the Kristoff. Another team had acquired local clothing in the sizes specified, while a third put together the weapons and equipment needed. Finally, the last team had stolen the necessary vehicles and licenses plates to swap, and they were stashed in a secret garage waiting to be deployed. There would be absolutely nothing on or about the team that wasn't local and anonymous. No personal identification or belongs. Even the cigarettes were Pall Malls, locally made and purchased at a local shop.

They won't even know we were there.

8.04   AMAR ENERGY SERVICES, HOUSTON, TX

The driver was anxious as he approached the gate to Amar's Rig Services Center in Channelview, about 10 miles east of Houston. After the flawless pick-up in Henderson, the Phoenix one hadn't gone so well. He was lowering the heavy lead shield into the second steel bin when the lifting bail on the shield had broken. The shield dropped several inches before it hit the bottom on the bin, and the driver saw the lid of the shield move. Having no idea what was inside, he panicked, fearing it might be anything from some poisonous gas to an alien life form, either of which would escape and kill him.

The panic caused him to do the right thing instinctively – he slammed the bin cover closed and secured the latch. Then he stood back and examined himself, half expecting rashes to appear or lumps to crawl around under his skin like he had seen in so many horror movies. After several seconds of nothing happening, he realized he needed to get out of there, to get rid of this truck and whatever was in those bins, and get back home to Las Vegas.

The 24-hour drive from Phoenix had been nerve-wracking, trying to watch the road and stay awake and check for alien life forms all at the same time. As he approached the Amar gate, he looked again at his hands and arms just to be sure nothing had changed. Satisfied, he rolled down his window, letting the hot and heavy Houston air into the air-conditioned cab, and handed his paperwork to the guard. Sweat broke out on his forehead as the guard read, not all of it caused by the heat and humidity.

After leafing through the three pages of manifest and authorizations, the guard handed the papers back to him and said, "Do you know your way to Building 9?"

"Yeah, been there many times," the driver lied. He did know the way, but only because he'd been given a detailed map and description of the route and had carefully memorized it.

"OK, Bud, you're clear," the guard said and went back into his small shack. As soon as he'd closed the door, the gate started its slow slide and when it cleared a lane big enough for his truck, the driver waved and went through.

Building 9 was the maintenance shop in the far southeast corner of the large facility. A maintenance van parked there, even for an extended period, was unlikely to attract any attention. The driver had been told where to park, with alternates in case something was already there, and he found his designated spot empty. Breathing a sigh of relief, he locked the truck and quickly walked away, holding his breath until he thought he might pass out. Halfway there, he remembered he was to leave the tool bin open, and he stopped. He looked back at the truck and thought about it for a moment. When he realized he was scratching his arm hard enough to draw blood, he made a decision and turned and kept on walking.

No way he was going near that thing again.

8.05   GRAINGER RESIDENCE, FRENCHTOWN, MT

Tag sat alone in the empty house, in his favorite chair, worried. Something was very wrong, and he didn't understand it. He had been betrayed and his people arrested and some of the bombs found, and that could only be the work of Ibrahim. But why? And Ibrahim had gone into hiding. Again, why? And this morning, he'd tried to kill Tag. None of it made sense. If Ibrahim was cooperating and fingering his team, why just some of them? And why hide? And why kill Tag?

But there was no other explanation that made sense, and the authorities were getting too close to his people, to his army. He had to act to protect himself.

The others had left with the bodies over an hour ago, and he'd received a call ten minutes earlier confirming that the drive to Missoula had been uneventful. They had loaded their cargo discretely and were airborne. He didn't want to rush anything, so he was giving them another fifty minutes to complete the 140 mile flight to the Idaho drop point. They were already at risk with the roll-up of nine team members, two more being betrayed by the first ones captured, and he needed to do something to put the focus back where it belonged, on the A-rabs.

At 3 PM precisely, he made the call. In Huntsville, Alabama, his contact knew what to do.

***

The call from Tag's contact came to the duty officer at the Huntsville FBI Field Office at 3:09 PM, Eastern Standard Time. The recording captured a calm voice with a slight Middle-Eastern accent.

Without preamble, the caller asked, "Is this call being recorded?"

"Yes sir," came the answer. "For your safety as well as ours."

"Good, then I won't need to repeat myself. Some of the missing cesium may be found in the parking lot at Amar Energy in Channelview, Texas. For verification, I can tell you that it is in glass jars inside a lead shield measuring 13.5 inches in diameter and 19 inches high. The shields are in the tool bin in an Amar Energy service truck."

The call disconnected before the FBI officer could ask any questions. A trace was unsuccessful. All that was known was the call was made from a cell phone somewhere locally.

8.06   CNN News Headquarters, Atlanta, GA

 **Vacation and Entertainment Spending a Bust**

Vacation and entertainment venues report dramatic drops in attendance

NEW YORK (CNNMoney.com) -- Across the nation, summer schools, camps, and family friendly vacation destinations are seeing 50% or higher cancellations for the upcoming holiday weekend, even when travelers are facing the loss of deposits and non-refundable airline tickets. Airlines are reporting as much as a 60% drop in fares to such vacation destinations as Orlando and Yellowstone National Park. Direct TV and other in-home and Internet-based entertainment systems across America are seeing huge spikes in consumer demand following the dirty bomb attacks, while shopping malls and movie theaters across the nation realize significant drops in attendance. According to the International Council of Shopping Centers, consumers have hunkered down and are insulating themselves and their families from public sites.

8.07   U.S. CONSULATE, VANCOUVER, BC, CANADA

The conference room at the U.S. Consulate in Vancouver was not big enough for all the people trying to crowd in for this unprecedented meeting. When the hangers-on were eliminated and the final roll call was made, seven people answered, and Cal wondered how anything would be accomplished with this group.

The FBI had two people present, Buck Buchanan and the Supervisory Special Agent from the Vancouver sub-office conveniently located in the Consulate. The Royal Canadian Mounted Police were only allowed one, so they rolled out the biggest gun they could find in British Columbia on short notice, the Provincial Commander in Vancouver. Hadi's lawyer, Colin Avery, was there, and if the membership in this very exclusive group had ended there, Cal would have been optimistic. But having Brenda Delagrave from the Canadian Department of Foreign Affairs in Ottawa and Peter Tucker from the U.S. Consulate in Vancouver added the catalysts that were sure to result in some drama.

The agenda was simple, on paper, anyway. Review and discuss the terms that had been worked out in crisis meetings in Washington and Ottawa, and the plan for implementing those decisions in a meeting with Hadi scheduled through his lawyer for 3 PM. The decisions made had pleased no one in full, so there were bound to be grievances aired and conclusions reviewed, even though nothing would change. The President and the Prime Minister had each signed off, and no one was going to trump that.

Actually, Cal thought, the one person who would be happy was Hadi, now identified as the ex-Marine, Martin Washington. He got what he asked for, in full. His lawyer should have been happy, but to Cal he seemed somehow disappointed and angry. Delagrave also had an attitude. Cal didn't know if she was tired from the quick 3,000 mile flight to be there or if she was anti-American in general or just in disagreement with what was happening. In any case, she had taken pains to let everyone know that at the first glitch, she was walking and taking the deal with her. Peter Tucker would have been more at home at a country club massaging trade interests or something, and he mostly kept quiet. The RCMP and the FBI also said little, their role being law enforcement and finding the cesium, not caring whose toes got stepped on in the process.

The RCMP Commander did make some waves when he asked a simple question that no one had considered – what if Hadi had some of the cesium with him and this was some suicide mission? A quick scramble turned up some radiation detectors from the local fire brigade, and these were given to the Marines guarding the entrance.

At 2 PM, as arranged between Hadi and Avery, Avery's cell phone rang. He answered and confirmed it was Hadi and then put it on speaker so everyone could participate.

"Mr. Washington," he said, "I have everyone gathered and listening, and …"

"Wait," Hadi interrupted. "How did you know my name? I'm Hadi to the FBI, and I never told you."

"Oh, of course. The U.S. authorities told me. They have apparently had you identified for some days now and have been searching rather intensely for you. Your entry into Canada pre-dated their search and was somehow overlooked. I have Dr. Bellotta as you specified and representatives from U.S. and Canadian governments and the agreement signed by both the President and the Prime Minister. So, we will expect you here in an hour to surrender and answer their questions."

"Are you totally satisfied with the agreement? It includes everything we discussed?"

"Yes, and we have Ms. Delagrave from the Prime Minister's office to assure that everything is as agreed. Now, if you will make your way to the U.S. Consulate at …"

"What? No. Forget it. That's U.S. soil. I show up there and they can do whatever they want. I'll never get out. Find someplace else and I'll call you in thirty minutes."

The phone went dead.

***

Hadi paced his small room like he was running very short laps. One two three turn one two three turn. It was a trick. Either they'd fooled his lawyer, or he was in on it. No way was he going to set foot on American soil ever again, not even American soil in Canada or anywhere else.

Suddenly he didn't like his odds of this working. And they knew who he was and were searching. Canada wouldn't be big enough to hide him, now. One two three turn one two three turn.

And he had a plan.

***

Avery spoke first. "Options, anyone?"

"We go to a different consulate," Brenda offered. "I'll call the PM and have them set something up."

In his head, Avery danced a little jig. Unless this agreement and meeting somehow failed, there would maybe be thirty people in the world who knew what was happening, and they were absolutely prohibited from breathing a word of it. So much for the biggest trial in Canadian history and the notoriety that would have resulted. But now, he might get his trial after all.

Avery's cell phone rang promptly after thirty minutes, and he went right to the speaker.

"What have you got," Hadi asked.

"The British Consulate. They've agreed to ..."

"Forget that, too. The Brits are in America's pocket. Make it the Swiss Consulate or we can forget it, and you'll never find me, Martin Washington or not."

"One moment while we discuss that," Avery said, putting the phone on mute.

Everyone quickly assented to this latest twist, and Avery opened the line.

"OK. We'll contact the Swiss and set it up. It may take some time. It's almost 6 PM in Ottawa and, let's see, 11 PM in Geneva. Call me back in two hours and we'll confirm the time that you can meet us there."

"That's not necessary. I'm already there."

8.08   HOTEL KRISTOFF, MARACAIBO, VENEZUELA

Ibrahim sat at his desk without moving for nearly twenty minutes, eyes closed, coffee cooling. Anyone entering the room would have thought him asleep. No sign of his tumultuous thoughts was evident in his face or body.

But tumultuous they were. The day had been a disaster, his men executed, he was certain. Bombs were missing and the plan was falling apart. Something had to be done. Several somethings. Ibrahim had been in his office most of the day, making some calls, incorporating new information into his constantly evolving plan.

First and foremost, he had decided, Grainger would die, and he would die horribly. Not today, or even this week, and maybe not this month or year, but the operation would be commenced, and nothing would stop it. Whether it would take one man or an army, Ibrahim would make sure that they would keep coming until Grainger was dead.

Next, his missing cesium would be found. He had to know how much Grainger had stolen, and how much the authorities knew. His soldiers had been dispatched after the call to Grainger, and others sent to each and every remaining bomb location, whether the authorities were watching or not. Better to know and act than to guess and wait. Without the necessary radiation detection instruments, they would have to make a visual inspection of the drum contents, not knowing that what they were looking for would likely kill them when they found it.

It was almost 4 PM when Ahmad, his senior remaining collaborator, had called with the latest report on the status of the remaining bombs, and it was not good. Of those checked so far, three were intact and two were empty, and there were still three that hadn't been checked. Including the two the FBI had discovered empty, Grainger had moved at least four of the bombs. *To where* was the question that plagued Ibrahim.

"Arrange an anonymous tip to the authorities," he told Ahmad. "Reveal the locations of just the two missing bombs they haven't uncovered. Watch the other bombs in case Grainger tries to move them."

Ibrahim decided he would ride out the plan. He had little choice. Whatever Grainger had done with the cesium, he still intended to detonate the bombs, and that would further Ibrahim's goals regardless of the target. And blame would certainly be placed on Muslim terrorists, whether al Qaeda of North American or of the Arabian Peninsula, in the end it really didn't matter. The U.S. would be forced to respond somewhere, and that would seal the fate of America. And if they didn't respond, they would be seen as empty threats, unable to even protect their own cities.

Finally, he would arrange some additional security. If he was targeting Grainger, he had to believe that Grainger was targeting him. Of course, Grainger's first problem would be finding him. Ibrahim didn't think Venezuela would be on Grainger's radar.

Ibrahim's phone rang, and he hoped for some good news about his latest moves. He didn't get it.

"Sir," Ahmad explained, "the manager at the Amar maintenance facility called and said the FBI is there and has ordered an evacuation of the building. He said they found some of the stolen cesium in the parking lot. He is asking for instructions."

Ibrahim was stunned. Grainger had once again beat him to the punch.

8.09   AMAR ENERGY SERVICES, CHANNELVIEW, TX

The Amar Energy maintenance facility was centrally located in the Brown Shipbuilding Industrial Park. The nearest residential area was a little over one mile directly north, and another was about two and a half miles south. It had taken the FBI, supplemented by what seemed to be the entire Houston Police Department, just twenty-eight minutes to converge on the building once the notification reached them at 4:16 Central Time.

They had confirmed that there were indeed two lead shields in the tool bin of an Amar truck parked in the back of the building, facing the western channel between Bear Lake and Crystal Bay, about 300 feet away. The Houston Fire Department HazMat team arrived while they were confirming this, and their sensitive monitoring equipment detected radiation readings slightly above normal background radiation, as would be expected from a well-shielded cesium source.

Starting with the Amar building, the Houston police had commenced an immediate evacuation working outward, the police enforcing strict control over the sequence of the buildings to assure no traffic jams or panic. In answer to the inevitable and repetitive question, they gave the standard bar-closing response – *I don't care where you go, but you can't stay here.*

Based on wind predictions and a projected plume path, the industrial park had to be cleared to one mile east and west of the building. The problem was the residential areas to the north and south, and there the evacuation process would be much slower.

***

Tag watched the live coverage on CNN. It was almost like having his own surveillance team. Actually better – they had more cameras and multiple commentators reporting on the activity in real time. At 4:15 PM his time, 5:15 in Houston, Tag made his second phone call.

No one answered, but he didn't expect one.

***

Special Agent Eddie Sparks was in charge, and he was very pleased with the progress. They had only been there thirty-one minutes, but things were getting done, quickly and efficiently

Based on the information he'd received from his Field Office, he knew he needed to disarm the bombs. They were cell phone detonated, and an antenna wire would be found snaking outside the shield plug on top. His SABT team simply had to remove that and then they could proceed with removal of the weapons. In the meantime, he'd arranged for total suppression of cell service in the immediate area and he was waiting for confirmation of that before sending anyone in to pull the wire.

Eddie had three cameras facing the truck and he occasionally glanced at the monitors in the command vehicle while he directed the evacuation and planned the approach to the bombs with his RAP team leader, the Houston bomb squad and HazMat commander. One camera had been mounted atop an Amar crane, giving them a good close-up view of the tops of the tool bins where they had been told the cesium was. With the information provided from the examination of the captured Philadelphia and Seattle bombs the day before, they had estimated the likely results of the bombs detonating. The black powder propellant, even confined by the lead plug, would not have sufficient heat and energy to detonate the semtex, so even with the bombs exploding, the shields and tool bin would contain much of the energy. It was estimated that the lead plug would be launched only sixteen feet or so with no obstacles, and the closed tool bin meant that it might not go anywhere. Based on the amount of explosive found in the other bombs, they estimated that, if exploded with the tool bin open, the plume would extend thirty to forty feet above them at the most.

The plan was to load the shields in an approved radioactive materials shipping container. They would easily fit in one that the South Texas Project Nuclear Power Plant, located 90 miles southwest of Houston, had agreed to loan them. It was en route and expected to arrive within an hour. Once sealed inside the container, even an explosion wouldn't breech the seal and the material would be contained in any event.

So Eddie was pretty happy with the way things were progressing. He glanced at his watch and noted that it was rush hour and the evacuation would be slow. He heard the muffled boom and looked at the monitors in time to see the smoke and debris rising above the truck.

Oh shit, he thought.

8.10   CONSULATE OF SWITZERLAND, VANCOUVER, BC, CANADA

A lone Swiss soldier, armed with the standard Belgian FNC NATO-approved rifle, stood guard outside the room where Hadi was waiting. Cal and the others had met with the Swiss consul before being escorted to the meeting room, and were told the conditions as they had been explained to him by the Swiss Ambassador in Ottawa who had gotten his directives from Geneva. These were pretty simple – no weapons of any kind, law enforcement or not; the Consul was to be present for the meeting; no physical interrogation techniques of any kind; and the Consul had the authority to call a halt to the proceedings at any time. No one was happy with these, but Hadi's choice of the venue left them with no alternative.

Hadi stood when the eight-person entourage entered, and he seemed nervous and scared to Cal. *Of course*, Cal thought, *who wouldn't be?* Eight people seemed like overkill to Cal, but he understood everyone's need to be involved to protect their jurisdictional interests.

The Consul took the host role and introduced everyone. Cal saw Hadi focus particularly hard on him after he was introduced, and figured that was because they had spoken previously. But he got a surprise.

"I would like a few moments alone with Captain Bellotta," Hadi said, using Cal's former military rank. Everyone looked around, and Brenda Delagrave spoke up.

"No. We have agreed to certain concessions in return for your complete cooperation in locating this cesium. There will be no new conditions, no private meetings. You will speak candidly and be fully forthcoming to all of us."

Peter Tucker, an almost non-entity in the process up until now, replied. "I see no harm in a brief discussion with Dr. Bellotta. It's not like we won't get what we came for. If he has something to say privately, let him. If it is germane to finding the cesium or to the agreement, then Dr. Bellotta can brief us all."

Buck Buchanan started to speak, but was interrupted by the Swiss Consul. "I'm sorry, Agent Buchanan, but we don't need further discussion. If Mr. Hadi wants to meet privately, then so be it."

He went to the door and spoke to the soldier and then turned back to the group. "Sergeant Abert will escort you to another conference room and bring you back."

The sergeant led Cal and Hadi to another room and left them alone. They sat without speaking for several moments before Cal broke the silence.

"What is it you want to talk to me about?"

"Captain," Hadi answered, "I would like to explain some things. I know that you know my birth name, and you must know my military record by now. There was a time when I wanted the Marines to be my career, to serve with honor. I have studied military history, and I know the things that went on in Viet Nam. Massacres of civilians, torture and murder of suspects, the total breakdown of military discipline and law.

"I thought we had learned from that experience. But then I was sent to Afghanistan. The things we did there would make you cry. I didn't do them myself, I made sure of that, but I was there and I didn't try to stop it. Those that did, that reported the abuses, got themselves transferred for their trouble and their careers ruined. And the abuse didn't stop, the abusers were never called to account. In the end, I took the matter into my own hands and betrayed my comrades. I'm not sorry they are dead. The things they did would earn a lethal injection back home. But I am sorry I betrayed them. I wish I had spoken up. I wish I had been a better leader. But like I said, I wanted to be a career Marine, and doing that would have ended my career. I would have been a 20-year corporal."

Hadi stopped and sat silent while Cal digested this. *No excuse*, he thought, *but as close as you can come to one.*

"Anyway," Hadi suddenly continued, "I couldn't live with myself after that and didn't re-up. I came home and got away from my past life, tried to make myself disappear. That's when I joined the Mosque and started getting serious about my religion. That's how they found me. That's how they recruited me. They knew what I'd done in Afghanistan and had recordings from my meeting there. And they threatened my family. I was scared all over again. I just want all of this over."

Cal said nothing, having no response if this were true, and no way of knowing one way or the other. He simply knocked on the door and the sergeant escorted them back.

***

The others stopped talking when Cal and Hadi entered the room. Avery immediately went to his client and pulled him aside.

"Look, you don't have to take this deal. These people will give you more, probably a lot more. I've talked to the Swiss Consul while you were out and he said they would give you asylum here for a few days if the negotiation stretched out."

"No. I'm going to sign whatever the deal is. I'm done with this."

"I understand, but there is another angle you should consider. This agreement has all parties muzzled – no one can ever talk about it. If you were to take that out, the potential for a book deal and speaking tour is huge. Millions of dollars."

"No. And that's final. I'm not trying to make money off of this. I'm trying to put this behind me."

"OK, if that's what you want. But I think …"

Hadi looked up, his face not six inches from Avery's.

"No. End of discussion."

And he walked away.

***

Cal watched the lawyer sidebar with Hadi and wondered what that was all about. When it ended, Brenda Delagrave decided she would take control.

"Are we ready? Mr. Hadi? You know the terms and we have all agreed to them. Once the agreement is signed, you will be held in protective custody by the RCMP here in Vancouver until we have checked your information. We may have more questions for you, and you agree to be fully cooperative with any follow-up. Once your information is validated, you will be released and provided a new identity, including a Canadian work visa and the $100,000 payment in Canadian dollars. For a period of five years, you will be required to report in to the RMCP every month so we have a record of your current location and status in case you are needed for any of the legal and investigative activities that will follow the recovery of the cesium. You're clear on all that?"

"Yes," Hadi simply answered.

"OK, then," Brenda said clasping her hands in front of her as if applauding her own performance. "Let's get this done and get on with finding these devices."

Cal watched as Hadi signed the agreement without reading it. Either he trusted his lawyer or he no longer cared, Cal thought. That done, Brenda once again took charge.

"All right. Mr. Hadi, if you would, please go ahead and tell us the information you have on these vehicles and their locations."

Hadi spoke from memory. "A Ford F-250, white with a crew cab. Washington license number Sierra November 92003. A sign on the door reading Kwik-Lube with an address on North East 45th Street in Seattle. Dodge Ram 2500, blue with a crew cab. California license 5 Alpha Romeo Lima 231. A sign on the door and tailgate reading Marconi Industrial Supply with an address on Bayshore Highway in Burlingame."

Cal wrote down the information as Hadi dictated, listing the details of all sixteen trucks, including the four suicide bomber vans. He was impressed at the information, not so much for its content as for Hadi's total memorization of it. All Cal could think was that he must have been obsessed with securing the knowledge and afraid to leave a record of it anywhere.

"Two questions," Buck asked when the listing was complete. "First, what do you know about when and how these devices will be deployed?"

"Nothing except there were two different containers used. The ones that went with the pick-up trucks had something electronic already installed in the shielded pipe with a wire that could be an antenna. To be honest, it looked kind of like a homemade mortar to me. I don't know anything about when."

"OK. What about the others? Do you know any of the people you worked with, or anything about them?"

"I'd never met any of the others. They were all Arabic except for the American Muslim. We were under strict orders to use only the Arabic names we were given and not to talk about personal things. When the drivers came to pick up the cesium, we were all in balaclavas, hoods, and so were they. Again, we were under orders not to talk to each other, so I never saw nor heard them."

"And the people who recruited you?"

"They came to my apartment one night, two of them, and, uh, persuaded me to cooperate. They left, and all conversations after that were by phone. They called me. I had no way to contact them."

"OK then. The RCMP will take temporary custody until we verify all of this. Let's go, Bellotta."

8.11   FBI Suboffice, U.S. Consulate, Vancouver, BC, Canada

Peter Tucker, not accustomed to urgency in his job, had to nearly run as Cal and Buck hustled out of the Swiss Consulate and got in the waiting car for the 700 yard ride to the U.S. Consulate and FBI suboffice. The rush was to get to the secure conference room at the consulate and report in the bomb information as quickly as possible, wanting to get all of them found and secured before they were used.

When they got through to Pamela Hastings in D.C., they found out they were already too late.

"Have you heard the latest," Hastings asked.

"No. What? We just got out of the meeting with Mr. Washington. We've got the information on all twelve remaining bombs."

"Make that ten remaining bombs. Two were detonated not twenty minutes ago. This time in Houston. Our local agents were on the scene looking for the bombs on a tip when they went off. There were two bombs in the one truck, probably being stored for future use, but we don't know that, and we don't know if all were detonated."

"Houston? Do any of our projections include Houston today?"

"No, Starlight projections didn't give us any nexus in or near Houston around now. We went looking based on an anonymous tip, so maybe the bomber decided to blow it when we got too close. That means they were under observation, and we're rounding up everyone within range for questioning. It was an industrial area and they'd already started evacuation, so we could easily have let someone get away. SIOC is starting the SVTC in ten minutes. Call in."

***

As soon as Cal and Buck were conferenced in, they could hear the turmoil in the background. After a moment, they heard someone banging on a table top and shouting, "OK everyone, let's get settled and we'll start."

That took several moments and when it had quieted, Hastings took the microphone and started.

"As you all have probably heard by now, we've had another RDD detonation in Houston today. Here are the facts as we know them at this time. There were two separate devices on an Amar Energy truck parked in back of their maintenance facility east of downtown Houston. The devices were inside a closed tool bin at the time of detonation and this contained the blast and the spread of the cesium. On explosion, it appears that the shield plug or plugs were launched through the lid. Some or all of the cesium escaped through that. The National Guard CST and DOE RAP teams are on-site surveying the area, and we'll know the extent of the problem within hours. Because of the tip, we had already begun evacuation, so we do not have any casualties, nor any threats to public safety outside of the immediate area. The tipster hung up before we could get a name, but he was very specific, describing the internals of the drums and the cesium container in detail, so we assume he's someone on the inside. Buchanan, you there?"

"Yes, Pam. Bellotta and I are in the Consulate in Vancouver."

"Good. Send us the recording of the meeting with Mr. Washington and we'll see if we can get a match with this Hadi guy. If we do, that's a whole new ball game. So, moving on. Amar Energy is the family business of one Ibrahim al Hasan who, you will all recall, was questioned in regards to the document we captured outlining this plot, and who subsequently disappeared under very suspicious circumstances.

"This morning, NSA got a hit on his location and we have teams following up. I am not in a position to share details of the locations identified or the operations to follow with respect to dealing with al Hasan and company. This explosion at Amar adds some urgency to that mission.

"Now, we've also made some progress with the questioning of the leader of the Pastor theft. Buck Buchanan and Cal ..."

"Wait a minute," Cal heard someone shout. "What do you mean, 'following up'? Where is al Hasan? And why don't the Saudis just hand him over?"

"I'm not getting into that at this point," Hastings answered. "I can't speak for the Saudis, but our mission is classified and no one here is to speak of it until advised otherwise."

"Are you implying that we're snatching him from somewhere? You can't do that! Saudi Arabia is an ally. And al Hasan is Royal Family and a diplomat. There are no grounds for such a drastic step. Are you arresting the owners of the other businesses where the cesium was stored? What makes al Hasan different?"

"What makes him different is the suspicion of his terrorist ties and AQNA involvement in the cesium theft. And we have questioned the other business owners, and they are being dealt with appropriately. Al Hasan has chosen to flee and …"

"Flee? Is that what this NSA intercept shows? You are planning a snatch!"

Anger vibrated in Hastings' voice as she answered. "I said no such thing, and we will not speculate on this. Let me remind you, there is still over 40,000 curies of cesium out there, and we've been damn lucky so far that no more innocents have been killed by it, or some critical infrastructure crippled. We cannot afford to waste time rehashing something that has already been reviewed and decided. We are proceeding."

The discord again increased in volume, and Hastings had to pound the room back to silence,

"Excuse me," Cal interrupted. "Cal Bellotta here. Look, I agree that we need to pull out all the stops on this, but the urgency to question al Hasan might become moot. We have identified all of the bomb vehicles now, and their probable location. I suggest that we go ahead and keep al Hasan bottled up until we see what we learn here."

"Bottled up," someone asked. "How do you bottle up his cell phone? These devices are activated by cell phones. He might just decide to blow the rest and ride his diplomatic immunity out of the country."

"This is Buck Buchanan. I agree with Bellotta. And yes, we can bottle up his cell phone and anyone else's, wherever he is. Radios, Internet, satellite, we can block them all. We can put them back to paper and pencil communications. I say we shut him down and see what we learn up here."

Hastings took control of the microphone and closed the discussion.

"I will advise the Director of these points. Now, let's move on. As Bellotta noted, we have all the cesium vehicles and destinations identified and teams will be moving on this within the next few hours. We are clearly dealing with an al Qaeda threat, but we still don't know where this is originating."

Hastings went on to brief everyone on the plans for the cesium search and the efforts to contain and mitigate the Houston detonations. Cal decided it was not the time or place to debate the WAR versus AQNA issue and let it go without comment. With murmured grumbles and conversation, the SVTC wound down and eventually ended. With the question of rogue diplomats and Saudi Royal Family and the urgent search for the cesium, Cal wondered how bad it was going to get in the next few hours.

8.12   HOTEL KRISTOFF, MARACAIBO, VENEZUELA

Stully scanned the expansive lobby of the Hotel Kristoff while the registration clerk checked him in using his phony Simon Goetz passport. He noted the entrances and the security cameras, but saw no overt security personnel, as expected in a somewhat obscure tourist location. Besides his carry-on roller bag, he had two small parcels, clearly marked United Airlines QuickPak. In Houston, he had disassembled his travel pistol, a Glock 23, putting the plastic parts in one box and the metal ones, including two fully-loaded clips, in another. At the United Air Freight counter, reasoning that cargo security would be lax, he had arranged for them to be expressed shipped to Maracaibo on his flight, to be picked up at the airport by a Mr. Simon Goetz.

It was after 11 PM and Stully was in a hurry, but displayed no impatience that might get him remembered. While he had kept the dead boy's identification, and the location of the body was somewhat hidden, he knew he couldn't count on much lead time until he was found and identified and the news reached Laila. That would ruin his plan, and he didn't have a good back-up. He needed to get to her tonight to be certain she would respond.

Declining bellman assistance, Stully took his key and went to Room 327. After examining the room and determining that the windows did not open for a possible escape route, he unpacked and re-assembled the Glock, checked its action, and hid it in the wire frame protecting the coils on the back of the small, under-counter refrigerator in the room. Then he went to reconnoiter the landscape.

***

When she felt the slight vibration against her thigh, Laila immediately awoke and went to the bathroom in her room. The secret cell phone was concealed in its nylon holster and held to her leg by a Velcro strap under her nightgown.

In the bathroom, with the door locked, she reached under her nightgown and took out the phone. Alain was the only person with the number so she had no doubt who it was. She hadn't heard from him since early the day before, and she was anxious to know if he was able to come to Maracaibo. The clock on the phone said it was just after 1 AM.

The text message simply read "rm 327 cn u cum" and she knew he'd made it.

Laila quickly changed into jeans and a pullover and slipped some flats onto her feet. Peeking out her door, she saw the doors to the other two bedrooms closed and she quietly slipped out of the suite and raced down the hallway to the elevators.

Pushing the down button over and over, Laila kept repeating *musstajal*, hurry.

She stopped in front of the door to 327 and composed herself, catching her breath. She knocked and waited, hearing footsteps in the room, each one bringing her beloved Alain closer. The door opened and she looked at the man standing there smiling and then at the room number on the door and said, "I'm sorry. I must ..."

She never finished. So fast she didn't know what happened, the man grabbed her shirt and yanked her into the room, closing the door behind him. She turned and was about to scream when she saw the pistol in his hand, and her first thought was *Alain!* Her second was *Daddy, what have you done now?*

"You have the right room, Laila," he said. "Just the wrong person. Now, please sit on the couch and you won't be hurt."

"What have you done with Alain?"

"Please sit and I will explain. Your Alain is fine, I just borrowed his cell phone."

Laila sat in the middle of the couch, hoping the stranger would do the same. He did just that, sitting on her left, casually pointing the gun at her.

"I am here to speak to your father. Please let me have your room key so that I may introduce myself to him."

"He's not there," Laila said. "He's in his office suite downstairs, like he always is."

"Well, then, we'll just go up and wait for him."

"He won't be back to the room tonight. He sleeps there most nights so he can talk privately on the phone to his people back home in Saudi Arabia."

"Call him and tell him you need to talk to him and you're coming down."

Laila reached in her pocket for her cell phone and the man swung the gun up, pointing at her face. She froze.

"What are you doing?"

"Getting my phone."

"The room phone is next to you. Use that."

"If I do, his guard will answer and I may not get to talk to my father. He will answer a call from my cell phone personally."

"OK, go ahead."

Laila took out the iPhone with its yellow plastic case and swiped the screen to bring it to life. As she did, she fumbled it, but caught it before it landed on the man's lap, but instead of dialing a number, she pressed the large button on the side of the case and jammed the top of the phone into the man's thigh. He instantly went rigid, the contracting muscles in his hand pulling the trigger on the silenced pistol, but his bullet missed everything except the wall. Laila released the button on her Yellow Jacket iPhone Taser and the man immediately slumped, dropping the gun.

She jumped up and grabbed the gun and backed away, pointing it at him with little control over its wavering barrel. Glancing at her phone, she speed-dialed her father's number and hoped he would answer the unfamiliar Caller ID.

"Daddy? Come quick. Someone tried to kill me. He's looking for you. Please hurry."

"Laila? What are you saying? Who tried to kill you? Never mind. I'm on my way."

"Daddy wait! I'm in room 327."

***

Simon Tully Lennocks, as Ibrahim knew him from the passport they had found, was duct-taped to the desk chair and an old sock stuffed in his mouth, facing the couch where Ibrahim comfortably reclined. Lennocks was bloody, mostly around the head and mouth, but conscious, and he stared hard at Ibrahim.

"Well, Mr. Lennocks, since you won't talk, you have no value to me at all. Even if you did talk, your value would still be very low, say around that of a small mouse that was about to become dinner for a pet snake. You really don't have any information that I need, nor can I bargain your life for any favor as your employer has nothing that I want, except his life.

"Yes. I know who sent you here. There is only one man who would employ a creature like you, someone so bane as to deserve no mercy. And, of course, your cell phone confirms it. These calls to the 406 area code. If I am not mistaken, that is Frenchtown, Montana."

Lennocks kept staring, and Ibrahim smiled, and said to Tariq, "Mr. Lennocks is a very hard case, don't you agree? What do you think you could do to test that?"

Lennocks' legs were taped to the chair legs, spreading them slightly apart. Tariq stood near the left one and jabbed his fist hard into Lennock's groin. His eyes grew wide and an ugly, deep-throated sound tried to get through the dirty sock without much success. His eyes watered uncontrollably and he bent forward as much as his restraints allowed, which wasn't much.

When they'd arrived and found Laila and the unconscious Lennocks, Ibrahim had questioned the girl quickly and learned just what had happened. He had then sent Tariq to escort Laila back to her room in case there were any others with Lennocks, although he thought that unlikely. When he returned with the duct tape, they had bound Lennocks before he recovered. Questioning had gotten them no information, even with the escalating motivation that Tariq applied. A thorough search of the room and Lennocks' tablet computer and possessions confirmed that he was alone.

Ibrahim waited until he thought Lennocks was able to focus on the matters at hand and then spoke to him again.

"You know your greatest sin, do you not? Coming to try to kill me? No, that was your job, and bungling that was not a sin so much as a failure. No, your greatest sin, and the one that will cost you your life, was laying your hands on my daughter. But let's see if you can't provide me some benefit before you die."

Ibrahim took Lennocks' cell phone and selected the 406 number and pressed dial. It was answered after two rings.

"Is it done?"

"Is what done, Mr. Grainger? Oh, you mean am I dead? No, I am quite well, thank you. I have a Mr. Lennocks here who tells me, with some reluctance, that you are his employer. Is that correct?"

"Ibrahim. Don't know what you're talking about. Maybe I could talk to this Lennocks guy and find out why he would say that."

"No need. We have talked to him and we're satisfied that he has told us everything he knows. So, would you like to hear him die?"

Ibrahim nodded to the body guard who pulled the sock from Lennocks' mouth at the same time he stabbed him in the throat with his own SOG knife.

Ibrahim held the phone up so Tag could hear the gurgling sounds as Lennocks tried unsuccessfully to breathe through the torrent of blood in his windpipe.

"So, that is done. Now we have just one last piece of business to conclude. There is a *fatwa* issued on you today, Mr. Grainger, by a much respected *mufti* in Yemen. You know *fatwa*? That is an irreversible edict in my religion, a final opinion, much like your Supreme Court. But in the case of a *fatwa*, we do not wait for police to carry out the command. No, all of the faithful are expected to do that.

"They will come for you. Maybe not today, but soon. Maybe they will walk down the middle of the street in that inconsequential little town of yours, killing anyone in their way. Or maybe they will be sneaking up on you in the dead of night and slitting your throat while you sleep. Maybe you will be able to defend yourself, kill them instead of being killed. But that will not stop them. My people will keep coming until the *fatwa* is honored and you are dead and in hell. You cannot stop it, you might only delay it briefly.

"In any case, goodbye Mr. Grainger."

Friday, July 2

8.13   Sybrium Container Solutions, Breezewood, PA

It was 2 AM when three large SUV's drove into the loading area at Sybrium Container Solutions. A roll-up door was raised, opening into a darkened warehouse area, and the vehicles all drove in, the door closing behind them.

Once inside, the light came on and a lone figure walked to a forklift that had a small hook and cable attached to the lifting forks. Three large cylinders, the shields each holding their 4,000 curies of cesium, were lined up next to the hook. The forklift operator lifted the first and the lead SUV drove under it. The driver got out and took a small step stool from the back seat and positioned it next to the SUV's cargo area. He climbed the two steps until he could easily reach across and remove the three-foot square flexible magnetic sheet, exposing a ragged, 18-inch circular hole in the roof.

He climbed down and gave the forklift operator the signal to lower the lead shield through the hole and onto the SUV's floor. The SUV visibly sank under the weight, giving it the raised front look of a plane taking off. The driver reached inside and removed the hook, signaling the operator to raise it. He then placed a cardboard box upside down over the shield, concealing it, replaced the magnetic sheet to disguise the crudely cut hole, folded the stool, and drove forward, making room for the next SUV.

The process was repeated two times, and twenty-three minutes after they had arrived, the SUV's exited the again darkened warehouse.

8.14 BBC NEWS HEADQUARTERS, LONDON, ENGLAND

B B C CHINESE NAVY GOES ON HIGH ALERT

CHINA DEPLOYS ITS BLUE WATER NAVY TO PROTECT ITS COMMERCIAL CHANNELS

The Chinese Navy moved in force today into the Sea of Japan and off the South Korean coast as a "defensive measure" against escalating tensions and political uncertainties caused by the radiation attacks on the U.S.A. ASEAN and the U.S. asked China to "stand-down" and to avoid increasing tension in the already volatile region. Oil and mineral rights disputes and border claims among Asian countries have simmered for years, and the Japanese Foreign Minister accused China of using the terrorist attacks in America as a pretense to send in its armed forces to support its claims of hegemony over the area

8.15 HOTEL KRISTOFF, MARACAIBO, VENEZUELA

There had not been a lot of time to get things organized and ready, to check and double-check their weapons and equipment, to review the floor plan of the Kristoff and the street plan of the surrounding area, to position the vehicles and drivers, to establish and drive the escape route, to reconnoiter the hotel itself and take and review pictures of the interior and exterior, and to brainstorm problems and contingencies. It was 2:15 in the morning before they were satisfied, loaded and ready and left the InterContinental hotel where they were staying for the eight-minute drive to the Kristoff.

When all was said and done, the plan was, by necessity, simple. The teams, faces concealed from security cameras, would enter the hotel by multiple entrances. There were plenty to choose from in the sprawling 300-room low-rise building. The problem of the electronic locks had been anticipated by the advance team and guest room keys obtained that would open the doors. With two rooms to cover, they would work in three-man teams, entering both at the same moment and preventing any communications between the rooms or to the outside world.

Shortly after 2:30, they were ready, each team stationed outside one of the rooms wearing hoods to conceal their identities and within sight of each other in the long corridor on the sixth floor. As a last step, each team used a contact surface microphone and mini amplifier to listen for activity in the rooms. The

Team 1 leader at the main suite clicked his 'talk" button twice, the signal to freeze, and then three times, indicating they withdraw. They gathered at the elevator at the end of the corridor.

"There's activity in the main room," the leader said. "It sounds like crying and someone talking. A woman. Did you have any contact?"

The other team indicated no, and the team leader made a decision.

"All right, we'll have to risk it. OK, everyone back into position."

Again they deployed, and on the go signal, opened the doors using their pass keys and stormed into the rooms.

***

Team 2 had a larger main sitting room, one bedroom, a bath and two closets to clear. It took just seconds to determine all were empty, disable the phone and head for the main suite.

***

Team 1 burst into the room and was confronted with the one sight they had not prepared for - everyone except for the targeted men gathered around a distraught teenage girl. The boy was the only one to react, making a dash for one of the bedrooms before being knocked down by one of the Krait men. Instantly the team leader ordered two of his men to gather and watch the women and boy while the others cleared the three bedrooms, baths and closets. That took another one minute and twelve seconds, and then things stopped.

"Team 2, take the mother into the bedroom and find out where the men are. We'll stay here and watch the others."

At that moment, the phone rang, and the team leader's brain murmured to him, *what now?*

***

Taja answered on the third ring, and Ibrahim's first question was, "Is Laila all right?"

"Yes," Taja answered tentatively. "We are all here. The man did not harm her."

"We will be done here very soon. We must consider moving tonight. I don't know for certain that this man was alone."

"We can do whatever is necessary, just as we did in Jazan."

Ibrahim tensed, but replied without hesitation or a change in inflection, "I know I can count on you, just as you can always count on me. I must go now. I will be there shortly," and hung up the phone.

Turning to his bodyguard, he said, "Contact the outside guard and find out if he is unharmed and if everything is clear. If so, have him get the car and wait for instructions."

As Tariq reached for his push-to-talk cell phone, he asked, "What is wrong?"

"She used a code. They are under duress and we must run. I told her I would be back to get her and the children out."

Ibrahim picked up the room phone and dialed zero to get the front desk. He cupped his hand over the mouthpiece and whispered urgently, "Please help. They've killed an American in room 327 and now they're in room 648. They have guns and they're holding hostages. Please hurry. They're going to kill them all."

Ibrahim hung up without waiting for a reply. Tariq said, "Everything is quiet outside. He is ready."

"Tell him the police are on their way and to wait for us on 68th Street near the north side entrance. We must go before hotel security gets here."

***

The team leader hung up the extension phone and raised his hand as if preparing to strike Taja and said, "Where is he? And what was that about Jazan?"

Taja bowed her head and talked to her folded hands and said, "That is my place of birth, a seaside town on the Red Sea. When I was young, younger than Laila, I was attacked by some tourist infidels and my family was forever humiliated."

She stopped and then slowly raised her head and spoke with a venom the team leader saw only in the most hardened of fanatics.

"Just as you and that man have corrupted Laila and forever humiliated our family. Ibrahim saved me then, and I can always count on him. He will save us this time, as well."

"Where is he?"

"I don't know. He has secret places he goes to do his work."

He hesitated and then came to a decision.

"Get them all into that bedroom," he said, pointing to the one furthest from the door to the suite and the two men he wanted to do the job. "Use the cuffs and tape their mouths closed. The rest of you, set up. There, there, and there. Wait for my signal. It will be when they are in the room and the door closed. Go."

With everyone set, there was nothing to do but wait for the men to return.

***

Ibrahim and Tariq jogged quietly to the north end of the corridor where the small foyer and elevator were located. Ibrahim opened the fire door to the staircase and listened for a moment.

"It is clear. We take the stairs then out the door to the car. Keep quiet."

They hustled down the stairs, trying to use both speed and stealth, and getting neither. At the first-floor door, Ibrahim hesitated. Once they entered the foyer there, they would be in full view from both the hotel to the south and the outside through the glass door exit. He looked as best he could and said, "It seems clear. Check outside and make sure the driver is there."

Tariq stuck his head out the door and looked both ways. The car and driver were there, just twenty feet away, and he signaled Ibrahim to follow. They jogged across the grass and jumped into the back seat. The car was moving before the door was closed.

As they crossed Eighth Avenue, the driver said, "The street ends here. I can only turn right. Where are we going?"

"76 Third Street."

"That is in the other direction. I must turn around."

"Just stay well clear of the hotel and get us there without notice."

"That will be difficult at this hour. As you can see, there is no one out. We will not be hard to find if the police are looking."

"They are, but not for us. Just drive carefully."

"Where are we going, if I might ask *sayyd*," Tariq asked.

"You may. The Cuban Consulate. I have done business with them before, and I made arrangements in advance should something like this occur. I will alert them we are coming."

Ibrahim took out his cell phone and autodialed a stored number.

***

It had been nine minutes since the call when the Krait leader, out of sight behind the small bar in the main room of the suite, began to get nervous. This was taking too long, and they were in an indefensible position should anything go wrong. Then he heard the sirens in the distance and knew something had.

"Everyone, on me," he shouted and the others appeared from behind closed doors and furniture. "Check the window. Something is wrong."

"There are police cars coming," the lookout reported.

"Shit. She alerted him. That Jazan stuff was code. All right, we go. Orderly, understand? Down the stairs and out the west entrance. We are not provisioned for a fire fight. Shoot only if you have to, and save your ammo. Call the driver and have him meet us at the 9th Avenue rendezvous point. OK?"

"What about them," one of the men asked, indicating the bedroom where the family was secured.

"Leave them. They are not our target. OK. Go."

Moving quickly, sweeping the corridor and guest room doors, the six men moved down the west wing to the stairs. A quick check confirmed there was no overt movement on the staircase and they started down, keeping their distance from one another and constantly watching doors and windows and the stairs for any threat.

The first two team members had cleared the first-floor landing and were out the exit when the door to the corridor behind them burst open and two surprised policeman shouted something in Spanish. The third team member, still on the stairs, shot the lead policeman, but before he could swing to the second, he ducked back into the corridor, the door half open with the dead body blocking it. A hand appeared with an automatic pistol and started firing randomly. Unfortunately for the Krait man still on the stairs, his chest was in the way and he was dead before his body landed at the bottom.

The hand withdrew and the firing stopped. The remaining Krait team members on the stairs rushed down, two of them grabbing their comrade and dragging the body with them, slowing their progress across the concrete patio around the swimming pool. Two more policemen came out the same exit and immediately started firing at them. Return fire pushed them back inside, but one of the men dragging the body took a hit in his right calf.

"Leave him," the other said, helping the wounded man down the space between the buildings and out to 9th Avenue.

Two unmarked cargo vans were parked facing north on the one-way street, and the five remaining men climbed into them and sped off. Inside, they quickly stripped off their clothes and changed into tourist-leisure slacks and shirts. The wounded man was attended to with a field dressing to stop the bleeding, and the other helped him dress.

At University Avenue, the vans turned right and then pulled into a large car dealership. All five men got out and into two rental cars, and the vans left with their old clothes and all their weapons. The fire department would soon be called to the parking lot at the Psiquiatrico Hospital to extinguish two vehicle fires.

As the two rental cars continued down University Avenue toward the InterContinental Hotel, one of the men mumbled to no one in particular, "I guess they'll know we were here."

8.16   WAR Compound, 6 miles NE of Whitefish, MT

The road had no name, it was just The Road, and everyone knew which road they were talking about. Once you got off Trumbull Canyon Road, names became useless and landmarks became the only tool for direction, so you were told to turn right at the six-foot tall granite outcropping with the skull and crossbones painted on it. Very few people were told that - turning right there got you into *Injun Country*, as the locals in Whitefish, Montana called it, a very dangerous place to be if you weren't invited.

The caravan that did turn right that morning was invited, in fact it included the chief inviter himself, Tag Grainger, riding in the Hummer H1, the military version. The two other vehicles were also 4-wheel drive, high ground clearance SUV's, because no other vehicles would be able to negotiate The Road. It wasn't designed for a quick getaway; it was designed for an agonizingly slow approach.

As they bounced and slid the last three-quarters of a mile to the mountain refuge, Tag relaxed, knowing that there were at least two, and as many as four, sets of eyes, each supplemented by laser sighting scopes ready to be turned on, on them at all times. Trained eyes that knew the identity every resident and invited guest and could tell if there was any coercion being applied to them by others, visible or not. Discrete signals, given at precisely specified points, assured those eyes that all was well. Missing those signals would mean that any unfamiliar face would shortly have a red dot marking the point where the bullet would hit a second later. Injun country.

The compound came into view in segments as they cleared the dense natural forest into the manicured area where trees and brush had been partially cleared to provide fields of fire. Eleven buildings were arranged in a planned defensive layout, providing fallback routes to consolidate forces and protected avenues for escape from attack. Ninety-nine people called this home at the moment, all dedicated soldiers of WAR and their immediate families.

The vehicles headed directly for the two-story main house where Tag's apartment was, along with quarters for three live-in guards and the offices and communications center of WAR. This was the focal point of the defensive design, the last outpost should they be attacked and pushed progressively back. This was where the survivors of such an attack would die.

Near the main house, a large barracks for the forty-two men provided protection from a frontal attack, and a smaller one for the seventeen women guarded the right flank. Three multi-family structures housed thirty-six men, women, and children covered the left flank, and the maintenance shop and generator building, and the kitchen/mess hall enclosed the circle in the rear. Stables housing twelve Appaloosa horses trained in mountain trail riding were located between the main house and the maintenance shop. There were two clear trails, protected by thick forest and additional ground cover, that ran north on either side of the mess hall, giving twelve people the possibility of breaking out of any siege and either forming a cavalry for a surprise counter-attack, or getting to the Canadian border, just forty very rugged miles north.

Tag got a pot of coffee from the kitchen and went right to the roof walk, a twelve-foot by ten-foot rooftop platform that overlooked the compound, providing a quiet and private place for Tag to think. He had a new problem, one that he'd never considered before, and he needed a plan. The A-rabs were going to kill him, sooner or later, unless he stayed in the compound until God took him naturally. There would be no stopping them. But he couldn't stay there. He had to move around if his plan was going to work. And he wanted to be present, watching and participating, as the milestones in the formation of the Christian Covenant of America were reached.

So Tag had two problems. First, how to avoid raghead assassins for as long as possible, and two, who was going to take over and carry the plan to its conclusion. One pot of coffee was not going to be enough.

8.17 FBI Headquarters, Washington, DC

As he fell asleep, Cal's fingers, intertwined behind his head, began to relax. His feet were on the desk in his temporary office at SIOC, and he was leaning back in the comfortable executive chair doing the only thing left that he could do to prevent the dirty bomb catastrophe - think. All the action pieces were in place and moving. All the bombs had been accounted for except the three that had headed for the East Coast from Denver, Kansas City and Detroit. Law enforcement agencies and the military were searching for those three with every resource they had. Ray was at the IDC coordinating the massive data input from every source, trying to identify the truck that had brought the bombs to the area and find its current location. By now, Cal figured, the

President and other senior government officials were hidden away in the various retreats that security required in such a situation.

When sleep relaxed his fingers enough for gravity to overcome friction, Cal's arms released and he awoke with a jerk, his feet thumping on the floor as he sat up. He put his elbows on the desk and his face in his hands and unsuccessfully tried to remember when he had last been this tired. It wasn't just the sleep deprivation or the constant trips back and forth across the country or the non-stop meetings - it was the stress that took this fatigue to new levels.

Somewhere out there were 12,000 curies of cesium sending billions of gamma rays out into the environment. And just six inches of lead prevented Cal from knowing exactly where it was. Six goddam inches! You would think that much gamma energy smashing constantly into a heavy metal would produce some reaction that they could trace. Heat or some gamma-induced secondary radiation like *bremsstrahlung*, the electromagnetic radiation released by charged particles hitting other charged particles. Something! But if there was, Cal didn't know about it.

But that doesn't mean it doesn't exist, Cal realized. *It just means that my knowledge is limited*. It was time to expand that knowledge.

Cal picked up the phone and called the director at Oak Ridge National Lab. Forty-five minutes later, he was in a SVTC with the heads of all nineteen DOE national labs and their research directors, reviewing every secret project and every experimental technology, trying to piece together something that would work.

***

If Cal thought he was tired before the phone conference, the stress of two hours of trying to keep several dozen geniuses on-point had made him wonder if it wouldn't be better just to let the damn bombs go off so he could forget about them. Forgetting about them seemed like his best course of action because he was out of ideas. Time to let the authorities handle it on their own and go home to Claire.

Then the phone rang.

"Dr. Bellotta," the slightly familiar voice said. "This is Larry McKinnon out at Los Alamos. Look, I couldn't say anything with everyone listening because this project is so buried you couldn't find it with ground penetrating radar." Cal ignored the bad science humor. "We do have a project that is showing some early positive results, but it isn't detecting the radiation or its effects so much as it is looking at the shield material.

"Let me explain real briefly. You heard that one of the detection programs being pursued at Sandia is the use of muons, essentially heavy electrons that are all around us, streaming in from space and passing through matter with little interaction. The goal is to detect heavy metals such as plutonium or uranium that might be used in a nuclear device or lead used to shield it by watching the distortion of the muon path caused by the dense material. The problem is that this technology requires two detectors, one on each side of the material, and some time to collect the data. In theory, it could be a drive-through detector for suspect packages.

"Now, of course, that doesn't help you. You can't make everyone in DC drive through and stop while they are scanned. We are working on a Top Secret advanced concept using the distortion of natural muon radiation by dense objects. It relies on motion, and instead of having two fixed detectors and a stable object, we use two directional detectors to monitor the change in muon distortion and map the ambient density of the observed area. Think of it like an infrared camera. What you see with infrared is a color variation that changes with the heat signature of the focal area, like you see on those police chase shows where a fugitive at night looks all red against a green background as he flees. With the muon detector, you're seeing a "density map" and the changes in the density caused by the movement of very dense material can be visualized by the computer to display the motion. Essentially, your cylinder would show up as a high density locus and its movement could be followed as it passes through the surrounding environment, generating a changing density map as it goes.

"This is all very theoretical at the moment, and we have some prototypes cobbled together, but it's not ready for actual use. But I thought you should know about it anyway."

"Let me see if I understand. You say you could track the lead shield as it moves, say in a truck, by the density of the lead? How could you know it was lead and it was the shield?"

"Well, we're not totally there yet, but theoretically the lead will have a different distortion than say, bismuth, which is very close to lead in atomic weight, so we could identify the specific material. Right now, we can't do that, but we can differentiate at about 10 or 12 Daltons. That's the unit of measure for atomic weight. So we could tell the difference between say your lead and industrial metals like iron or steel. Also, the distortion is specific to the material, so you can see the vague shape with our current resolving algorithms. This will get better with time and testing."

"Hold on a moment, would you," Cal asked as he awakened his computer from the sleep mode it had fallen into while he dozed.

"Kirtland Air Force Base is a two hour drive for you. How fast can you pack that thing up? I can have transportation ready to drive it there and then get it to Andrews so we can give it a try."

There was a long pause before McKinnon spoke again. "Maybe I shouldn't have called. You need to understand, this is not a viable technology at the moment. There is no *thing*, as you call it. Right now it's a bunch of discrete pieces held together by cable ties on a metal frame. There's more duct tape on this than there are nuts and bolts. I'm not entirely sure I can move it."

"Listen, Larry, I've got nothing else at the moment. Nothing. Tomorrow is the Fourth and that's when they're going to set these things off, disguised as fireworks. That's 12,000 curies of cesium chloride in a low air-burst over Washington, DC. Think about the consequences of that for a minute. And we're relying on luck at this point, so your thing is already an improvement. Maybe it won't work and we'll waste some government time and money. But maybe it will, and we'll save a lot of lives and property."

"It's simply not possible. I would need a half dozen of my best techs to take it apart, and then they would have to fly with it and oversee the handling and put it back together. And even then, something will get out of specification from the trip and they'll have to diagnose the problem and try to rig some fix. And then it will need calibration. It would be three days before it would be ready to *maybe* work. And then you're going to put it in a helicopter? The vibration alone would mean a tech would have to constantly adjust the energy compensation to correct for the vibration. Really, it's not feasible. I'm sorry."

"This is a DOE program, correct? DOE is Executive Branch. You saw the authority the President has granted me. Please don't make me use it. Let's work together on this. I can have all sorts of resources put at your disposal instantly. This could be the opportunity to leapfrog this technology, and maybe avert a catastrophe."

Again, there was a long pause and Cal let the silence continue.

"OK, then. I'll email you what I need. I'm going to contact Kathy Daly at Sandia. They have some new plastic scintillators that they've doped with chemicals that should improve the resolution of the image. This is not going to be easy, so you'd better have some back-up ready."

SATURDAY, JULY 3

8.18   ANDREWS AIR FORCE BASE, CAMP SPRINGS, MD

Kirtland AFB was not a cargo plane center, as the eight technicians and scientists had learned on arrival in the back of two military trucks. The two hour trip to the base had been uncomfortable, the trucks seeming to have no suspension at all and every expansion joint on the highway was a slap to their bodies. They had disassembled the muon detector and packed it as best they could, it never having been designed to move. Technicians carried several of the more delicate parts on their laps.

The C130 cargo plane that happened to be at Kirtland was their only choice, and even then only after it was appropriated on some very high orders. It proved no better than the truck. Worse, in fact, with rudimentary sling seats and no apparent sound insulation. Adding the five hours of that trip to the two hours in the truck and the four hours of packing the instrument, everyone had been working or bouncing for eleven hours, and for most, this was after a full day of regular work. The mood when the cargo doors opened at 5 AM was fragile, at best.

Cal was waiting at the bottom of the ramp when it lowered and he was met by what looked like an all-geek press-gang—dirty, sullen, and almost scary.

"Who's in charge," Cal asked the first person off the plane and got a thumb gesture towards a short, chubby man who looked to be dressed to attend a summer cocktail party at the British ambassador's residence.

"Hello. I'm Cal Bellotta, your contact here. Sorry about the rush, but time is pretty tight."

The man, dressed in a seersucker suit and a baby-blue bow tie, smiled as he shook Cal's hand with a little more vigor than required.

"Dr. Bruce Caldor. Pleased to meet you. Now, where do we set up?"

"Good to meet you Dr. Caldor. We've got facilities set up at RSL, the Remote Sensing Lab, here at Andrews. They've also made their staff and equipment available, so you should have everything you need."

"Please, call me Bruce," he said with genuine good humor. "The RSL? Very good. I'm familiar with their work, know a few of their people. Can we get some facilities for my team to clean up? And then some food? It has been a particularly difficult night and everyone is a little on edge."

"I understand. We've arranged quarters for you on base. Why don't we get the equipment over to RSL so it's secure and then your people can take an hour or two to get settled and have a meal. It's a little after five now. Say 8 o'clock to get started?"

"Eight it is, then. Let's get cracking, shall we?"

Caldor directed, or more accurately, politely asked, for the technicians and scientists to gather the equipment and, with the help of several airmen, load it onto the waiting truck. Cal watched the pieces come off the plane and his optimism faded with each load. There wasn't a single complete device of any description, just a structural steel frame that stood about four feet high and wide with some steel pieces to keep it upright. A few panels were still bolted to it, but for the most part technicians were carrying individual components and wires and clamps. Cal began to understand Larry McKinnon's reluctance to send this ... device.

Caldor must have seen Cal's expression because he reached up to the much taller man and patted him on the shoulder lightly and said, "I know it doesn't look like much, but just wait. You'll be amazed when you see it work."

Cal thought amazed might be an understatement.

8.19   WAR COMPOUND, 6 MILES NE OF WHITEFISH, MT

The Montana State Police Tactical Command Vehicle was parked about 2,000 feet from the end of the paved road and the start of The Road. Right behind it, the MSP SWAT vehicle was alive with activity as its occupants, along with the FBI SWAT team, suited up and coordinated their hand signals and radio frequencies to make sure they could communicate.

The FBI contingent, including Ed Wachs, the Assistant Special Agent in Charge, a Special Agent Bomb Tech Team, a WMD trained Hazardous Evidence Analysis Team, and a 12-man SWAT team, had flown into Glacier International Airport from Salt Lake City during the night and met up with FBI agents from the Billings, MT office and State Police for the 18-mile drive to Wherever They Were, Montana. They left the location name to the locals, caring only that there was nothing but very rugged forest all around them.

The senior agents and the State Police Captain remained behind at the Joint Operations Center they had set up in one of the three hangars behind the general aviation terminal. Also in the center was Col. Adam Cliffords of the U.S. Army's Northern Command out of Colorado Springs. He was there to coordinate any special operations requiring military assistance. The Northern Command's involvement was a result of their civil support mission where, in compliance with the Posse Comitatus Act, DoD assets were provided for specific, limited, and local action in an emergency that exceeded the capabilities of civil authorities. Terrorists holed up in a fortified compound and in control of weapons of mass destruction which they had shown the intent and capability of using qualified under that exception.

"Hell, why can't we just call up the Guard and go in? They could be here and ready in four hours. We do it your way," he indicated Col. Cliffords by a nod of his head, "and we'll be here for 20 hours cooling our heels while that little asshole does God-knows-what."

"No disrespect to the Montana National Guard, sir," Cliffords said, "but they would be annihilated before they got close. Or somebody would be. See this," he asked, putting one of the infrared photos on the table and overlaying an outline transparency of the compound as they had mapped it so far. "There are eight buildings, arranged in a very defensible array. And between, see these rows of heat signatures? Those are almost certainly heavily-armed defenders, dug-in in trenches."

He switched the infrared picture for an aerial photo and used the same overlay.

"Now look here, and here and all around. They've set up very effective overlapping fields of fire using the woods and terrain to direct to flow of attackers right into their guns. They've got these two pathways here and here. I expect those are sheltered and will allow a force to move out and flank any attackers, possibly using the horses we expect are located here. Mounted cavalry would be much more effective in this terrain than armored vehicles.

"The only way to get into that compound during daylight would be heavy munitions, and that means they would have to slaughter a lot of civilians and then come in fast and hard behind the bombs. You could survive and succeed militarily, but I doubt you could do so politically."

The FBI SAC said, "We'll use the time to surveil the compound and establish regular schedules and movements within the compound. We'll keep them occupied with occasional helicopter forays. By tonight, they'll be exhausted and that will make our job easier. And the information we gather should allow us to plan the most effective way to subdue these people with as few casualties as possible."

"I guess," said the MSP captain. "But the same holds true for my boys. We sit around here for twenty hours and they're not gonna be at their best when we go in."

"You're right," Cliffords said, "and I suggest you release your SWAT members until tonight and let them get some food and rest. We have the compound under constant view, so nothing is going to happen without our knowing beforehand. This is the only trail in or out, so if they try to break out, we can handle that with just your troopers and the FBI guys. Tonight, you and the FBI team will be on clean-up duty. My guys will secure the compound and only then will you move in and we will withdraw immediately. Otherwise someone will go down in friendly fire."

"The objective is Tag Grainger alive because as far as we know, he is controlling the DC weapons," the SAC added. "Secondarily, they will have records, probably computerized and probably in some bunker. If they haven't already, they will destroy these at the first sign of an attack. We really need those intact."

"Yes, sir. I understand that," Cliffords said. "We will be inserting an initial team whose objective will be any command and control resource. They will find and secure it, and that will be the trigger for the main assault."

The captain looked down at the map and back at the Colonel. "Insert a team? How in the name of all that's holy are you going to do that?"

"That isn't important right now. We can, and we will. Your job will be to get in there quickly once we've pacified the compound so my guys can withdraw with minimal exposure. To media and other civilians and even your teams, I mean. The less anyone knows about our involvement, the easier it will be to answer the inevitable questions that will follow."

"I thought this was kosher," the captain said.

"Of course it is," the Colonel answered. "We're operating under the legal mission of Northcom and within established law. Our standing orders are local, legal, and limited. We operate within the same Joint Task Force as you for this specific mission, we have strictly defined and limited objectives, and we relinquish command as soon as possible. We'll be in and out before you know it. Well, not really. You'll know we've been there."

***

The two agents were alert, but saw nothing but trees and undergrowth and heard nothing except the strain of the Jeep engine as it climbed in low gear range to negotiate the barely-passable trail. According to the satellite images and hand-drawn map they had, the compound was about 600 yards ahead. As the trail turned right, they could see a break in the forest cover and the higher elevation of the mountain ahead. At that moment, the Jeep jerked and stopped dead. The driver's first thought was that he had hit a rock and damaged the undercarriage. But then the deep echo of the .50 caliber round reached them and he knew they were under fire, and that there was likely a big hole in their engine block. The second round blew the windshield at dead center, and both agents bailed, gaining whatever cover they could.

"Command this is Point. We're taking fire. The Jeep is disabled. Over."

"Point, Command. Any casualties? Can you see the shooter?"

"Negative, Command. We're both unhurt. It sounded like a fifty. He's likely somewhere up the peak to your northeast, could be as much as a thousand yards."

"Can you withdraw?"

"Negative. I don't think he was trying for us. His two shots were very good and he could have taken us out easily. But I don't want to test that theory."

"Roger, Point. Stay put. We'll get back to you with a plan."

8.20   U.S. Army Information Dominance Center, Ft. Belvoir, VA

Ray ignored the ringing telephone, just as he had ignored the earlier intruder inquiring about his all-nighter and if he was OK. The idea had come to him after talking to Cal early that morning, and wishing it had been as easy for him to identify the truck as it had been for TIDE to identify the terrorist using facial recognition software. And then he thought, why not?

He'd spent the next four hours dissecting the code for the 3DFL software and then writing his own for any inanimate object. In the end, the program would let him define parameters like dimensions, shapes, colors, text, materials of construction, purpose, and all the other descriptors that he could think of, and then match these against pictures and streaming video and even eyewitness accounts to find hits.

The program had been running all the surveillance videos from truck stops, toll booths, and inspection station cameras along the suspected route of the truck and matching them against the eyewitness accounts from the locations in Denver, Kansas City, and Detroit where the cesium had been picked up, and from manufacturer's data on the truck, a blue Kenworth cab-over with magnetic signs on both doors with unknown text and graphics. The trailer also had some unique design features to accommodate the internal bridge crane, and Ray had been able to narrow the search further using manufacturer's data on that, as well.

The program had been running for several hours on the Starlight system and Ray thought he had his answer - it was a 2004 Kenworth T800 pulling a Fruehauf trailer owned by Signal Freight in Golden, Colorado. The trip manifest for the dates in question had it dropping its load at Breezewood,

Pennsylvania. The only problem was that the trucking company had no record of any stops en route, and the driver was nowhere to be found.

8.21 CNN News Headquarters, Atlanta, GA

 **Immigration Near Record Lows**

Mexico, Canada, South America all report record influx from the U.S.

ATLANTA (CNNNational.com) -- Accelerating a trend that began with the U.S. economic downturn and reduced job opportunities, the flow of legal and illegal immigrants into the country has reversed, according to the Immigration and Naturalization Service records. Currently, emigration from the U.S. exceeds immigration coming into the country by over 200% as the economic incentives to leave the country are reinforced by the fears of terrorist dirty bomb attacks. Using indicators such as postal service information, utility usage, and cell phone traffic, officials are estimating as much as a 6% drop in big-city populations, especially over the last few weeks. Officials say they have corrected these numbers for normal vacation travel, and the actual numbers could be even higher as other indicators show a virtual crash in vacation travel this summer season. This could mask even higher emigration figures as many people leaving the country could be mistaken for vacation travelers.

8.22 Cuban Consulate, Maracaibo, Venezuela

The Krait team was not enjoying their trip to Venezuela. In addition to reporting their failure, they had to hide their wounded member in a local safe house and then substitute two of their local assets for the missing team members so they would appear to be the full team of Canadian engineers. The local police had questioned them earlier in the day, and while their documents and cover story had held up then, the team leader knew that wouldn't last. The first time someone asked them a question about oil sands, their ignorance would be evident and the cover blown. Thankfully they had worn the hoods and the family wouldn't be able to ID them.

Even so, they had been tasked to surveil the Cuban Consulate until other arrangements could be made. NSA intercepts had put al Hasan there, and their employers wanted him bottled up until a new plan could be arranged. The Krait team leader didn't care about any of that. He just wanted to get back on the Petro Canada plane and beat it out of there. Instead, he was on the roof of an outpatient clinic two doors down from the Cuban Consulate watching the front door while another team member was on the far side watching the rear. Fortunately the Consulate was just an apartment in a building with no elaborate security, or any security that could be seen.

It was lunch time and they were expecting their relief, so when the door in the small shed that covered the staircase opened, he thought they had arrived. Instead, a stranger emerged and looked back and forth at both of them and then approached the leader.

"Who are you," he asked in Spanish, "and what are you doing on my roof?"

Anticipating just such a situation, the leader had prepared a very thin cover story, and answered, also in Spanish.

"We are American private investigators," he said as he showed him one of his many phony IDs. "We were hired by a rich American woman to follow her husband here. He comes to Maracaibo frequently and she thinks he has a woman here. And she is right. We're watching him and getting evidence so she can divorce him and get his money."

Ah," said the man. "Like Magnum, PI. I see him on TV. That is very adventurous. But still, you should not be on my roof."

The leader could translate this in any language and gave him the ten folded American ten-dollar bills he had prepared for this occasion. The man took them and looked at them for a moment and then said, "But there are two of you."

The leader reached in his other pocket and took out the other folded bills he had ready and handed them over.

"That is all, you understand," he asked the man, who put both wads in his pocket.

As he walked away, he said, "Yes. That will cover today."

8.23   WAR COMPOUND, 6 MI. NE OF WHITEFISH, MT

Tag gathered his senior staff for lunch. He wanted to review the situation and assess the mood of the troops and their families. The first sign that something was wrong had been the sudden loss of Internet and cell phone communications. The explanation had been technical problems, and everyone seemed to believe that. But then one of the perimeter snipers had reported a large law enforcement presence on Trumble Canyon Road leading to the compound. That had led to much speculation, and Tag needed to know what people were thinking. The meeting, held in Tag's private quarters, included Josef, the only other person there who was fully aware of the DC plans, Donald Horner, in charge of the compound defense, and Millie Dempsey, responsible for the women and families. Two of the younger wives served the lunch and kept the beverages refreshed.

"Mr. Grainger," Millie started, "can't we evacuate the women and children. They are not necessary for our defense, and they are so frightened, especially the mothers for their children. They don't want to see them die here."

"Die! We are not going to die here, Millicent," Dave Horner interjected. "The government wouldn't dare attack us. We have done nothing illegal and there is no reason for them to even be here except for harassment. No, we are too well defended for them to try anything without some very powerful reason, and we have not given them one. So tell your women to get a hold of themselves."

"Is that true, Mr. Grainger? Are we really just being harassed?"

"I don't believe it is as simple as that, although Mr. Horner is absolutely correct about our defense. We are very secure here. The government would need to use a very strong force to defeat us, and I believe that will keep us safe. They don't want non-combatants hurt any more than we do. It is, after all, why we went to so much trouble to design and build this refuge.

"But Mr. Horner," Tag continued, turning his attention to him, "We can't be lax in our readiness. WAR has been very successful these past two years in gaining increasing popularity among real Americans. They see what the government has to do to maintain its hold on power, and they like it less and less as our freedoms are violated and our hard-earned money stolen. I believe that the Zionist Occupation Government would go to great lengths to trump up some justification for attacking us. Just look at what is going on with these Arab terrorists. We haven't seen any arrests yet, and no assurance that we ever will. I would not be surprised to find the government trying to blame us for those attacks. So, Mr. Horner, make sure your men, and Mrs. Dempsey, your women, are alert and ready."

"Yes, of course we will be ready."

"Good. Everyone should get some rest today. If they do attack, it will be at night and we need to be prepared. And Mrs. Dempsey, please tell the women that we cannot do anything except prepare and pray. Once we let the government control our private lives, either by unconstitutional laws or the threat of force, then we have lost and we might as well put on the shackles and bow down to the Zionists and their mongrel supporters. No, we will stand and fight if we are attacked. We have friends who will do what they can to protect and support us. But here, today, we are on our own, and we will show the world that we stand for something, for the values and beliefs of our forefathers, and we too are willing to lay down our lives in defense of those sacred principles. I will be here with you, and I will do the same."

Lunch and inspirational speeches finished, the two guests and the servers left, and Tag got down to business with Josef.

"I am going to die here, today, Josef, and it must be done right."

"I am with you, Tag. We'll show the bastards that they can't scare us into submission."

"No, Josef, I want you to survive this, with as many of our people as possible. Put up a good defense, kill as many of them as you can, but surrender before too many of our own people die. Marcus is in Washington, ready to take command of WAR and to use this provocation and the dirty bomb attacks to stir up support. He will need your help. He will need the eyewitness testimony of the people here. He will need pictures of the casualties.

"And Margaret has established her political leadership, and she, too, will carry our message. They want just me, Josef. They now know, or at least think, that I am in control of the remaining dirty bombs, and they will stop at nothing to find out where they are. Marcus is monitoring things here through our police informants, and when he knows we have been attacked, he will make the necessary arrangements to protect the weapons and get them deployed and used.

"They also want our computers, our records, and they would use those to try to defeat us. That is where I will make my stand, in the communications bunker. They will kill me there, but not before I have blown up the room and as many of them as possible. Only you and Marcus know where the back-ups are. Keep them safe."

"Tag," Josef said, "we can do all of that without you dying. The movement will need you more than ever to carry on after this."

"No, I've made my decision. It is time for new leadership, and I have made the arrangements. It is better this way than by some raghead assassin slitting my throat in the middle of the night. I will not live cowering from those anti-Christs. Marion is taken care of, and my daughters have their own lives. This is my moment, Josef. The moment that will galvanize our people to take command of their own lives. The Christian Covenant of America starts here."

8.24 PENNSYLVANIA STATE POLICE STATION, EVERETT, PA

The Pennsylvania State Police Station in Everett was as close to chaos as it had ever been. Sixty-three of the eighty-one employees of Sybrium Container Solutions were scattered about in every room, including the toilets, the furnace room, and even in individual police cars in the parking lot. The thirty-two officers available were supplemented by fourteen FBI agents and four local Everett Police Department officers, dragooned into service when the order had come down to detain and question each and every Sybrium employee until every detail of the cesium that was no longer there could be extracted.

Sybrium was closed on Saturdays, but that barely slowed the police and agents and techs from RAP with their radiation detection instruments. The front door was battered down, and law enforcement quickly cleared the building to allow the techs to do their job. And their work proved conclusively that there was no cesium there and no evidence that there ever had been. That left human intelligence as the only clue, and the result was the current chaos in Everett.

Cpl. Victor Rodriguez was questioning one of the loading dock foremen and getting a bad feeling about the guy. His bluster seemed to be masking some nervousness, and Rodriguez decided to upgrade this one.

"OK, Mr. Salters, we're going inside now and someone else will want to talk to you further."

Rodriguez got out of the front seat and went to the rear door to let Salters out. When he did, the big man tensed and looked around, and Rodriguez' hand went to his gun.

"Mr. Salters! Look at me. We're going inside. Please cooperate and we'll get this done quickly."

Salters looked at Rodriguez, and at his hand on the butt of his pistol, and seemed to deflate slightly. Rodriguez directed him inside staying a step away for caution. There were no chairs available and Rodriguez told Salters to sit on the floor and wait. Keeping an eye on him, Rodriguez told the sergeant that he had a live one and needed an FBI agent, now.

Special Agent Leigh Evans took Salters into the station commander's office and sat him in a visitor's chair. She took an instant dislike to the guy but forced that out of her mind, trying to remain objective for the questioning. Then she thought, *Screw that. I'm going to rattle this guy's cage and see what he does.*

"Bet you ride a Harley on weekends, don't you?"

"Yeah. What about it?"

"Nothing. Just the mustache, the beer belly, the crappy tattoos. You look the part of the old fat guy trying to be the bad boy. So, give me your full name and social security number."

"Am I under arrest," Salters asked. "Cause if I am, I want my lawyer."

"Full name and social, Mr. Salters," she said, and Salters told her after a slight hesitation. Evans typed into the laptop computer she had on the desk next to her and waited. And then waited some more. Salters became more agitated as she sat silently, staring at the computer screen.

"I said I want my lawyer."

"No, you didn't," Evans answered without looking away from the computer. "You said you wanted your lawyer if you were under arrest, and you're not. Just some routine questioning."

"Well, I changed my mind. I want my lawyer."

Evans turned away from the computer and leaned forward in her chair, elbows on her knees.

"Listen, Salters. I want to be home with my family, but I'm stuck here with you. The point is, you can't always get what you want, and I'm under no obligation to get you a lawyer until, if, and when you are under arrest. So just answer my questions and we'll get this over with."

"If I'm not under arrest, I'm leaving. I know my rights."

"No, you don't. You think you do because you watch *Law and Order* on TV or something, but you have no idea what I can do to you here and now under the Patriot Act. You're under suspicion of harboring weapons of mass destruction. Shit, I could send you to Guantanamo Bay right now and no one would ever see you again."

"Weapons of mass destruction? You're crazy, lady. I never even seen any kind of weapon 'cept my own. And they sure as hell aren't gonna mass destruct nothing."

"Oh, wait, here it is," Evans said going back to the computer and tapping a few more keys. "You bank at First Commonwealth in Bedford, don't you. Wow, you put in four cash deposits of $9,500 each since the twenty-fifth. That's like, every other day. And funny it's $9,500 each time. Just under the $10,000 Federal reporting limit, isn't it? Let's see, four times ninety-five hundred, that's $38,000. What, did you use the other $2,000 on beer for your biking buddies?"

"I want my lawyer. You got no right to be lookin' at my personal business."

"Yeah, well, you do that and there goes your $38,000 windfall at $300 per hour."

Evans took out her cell phone and dialed a number. "We've got him. I'm in the commander's office. No, he's not talking, but he's got a real nice cash situation and he keeps asking for a lawyer. We don't need to do that under the Patriot Act, right? I thought not. Come on in and meet our Mr. Salters."

Evans sat back and crossed her arms and stared at Salters.

"I want my fuckin' lawyer," he shouted, getting red in the face and looking dangerously explosive. Evans didn't move or speak, and the door opened and a tall, balding agent in a dark suit came in, looking the part of the person in charge.

"Sorry we're not going to be able to comply with your request, Mr. Salters. I'm Special Agent Forbes, and I'll be asking you some more questions, so please just wait a moment while I talk to Agent Evans."

They moved behind the commander's desk and spoke in whispers and then Evans showed Forbes the computer display, and he nodded and said out loud, "Good work. That's enough to invoke the Act. We'll take him to Harrisburg and process him there."

"I ain't going nowhere. I want my lawyer!"

"Mr. Salters, I am placing you under arrest under the provisions of The Patriot Act for possession and intent to use weapons of mass destruction. You will be taken to the FBI Field Office in Harrisburg for processing and further questioning. You will be interrogated without benefit of counsel, and then a determination will be made as to your disposition. That could include everything from release to incarceration in a Federal holding facility until such time as a decision is made on charges and a Grand Jury is impaneled to hear the evidence against you. At that time you will be able to engage counsel. However, your bank accounts will be seized as of today, so finding one might be difficult. If you cannot afford counsel, of course, you will be represented by a public defender. So, do you understand what I've just told you?"

Salters sat and stared at Forbes for a moment, like he was trying to understand what was happening to him, which was exactly what he was doing.

"I didn't do nothin'. The money was owed to me."

"Are you saying you want to talk about this, Mr. Salters," Forbes asked.

"Yeah, I'll talk about it. Like I said, that money was owed to me."

"OK. By whom, and what for?"

Salters seemed surprised by the question. "None of your business. It was owed to me and you can't prove otherwise."

"You clearly haven't understood what I've been telling you. I don't have to prove anything. I don't have to get you a lawyer. I don't have to consult with my superiors."

Forbes stepped close to Salters chair and leaned into his face.

"What happens to you from here on out is totally up to me. Right here. Right now. I make one decision and you're in solitary in a Federal facility and no one talks to you except me and my associates. I make another decision and you walk out of here with your $38,000 in the bank. Now, do you have something to say to me that will affect my decision?"

Again Salters sat and stared, and finally said, "Yeah. He just asked me to store a couple of drums until he sent someone to pick them up. No law against that."

Behind Forbes, Evans turned on her digital recorder and set it on the desk.

"Who is he, Mr. Salters?"

"I don't know. Some guy I met on a Poker Run up to Punxsutawney. Gave me $40,000 in cash and told me to take real good care of them."

"And did you?"

"Yeah. Some truck delivered them along with a regular shipment and I put them in the cage we have for toxic shit."

"When was that?"

"It was a Friday. The same day them dirty bombs went off."

"What happened to the drums?"

"Someone picked them up yesterday morning."

"Yesterday? Who picked them up?"

"The guy called me Thursday night and told me to be at the plant at two in the morning and to expect him to come by and get the drums. Said I needed a fork lift to load them and that was it. Three SUV's arrived sometime before three and I let them in and loaded the stuff like they wanted and they left. That's it."

"You put the drums into SUV's?"

"Not the drums. Some metal thing that was in 'em. I tossed the drums out back with the other empties to be recycled."

Without a word from Forbes, Evans dialed her cell phone and sent agents out to find and secure the empty drums.

"OK. What about these SUV's. What can you tell me about them? Make, model, color, everything."

"I didn't pay no attention to that. They was all big ones, though. Escalades or Navigators or something like that. I did notice the weirdest thing. They had cut holes in the tops and put some magnetic panel over them. They took the panel off and I lowered the metal can through the hole. They was heavy, I can tell you that. Forklift had to work, and them SUV's settled real far on their springs when I set them down."

"What can you tell me about the drivers?"

"Nothin'. They never got out. Only my guy. He was drivin' the first SUV."

Forbes turned to Evans and said, "Stay with him. I'll be right back."

8.25   WAR Compound, 6 Miles NE of Whitefish, MT

Cpl. Terry Murcheson and PFC Omar Francis stood by the side of Trumble Canyon Road, about 3,000 feet north of The Road, and watched the Hummer turn around and return the way it had come. When it was out of sight, Francis checked his GPS and locked in their starting point. Murcheson checked his M110 Semi-Automatic Sniper System to make sure it was secure and protected in its lightweight padded case. It was a system because it included the Knight's Armament M110 semi-automatic sniper rifle, a Harris swivel bipod, a Leupold 3.5-10x scope, and an AN/PVS night sight. Murcheson's shot would be at night, but he never took chances and the daytime optic was there because it was only 2 PM and they had seven hours of daylight full of unforeseen circumstances, like having to fight their way out. Francis has a standard-issue M4 carbine for more firepower, but Murcheson wanted the ability to suppress any attack before it got within range of the M4.

Weapons slung, they started their 1,500 foot trek - 1,100 forward and 400 up. Within 150 feet, they were in thick woods, unable to clearly see more than about 100 feet in any direction. The GPS kept them going in the right direction, and Francis, taking the lead, figured they were traveling one foot sideways for every two feet forward, adding 50% to their trip. He wondered if the other two sniper teams had similar terrain to negotiate before they were all positioned to provide cover for the insertion that night.

The incline at this point wasn't bad, but it was constant, and they knew it would get worse as they worked themselves up the mountain to the promontory that their computer maps back at Ft. Harrison in Helena had shown to be the best vantage point above the compound. The problem with vantage points, Francis thought, was that they were always a disadvantage to get to, and this one was no exception. The approach to this promontory was required climbing most of the 400 vertical feet in a 500 foot horizontal distance, making it a 37° angle. They were literally mountain climbing.

They had been moving slowly up the mountain for about thirty minutes, taking their time because they had plenty of it and didn't want to wear themselves down, when their earpieces both sounded simultaneously.

"Badger, this is bison. Hold at current location."

They were Badger, and their control back at Ft. Harrison was Bison.

"Roger, Bison. Holding here. What is the problem?"

"We have a target at your 10 o'clock, 900 yards and moving in your direction. Maybe 500 feet above you."

"Do you have analysis?"

"Yes. Single person, moving along a trail, appears to be carrying a long barrel weapon. The trail he is on heads directly toward you and then hairpins back. The hairpin is 80 feet above and 200 feet southeast of your destination. It is, in fact, your alternate destination should your primary prove unsuitable. Our analysis is that he is deploying for observation and defense."

"Roger, bison. What are your orders?"

"Take cover and concealment measures and standby. We're working on that now."

Murcheson and Francis settled down under a large pine tree, Francis aimed toward the target, and Murcheson in the opposite direction. The cameras and infrared detectors on the drone circling 15,000 feet above them, and 19,000 feet above sea level, were much better sentinels than they were, but it always felt better to see for yourself, even if you couldn't see anything.

"This is not good," Francis said.

"Yeah. I'm glad I'm the shooter. That means you get to do the hand-to-hand."

"There will be no hand-to-hand. My little buddy here," Francis tapped the Beretta M9A1 pistol in the holster at his belt, "will see to that."

"What if they want him alive?"

Francis hadn't considered that possibility and went silent. The silence went on for six more minutes before Bison spoke again.

"We estimate he will be fifty minutes to station. Can you get there in thirty?"

"Negative. We're less than halfway to the primary destination and you say he is another 200 feet from there. We will be approaching uphill to his stationary position."

"I'm sending new coordinates to your GPS. They will take you around the peak at your 9 o'clock and put you on the same trail, approaching the location from above and behind. You are to capture the target if possible. Eliminate him if not. This position will be your new primary."

As they got up to move, Murcheson smiled at Francis. "I guess your little buddy doesn't get to come out and play today."

***

In the FBI's Joint Operations Center, Col. Cliffords, the Northcomm liaison and Agent Wachs watched the real-time output from the drone and listened to the commentary from Ft. Harrison. They had just participated in the decision to change the sniper team's mission to include possible combat and a new primary shooting location. Cliffords didn't like change in the middle of a mission, although he could recall none where it hadn't been necessary.

"All right. Nothing we can do about that. Let's get back to our problem."

Cliffords tapped some keys on the computer and the screen went to a replay of earlier infrared surveillance. He fast forwarded it and faint red smudges that were people and horses within the reception of the drone's heat-sensing cameras, along with the occasional dogs and cats, moved around the screen like they were electronic pinballs controlled by invisible bumpers and flippers. He slowed it to normal speed and pointed to a red signature that just appeared and then faded to a smaller one which moved away.

"There. We're guessing that is the door to an underground bunker, probably the command and control center. The bright flash is the door opening, letting the heat out. There is a window here," he said and pointed to the spot where the red smudge had appeared, "so we're not seeing the actual door and person, just the effect of the heat transient. And then the person moves up some stairs and you can see the signal brighten as they get closer to the window."

He fast forwarded again and stopped when a red smudge retraced the previous path, ending with the same bright flash and then nothing.

"That was someone going in. This gets repeated occasionally, so people are moving in and out. So far the count is that there is one person in the room, but we don't know if there was anybody already in there when we began surveillance, so the number is a guess.

"We don't know anything about the door, but we have to assume it's metal and locked. Otherwise, why have a bunker at all? The walls are clearly concrete or something similar because there is absolutely no heat signature at all. In fact, the walls seem to be a bit cooler than the ambient air temperature which would support the conclusion of a below-grade bunker."

Wachs stared at the screen for a moment, watching faint red smudges move in seemingly random patterns.

"We have to get those computers," he finally said. "Even if we take him alive, Grainger is not going to tell us anything in the time we have left. He's an old man and any extreme interrogation will kill him. And if he dies in the assault or even after, we have to assume his people have orders to detonate the weapons. Can you get into that room and secure it before they have a chance to destroy everything?"

"You mean if they haven't already? There is no guarantee we'll get anything out of there. But I can tell you that unless they've prepositioned thermite grenades and have a remote detonator, they won't have time to do much of anything from when we blow the door until they are dead or disabled."

"OK, but how will you get to the door without raising an alarm?"

Cliffords tapped some more keys and the view changed to a camera above the compound. Wachs could clearly see people moving around outdoors, but he couldn't tell if they were men or women. On the top of the main building, a single person sat on what appeared to be a platform.

"The buildings are arranged in a rough oval with the main building in the center. On the right, the east side of the compound are the family living quarters, there multi-family building with probably nine families in total. On the left are a smaller barracks, we think for the single women, and the kitchen and mess hall. In between those two building is what appears to be stables for twelve horses. In front of the main building is the men's barracks and behind is the maintenance shop, generator, and a water pump pulling from their storage tanks here, just north of the shop and slightly above the compound. And these," he said, pointing to straight, wide paths connecting the men's and women's barracks to the main building, "are trenches, probably for movement between buildings during any attack. They connect to basement-level doors in all three buildings, so they are not exposed coming or going.

"See this on top of the main building? That's some rooftop observation platform," Cliffords continued. "It is manned constantly, and there is a hatch and ladder leading to the second floor. Then stairs here and here," he said pointing to areas on the screen at the front and rear of the building. "The plan is to rely on an airborne led operation, a HAHO team. That's a High Altitude, High Opening parachute drop that is very precise and very stealthy."

It was after 4 PM when the helicopter finally started spinning its blades. Cal and Bruce Caldor watched, but most of the others were sitting or even lying down on the gleaming linoleum floor of the RSL hangar, too tired by then to watch, and only hoping this test would prove successful so they could get some sleep.

They were several hours behind schedule as there had been problems getting the high voltage setting correct on the power supply. Even now, a technician was going with the crew for the sole purpose of turning it up or down to compensate for the drift caused by the vibration of the helicopter.

The plan was to sweep the area around the RSL building and try to get a density map. Two lead containers had been borrowed from the RSL storage room, and they approximated the size of the cesium shields they would be trying to find. These were in the back of a pick-up truck belonging to one of the RSL techs, and he was to drive it down the approach road while the helicopter made several passes from different angles and speeds to test the response characteristics. This was new territory for the Los Alamos people as they had only tested with the device stationary, moving various objects past the detectors to simulate instrument motion.

As the truck and helicopter followed their choreographed routes, Cal listened to the radio chatter between the pilot and the lead tech on the ground. It didn't sound encouraging. After 20 minutes, he heard the tech say, "Bring it back. We'll have to try the Sandia detectors."

Caldor went and spoke to the tech and, after some impatient gestures that Caldor took in stride, he returned to Cal and said, "The response time is totally inadequate. We would have to hover over every vehicle for 900 milliseconds to get any accurate resolution. We're going to have to try the Sandia detectors. They have a quicker response, but it will take some time to install them and get the voltage settings right. I don't know if my team can keep at it without some rest."

"Could the RSL techs do the installation while your team grabs a couple of hours?"

"I suppose so. They know their stuff and they've been working with us all day. Yes, that would be good. It will probably take four hours to make the change. I'll send my team back and have them return at nine. I'll stay and work with the RSL people to make sure everything goes right. You should probably get some rest yourself. There's nothing you can do here until we're ready for the next test."

Cal nodded and went in search of a couch.

8.27   9900 Stoneybrook Drive, Kensington, MD

The press conference was being held on the patio of the visitor's center at the extravagant Washington, DC Temple of the Church of Jesus Christ of Latter-day Saints, the Mormons. The arrangements had been made in haste, and church officials knew only that one of the politically-prominent church members was announcing the formation of a new Christian political action committee and wanted the temple's soaring spires as the backdrop. No harm in that, they thought.

Margaret Hancock stood at the microphone-laden podium with church officials and her entourage behind her, and spoke from prepared notes. This was her moment, the commencement event for her new dream, and she wasn't taking any chances with a mis-spoken ad lib.

"Today I am announcing the formation of a new political action committee called the Christian Covenant of America. As an elected official, I am barred by law from participation in such a PAC, so I am simultaneously announcing my resignation as the Lieutenant Governor of the great state of Idaho. I will be assuming the privilege of leading the CCA to a new chapter in American history. A chapter where we regain the lost faith and morals of our ancestors. A chapter where once again Christian principles and precepts guide, and yes, even command our actions.

"The mission of the CCA is no less than the establishment of Christian doctrine as the law of the land. Of Christian charity as the obligatory means of loving thy neighbor and caring for all. Of Christian strength as the bulwark against the encroachment of evil and depravity. Of Christian love as the guiding principle of the American family.

"The CCA will be a new and radically different kind of PAC. We do not seek to support any specific candidate. We support an idea. We do not seek to influence Congress or the Executive. We seek to influence those around us with our Christian example. We do not seek to pass or overturn any specific law or regulation. We seek to invoke the law of God. And we will not be enlisting the powerful to affect change. The most powerful one is already on our side.

"The CCA is a grassroots association of Christians whose goal it will be to find and join with our like-minded brothers and sisters in communities where all our neighbors share our values. In communities that will grow and prosper and spread the word of God and America. And we will use our resources to support those communities, and those that want to join us.

"CCA will be headquartered in St. Paul, Minnesota, and I will be relocating there as soon as possible to personally see to it that our message is spread to Christians throughout America. We have today opened the doors to our satellite offices in Bismarck, Pierre, Helena, Boise, Cheyenne, and Salt Lake City. You may recognize those cities as the capitals of their respective states, and that is where we will be starting and concentrating our efforts.

"Let me tell you from my heart that I have never been so motivated, so determined, so certain that we are doing the right thing. We only need to look at the recent attacks on America by foreign terrorists with weapons of mass destruction to understand that America is not working well at the moment. Decades of ambivalence by the good Christian backbone of this country have dulled our morals and our determination. People, some with good and Christian intentions, some not, have taken us down a path of compromise and miscegenation. While we have struggled to maintain our Christian values, others have stolen our rights and our principles and our wealth, one little bit at a time so we hardly noticed.

"That stops now, and I am here to lead the Christian Covenant that will guarantee that."

8.28   WAR Compound, 6 Miles NE of Whitefish, MT

Bradley Allen loved his job. Who wouldn't? He got to hike in God's country all day, high up where he could see and not be seen. Alone for most of the time, with only God for company. And he got to carry a really big rifle, and even fire it from time-to-time. He had food and water. He had shelter at night. He had like-minded people around him when he wanted company, which was not often. And he got to hike all day.

Bradley knew his area. He was responsible for the northeast quadrant of the area surrounding the compound, and he hiked it every day, exploring and watching. He knew the local animals, and he thought they knew him. He was part of the landscape. Bradley was 23 years old and a trusted sentinel and true believer in the principles of WAR.

Today was special, and Bradley spent more time watching than exploring. He and the other sentinels knew law enforcement was nearby, watching, waiting. He'd seen their vehicles occasionally on Trumble Canyon Road, about 700 feet below his trail. He'd been briefed by Josef himself on their duty tonight. Bradley knew right where he wanted to be if and when they came. It was his favorite spot, and outcropping dropping 150 feet almost straight down, overlooking the compound and the approaches to it. He would often sit there for hours, using his rifle's telescopic sight to watch the activity in the compound, people moving around, doing their chores or just visiting, totally unaware that he was watching. It was as close to being God that Bradley wanted to get.

Today was different. He knew that somewhere above him, someone else was playing God and watching him. But Bradley was a survivalist. He read the online forums, he knew the tricks. He knew how to defeat those watchers, at least for a while. He had a camouflaged thermal blanket. And he had a cave. The blanket would hide him for a while before it heated up, but that wouldn't be until he was inside his cave, where the blanket would hide any slight increase in the temperature of the interior. Bradley would hole up there until midnight, and then move to his spot. They would spot him sooner or later, but he was hoping the outcropping would give him some protection from their smart shit, at least long enough to use the Barrett 50 he carried, and to deliver a few of the enemy to God for judgment.

The cave was about 200 feet away when Bradley figured it was time to go invisible. He took the blanket out of his pack and spread it on the trail to reach ambient temperature and become part of the background. When he figured it was ready, he picked it up and held it over his head like a cape and started jogging to the cave. It wasn't perfect, but he figured it was good enough.

***

"The target has disappeared, Repeat. The target has disappeared."

Murcheson and Francis stopped climbing and looked at each other in disbelief.

"Disappeared," Murcheson said into his microphone. "What do you mean, disappeared? He can't just vanish."

"He did. There one moment, gone the next. He's got a hidey hole that doesn't show on IR. We switched to visual and there's nothing there. We thought we saw some movement, but the replay doesn't show anything significant. He's gone."

"You have his last location fixed?"

"Yes, we do. Downloading the coordinates to your GPS. You're less than 600 yards from the spot. Take care because he's probably gonna see you before you see him."

"Thanks for that. Francis is taking point."

"Roger that. You now have our priority for viewing, so we'll keep an eye out. Let you know if we spot anything."

Francis gave Murcheson the finger and took point as they started toward the new destination.

***

They lay on soft pine needles under different trees, about 20 feet apart and about 100 feet away from the point on the trail where the target had disappeared. They each carefully examined the terrain, Murcheson using his Leupold optic like a telescope, and Francis using his binoculars. Hand signals told each other the same thing - *I see nothing*. They had three and a half hours of daylight left, and another four hours after that until the shooting started, but Murcheson had planned to use that time to memorize the compound and prepare for action. After he took out the sniper, his orders were to support the Special Forces who would be making the actual incursion.

After waiting and watching for a full thirty minutes, Murcheson signaled Francis ahead to examine the spot where the target had disappeared while he stayed under the tree and provided cover. Francis gave him the finger again and went to look.

"Right there," the controller told Francis when he reached the spot. He crouched just off the trail and looked carefully around. Seeing nothing, he went onto the trail and started looking for signs that someone had been there and which direction they had gone. There might have been some disturbance of the underbrush at one spot, but Francis wasn't sure.

"Nothing," he whispered into his microphone.

"All right," Murcheson answered. "Proceeding to our destination. We'll deal with this guy when we have to. Keep an eye on us, bison. I don't want any surprises."

8.29   CNN News Headquarters, Atlanta, GA

 Prank Turns Deadly in Local Theater

Movie-goer held for questioning in teen-ager's death

ATLANTA (CNNLocal.com) -- A teenager's prank cost him his life today at screening of the 2010 Matt Damon movie, *The Green Zone*. A 17-year-old boy (name withheld due to his age) crashed into the theater, witnesses say, wearing military-looking dress and a ski mask. He was brandishing what turned out to be a toy gun and screaming unintelligible words that the audience took to be Arabic. He leapt onto the stage with the movie running behind him and raised the weapon. At that point, one of the audience members took out his licensed pistol and shot him. The boy was pronounced dead at the scene. Police took 42-year-old David Lee into custody for questioning. James Olson, owner of the independent theater, said they were showing the old movie about terrorist weapons of mass destruction because he is having trouble getting any new movies. Hollywood's virtual shut down of new releases due to poor attendance at theaters is making it difficult to attract movie-goers, and he thought the topic might be popular in today's climate. A spokesperson for the boy's family declined comment.

8.30   REMOTE SENSING LAB, ANDREWS AFB, CAMP SPRINGS, MD

It was nearly midnight before the Sandia detectors were finally installed and calibrated and everything was working well on the ground. It was again time to launch the helicopter and see what problems motion brought to the equation. By now, the Los Alamos and RSL teams looked like refugees, with various levels of dirt, grease, and facial hair providing that image overlaid on slumping posture and sluggish movement.

The test was to be repeated, this time in the dark, and this time with Dr. Caldor in the helicopter to monitor the device first-hand. Cal noticed that Bruce, still over-dressed in a tactical-looking outfit out of one of those high-end safari magazines, was not eager to get aboard and guessed that helicopters were not his favorite mode of transportation, or possibly he had never been on one. In either case, Cal gave the guy a lot of credit. He had rested less than any of them and was overcoming some level of fear to try to get his project working.

The helicopter took off and the truck started its run, and Cal watched. There was no radio chatter this time with Caldor aboard. It was more difficult to watch the progress as all he could see were the lights of the helicopter and the truck and it appeared that they completed the pre-arranged route. The truck returned to the RSL hangar, but the helicopter made several more passes over the area, sometime stopping to hover, and at others flying over the same area at different speeds. Cal decided this was a good sign and Caldor was simply fine-tuning the instrument.

When they landed Caldor jumped out and strode toward Cal with a determined expression.

"Nothing," he said. "The resolution time actually deteriorated. We're at over 1,100 milliseconds to get an image. We'll need an improvement factor of at least five if this is going to work, and I don't know how to get it. Even five is marginal. I'd like it to be six or better. I'm sorry, but I'm at a loss. I don't know what more we can do."

"Let's get everyone together," Cal said, "and see if anyone has any ideas. And can we get Sandia on the line? Maybe they can help."

Half an hour into the group discussion, with several scientists and engineers from Sandia National Lab on the speaker phone, it became apparent to Cal that this was a dead-end. The speculation about the problem and the suggested solutions were all at least several days in the doing, and he didn't have several days.

"All right, everyone. Let's get some sleep. You've done good work here today, and I really appreciate your efforts. It looks like we're just not going to be ready in time. Get some sleep and we'll get together at seven tomorrow and see if we have any new ideas. Thanks."

This time Cal headed for his own bunk on base. No need to sleep on the couch nearby when nothing was going to get done.

Part Nine – Independence Day

9.01   JW Marriott Hotel, Washington, DC

Officer K'tema Mbeki, K-man to his friends, made his 2 AM rounds through the underground parking garage at the JW Marriott Hotel. He was off-duty, but in keeping with DC police policy, he was allowed to wear his uniform and service weapon on his second job as a private security officer. He worked weekend nights, the least popular shift, but the one that fit best with his regular duty and the needs of his family.

K-man was a diligent and serious cop, determined to do a good job and advance in the department, so he always checked the DC Metro Police Intranet before any shift to make sure he was aware of current alerts even though he was not on official duty. Among other notifications, tonight he'd seen a BOLO, be on the lookout, for large SUV's that seemed to be heavily loaded. Confirmation of the target vehicles would be a magnetic panel on the roof covering a hole. He had thought the alert rather odd, but hadn't given it much thought.

Until now.

He looked at a black Cadillac Escalade parked near the garage exit and considered the situation. It was facing out and riding very low, mostly in the back, and K-man looked carefully around the garage to see if there were any threats. Seeing nothing suspicious, he approached the Escalade from the driver's side, hand on his pistol, eyes scanning the area. The rear windows were heavily tinted, probably more than the law allowed, but he doubted that was the cause of the BOLO. More likely it was something they concealed, and K-man didn't want to be surprised by a truck full of armed hostiles.

The front seemed to be empty, but he couldn't see below the door sill so he couldn't be sure. He stopped in front of the Honda parked next to the Escalade and waited, hoping to spook anyone inside who might be watching him. When nothing happened, he went to the window and glanced inside, pulling back after a quick look. There was no one in the front so he went back and took a longer look through the windshield.

The back seats were folded down, creating a large and visible cargo area. It was empty except for a cardboard carton in the middle. K-man was also a smart cop and it didn't take long for him to do the arithmetic. No cardboard carton could contain something heavy enough to compress the Cadillac's springs to that extent. Something that heavy that was also small enough to be hidden under a single cardboard carton meant it was made of something very dense - like lead. Lead meant the other BOLO that had had the department hopping for the last two weeks – the stolen cesium.

Certain there were no bad guys inside, he was willing to get a little more intimate with the big SUV. It was six feet, four inches tall, but so was K-man, and he could see the panel on the top. He carefully lifted the edge, hoping there were no booby traps, and saw the gaping, jagged hole cut haphazardly in the roof. He replaced the panel and retreated quickly to the opposite side of the garage where he could keep the vehicle under surveillance from a safe distance.

Positioned where he could see the Cadillac and the exit and the approach from the elevators, K-man dialed 911.

"Officer Mbeki, badge number 11481. I am at the northeast corner on level 2 of the parking garage at 1331 Pennsylvania Avenue Northwest. I have a black Cadillac Escalade matching the BOLO under observation. Confirm heavy weight in the cargo area and a magnetic panel covering a hole in the top."

"BOLO requires me to contact the FBI for instructions," the dispatcher answered. "Do you need immediate assistance?"

"Negative. Keep this line open and advise when you have instructions."

***

The call came through to the Metro Police liaison at the SIOC and she went immediately to the SIOC commanding officer and reported the discovery of the SUV.

"Stay with me," he told her. "We're going to need to coordinate with your people. Do we have contact with the officer?"

"He's off duty and working a shift as a security guard so we don't have radio contact. The dispatcher has him on a cell phone."

"OK. Have him take a few photos of the vehicle from different angles, including a roof shot, and get them here ASAP. Then have him find a good concealed spot to keep an eye on the target vehicle until we can get a SWAT Team there to relieve him. Quietly. Understand? No black & whites, no uniforms. I'll notify the others to join us. You're going to want to get your commander on the line with us. He's going to have some decisions to make."

While she went to make the arrangements, he picked up the phone and called his comms supervisor.

"I need a communications van with cell phone suppression to secure the JW Marriott Hotel, and a four block area extending from 14th and E Streets Northwest. No signals in or out until you get the all clear from me, understand?"

Within three minutes, SIOC had established a SVTC with representatives from the DC Homeland Security Bureau, the DC police, and the uniformed Secret Service police. After briefing everyone on the situation, the SIOC commander threw out his plan.

"We have WMD teams from Quantico deployed here for the search and to disable the bombs. I want to secure access to that floor and then sweep the whole garage from the mobile unit. We'll look for it all – infrared, electromagnetic, explosives, radiation. And, of course, the other SUV's. Once we've cleared it, I want the bomb techs to go in and check for booby traps and to remove the antenna. This needs to be very low profile. We can't alert the driver or we'll lose a good chance to find the other SUVs."

The Metro police commander spoke up by phone. "I don't think that's acceptable. We have a full hotel for the holiday and you're putting hundreds of lives at risk. We need to shut the area down and evacuate. Hell, we need to shut down DC."

"You know we can't do that," the FBI agent answered. "They don't know we're onto the SUVs and if they find out, they'll detonate their weapons at the first target of opportunity. Look, our WMD team from Quantico are the best. Their gear can detect even the slightest amount of radiation and telemeter it back to our labs for instant analysis. If there is anything there, we'll know it immediately and then we can consider an evacuation. In the meantime we're suppressing all cell phone transmissions in the area so they can't detonate."

"I don't like it. We don't know that there isn't some booby trap that will set it off if you tamper with it."

"Yes, we do. We've examined the bomb from Philadelphia and it's semtex. It requires a lot of electrical energy to work. If the cell phone doesn't activate the detonator, the only danger is from the black powder in the tube to launch the device. With the shield plug in place, it won't go very far, and even if all of this went wrong, we're in an underground parking garage with no people there."

***

The couple, dressed casually, walked directly from the elevator toward the Honda parked next to the SUV. She carried an oversized handbag and he had one hand in his jacket pocket. In the corner, hidden by shadows and the sedan he was hiding behind, K-man had his service automatic out and he watched their progress and the rest of the garage for any movement. As ordered, when they stopped at the Honda, he casually walked down the exit ramp to meet the FBI agents for a debrief.

The couple split up and the woman went to the driver's door of the Honda, right next to the SUV. She fumbled in her purse as if looking for her keys while the man stood and waited. After a moment, he signaled her and she took out a camera and snapped shots from every angle and sent them back to the WMD teams waiting discretely near the garage exit. She then took a tube-shaped metal device from her purse, attached to a coil cable that extended from inside, and she quickly scanned the window in the rear door, looking into her purse and then nodding to the man.

In Detroit, Michigan, a customer support agent from OnStar pushed a button, and the doors of the Escalade unlocked with an audible click. The couple then left, following K-man down the ramp.

A two-man bomb tech team passed them on the way in. They did a quick and thorough examination of the SUV and, not finding any triggers or traps, opened the door and one of them climbed awkwardly into the cargo area. He lifted the carton over the top and off the lead shield.

"The wire is held firmly in place by the shield plug. I'm going to have to use the pliers and pull, but I'm not sure I can get it out even then."

Using the pliers and both hands to hold them firmly closed, he pulled steadily on the wire, increasing his force a little at a time. Suddenly, the wire gave and he lost his balance and fell backwards.

"Shit!" he yelled, and sphincters at the other end of his radio slammed closed.

"What happened," he heard in his earpiece.

"The wire broke. I've got maybe a four-inch piece and I can just see the broken end under the shield plug. We're going to have to lift the plug slightly to free it up."

The other man climbed in and they positioned themselves on opposite sides on the shield.

"You'll have to lift and tilt the plug until I can get the pliers into the opening. Slowly, OK. Go."

He pulled the plug toward himself to see if it would tilt enough to expose the wire, but the man shook his head and said, "Not enough room. You'll have to lift a little as well."

He nodded and lifted the plug ever so slightly.

"Good, just a little more," and he lifted further.

"Damn. You can let go. The wire fell into the shield when we lifted the plug," he said into his microphone. "That's as good as removing it because it's now shielded. We're done here."

9.02   WAR Compound, 6 Miles NE of Whitefish, MT

When Bradley Allen woke up, it was dark, just as he'd planned. His watch, silently vibrating on his wrist, told him it was 11:30, the alarm time he'd set. Based on his research, which was mostly popular thriller novels and survivalist forums on the Internet, he figured the enemy would come in the very early morning hours, and he intended to be rested and ready at his post.

He also guessed that they had drones watching every movement in the compound. He was hoping that they were keeping a tight focus there to get the maximum resolution and that he would go unnoticed. To promote that, he intended to use his thermal blanket trick for the dash to the overlook and then, between the blanket being hung like a curtain from the outcropping and the stored heat in the granite, he would hopefully go undetected, at least long enough to do some damage.

He checked his Barrett .50 caliber sniper rifle, bought with every dime he'd ever saved, and crawled out of the cave holding the blanket over his head. He got up quickly and jogged down the trail that he knew very well, the blanket streaming above him. He'd covered most of the 300 feet to the outcropping when a red light flashed across his vision and a dot appeared on his chest.

"Lay down your weapon," someone who Bradley couldn't see ordered, but Bradley stopped and stood still, the thermal blanket draped partially over him and the Barrett in his right hand.

"One more time. Lay down your weapon or I *will* shoot you."

Under the blanket, Bradley clicked the Barrett's safety off and slowly leaned over to set the rifle on the ground. Maybe he wouldn't do any damage to the enemy, but he was sure as hell going to damage their plans for a surprise attack.

Just as the rifle came to a rest on the ground, Bradley pulled the trigger, and the Barrett's resounding .50 caliber boom echoed across the canyon below, loud enough to awaken those who slept there.

***

The gunshot startled Terry Murcheson and he instinctively swung his own weapon from the compound toward the direction of the sound. He'd barely started that move when he heard three rapid tufts of sound, so quiet they were almost lost in the echo of the other gun. He stopped and stayed still and quiet, keeping his own position secret until he knew what had happened.

"Bison this is Badger 2. Target is down," Francis reported over the radio. "Thanks for the alert he was coming. He got off one shot. The compound will have heard it."

"Roger Badger 2. We saw the muzzle flash and yours as well. Big gun, right?"

"Sounded like a 50. Very goddam loud. Checking the target now."

Wearing his night vision goggles, Francis climbed down from the outcropping over Murcheson's position and approached the body on the trail, his carbine pointed and ready in case it moved. It didn't, and the three holes in its chest were clearly the reason why.

"Target is down and out," he reported. He quickly searched the body and recovered the dead man's two-way radio and returned to his spotting duties for his team mate.

***

In the JOC, they heard the exchange between Francis and the controller in Helena.

"There goes any surprise," Cliffords said. "Not that there was a real chance of surprising them, anyway. All right, let's review quickly. Helena, are you on the line," he asked, apparently to the air.

"We're here, Colonel. Go ahead."

"Any chatter on their radios?"

"Affirmative. They definitely heard and are aroused and alert. We're seeing significant movement. It looks like they are assembling in two buildings, the main building in the center, and the v-shaped building on the south side. We have tentatively identified that as a men's barracks. The other buildings seem empty except for the horses in the stable and the three structures on the eastern perimeter. Those three buildings appear to be multi-family residences, either duplex or triplex. By our current count, there are thirty-seven people in the main building, thirty-three in the men's barracks, and twenty-nine in the three eastern residences.

"Shit," Cliffords mumbled. "I don't like this one bit. Captain Allison, are you there and up to speed?"

"Yes sir, Colonel. We are re-working the plan based on this new intel and we'll have it ready in fifteen."

"Control, they will have heard one shot and no return fire and will certainly think one of their snipers took out a target. Are you getting anything on the radios?"

"They tried to raise each sentinel and got through to three. They must know the fourth is down and associate it with the gunshot. I'd guess they have a pretty accurate idea of what's happened and where. There were some deployment commands, but we don't know specifically what they meant. Could be *run for cover* or *don't shoot until you see the whites of their eyes.*"

"All right, let's cause a little confusion. Can you interfere with their radios enough to deteriorate transmission but still allow it?'

"Sure. No problem."

"OK. Do that and have Badger use the radio to report in as the sentinel and say that he's had an accident in the dark and his gun discharged. Tell them he's hurt and can't move. Then end any communication with him. Give them something to argue about.

"And Captain, I'm delaying the assault. Let them sit for a few hours and see if some of the adrenaline wears off. Reschedule for zero three five five. Can the HAHO team circle that long," he asked, referring to the High Altitude, High Opening Delta Force paratrooper team that was designated as the assault force.

"Affirmative. They have plenty of fuel for loitering and return to base."

"Good. Let the Badger, Lynx, and Moose sniper teams know. Oh yeah, is the sentinel still on the roof?"

"Affirmative. He moved around after the gunshot, but he's still there."

"Well, he just got three extra hours of life. Call me with the new plan as soon as you have it."

***

Fourteen minutes later, the secure communications connection sounded in the JOC and the comms tech turned on the microphones and speakers so Cliffords and the others could hear Captain Allison, one minute ahead of schedule.

"Sir," he reported, "we have prepared a new plan of attack. This is no longer a traditional Delta action where stealth, speed, and technology are our advantage. The stealth is gone, and while we still have speed, that could just mean we run into a trap faster. On top of that, the enemy has technology counter-measures in place including night vision, infrared, and respiratory protection against any use of disabling agents.

"This has become a traditional military engagement where tactics and firepower will prevail. We have an unprecedented fifty-five man Delta team assigned to this assault, and there is no time to deploy any other force, so we will use them in unconventional ways, at least for Delta.

"To use the Gulf War term, we will rely on shock and awe. And you can be sure we will deliver. Here's the plan."

9.03   FBI Headquarters, Washington, DC

Things were taking way too long, and the duty agent's legs bounced up and down under the desk while he waited for the two agents in Sterling to report back. They were en route to Carmax in Sterling, Virginia where the SUV found at the Marriott had been purchased less than a week before. The Virginia Department of Motor Vehicles supervisor had been pretty annoyed when she was awakened at 3 AM on July 4th and escorted to her office to track the VIN number from the Escalade with the stolen cesium. She had no idea why she was doing this, only that orders had come down to cooperate fully. Once they had the DMV records, they had a name and a trail to follow.

But that was two hours ago and so far the name had turned up nothing, including no guests or employees at the Marriott. They still had no idea who had brought it in. Fingerprints, hair, DNA, everything in the car was being run through the mobile FBI forensics step-van lab sitting right outside the hotel, but there were a lot of samples and he expected most would belong to Carmax employees. The SUV was still in place and under covert surveillance after the forensics and WMD teams had done their job and cleaned up any traces of their presence.

As if he'd willed it, the speaker for the radio link to the agents came alive.

"Agent Donaldson here. We've got the records on the SUV's. All three were bought at the same time by a Donald Wilson of Winchester, Virginia. We're transmitting the information on all of them."

We've got them, he thought. With the SUV Vehicle Identification Numbers and the owner's name, there would be a paper trail. And with a paper trail, it was just a matter of time before they had all three vehicles and all three bombs. Just how much time would depend on a little luck.

9.04   WAR COMPOUND, 6 MILES NE OF WHITEFISH, MT

Murcheson's watch, a Casio G-Shock digital that kept dead-perfect time, clicked to 3:17. The crosshairs of his night scope were on the back of the head of a man sitting on a folding chair on the rooftop platform, occasionally looking around through night vision goggles. He had something hanging around his neck that looked like a gas mask, and Murcheson had forwarded that information to Helena several hours ago.

"Nothing moving," Francis said as he scanned the compound with his own night vision binoculars. No movement wasn't really important at that moment, it was more of an acknowledgement that he was watching.

In their earpieces, they both heard the Ft. Harrison controller say, "HAHO away. Twenty-eight minutes to contact."

Murcheson checked his watch again even though the controller in Helena would keep him informed of the exact moment he was to take his shot. Shit happens, and he wasn't going to let some freak comm blackout drop the team into a live LZ. Francis did the same to double check the shoot time. No one was taking any chances.

At 3:44 exactly, Murcheson's earpiece came alive. "One minute to contact. You're clear to engage."

It was time to take his shot.

And the target stood up.

With the team coming into the sentry's vision any second, and with no time to think about it or to wait for his movement to stop or to re-target properly, Murcheson took the shot. Center mass allowed for some margin for error, but as soon as he squeezed the trigger, he knew it wasn't a kill. *Thank God for semi-automatic*, he thought as he squeezed off two more silenced shots into the body that had fallen onto the platform. He was dead now.

Murcheson flipped on his laser targeting device and placed the dot on the center of the platform.

***

The HAHO team leader, descending through the night sky at nine feet per second, checked the GPS on his right hand and then the altimeter on his left. He was seven seconds ahead of his teammate to allow him time to clear his 'chute before his partner arrived. He focused hard on the red dot he could clearly see through his infrared goggles and tugged lightly on the lines of his ram-air parachute to keep himself aimed at the target, about 500 feet and one minute below him.

As he approached, he could see the body of the dead sentinel and maneuvered to avoid it and a possible sprained ankle. He stuck his landing better than an Olympic gymnast and hauled in the parachute while moving out of the way for his teammate.

They were the advance team, and what level of stealth the other teams would have would be provided by this team securing the high ground, keeping the enemy limited to ground-level vision. They knew that the sniper teams in the mountains above them were at that moment eliminating enemy sentinels like the one encountered earlier and killed.

They shed their parachutes and made their weapons ready,

***

Murcheson saw the two Deltas land and set up. He immediately refocused on the western- and southern-facing doors and windows. In less than a minute, four more HAHO teams, forty-seven of the most highly-trained and effective fighters in the world, would be landing within range of fixed, armed, and hostile positions. His job, and the job of the other two sniper teams, was to suppress any resistance by making it impossible for anyone to stick his or her head up without finding a 7.62 mm hole in it.

"Heat signature 11 o'clock high," his earpiece said and Murcheson swung to the second-story window at the rear of the main building, his '11 o'clock high' orientation. A shape moved across the dark window and Murcheson shot it, seeing the glass shatter and the shape disappear, but hearing nothing from this range. He knew other windows and doors on all sides of the two fighter-occupied buildings were having the same scenario played out, and he could only imagine the turmoil that must have been starting in the house.

"Heat signature 3 o'clock low," he heard, and shifted his aim.

***

The leader of the second-wave HAHO team, corkscrewing down at a slower rate, got the command from the Ft. Harrison control to proceed and tugged on the left control line of his parachute. He immediately straightened his descent and headed for the open lawn behind the three family housing buildings, and touched down fourteen seconds later, followed by his twelve teammates.

Freed of their 'chutes, they deployed as planned, one automatic weapon each on almost opposite sides at the perimeter to establish an imaginary line segregating the civilian area, and one on each side of the center house between the houses on either side of it. This created a semi-circular no-man's land with fields of fire crisscrossing it at about sixty degree angles. The drawback of this array was the possibility of friendly fire casualties as the teams were all sort of facing one another, as if seated around one-half of a round table. To guard against accidents, all team members were "blue-tagged" and their location displayed on the screen at Ft. Harrison control. From there, controllers could keep them informed of any threats, including the possibility that one of their teammates would be shooting at a target in their direction.

The job of the other nine men, including himself, was to secure the three residential buildings. Three men assigned to each of the residences were to eliminate resistance and safeguard the civilians. For that purpose, one man on each team was armed with M1014 Combat Shotgun using 12-gauge, non-lethal beanbag rounds to subdue any non-combatants who posed a potential threat. A second team member also carried the M1014, but the initial two rounds in his magazine were breaching rounds designed to be fired about six inches from a door latch or hinge, destroying it while dissipating on contact so as not to endanger anyone on the other side.

Their operation would begin four minutes before the assault. Once inside, they would act in concert to get all civilians to the eastern side of the building, away from the anticipated fighting to their west, and down on the floor to provide minimum exposure to any stray bullets. Their orders were crystal clear on one subject – this would not be another Waco, where seventy-six Branch Davidian cultists, men and women and children, had died in a suspicious fire after the FBI's 51-day siege to enforce a search warrant for some very significant weapons violations. No civilian casualties was the goal.

Eighty-three seconds after landing, three front door knobs and latches disintegrated and the doors swung open.

***

The final wave of HAHO troops was actually three separate teams deploying on the "military" two-thirds of the compound. These were the teams who would assault the buildings and secure or subdue their occupants, recover the computer equipment, and capture the WAR leadership for questioning about the three weapons in Washington. One of those two objectives – live leadership or intact computers – was their primary goal, and they were the shock and awe part of the plan

Sergeant Frank Vargas led his six-man team to the rear door on the building they thought were stables. Intel had indicated twelve large animals inside, actually twelve large, moving heat signatures that were compatible with the profile of a horse. Or a cow. Or a large llama. The latter two were mostly jokes bantered about by the analysts, but it indicated a level of uncertainty that Vargas didn't like.

Behind them, four machine guns positions were set up at the perimeter to provide covering fire, and another six-man team cleared the unidentified building that was thought to be a mess-hall and kitchen. These two buildings completely obstructed any view from the two occupied buildings, and surveillance had indicated the stables and mess hall, if that was what they were, were vacant of humans. Vargas had less than two minutes to clear the building, but he was not taking any chances. Two men would enter the building with night vision goggles and confirm the intel, and then the others would enter.

Vargas had picked Justin Cassidy to accompany him. He'd chosen him because he was born and raised on a cattle ranch in Texas and knew his way around horses, just in case anything had to be done to control them. Short of shooting them in the head, which Vargas wanted to avoid as potentially very bad press.

The door was unsecured and opened into what appeared to be a six-foot wide corridor that was about eight feet long and then opened up to the right and left. Across the open area, an identical corridor led to another door on the other side of the building.

"Looks like a stable," Cassidy spoke into his mic. "See the gear hanging on each side? That's some tack, you know, horse saddle stuff. And those are cross ties to keep the horses fettered."

They moved cautiously to the open area, hearing movement and hoping it was just the horses. As they did, the sound of breaking glass, more windows being shot out to provide their cover, spooked one of the horses and it kicked the wall of its stall, sounding like a gun discharging and causing both men to instinctively duck. After a nervous second, they proceeded to the open area and could see agitated horses in each of the stalls, sticking their heads out, bobbing them up and down nervously, and then retreating back out of sight.

"Bravo 1, on me," Vargas said into his mic and the other four fighters quickly entered the door behind them. When they were all there, Vargas pointed at three of them, including Cassidy and indicated they were to search the stalls on the right. He took two men to search the ones on the left and moments later the stables were confirmed unoccupied.

"Bravo 2," Vargas heard. "Mess hall is clear. Proceeding to Bravo 1."

The plan was for the two teams to breach the front of the main building while another six men from the Alpha team breached the rear. In addition to the front and rear entries, there were two cellar doors, one at each front corner, that opened into two trenches that connected the men's and women's barracks to the main building. These were thought to allow covered movement between the buildings in the event of an attack.

At the same time, the Charlie team would be assaulting the men's barracks. In all, thirty-two Delta fighters would be stampeding into two buildings from six different directions after clearing their path with XM25 Air-burst grenades that would literally blow the doors off the buildings, and under covering fire from three sniper teams and eight machine gun positions. It would absolutely be a scene of shock and awe, and the challenge then became to clear the many rooms of any enemy before they could recover.

***

Everything had gone silent in the main building, and the WAR defenders had realized that walls were the only thing between them and whoever was out there with magic bullets that found them the instant they moved from behind anything solid. It had taken four casualties to determine that, and three of those were dead. The radios had become useless the minute the first bullet had hit, and they had no specific information on the status of the defenders in the barracks. Even an attempt to use the trenches to communicate had cost them one more death as snipers in the hills had the angle to see movement there and stop it. Their own snipers were also silent and presumed dead.

Josef knew it was only a matter of time before there would be a forced entry, and his job was to put up a credible fight and accept just enough casualties to rally sympathizers to their cause, and reinforce the opinion that the government should spend less effort murdering patriots and more subduing the real enemy, like the terrorists who would shock the nation that very night. In his own head, Josef had arbitrarily selected twelve dead as a reasonable number. By his guess, he'd already reached eight - two in his own building, the sentry on the roof whose body had rolled off and lay on the front lawn, the runner in the trench who'd tried to get to the barracks, and the four snipers. It was fully possible, he knew, that he'd already reached his target number without once seeing the enemy.

He had started with forty-one people in the building, and he was down to thirty-six still able to fight. It was time for Plan B, and he was sitting in the office trying to figure out what that might be.

***

Precisely at 0355, five explosions rocked the two occupied buildings. They would have been simultaneous explosions except that one of the XM25 operators was responsible for two doors, the western cellar door, and the front door of the main building. It took him three seconds to realign from the cellar door to the front, for the laser targeting system to acquire the new target and set the exact detonation point, for the XM25's 6-grenade magazine to cycle another round, and for the round to reach its precise location 18 inches in front of the door before exploding.

The assault teams were moving even before the grenades were launched and burst through the gaping gaps just six seconds after the explosions. In the main lobby, extending the depth of the building to the similar back door, they found thirty-four unconscious or dazed people, and what was left of two doors. And then the sixth explosion rocked them, an explosion they had expected as the cellar assault team blasted the door to the suspected communications bunker there.

And then they were rocked by the seventh explosion, one from the cellar that was not expected, and they knew like in all military engagements, the plan was the first casualty.

***

Frank Vargas led his team into the cellar and quickly determined it was empty, with rows of industrial shelving containing supplies that he didn't take time to identify. Their target was the only closed space, a room built against the rear cellar wall with one door in the middle of the wall facing them. They had prepared for this to be a reinforced bunker, and it turned out to be accurate. The XM25 would not have sufficient explosive power to blast a steel door set in a concrete wall, so the sapper on their team set the C4 explosive charges and wireless detonators at each hinge area and latch. One last charge was set along the bottom that would detonate a fraction of a second after the others, lifting the now unhinged door out of its frame for clear access. It took him less than thirty seconds, and the team retreated to the trench while he detonated.

The explosion rocked the shelves, knocked boxes and containers to the floor, and the door lay mostly on the floor but raised on one side where it had come to rest against the frame. Access was clear and Vargas and Cassidy charged ahead while the others set up for cover.

As Vargas entered the room, his vision was blocked by smoke and dust, but he could see that it was in fact a command bunker with electronic equipment for security and communications and several computer server racks with multiple computers. *That's what we came for*, he thought to himself. Cassidy followed him in and they moved apart to clear the room. In the far corner, two desks had been turned onto their backs and a large photocopier set in front of them, a strange arrangement that hadn't been caused by the explosion, Vargas knew.

As he watched, a single hand was extended above the barricade, and Vargas went on an even higher level of alert.

"Behind the desk. Put your hands where I can see them and come out slowly," he shouted.

Whoever was there obeyed and he saw two hands, one closed in a fist and holding something.

"Drop what you're holding and come out slowly," he ordered again.

Instead, the thumb of the right hand raised, revealing a button, and then snapped down, pressing it, and Vargas, Cassidy, Tag Grainger, and any hope of finding the weapons, died in a tremendous explosion.

9.05   REMOTE SENSING LAB, ANDREWS AFB, CAMP SPRINGS, MD

Cal was surprised to see Bruce Caldor and several of his techs at work when he walked into the hangar. Caldor, dressed in firmly-pressed, civilian-styled jungle fatigues' was smiling and busy and actually waved at Cal when he noticed him coming in.

"I couldn't sleep very well," he told Cal, "and I went back over everything and it finally dawned on me. The Sandia detectors are more sensitive and have no lag time in their response, so the signal is sent within milliseconds. Therefore the problem must be with the photomultiplier tubes getting and processing the signal. I went back over the specs and there it was! An impedance mismatch. The detectors operate at 50 ohms, but the PM tube needs 400. The result? It takes almost 1,000 milliseconds for the PM tube to catch up to the detectors. We're installing new PM tubes now and we should be able to get response time down to 100 milliseconds or less, well within the range you need."

By now Caldor was rubbing his hands together like he was anticipating a Christmas present.

"That's great. How soon do you expect to be operational?"

"It will take several hours more to mount and connect and calibrate everything, so we should be ready by about nine to run new tests. Then we're ready to go."

"The sooner the better, Doctor. We've got one instrument, two weapons, and a large city to cover. We expect they are planning detonation to coincide with the fireworks display at about nine tonight. We've got less than twelve hours to find them."

9.06 FBI HEADQUARTERS, WASHINGTON, DC

Back in college, studying political science, the FBI ASAC for the DC headquarters had done a paper on intergovernmental relations using DC city government, the surrounding counties and states, and the Federal government as his case study. The topic had been public transportation, and he could now see that he had greatly overestimated the ability of these groups to cooperate.

It was 7 AM on a holiday Sunday morning, the 4th of July, and that might explain some of the problem, he thought. The room was a mix of almost fifty elected officials and emergency response and law enforcement professionals, and the different motivations and priorities of these disparate groups might explain some more. But he was beginning to think it was simply that each and every one of them was senior enough that they were used to getting his or her own way, and in this forum, they weren't.

The debate had been going on for nearly an hour, and as far as he could see they were no closer to a resolution than when they had started. The question was simple—were there going to be fireworks tonight or not? If they were going to shut down DC, then they needed to start very soon or it would be too late. It was already too late for the out-of-towners who packed the hotels in anticipation of the celebrations that day and night. The question was whether the locals from surrounding Maryland and Virginia, and even Pennsylvania and Delaware and New Jersey and West Virginia, would be allowed in. Tourists were already on the road heading for The Mall. It was decision time.

The breakdown of opinion was divided into three groups. The majority of emergency professionals wanted the activities delayed and DC mass transit systems shut down, no one in or out without extreme need, and the roads closed except for emergencies, everyone asked to stay at home and shelter in place. The mere thought of the chaos that would cause motivated the politicians and their appointees to divide into the other two groups.

The smaller of these two groups took a stand and said things should go forward. They knew that one of the three bombs had been found early that morning and law enforcement was hot on the trail of the others. They reasoned that they would almost certainly be captured and the blowback from a cancellation for no reason would cost them votes and expose them to public ridicule.

The larger group simply couldn't, or wouldn't, take a stand. They listened, and if called upon, generally prevented any meaningful progress. If someone had been clearly in charge, this might have been overcome. But the counties didn't answer to the DC Mayor, and the Feds couldn't order the Mayor to put his citizens at risk, et cetera, et cetera, et cetera.

The FEMA Administrator and his Director for CBRNE Operations discretely left the room together and called the DHS Secretary and explained the problem. She, in turn, gave FEMA the green light to exercise some untested authority and invoke a Soloman-esque solution. He returned to the conference room at FBI headquarters where everyone was gathered and commandeered the microphone.

"Ladies and gentlemen," he almost shouted to get everyone's attention. "I'm Stuart Bosman from FEMA. I've just spoken to the Secretary of Homeland Security who is presently with the President and other senior leaders in an alternate command post outside of the DC region. We have gained the President's approval for the following actions. In accordance with my authorities as the FEMA Administrator, we are, under the authority of the Stafford Act, declaring the larger DC metropolitan area a critical national emergency situation as of noon today. FEMA, acting on DHS's behalf, will coordinate all emergency response and recovery assets and resources. Concurrently, and again in accordance with law, the FBI will direct state, local, and Federal law enforcement in support of shelter in place and evacuation related orders consistent with this emergency. We will be closing down all access to DC, including roads, bridges, trains, and airplanes. All private boat traffic will be ordered ashore. All public events scheduled for today will be cancelled or postponed.

"In the meantime, DHS representatives will be assigned to each of your agencies to coordinate roles. This is being done on the authority of the President, and we expect full cooperation from each and every one of you and from all of your staff and personnel. If before noon we have secured the weapons, this order will be immediately rescinded. DHS representatives will be contacting local media to announce this plan. That is all. If you have any questions, please direct them to the DHS liaison assigned to your agency or jurisdiction."

With that, he turned off the microphone and left the room.

9.07   WAR Compound, 6 Miles NE of Whitefish, MT

Private Garrett Eastwood would be the second-to-the-last casualty of the assault. The count of the WAR dead, wounded, and captured had come up one short, and Eastwood and his backup were searching the second floor of the main building, looking for what they hoped was a dead body and not a live bushwacker. There had already been two ambush attempts by hidden WAR combatants, and Eastwood figured there was one more out there somewhere. Both ambushers had been killed, but not before one of them had wounded another Delta soldier.

The women's bathroom was a large area with enclosed stalls, a row of six sinks in a single, long counter, and a communal shower. The stalls had been cleared and all that was left was what looked like a supply closet. Standing to the side and with his backup providing cover, Eastwood yanked the door open and it swung 180°, crashing against the wall. Nothing happened.

His backup nodded once and Eastwood peered around the corner, seeing nothing but piles of towels and toilet paper and cleaning supplies on shelves in a deep closet. What he didn't see, on the top shelf, above the doorframe, was the small woman with a Glock 17. She shot Eastwood twice in the top of his head before she was decimated by a 1.8 second burst, eighteen bullets, from the 30-round magazine of the MK 16 SCAR carried by the backup, becoming the last casualty.

***

Colonel Gary Jameson found some privacy in the same office where thirty-five minutes earlier Josef had struggled with Plan B. It was Jameson's task as the Special Operations Command Officer on the scene to report back the results of the mission. Talking over his Q-Sec secure cell phone, using the same cell tower that they had earlier suppressed, he spoke with his military superior at joint command back at Ft. Harrison in Helena.

"No, Sir, I would not describe this as a success. We failed to fully achieve either objective and I have nine casualties, including three dead. We also have twenty-one dead civilians and twenty-two wounded. Five of the dead were the result of their gathering almost all of their people in the main lobby just prior to our entry. Apparently they were going to surrender but they picked a bad time and place to do it. The remainder died in combatant roles, either fighting or positioned to.

"My own casualties include two dead in the destruction of the command bunker by a single WAR combatant that also resulted in four minor wounds by the concussion in the cellar. Interrogation of the captives indicates that the dead WAR combatant was Grainger, the leader of the group. The third death happened just moments ago as the result of an ambush by a female WAR fighter. She, too, is dead. Our other wounded were the result of a booby-trapped stair in the men's barracks that caused a one-story fall and a broken leg, and one man hit by one of the ambushers.

***

In Washington, eight people were gathered in a secure conference room in the White House Eisenhower Executive Office Building, monitoring the communications and video feeds from the combat scene.

"Shit," one of them mumbled to his lap. Lifting his head, he stated more clearly, "This is not good."

"It's defensible. They were clearly combatants and refused to surrender, even to the point of setting ambushes after the capture of most of them. This is no Waco. We're completely clean here."

"I don't mean that! The operation was carried out as well as possible given the circumstances. I mean Grainger killing himself and destroying any record of those weapons. We know there are two more bombs right here in DC, and that was our best shot at finding them by planning, not luck."

"It's not that bad yet. We've got the one bomb and that means we have leads on the other two. All indications are that they are scheduled to detonate tonight, probably at the finale of the fireworks. If they stick to that schedule, that gives us almost thirteen hours to find two vehicles in a fairly small part of the District. Between cops and surveillance, we should be able to do that."

"The problem," he answered, "is the 'if' in your assessment. Once they know about the action this morning, and there is no way that will stay quiet, they may well change their schedule. And if they are communicating and find we've got one of their SUV's under surveillance, then they may very well change their targets. This could turn into a free-for-all with each of them just going somewhere and detonating their bomb. We don't have the luxury of thirteen hours. We have to count every minute until this is over as a gift from God. And we'd better use that gift well."

9.08   HYATT REGENCY HOTEL, WASHINGTON, DC

From his room on the second floor of the Hyatt Regency Hotel, Marcus made his 9 AM scheduled phone call. He always wanted to be on the first floor of any hotel, giving him more escape options, but the Hyatt was all public space and retail stores at ground level, so he'd gotten as close as he could, figuring he could survive a one-story jump and still run. He'd never had to exercise an escape option, and as far as he knew it wasn't going to be an issue here, but it always added to his sense of adventure and risk to believe he might have to.

The call was answered on the first ring, these being carefully scheduled and necessarily clandestine, and a sergeant in the Kalispell Police Department passed on the news.

"The Feds overran the compound at four this morning, our time, so seven yours," he added, unnecessarily. "I just got the word a few minutes ago. I have no information on casualties or intel, but you'd better assume you're blown."

Marcus hung up without ever having said a word. He'd been more or less expecting this since talking to Tag the day before, but the news was still a shock. There was no time to worry - he had a job to finish and he had to move if he was going to do it. His suitcase was packed, his bill paid, and nothing stopping him, so he left, using the stairs because of another imaginary precaution.

In his rental car and cruising aimlessly, he made the calls, all identical, in sequence.

"Code Yellow," he said three times to three different cell phones that were each answered with the code words *Eagle One*, or *Two* or *Three*. Code Yellow was the first back-up plan and called for the immediate deployment to the primary location and detonate the weapon on a pre-arranged schedule that gave everyone time to get to their location, park their vehicles, and prepare the weapon for launch. Each driver was supposed to call back ten minutes before the hour to be sure all were in place and the attack would be coordinated. It was 9:10 in the morning, and as the attack would take place at 10 AM, he had forty minutes to kill until the next calls.

9.09   MAYFLOWER RENAISSANCE HOTEL, WASHINGTON, DC

Officer Sandy Ellison was doing as she had been told at roll call that morning if she spotted a suspicious SUV. She was to get to a secure location where she could observe without being observed and call it in. That was not as easy as it had sounded. It was going on 8:30 and there was a lot of traffic, foot and otherwise, in the parking garage at the Mayflower Renaissance Hotel. She had done the best she could, and she hoped Avis would understand the broken rear window when they got back the Chrysler 200 she was hiding in. And she really hoped the renter would not show up before she'd gotten some orders and back-up.

When she'd called it in, she'd been immediately patched through to an FBI Special Agent in something called "sigh yock" that she'd never heard of.

"It's a late model Lincoln Navigator. Dark red. Virginia plates XJC-3958. Look, my dispatcher has all of that. Just tell me what to do. There are people and cars everywhere and someone is going to spot me soon."

"We've dispatched a team to inspect the vehicle and secure the area. Just stay put until they get there. We've suppressed cell phone signals in the area so you'll see a lot of frustrated people waving their phones around. Don't worry about that. Do not let anyone into the car. Understand? Anyone tries to get in, you stop them. Friendly if you can, but these people are terrorists and not likely to cooperate. Do whatever you have to, but that car doesn't move."

"Can't I just go and let the air out of the tires? One quick stab with my knife and it's not going anywhere."

"Officer Ellison, that is a very good idea. Can you do it without anyone seeing?"

"I'll have to wait for a break in the traffic, but yeah, I probably can. Driver's side front so he can't miss it when he comes."

"I'll stay on the line. Our team is en route, but they're fifteen minutes out."

She watched the exit ramp in both directions, and when it seemed there were no cars coming or going and no foot traffic in sight, she got out of the Chrysler and opened her Swiss Army knife while she dashed across the garage to the Navigator. One quick stab and there was a pop and a whoosh of air.

"What the hell do you think you're doing," the man jogging toward her yelled.

Ellison had her Glock 17 out and in the position before she finished shouting, "Stop right there and put your hands where I can see them."

The man kept on coming, if anything increasing his pace. Confident in her skills, especially at this close range, Ellison dropped her aim and shot him in the right thigh and he went down hard, not ten feet from her, lying on his stomach.

"Keep your hands where I can see them," she ordered. And he ignored her, trying to roll to his left, putting his back to her, and reach into his right pants pocket.

"Stop and raise your hands. NOW!"

The man continued to ignore her and struggled with his pocket, finally getting his hand in. As he started to remove it, Ellison hesitated. Shoot a man in his back? She'd never considered the possibility. But this wasn't just a man, he was a terrorist, and he probably had a detonator. All of that went through her mind in the time it took her to put three 9 mm bullets into that same back.

***

Special Agent Mark Traynor was speaking to Officer Ellison, getting personal confirmation of her story before releasing her to the DC Metro Police and their investigation of the shooting. Traynor was confident it was justified based not only on her story, but also by the transcript of her confrontation from the phone recording with SIOC. After the interview, Traynor made a note to tell someone to take a look at her as a possible recruit for the Bureau.

Immediately after the mobile unit had cleared the area, the bomb techs had removed the weapon's antenna and the cell phone suppression lifted. With no need to be stealthy to prevent alerting the driver, they were able to make a more thorough search of the vehicle. While that proceeded, the medical forensics team examined the body, recovering a cell phone that he had been reaching for in his pocket, and his wallet. The urgency with which he'd tried to get at his cell phone indicated to Traynor that he had intended to detonate the weapon where it was.

"Get me a list of his incoming and outgoing calls," he said to one of the agents examining the body. "And his contact directory."

They had checked with the hotel and found the driver had registered Friday night with a reservation guaranteed by the credit card in his wallet, and had checked out just before Ellison had shot him. His roller bag was found where he'd dropped it to chase her, and it was being searched before going to the FBI's labs for thorough examination, and his name and address in Pittsburgh were already being investigated by the Field Office there. And there was a flatbed truck standing by to take the SUV to Quantico for thorough examination, bomb and all. It would be quite a procession, Traynor knew, with police and Hazmat and FBI escorts in a rolling roadblock of I-95, but it was more efficient than transferring the shield in downtown DC. And quicker. Time was the enemy now, as much as the terrorists.

All in all, Traynor was happy with the progress, even if they would have preferred the driver alive. And then, even that didn't matter.

"Hey, Mark. You'd better come look at this," an agent in the passenger seat of the SUV called.

Traynor went over and the seated agent handed him a device that looked somewhat like an old-fashioned cell phone. A small LCD display, an extendable antenna, a full keyboard and a brand name he didn't recognize.

"What is it," he asked.

"I have no idea, but given the situation, I'd say it was a back-up detonator."

"Get a picture of it and send it over to the lab. And get this put into something safe and have someone take it over there. And for God's sake tell them not to play with it on the way. "

"That's not all," the agent said. He was pointing to the factory touchscreen in the center of the dashboard with the GPS system displayed.

"It's showing directions from here to the Capital Hilton. That's only three blocks or so. What do you suppose he was going there for? And when?"

"Does that thing store a history?"

"I would think so. Mine does, and it ain't a Lincoln."

"Call it in. Get someone on the horn with instructions on how to download its memory. Let's see if we can get a little history on this guy. Oh, and while you're talking to them, get someone on his phone history, including any location information."

"What about the other one? Do you think it might have something similar?"

"Good. Very good thinking. Tell them to get inside that one and find out. They won't have keys, so someone has to have a way to get power to it."

"I'm on it."

9.10   REMOTE SENSING LAB, ANDREWS AFB, CAMP SPRINGS, MD

They must have elected Buck to be my handler, Cal thought when he saw Buchanan's name on his caller ID. Buck had probably only arrived in DC the day before, and already they had apparently assigned him babysitting duty.

"Hey, Buck. Welcome back."

"Bellotta, you are a pain in the ass, do you know that? I'm told you have half of Los Alamos and some of Sandia out there at Andrews. What the hell are you up to, now?"

Cal had considered the option of actually going through channels to line up the resources for this last-ditch effort, but he figured the time wasted explaining it and justifying it and arguing with the inevitable obstructionists just wasn't worth it. Instead he'd relied on his letter from the President and his personal relationships with national lab leadership and gone off the reservation. Again.

"I'm not up to anything, Buck. Just out here at Andrews experimenting with some detection technology with some of the national labs folks. Why?"

"Some DOE joker called DHS about you poaching all their scientists and it got kicked around and since you're assigned to me, it got dropped on my lap. I don't have time for this. We've still got bombs out there due to go off today."

"Yeah, Buck, I'm aware of that. Tell it to your DOE flunky. We're a little busy just now."

There was a brief silence and Cal could see Buck rolling things around in his head, trying to decide what was important, not necessarily what was procedure.

"Tell me what you're doing and how it's gonna help us find this shit before it become part of the scenery here."

Cal explained the meetings he'd had with the national lab scientists and what they were working on and how they thought it might actually work if they could get things to mate up.

"How long before you test it?"

"We've tested it twice so far and the results aren't fast enough to make it practicable. We're an hour away from testing it again."

"What kind of area can you cover with it?"

"It has to be a pretty tightly focused beam, so we can see about a football field sized area with the helicopter at say 700 feet with a ground speed of probably 50 miles per hour."

"Let me get my calculator. OK. DC is approximately thirty-six square miles so you could fly across it in 7.2 minutes. With turn-around time, let's say 8 minutes per pass. One pass covers a 300 foot strip, so to cover the city, you'd have to make, just a second. About 100 passes. How many of these things do you have?"

"One."

"ONE? You're going to cover DC with one? That's, wait a second, thirteen hours to cover the city. And you'd have to be lucky enough to pass over the bomb on the first pass."

"That's a bit of an exaggeration, Buck. These guys aren't going to be setting these bombs off in Cathedral Heights or Lincoln Park, are they? The area we have to cover is much smaller. We should be able to cover the likely target area every hour or so."

"Do I understand this technology right? Could your detector see this high-density lead shielding material in, say, the parking garage where we found the SUV this morning?"

"Probably not. As I understand it, it was in an underground parking garage under a high-rise hotel. No, the density differential under all that wouldn't be discernible."

"So these guys are gonna have to be out in the open for you to see them, right?"

"Yes, or at least concealed by less than a few floors of a building. We really don't know. This is all new and until we try it, we're only guessing."

"So you're going to have to be lucky enough to find these SUV's driving down Massachusetts Avenue just at the time you're flying over them. Do you know the odds of that?"

"Yeah, not very good. But I either do this or I go home and watch the news. What would you do, Buck?"

"I'm doing what I'd do. We've got one dead driver and another SUV under surveillance. We know the description and license of the third, and you can bet your ass we'll have him before they do anything tonight."

"What do you mean, a dead driver? When did that happen?"

"Just a few minutes ago. We found a second SUV at the Mayflower and the driver tried to kill a DC cop and get away. Why?"

Cal didn't answer for a moment, and then said, "They're on the move. Shit! They're on the move! They must know about the compound raid and figure we've got intel on them and they've accelerated their plans. You said you have one under surveillance? Has there been any activity around it?"

"No. Nothing as of now. What the hell are you talking about?"

"There is no need for them to be moving. You said it yourself. They are totally undetectable underground and they know it. It would be pure chance for anyone to find them. As soon as they start moving, the risk of exposure escalates. Why take the chance?"

"We don't know that he was moving. He might have been just putting his suitcase in the truck. He was killed before he got there so we have no idea what he was doing."

"Suitcase? He had a suitcase? Why would he put that in the truck and then wait around ten hours until nightfall? THEY'RE MOVING! The driver of your second SUV is probably on his way right now. We are out of time. You need to get every resource you can find checking every SUV in DC. I've got to go and get this thing up in the air. I'll contact you when I do. If the other driver shows up, call me immediately."

Cal hung up and went in search of Caldor. When he found him they were just finishing up clamping the last of the components into the helicopter.

"How soon can we take off," Cal asked.

"We'll be ready in about ten or twenty minutes. Then we can test it and if everything works, we'll be ready to go in less than an hour."

"Too late. You've got ten minutes to get this thing going. We're testing it in the real world. I'm going up with you and try to coordinate the search and narrow the area. The bombs are on the move and we're out of time."

Cal wheeled and walked away, dialing the IDC as he did.

"Ray? What's going on over there?"

"Not much. We're just watching right now. Nothing to analyze. Why? Do you have something?"

Cal quickly briefed him on the new situation.

"We have drones watching," Ray told him, "and we are running my object identification program against their product, looking for the SUV's. It is working OK right now, but we do not have a lot of traffic to study so it is easier. Once traffic builds, the task will become orders of magnitude more difficult. The only distinguishing feature is the hole in the roof, and while we can see the panel covering it, there is a definite lag between the observation and the processing and the identification because it is so faint from directly above. Enough of a lag that we could easily lose track by the time the program alerts us to a match. The best we can do is put you in the area."

"That's what I need! If we can cut the search area down, we have a much better chance of the muon detector seeing them."

"Do not get too excited. As I said, it is not perfect and the probabilities are not good. We will be processing data from tens of thousands of vehicles scattered over the entire metropolitan area and we could miss them if we're not looking in the right place at the right time. Get me something to narrow the search and our probabilities increase greatly."

"We know the location of two of the SUV's. Doesn't that help?"

"Two? I only have one. With two I can begin extrapolating possibilities and predicting results. Where is the second one?"

"At the Mayflower. They found it a few minutes ago and the driver was killed. Work from those two points and get back to me quickly with something. Anything."

9.11   CUBAN CONSULATE. MARACAIBO, VENEZUELA

Ibrahim knew his Cuban hosts were getting impatient. The Consulate, really just a couple of apartments where the Consul lived and conducted business, was not equipped for guests, and he and Tariq were taxing the patience of the Consul and his meager staff. Ibrahim knew this, and he had worked his cell phone hard the previous day, trying to find out what was going on, who was after him, and the fate of his family. The Consul's assistant had inquired discretely with the police and learned that there were two dead whom they had been unable to identify, and that Ibrahim's family had been moved to Caracas where they were being interviewed before exit visas would be issued.

As far as who was after him, he didn't know but guessed it was beyond the resources of WAR to put such a team in the field and hide their identity, so it had to be the American government. Of all the possibilities that he could imagine, this was the best as it would earn him entry into one of the friendly Arab countries and protection once he was there. The bulk of his phone calls the day before had been to his network of contacts to arrange just that.

It was almost 9 AM local time, making it 9:30 in Washington, and Ibrahim had a special interest in the news coming from the U.S. today. He had given Grainger's actions a lot of thought and was guessing he would be detonating the three missing bombs at one location, somewhere of particular interest to WAR, and the most likely location was Washington.

He was watching CNN International on the one available television when they broke into the talking head program.

"CNN has learned that, just hours ago, U.S. law enforcement and military units assaulted a militia compound in a remote area of Montana. The compound was the property of the American hate group known as the White Aryan Resistance, or WAR. We are told by our sources that there was a large number of casualties. We do not know the reason for the assault. However, this comes as authorities are still looking for the stolen cesium, and speculation among many here is that these are somehow connected. We're going now to our local affiliate in Kalispell, Montana for an update."

Ibrahim watched, stunned into immobility, as the local reporter filled airtime with no useful information, at least not useful to Ibrahim. Where were Grainger and his lieutenants? They were the only ones who knew all of the plan, knew about the alliance with AQNA. Were they in custody?

And if this was connected to the cesium, his plans for resettlement were also useless because no one was going to want to be associated with a failed plan that relied on infidels of the worst Christian kind. He would be a pariah in his own domain. Maybe even a target.

His family would…*Waa faqri! My family, they are in danger.* Ibrahim's thoughts slammed into his brain like a head shot. He grabbed his cell phone and started dialing. It was only 5:30 PM at home. Maybe he could still do something.

9.12 JW MARRIOTT HOTEL, WASHINGTON, DC

Harley Frazier was late. He'd overslept and hadn't been packed and ready when Marcus had called fifteen minutes earlier. He'd rushed the last bit of packing and skipped formal checking out of the JW Marriott, figuring they had his stolen credit card and phony name and would get their money somehow. In the garage, he was quick-walking to the black Cadillac Escalade, dragging the roller bag he'd been given so he'd look like everyone else coming and going, looking at his key chain to select the proper button on the unfamiliar remote to unlock the doors, not paying attention. He got it right and heard the two clicks, meaning all doors were unlocked.

When he looked up, the first thing he saw was the head of someone behind the front of his SUV who was pointing a gun at him. He glanced left and right and saw several more from behind and between the other parked cars. Before he could process this, he heard an explosion and knew he was being killed. But instead, something hit him hard in the back, and he lost control of his body, falling to the ground jerking uncontrollably. And that was the last thing he remembered until he awoke with his hands and feet in restraints and people moving around his SUV.

I am totally fucked, he thought.

9.13 U.S. ARMY INFORMATION DOMINANCE CENTER, FT. BELVOIR, VA

Ray set to work on extrapolating patterns based on two storage locations he'd been given, figuring there had to be some non-random reason for the locations. If he could discover it, he could postulate the third and give Cal somewhere to concentrate his search. Using a grid overlaid on a DC street map, he ran various pattern-matching algorithms and turned up nothing of significance. As far as he could tell, there were lots of targets within the projected area, but none stood out as located symmetrically, and his mathematical mind wanted symmetry in there somewhere. The best he could guess was the third SUV was somewhere in the vicinity of the General Jose San Martin Memorial off of Virginia Avenue in an area of parks and monuments and government building and no hotels, or the Henley Plaza Hotel near Mt. Vernon Square. They were over a mile apart, and extrapolating outward a little to account for error, left a search area of over 2.2 million square feet that encompassed nearly every imaginable terrorist target in Washington.

He was working on refining his search algorithms to tighten up the area when he got a message on his screen. It was from his earlier request to have all information on the SUVs sent to him immediately as it changed. The message read:

"GPS of the Mayflower SUV has two stored locations labeled Yellow and Orange. The yellow is the Capital Hilton at 1001 16th Street Northwest, and the orange is Franklin Square Park at 14th and Eye Streets Northwest. The Marriott GPS also included two stored locations. These are yellow in the 1300 block of Pennsylvania Avenue which is Freedom Park, and orange at 1111 Constitution Avenue Northwest which is the location of the Internal Revenue Service."

When he plotted these new locations, everything seemed to have shifted south and east of the initial locations. His algorithms went to work trying to discern patterns in the six locations he now had, and he got nothing.

9.14 WASHINGTON NAVY YARD, WASHINGTON, DC

With nothing to do except kill some time before the next confirmation calls, Marcus had wandered sub-consciously to the area of the Washington Navy Yard. An ex-sailor, it was one of very few places in Washington that he had been to before, and he just instinctively gravitated there. His thoughts, in the somewhat familiar surroundings, went back to Montana and the devastation he imagined. Some of the residents there were friends, and of course Tag was his closest friend, his trusted mentor. Now the responsibility of leading WAR through the culmination of their plans would fall to him, and he wasn't certain he was up to it.

His reverie was broken by the National Anthem ring tone he used for all WAR business. It would be the first of the confirmation calls. Answering "Eagle Base," he received the response "Eagle Three" followed by an immediate hang-up, per their protocol. *One down, two to go*, he thought.

He checked his watch almost constantly, wondering what the hold-up was. The calls were to be made on time whether the weapon was ready or not. If it wasn't, Marcus needed the time to change the plan to the backup, Code Orange. That plan assumed that one of the weapons had been somehow disabled and the two remaining drivers would re-deploy for maximum effectiveness with just the two bombs, bracketing the target instead of triangulating it.

Marcus called Eagle One to see what the delay was. He got the message that the phone was out of cell range and he should try later. That was very disconcerting. He couldn't imagine where on the planned route it would be out of range, but he didn't have time to think it through.

He called Eagle Two, and was relieved when it rang. He was less relieved when he heard the familiar voice of Harley Frazier answer with the common "hello." Marcus hung up immediately and dialed Eagle Three. He simply said "Code Orange" when he got the correct response and hung up, rescheduling the attack for 11 AM. He tried Eagle One again and still got the "out of range" message. He hoped it was because he'd had to divert to some temporary hiding place, maybe another underground garage where there was no reception. He wondered if the cell towers were being hosed-up on purpose. He texted "Code Orange" so that Eagle One would get the message when he was clear, if ever.

Harley was caught and Pat, Eagle One, was on the run, at least he hoped that was the case. Clearly the authorities had gotten some intel from the compound raid and the mission was compromised. The fact that Eagle Three was still free and mobile was a good sign. Maybe Eagle One would be, as well. In the meantime, Marcus had to act.

9.15   REMOTE SENSING LAB, ANDREWS AFB, CAMP SPRINGS, MD

"Bruce, we go now. Get your tech on board."

"Impossible. We haven't calibrated the unit. We won't be able to tell a car engine from our lead shield until we do."

Cal turned to his RSL contact and said, "Get the truck moving. We'll calibrate on the fly and then head for the target area."

"C-c-calibrate on the fly," Bruce stuttered. "You can't do that."

"Bruce, listen to me. In our previous tests you told me you simply had to scan several objects of known density, preferably a very high density. Look around you, this place is density central. We fly over something, you measure it, we radio down for someone to tell us what it was and someone calculates the approximate density, you plug in your numbers, and bingo, we're go."

"It isn't that easy. Those densities have to be precise, and the calculations checked."

"We're looking for a 1,300 pound lead shield with a density of half a pound per cubic inch in a field of car and truck engines four or five or six times the size and half the density. You can't tell me this thing won't differentiate between those, precision or not."

"All right, I suppose we can do that."

"And we want speed. We will be able to identify any false positives visually just by looking down, so don't worry about that. Just find me anything denser than an internal combustion engine and we'll figure it out from there."

***

Bruce was clearly agitated and uncomfortable. Cal didn't know if it was the helicopter ride or the imperfect parameters the muon detector was working from. The important thing was that the detector was working and they could map engines of all sizes along with occasional the load of structural materials and even granite monuments and boulders.

"Talk to me, Ray," Cal shouted into his microphone. "We're over Ft. Stanton Park coming up on the Anacostia River. Where am I going?"

"To the White House. More precisely, to a point 2,000 feet from the front door on a bearing of 247 degrees true. That is the Yellow location in their plan. There is another location Orange which is also 2,000 feet from the White House on a bearing of 225 degrees true. You'll fly right over that on your way to Yellow."

"How confident are you?"

"90 plus percent. When you treat the two sets of locations discretely instead of mixing them together they show two possible deployment schemes that are likely based on circumstances. Whoever is running the show no doubt picks the scheme and deploys the weapons. The NSA is running phone intercept searches of the words Yellow and Orange over the last hour in the metropolitan area. We'll know soon which is in effect."

"What do the drones see?"

"Just what you would expect, a lot of traffic. The object identification program will be sending you coordinates of SUVs with high confidence factors as quickly as we get them. You'll need to take it from there."

"OK Good work. We're coming up on the target area now. Let's keep this line open. Coordinates are being displayed now. We're go."

9.16 Washington Navy Yard, Washington, DC

It was ten past ten and Marcus knew the plan was blown. Only one bomb remained in play for sure, and he was getting less and less hopeful about Eagle One. Each call was now just ringing until the voicemail kicked in.

He was in charge now, there was no Tag to call for directions. The decision was obvious and inescapable - Code Red. Code Red was essentially every man for himself. Any drivers still free were to get to the nearest point to the White House as fast as they could and detonate immediately. Coordination became secondary to implementation. Marcus' role in Code Red was to get out of town as fast as possible and work his way back to the compound. *What compound*, he wondered, but put that thought aside figuring there was plenty of time to consider it as he tried to sneak across 2,000 miles of America with every last enforcement officer in the country looking at his picture.

He was prepared for this contingency and consulted his Washington Metrorail map for the nearest station and saw there was one at the Navy Yard, just a couple of hundred yards from where he was parked. He then looked at his Amtrak schedule and saw a train departing at 10:55 heading south. That worked for him, and he drove to the Metro Station and abandoned the rental car in the parking lot, figuring it would be days before anyone found it. Then it was just a matter of getting off the AMTRAK train before the authorities started searching them, and disappearing into whatever city that he was in.

Before implementing his plan, he took out his cell phone and started where he knew he might still get a response, dialing Eagle Three. "Eagle Three" came the answer, and Marcus said "Code Red" and hung up. His call to Eagle One was met with the same ringing and voicemail. Now it was time for Marcus to get out of range. He took the battery out of the cell phone and dropped it into a trashcan, and did the same with the SIM card at another receptacle as he walked to the station.

***

Alan Owens was parked at his Code Orange position, on C Street NW, in the shadow of the Daughters of the American Revolution Constitution Hall. A fitting location, he felt. He had plenty of time before the 11 AM detonation, and he was pretending to relax in his Chevy Suburban while actually watching for any signs of trouble. Code Orange meant that someone was blown, and the risk that he would be also had increased significantly.

His phone rang and he knew things had gotten worse. He answered and, as expected, heard "Code Red." He'd prepared for this in his head, and he had a little plan of his own that no one had suggested—the world's first drive-by dirty bomb attack. He figured that would be immortalized in Wikipedia and he would be famous.

He was five and a half blocks from the Eisenhower Executive Building at 17th and F Streets, and that was 500 feet from the front door of the White House. That was as close as anyone could get without an invitation or a small army. He would need a couple of minutes to stop and remove the roof panel and shield plug at the last minute. He knew as soon as he did that, someone somewhere above him would know instantly the cesium had been opened. He decided to stop half a block from 17th Street to prepare the weapon. There was no way they could get to him fast enough to stop him from there. Not even some drone missile, if they had the balls to shoot one that close to the White House. He would dial his phone so it was ready, drive the last half block, press "send" just before turning onto 17th Street, and be gone. Without the cesium, he could disappear from their instruments. He was eleven minutes from immortality.

Alan's excitement elevated as he counted down the streets—D, E, New York Avenue, and then F. He turned right and parked in a loading zone. *They gonna give me a ticket*, he laughed to himself.

***

"Cal," Ray nearly screamed into Cal's ear, "the NSA got the trace on Yellow and Orange. The same phone just issued a Code Red to one other phone."

"We don't have a Red location?"

"No, nothing. It's got to be in their heads."

"Or it's a free-for-all. Targets of opportunity. He'll be heading north from the Orange location. 18th is one-way, and C takes him away from the White House. We're on our way."

The helicopter pilot aimed for 18th Street and started north.

"We've got a drone target identified. It's just ahead, northbound," the technician called. At the same time the muon detector alarmed for the first time since leaving Andrews, and Bruce, clinging to his seat, let go long enough to pump his right arm like Tiger Woods sinking a birdie putt and quietly said, "Yes."

***

Alan got out of the SUV and started to stretch. Then the sound registered and he looked up and saw a military helicopter descending like a bomb, aimed right at him. *How did they do that*, he asked himself as he instinctively jumped back into the SUV and took off.

He turned hard right on 17th, the cesium still contained by the shield plug, preventing him from detonating. The Chevy wallowed under the weight of the lead and he pushed the accelerator until it hit bottom and rocketed down the street, weaving as best he could, side-swiping several cars, both moving and parked. His instructions had been to detonate the weapon no matter what. *But it isn't ready*, he thought. *It will just blow up in here and kill me.*

He had no destination, no plan other than to run fast. He didn't know DC, but he had taken the time to reconnoiter the area for escape routes, and he knew if he turned right on E Street, it went into a tunnel under Virginia Avenue and he could stop there, hidden from the helicopter, remove the plug and deploy the weapon.

Even as he formed the plan, he saw it wouldn't work. Traffic turning right was stopped, some jam up on E Street that would box him in, maybe intentionally. His new plan was to get somewhere where he could stop and pull the plug out and the panel off and become a rolling weapon of mass destruction. There were trees and parks south of his location, his only chance.

He tried to push the accelerator further, but the floor was in the way.

***

17th Street was a breeze for the helicopter. Buildings lined the western side, but the east was all the Ellipse and the Washington Monument and wide open except for that one tall thing.

The pilot could get as low as the trees and power lines allowed, which was far lower than the law did. But today he was the law, and he used the freedom to ride the rooftop of the SUV as it caused chaos on its race down the street.

"We have him," Cal yelled into his mic. "Heading south on 17th at D. We need armed support."

An unfamiliar voice said, "Break left, DHS. I've got him."

Until the AH-6 "Killer Egg" attack helicopter with FBI markings flashed by their right side, Cal hadn't known they weren't alone in the air. At that point, they all ignored their instrument and watched with fascination as the pilot tried to make the helicopter into another vehicle heading south on 17th Street.

"This is the FBI," they heard over their earpieces and faintly in the background, like an echo, and they knew it was being amplified at the SUV. "Pull over and stop the vehicle."

The driver ignored them and flew through the Constitution Avenue intersection, fortunate to have the green light.

"Tac Three, this is Tac Base. We have you on the screen. He has to turn right at the Tidal Basin. There are four tour busses and numerous civilians in the loading area of the WW2 Memorial. You are to engage as soon as you're clear, and before the DC War Memorial. Put him into the wooded area on the north side of Independence Avenue. Ground units will converge there. The driver is to be positively restrained until then. Take whatever action you deem appropriate."

Cal could see the little helicopter bank right and speed ahead, swiveling and hovering above the DC War Memorial, facing up Independence Avenue where the SUV would be driving almost directly toward it.

"Tac Three, Tac Base. He spotted you and has turned onto the Kutz Bridge ramp. He will be heading east on Independence Avenue. Engage at the east end of Kutz Bridge. Get him into the grassy area south of Maine Avenue if possible."

Again, the little helicopter seemed to move like a dragonfly, one moment here and the next, not here but over there. It sped across their view from right to left and pulled a tight arc, coming to a hovering standstill at nearly ground level about 400 feet from the bridge, over a grassy area where southbound Maine Avenue and eastbound Independence Avenue intersected in a fork. Cal thought the other drivers on the road must be stunned and wondered if they would have a traffic accident to further complicate things.

They could see the sniper at the right door, strapped in with his right leg on the strut, his rifle aimed at the oncoming traffic. Traffic was light and Cal could see the chaos unfolding. Cars veered to either side, eager to be out of the aim of the shooter they could clearly see.

***

In the chaos of spotting the helicopter waiting for him and then trying to muscle the overloaded SUV through a hard left turn to head the other way, and the near accident as he barreled through the stop sign onto Independence Avenue, Alan had lost sight of the helicopter. Trees on his right and left blocked his ground-level view, and he saw nothing above them. The road forked ahead, and Alan planned to go right and find some cover to deploy the weapon. Maybe under some of those trees if he could get this boat off the road.

The light at the pedestrian crossing was red and there were several cars stopped and people in the street. Alan jumped the curb and drove up the wide sidewalk to get around the cars, scattering the few early morning tourists and joggers. Ahead some cars in the street were veering left, as if to avoid something in the middle of the road. That was OK with Alan; it cleared the way for him.

He shot past the light, clearing the trees on his right, and saw the obstruction. It wasn't in the middle of the road, it was just feet above the grassy area on the right, and Alan could practically see right down the barrel of the gun.

***

Cal saw the muzzle flashes, and the SUV lurched, like it had hit something, and swerved hard to the right onto the grass, the right front tire shredded by the marksman's three shot burst. With the heavy load and high center of gravity, the SUV was not up to the maneuver and rose off the right wheels as it continued on its arc. The wheels rose further until it reached its tipping point and rolled over, completing a 270-degree roll and coming to rest on its passenger side.

The helicopter shifted its position to its left, giving the sniper a clear view through the windshield, and again Cal saw three muzzle flashes. *One emergency over, another just begun*, Cal thought as he pictured the lead shield falling left, then down, and then right as the SUV rolled. There was no way that glass jar was going to survive that.

Cal called into his mic, "Pull the helicopters back. Their prop wash will spread the cesium. How long until ground crews get here to secure the scene?"

"One minute, DHS," the agent on the other end answered.

"That's too long. There are pedestrians and vehicles in the area and they will be coming to check out the accident. Have the other helicopter land and the sniper can help me with crowd control until they get here. We need the emergency response units here now. The cesium is no doubt loose and we have to contain it."

Cal leaned to the cockpit and pointed down, and the pilot nodded. He pointed to the other helicopter and pointed down again, and the pilot nodded again and coordinated landing with the other helicopter. On the ground, Cal turned to Bruce and the tech and signaled them out, as well. Bruce jumped without hesitation, but the tech hesitated, looking around like he could see cesium in the air. He looked back at Bruce, who scowled at him, and shrugged his shoulders and jumped out.

Both helicopters took off and stationed themselves far enough away to keep their turbulence away from the SUV. Cal waved the sniper over and he came at a trot, still carrying his rifle and sidearm.

"We need to get everyone back. You," he said to the sniper, "what's your name?"

"Special Agent William Ng, sir."

"I want you to go back to the bridge and divert all eastbound Independence Avenue traffic back up the ramp around the Tidal Basin. No one comes through. OK?"

"Yes sir," he answered and trotted up the middle of the street, assuming oncoming traffic would avoid a heavily armed man in a helmet and military uniform. They did, and at the fork, he used his rifle and arms to direct traffic left, back north and away from the SUV.

To Bruce and the tech, Cal said, "We have to get these pedestrian and drivers away from the SUV. No one goes near it. One of you here, at the street. Get everyone to the other side and tell them to keep going. The other over there and make sure no one wanders in from that parking area next to the Basin. I'll be over here," and he indicated the pedestrian walkway at the end of the Kutz Bridge, "making sure everyone stays away. Ground crews and rad response units will be here quickly so we won't have to do this for long. OK, go."

They were only in position for a few seconds when the first DC Metro Police car arrived, followed quickly by several more and the fire department. The police and firemen were equipped with personal radiation detectors and quickly determined there was no radiation hazard that far from the SUV. Cal took one of them and made a complete circle around the SUV, about 20 yards away.

"No real hot spots, so the shield is either still in place, or it's positioned so the opening points up or down and I'm not seeing it. There are elevated radiation levels, just a couple of millirem, so the container is definitely open and some material has spilled out."

To the senior policeman, he said, "We're going to need to seal this area off. Barricades all around, preferably solid so we won't get spectators. Give me a 200-foot circle. That should be enough. That will be, what, about 600 feet of barricade."

"628.45, to be accurate," Bruce said. Everyone looked at him.

"What? Pi times the diameter. That's high school geometry!"

9.17   FBI HEADQUARTERS, WASHINGTON, DC

Through the day, the FBI's forensics and bomb tech teams swarmed the SUV, sealing the container and fixing the loose cesium powder to the interior with spray-on adhesive. Cal had been in the SIOC, overwhelmed by FBI, DHS, and FEMA personnel collecting evidence, managing the risks, cleaning up the details, and making sure there were no loose ends.

But, of course, there were. They had identified the DC WAR controller as Marcus Harrison and there was an intense search in progress without any leads as yet. The WAR compound was under quarantine and no one allowed in or out. The residents were all being thoroughly interrogated and many had been taken into custody under outstanding warrants or because of their attempts to kill the Delta soldiers in the pitched battle. There was already a demand that they be declared enemy combatants and tried in military courts. On the other side, a queue of lawyers had formed up, looking for clients to defend against just that possibility. *Montana isn't going to be big enough to contain the egos*, Cal thought.

Ibrahim al Hasan was in Venezuela, as Cal had learned for the first time, no doubt making secure arrangements to get to some friendly middle-east country. His family was back in Saudi Arabia and incommunicado, and no one knew the fate of Ibrahim's right-hand man, Ismail. The others in the al Qaeda camp were scattered, some still in the cave in Pakistan where they'd been tracked through the courier, who had returned to Yemen under his diplomatic immunity and was safely living there.

The RAP Curie Count Team had finished their calculations and they were confident that all of the cesium had been accounted for and there were no other weapons out there waiting to surprise them.

Cal had spoken earlier to Ray Nassiri and thanked him for his work. As Cal had told him, this would be a different kind of clean-up without Ray. When he met with senior leadership for after-action reviews, Cal planned to mention both Ray and Bruce, hoping to share some of the limelight with these two critical contributors to the successful outcome.

Tomorrow he would head back to Stevensville, and Cal was planning a really nice vacation with Claire.

Part Ten – Retribution

<u>Monday, July 5</u>

10.01 Consulate of Cuba, Maracaibo, Venezuela

Ibrahim hadn't slept. He'd been watching CNN International and monitoring al Jezeera and searching all the other broadcast news and Internet sources all night and now into the morning, inhaling anything about the WAR raid and the events in DC and the capture of the remainder of the cesium. He had it memorized, the coverage repeating the same things over and over again. But still he watched and searched, opening these oysters of information like one of them would contain the pearl that would save his life.

Grainger was dead, that was good. But one of his associates, Josef, was in custody, along with a large number of WAR soldiers. That was bad. And Marcus seemed to have disappeared. That was worse. Josef knew the whole plan and would no doubt be telling the story. Marcus knew Ibrahim and was no doubt plotting some revenge. And, of course, his name had come up as a "person of interest," and that was really, really bad. At least he knew who was chasing him.

His efforts of the day before had all been wasted. Once the WAR involvement in the cesium theft was revealed, his value to his *jihad* mission, and to the others who shared it, had been lost. He'd allied with the worst kind of Christian infidel, and that was bad enough. That he had failed even then was unforgivable. Sixteen dirty bombs, and only one had gone off according to the plan. While others had detonated, they were compromised and ineffective.

Yesterday he could have spun that as success. Today, it was an embarrassment, a betrayal.

And, his family. He didn't even know where they were or what would become of them. By now the Saudi authorities, possibly even Mabahith, had them. They would be used to force him to come in, and he did not see how he could avoid that. Even if he cooperated, there was no guarantee they would be allowed to live, and in any case they would be outcasts in their own homeland.

I must do something, he thought. He knew he was no longer welcome at the consulate, and any protection it had afforded him was over. With no other choice, with his jihadist brothers now shunning him, and the American authorities no doubt putting pressure on the Royal Family to do something public, he had no options. Today he would call his brother back home and arrange a final resolution.

10.02   NEAR HADDA STREET, SANA'A, YEMEN

Atiya Abdul Rahman arrived home from work to the small apartment he rented off Hadda Street. He liked his neighborhood, away from the guarded enclaves of the wealthy and the foreigners, and close to the hustle of Hadda Street. He was anonymous there, a place where he could drop pretense and quietly be himself, where he could study his history, where he could think about the future and his role in changing it. He could live an austere and virtuous life there.

Tonight he would eat at Yamal al-Sham, a small, quiet restaurant that served the Syrian food that he favored on occasion, especially the *shish toauk*, a chicken kabob served with garlic paste and vegetables. There were no meetings planned, and he wanted some time to reflect on the day.

The news from America was very disconcerting. While his involvement in the affair was minor, his superiors at the Ministry of Foreign Affairs were aware of his clandestine trip to Pakistan, and they were concerned that his involvement was known in America and he would somehow bring trouble to an already troubled relationship. The Americans were making a lot of noise about holding those responsible to account, just as they had after 9/11, and everyone was afraid this would result in more problems, more sanctions, more pressure to arrest and extradite Yemeni citizens, Rahman in particular. He had been told this would not happen, but that was small consolation, as he knew they would lie to him right up until the moment that he was in chains and on a flight to America.

Tomorrow he would make arrangements. He would arrange to leave Yemen later in the week, go somewhere isolated where he could live until this was all just a faint memory. He had friends in Quetta, in Pakistan near the Afghan border. They would shelter him for as long as necessary, years, if that was what it would take. He didn't think it would.

10.03   AL-HA'IR PRISON, 25 MILES SOUTH OF RIYADH, SAUDI ARABIA

Ismail paced the twenty-foot by ten-foot room. He walked a rough rectangle around the perimeter, there being noting except a sink, toilet, and small cot to inhibit his route. There were no windows, and one door that hadn't been opened since it had closed behind him nine days ago, although he had no count of them. After thirty circles, he paced in the other direction, all the while mumbling quietly to himself, sometimes a prayer, sometimes a memory, sometimes a song. His was the only voice he'd heard in those nine days.

The florescent light were on twenty-fours a day, flooding the room with a brightness that had developed weight, bearing down relentlessly on him. Security cameras in two opposite corners watched his every move, and he had stopped staring at them and pleading to them days ago. It hadn't taken long for Ismail to tell the Mabahith officer everything he knew. His naked wife and the brutal man and the threat of what would occur next was sufficient. Maybe it had occurred despite his confession. Maybe his wife and family were already dead. Maybe Ibrahim was celebrating the success of their plan. Maybe not. He didn't know what day it was, what time it was, how long he'd been there.

He only knew that he walked around that room 48,623 times. So far.

10.04   EIGHT MILES NORTH OF LANDI KOTAL, PAKISTAN

The cave was quite comfortable, certainly more comfortable than most bivouacs Saif al-Adel had occupied in his long and illustrious service to al Qaeda. It was a natural cave, accessible only by some difficult rock climbing from only one direction that could be watched easily. Inside, it had been widened and reinforced, and the entrance protected by a maze of rocks and sandbags. An ingenious system of water supply and sanitary drainage made it possible to stay inside for extended periods. Months, if there was sufficient food. The entry itself would only accommodate one person at a time, and Saif felt protected.

He had been there nearly three months, and soon it would be time to move again to keep ahead of his American pursuers. He had been taught that Americans were soft, that they would quickly tire of any action that didn't produce immediate results, that they were no match for the fanatical commitment to the Fifth Caliphate that he shared with his brother jihadists.

That might be true, he knew, but there were at least some Americans who weren't, who were as dedicated to his eradication as he was to theirs. They were relentless, and they had technology that he simply believed was a lie, propaganda to wage psychological warfare on him, to discourage and exhaust his resolve. See donkey dung from cameras so high they could not be seen, even with his telescope? He did not believe this was possible. But whatever they had, it would find him eventually, and so he had to move again. Maybe just another day or two, and then he would go. A courier was due soon with news of the dirty bomb attack and he was eager to hear that.

10.05 Braiman Prison, Jeddah, Saudi Arabia

The cell was approximately fifteen feet by twenty feet, and could humanely house four inmates. Bander shared it with twenty-two other men and one 11-year-old boy. His days were spent eating two meals of nearly raw chicken in a watery broth with occasional vegetables, and moving from place to place at the whim of the guards. And trying to stay alive.

Bander had been detained as soon as he disembarked at King Abdulaziz International Airport in Jeddah. After a day of questioning, accompanied by two broken toes when the interrogators didn't like his answers, Bander had been taken directly to Braiman Prison and was told he would be held there until his trial. His question, "For what crime?" was what earned him his second broken toe.

He had not seen his family and was unsure if they even knew of his fate. He had not seen a lawyer, nor had anyone mentioned anything about a formal trial with a defense. With the exception of the 11-year-old and a couple of aged and infirm men, Bander felt threatened by everyone in the cell and was constantly on guard.

He would have given anything to have been charged and tried and imprisoned in America.

10.06 Covent Gardens Apartments, Vancouver, BC, Canada

His name was now Arty Bishop, and he was working construction for the summer until classes started in the fall. He was enrolled in the School of Commerce at the University of British Columbia and planned to get a degree in Accounting. He was good with numbers, and he couldn't think of another occupation where he could get work anywhere and still be invisible. Did anyone ever feel threatened by their accountant?

He had money in the bank, an official identification complete with a verifiable history, a new place to live to go with his new identity, and a job to fill the days. He intended to live quietly and enjoy the life he felt he'd earned. Getting there hadn't been easy, and there had been casualties. The one he regretted most was Sgt. Martin Washington.

TUESDAY, JULY 6

10.07 EISENHOWER EXECUTIVE OFFICE BUILDING, WASHINGTON, DC

Deep inside the Eisenhower Executive Office Building, the White House's main office building, less than one hundred yards away from the West Wing's Situation Room and the Oval Office, a highly classified national security briefing was about to take place. The audience, including the Director of the FBI, the Attorney General, Secretary of Homeland Security, the Director of National Intelligence and the DoD Joint Chiefs of Staff, along with a dozen senior White House national security leaders, were all anxiously awaiting a presentation by a joint DoD - CIA strike team identified on the agenda handed out to the audience as "Retribution Pathways and Courses of Action Assessment."

As the lights were dimmed in the secured conference room, two men approached the matching podiums positioned on either side of the large rear-projection screen and proceeded to introduce themselves.

"I am John Warner, Director of the American Security Project. As some of you know, I have been detailed to lead this interagency strike force from the Special Operations Division of the Central Intelligence Agency. I am joined by Dr. Peter Flynn, our Deputy Director. Dr. Flynn is himself assigned to the project from the Department of Defense's Office of UAV Strike Operations."

Flynn waved into the audience and then Warner continued. "The American Security Project is the mechanism used to identify potential targets of national security interest, typically focused on an individual or small group of terrorists that pose a grave threat to the United States or our strategic interests abroad. Our job is to work with the intelligence, defense, and domestic security agencies and recommend to the President courses of action to neutralize our enemies located outside of traditional combat zones. The members of our project team identify, prioritize, and prepare the operational template to surgically excise these adversaries, the so-called "kill list." This is the recommended course of action that we offer to the President."

Warner looked up from his notes and, picking out no one in particular to focus on, said with great gravity, "Only the President has the authority to approve such by-name targeted actions. It is only a kill-list when he so determines it to be."

Dr. Flynn quickly interjected from the other podium on the stage. "The American Security Project team, which includes representatives from all of the agencies and departments here in this room, takes its responsibility very seriously, and today we are here to present to you our team's recommended retribution pathways, and courses of action against the short list of foreign masterminds and tactical leaders that our larger community has identified as primarily responsible for the recent wave of dirty bomb threats and attacks."

The slide show proceeded, and Flynn took the lead in talking around the images and short narrative bullets that were contained between the "Top Secret - Special Access" warning in the borders of each slide.

"First, here is the initial list of proposed targets. We fully expect this list to grow in the coming weeks and months, as our forensics and attribution investigations continue, and as our intelligence agencies, and those of our allies, begin the arduous process of culling through all the data, sources, and information possibly associated with these recent attacks. The following names and general geographic locations of these individuals and groups are identified on the proposed kill-list.

"First, Ibrahim al Hasan, assessed to be the leader of al Qaeda North America, presently located per NSA communications intercepts in Maracaibo, Venezuela.

"Next, Atiya Abdul Rahman, a Yemeni diplomat previously assigned to the Saudi embassy in Riyadh. He is presently located in Sana'a."

Each slide included a picture of the individual and a very brief description, usually just their title in their terror organization, or the role they played in the attacks. Flynn continued.

"Saif al-Adel, aka "The Sheik," the interim leader of al Qaeda Global and the final approval authority behind the AQNA attacks here, presently located in the mountains of Waziristan, Pakistan.

"Ismail al Ghamdi, associate of Ibrahim al Hasan and co-conspirator, presently in Saudi custody at the Al-Ha'ir Prison near Riyadh."

The slides stopped there, but Flynn continued his narrative.

"The use of armed drones presently located within range of these priority targets has been assessed as the most viable weapons platform, with respect to several metrics, including lethality, stealth, immediacy, and geo-political considerations."

Cal Bellotta knew he didn't belong here, among these very senior authorities, but he was there, anyway, quietly escorted into this seat in the far rear corner of the room by a White House National Security official after everyone else was seated. "Just listen," he'd been told. "The President thinks you've earned the right to know how this will end."

Sitting and listening, Cal reflected on a recent report he had read that stated that the Pentagon now has some 7,000 aerial drones, compared with fewer than 50 just a decade ago, and that the CIA had about thirty Predator and Reaper drones, operated by Air Force pilots from a U.S. military base here in the United States. This report by an independent think tank had focused on how targeted assassinations continued to test the legal limits of the President's authority to approve such kill-lists. *No doubt all the lawyers and politicians will be behind this*, he thought. He knew that even the ones who were dead set against the use of drones outside of combat zones would bite their tongues and remain silent after everything that had happened. To do otherwise would end their careers.

The next series of slides spoke of legal authorities. John Warner walked up to the screen with laser pointer in hand and proceeded to speak to the bullets, one after the other.

"To put it in legal terms, drone strikes in designated combat zones fall under Title 10 of the U.S. Code, which sets rules for the armed forces, while drone strikes in countries outside of official U.S. military supported war zones fall under Title 50, which provides authority for covert operations. These are covert operations, and not even our closest allies will be briefed before these missions are completed. I emphasize that. No one outside of this room and the President will know of this action prior to execution. No one. I trust you understand that restriction.

"Our targets are all outside of U.S. military combat zones, and the project team is unanimous in its recommendation that the drone strikes fall under Title 50, and the CIA will prosecute this operation with the full support of the Department of Defense.

"One pertinent provision of Title 10, and the reason for our application of Title 50," Warner concluded, "is that in order for U.S. armed forces to operate under Title 10 on foreign soil, they must get permission of the foreign governments. If the military controlled these drone strikes, they couldn't be conducted without this permission. That isn't going to happen, period, end-of-story."

The only signs on Building 14506 off Bong Avenue, the subject of endless bad jokes, simply stated Restricted Access. Both doors, one at each end, included security card readers and cameras. Anyone approaching Building 14506 tripped gravimetric sensors and infrared beams, so no one ever had to knock. If they had tried, they would have been turned away by the sign on the door and the voice on the speaker above it that reinforced the message.

Building 14506 was home-base for the U.S. Air Force 4th Special Operations Squadron. Code named *Red Eyes*, the 4th operated sixteen of the MQ-1C Grey Eagle Block 1 variant of the Predator UAV equipped with the AGM-114 Hellfire missiles. Deployed by Air Force cargo jets, and capable of flight from short runways, they were lethal projections of American power, and particularly effective at taking out critical targets anywhere in the world.

A special shift had been placed on duty at an unusual shift change time—noon, Central Standard Time. There were only fourteen men on this shift, all 4th Squadron officers, itself an unusual crew, plus some CIA liaisons. They were all escorted into the briefing room, a guard posted outside the locked door, and directed to be seated and pay attention to the large screen at the front of the room. After a moment, the screen came on and they were startled into complete silence.

"Gentlemen," the President of the United States started, "I wanted to speak to you live and personally today, and since I cannot be there, this is the only solution. You are about to be given an assignment of such gravity, of such sensitivity, of such importance to national security that I wanted to make it clear to you myself so there will be no question, no hesitation, no uncertainty. Very soon you will set about the business for which you have been trained and tested, piloting unmanned aerial vehicles.

"Today's mission is an extreme one, and you will be targeting and, to state it bluntly, killing several enemies of the United States that our intelligence and national security communities have determined beyond doubt were instrumental in the recent wave of dirty bomb attacks on our country. I ask you, no, I charge you, to do your jobs with the mastery that I know is your standard. We cannot, we will not ever, abide an attack on our citizens and on our soil without a retaliation that sends a message to those who would try. You, gentlemen, are the messengers, and I trust you to deliver that message well. This is a moment for swift retribution, and I have selected you and the 4th squadron to exact the necessary price from our enemies for this violation of our great nation, and the associated death and destruction of our peoples and our property. Gentleman, I salute you! May God bless you all, and these United States of America."

The screen went blank. There was silence in the room for a few seconds, as the profoundness of the moment was absorbed by each and every person in the room. They were about to complete a mission by direct orders received from the President. A mission they were likely never be able to share with others, a mission like no other.

***

The three-mile stretch of the Via al Aeropuerto from the edge of Maracaibo to the La Chinita International Airport was desolate, just unoccupied, uncultivated land. At 3:30 PM local time, 2 PM Lackland time, there was little traffic, and the black Mercedes on loan from the Cuban Consul was speeding unimpeded towards the airport entrance. To the driver half a mile down the road, heading towards it, the car just seemed to disappear in a huge fireball, and he drove off the road in shock. The police were only able to determine that there were enough body parts to belong to two people, and the Cuban Consul gave them the names of Ibrahim al Hasan and Tariq Rahal as the men he'd loaned his car to.

***

Neighbors on Morcos Street, just off of Hadda Street, were baffled by the localized destruction and theorized that the reclusive Mr. Rahman must have died in a propane gas explosion. The police were baffled because the debris didn't look like a propane tank, and they suspected the dead man was a bomb-builder killed in an accidental explosion. They never found any bomb-making material in the debris, but that didn't shake their faith in their conclusion. No one claimed his body, and the authorities ordered the investigation closed.

***

The guard watching Ismail noted that he had stopped pacing in his cell and was staring at the wall as if it was talking to him. He watched a row of monitors that showed seven other identical rooms, all lined up on the south-facing wall of the prison's southern wing, where they would get the maximum sun to heat the concrete, and where the temperature would reach 110° during the day and drop to a comfortable 80° outside at night. But not in these rooms, heated like an oven and then retaining the heat through the night.

He was still watching when the explosion rocked the fortified structure and the cameras in Ismail's room and those throughout the prison wing where he was located went out. *Escape*, he thought, and pushed his alarm button, staying at his post as he was supposed to, and also where it was safe from anyone trying to break the prisoners free.

When the other guards got there, they found the total destruction of Ismail's room and significant damage to the ones next to it. It was clear that there had been no escape attempt. If Ismail had been alive, he would not have agreed. He would have thought of it as a successful escape.

***

Saif al-Adel had finished his nightly Isha prayers and was preparing for sleep when the sentry posted at the cave entrance called to him, his voice full of urgency.

"There is a strange orange glow in the sky," he said, looking through the night vision goggles he wore. "And another. See, my Sheik. It is a sign perhaps from Allah?"

Saif could see a faint orange glow, more like an illuminated thin trail, in the east, and another in the south-east. He watched with some curiosity as they grew larger. After a moment, he could see that they were converging. After another moment, it almost seemed that they were converging on him. It only took a second for him to realize the meaning of that, and he ran for the cave entrance, calling the sentry to follow.

They ran deep into the cave, calling the others to follow into the man-made parts that led to the reinforced room. They were safely in and the door closed when the first Hellfire missile penetrated the entrance and exploded in the entry chamber, sealing the entrance under tons of rock.

Saif smiled, secure that he had outwitted the Americans again. Then the second Hellfire exploded behind him, sealing the small, secret escape tunnel, and Saif stopped smiling.

***

Arty Bishop, the former Marine, former terrorist, former informant, was preparing for sleep, tired from a day of working construction on a new apartment complex. As was his nightly habit, he recited his evening prayers and closed them with an old Arab proverb.

"Not realizing all of an objective doesn't mean some of it can't be realized."

The Star-Spangled Banner

O say can you see by the dawn's early light,
What so proudly we hailed at the twilight's last gleaming,
Whose broad stripes and bright stars through the perilous fight,
O'er the ramparts we watched, were so gallantly streaming?
And the rockets' red glare, the bombs bursting in air,
Gave proof through the night that our flag was still there;
O say does that star-spangled banner yet wave,
O'er the land of the free and the home of the brave?

On the shore dimly seen through the mists of the deep,
Where the foe's haughty host in dread silence reposes,
What is that which the breeze, o'er the towering steep,
As it fitfully blows, half conceals, half discloses?
Now it catches the gleam of the morning's first beam,
In full glory reflected now shines in the stream:
'Tis the star-spangled banner, O! long may it wave
O'er the land of the free and the home of the brave.

And where is that band who so vauntingly swore
That the havoc of war and the battle's confusion,
A home and a country, should leave us no more?
Their blood has washed out their foul footsteps' pollution.
No refuge could save the hireling and slave
From the terror of flight, or the gloom of the grave:
And the star-spangled banner in triumph doth wave,
O'er the land of the free and the home of the brave.

O thus be it ever, when freemen shall stand
Between their loved home and the war's desolation.
Blest with vict'ry and peace, may the Heav'n rescued land
Praise the Power that hath made and preserved us a nation!
Then conquer we must, when our cause it is just,
And this be our motto: "In God is our trust."
And the star-spangled banner in triumph shall wave
O'er the land of the free and the home of the brave!

Acronyms and Glossary

AMS – Airborne Monitoring Systems
APC – Armored Personnel Carrier
AQAP – Al Qaeda of the Arabian Peninsula
AQNA – Al Qaeda of North America
ASAC – Assistant Special Agency in Charge
ASEAN – Association of Southeast Asian Nations
BOLO – Be On the Look Out
Bremsstrahlung – radiation released from electron deceleration
CBP – Customs & Border Patrol
COI – Chief of Intelligence
CMRT – Consequence Management Response Team
COOP – Continuity of Operations Plan
CST – Civil Support Team
Dalton – The standard unit that is used for indicating atomic mass
DEA – Drug Enforcement Administration
DHS – Department of Homeland Security
DNI – Director of National Intelligence
DoD – Department of Defense
DOT – Department of Transportation
DNDO – Domestic Nuclear Detection Office
DOE – Department of Energy
Dosimeter – measures an individual's exposure to radiated energy
ECN – Emergency Communications Network
EOC – Emergency Operations Center
EOF – Emergency Operations Facility
FIG – Field Intelligence Group
FTTTF – Foreign Terrorist Tracking Task Force
FRMAC – Federal Radiological Monitoring and Assessment Center
Fusion Center – a law enforcement information sharing center
GETS – Government Emergency Telecommunications System
Geiger-Muller (GM) Tube – a sensing element to detect ionized radiation
HAHO – High Altitude High Opening parachuting technique
HMRU – Hazardous Materials Response Unit
HPGe – High Purity Germanium Detector identifies radionuclides
HSDN – Homeland Security Data Network a classified wide-area network
IAEA – International Atomic Energy Agency

IED – improvised explosive device uses in unconventional warfare
IND – improvised nuclear device is an illicit nuclear yield weapon
IDC – Information Dominance Center
INL – Idaho National Laboratory
Inverse Square Law – energy decreases as the square of distance increases
ISI – Pakistan Inter-Services Intelligence Agency
JAC – Joint Analysis Center
JOC – Joint Operations Center
JTTF – Joint Terrorism Task Force
LEO – Law Enforcement Online
LRM – Linear Radiation Monitor detects gamma and neutron radiation
LZ – landing zone is a designated area where an aircraft can safely land
Mabahith – secret police agency of Saudi Arabia
Micro-REM – one millionth Roentgen Equivalent Man (REM)
Milli-REM – one thousandth Roentgen Equivalent Man (REM)
NCTC – National Counterterrorism Center
NNSA – National Nuclear Security Administration
NSA – National Security Agency
NRTS – Nuclear Reactor Testing Station
NCT – Nuclear Counterterrorism Team
NEST – Nuclear Emergency Support Team
NIRT – Nuclear Incident Response Team
Posse Comitatus – laws restricting military force in domestic situations
PAG – Protective Action Guides support radiation protection
RadFL – Radiological Forensics Laboratory
RAP – Radiological Assistance Program
RDD – Radiation Dispersal Device, a so-called dirty bomb
REM – Roentgen Equivalent Man measure of biological radiation effects
SABT – Special Agent Bomb Technician
SAC – Special Agent in Charge
SCIF – Secure Compartmentalized Information Facility
SIOC – Strategic Information and Operations Center
STT – Specified Target Team
SSA – Supervisory Special Agent
Starlight – a visual information system
SVTC – Secure Video Tele-conferencing Communications
THU – Tactical Helicopter Unit
Thunderbolt – a no-notice exercise to test quick response forces
TIDE – Terrorist Identities Datamart Environment
TLD – Thermo Luminescent Dosimeter measures radiation exposure
TSA – Transportation Security Administration

Type B Container – a metal container for shipping radioactive materials
UASI – Urban Area Security Initiative
UAV – Unmanned Aerial Vehicles, also referred to as drones
VACIS – a gamma-ray radiography system used for cargo screening
WAR – White Aryan Resistance
WMD – Weapon of Mass Destruction
ZOG – Zionist Occupation Government

Cast of Characters

NLN, JOSEF	WAR LIEUTENANT	2.03
OWESCAR RICHARD	FBI, LEXINGTON, KY	2.10
PASTOR JR, KENNY	WAR CO-CONSPIRATOR	1.06
PASTOR SR, KENNETH	OWNER, PASTOR TECHNOLOGY	1.04
RAHAL, TARIQ	AQNA BODYGUARD	5.07
REASENS, JIMMY	FBI, KNOXVILLE, TN	2.01
SAAD, MERVA (RASUL)	AQNA SOLDIER	1.04
SLOCOMB, ALAN	KY STATE POLICE	1.11
SPELLMAN, LEROY	FBI LOUISVILLE, KY	2.13
STROBEL, JIMMY (UBAID)	AQNA SOLDIER	1.07
VARGAS, FRANK	DELTA FORCE HAHO TEAM	9.04
VINCENZO, JULES	U.S. STATE DEPARTMENT	3.09
WATTS, EDGAR	CHICAGO POLICE PATROLMAN	4.01

MINOR CHARACTERS

NAME	AFFILIATION	CHAP.
ABERT, NFN	SWISS GUARDS, VANCOUVER, BC	8.09
ADAMS, NFN	FBI SABT, KNOXVILLE, KY	5.09
AIKENS, ROGER	WAR DRIVER	1.08
AL HASAN, FARID	FAMILY	5.08
AL-ADEL, SAIF	AQAP LEADERSHIP	3.01
ALLEN, BRADLEY	WAR SNIPER	8.25
ALLISON, NFN	CAPTAIN, DELTA FORCE	9.02
AMOS, STAN	DEPUTY DIRECTOR, U.S. ARMY IDC	6.04
ANDERSON, JUSTIN	WAR DRIVER	3.04
ANDREWS, HARRISON	PAM MOONEY'S LOVER	7.04
ARMSTRONG, NFN	FBI, HOUSTON, TX	7.02
ARTELSON, NFN	GILLETTE, WY POLICE DEPT.	3.15
BANKS NFN	FBI, HOUSTON, TX	7.02
BARNABY, WILLIAM	NSA TIER 2 ANALYST	8.03
BATES, BILLY	WAR DRIVER	3.04
BELLECKS, NFN	FBI, ATLANTA GA	3.06
BELLOTTA, CLAIRE	FAMILY	2.05
BENSON, NFN	FBI, HOUSTON, TX	7.02
BERGESON, CLIFF	WAR DRIVER	2.15
BERNER, KEVIN	DIRECTOR, WMD DIRECTORATE	2.19
BIN DULAZIZ, AL-AZIZ	ROYAL EMBASSY OF SAUDI ARABIA	3.17
BOSMAN, STUART	DHS UNDER-SECRETARY	9.06
BOWMAN, MATT	CTO, TIDE	6.01
BRIDGES, NFN	SECURITY CHIEF, FERMI NPP	3.11
BURKE, HENRY	GILLETTE, WY POLICE DEPARTMENT	3.15

Byrne, Brenda	WAR driver	2.10
Chadwick, Richard	Victim	5.06
Chapin, Laurie	CNN Newscaster	7.16
Clark, Alex	FBI SSA, Boston, MA	6.09
Cliffords, Mike	NSA Tier 3 Analyst	8.03
Costas, Glen	FBI, Houston TX	7.02
Daler, Travis	Family	2.01
Daly, Kathy	Scientist, Sandia Nat'l Lab	8.15
Delagrave, Brenda	Canadian Foreign Affairs	8.06
DeLotte, Alain	Victim	6.05
Dempsey, Millie	WAR Lieutenant	8.20
Donaldson, NFN	FBI, Washington, DC	9.03
Dressler, Lou	WAR driver	2.15
Drury, Samuel	FBI, Boston, MA	6.11
Eastwood, Garrett	Delta Force HAHO Team	9.07
Edgerton, William	WAR member	3.03
Elkins, Lloyd	Gillette, WY Police Department	3.15
Ericson, NFN	FBI WMD, Knoxville, TN	5.09
Evans, Leigh	FBI, Harrisburg, PA	8.21
Fair, Pete	RAP Team Leader	2.11
Fellows, Claude	FBI, Kansas City, MO	7.03
Flynn, Amanda	Captain, USS North Carolina	1.01
Flynn, Peter	American Security Project	10.07
Fogarty, Art	WAR driver	7.21
Forbes, NFN	FBI, Harrisburg, PA	8.21
Frazier, Harley	WAR driver	9.08
Gerlach, Anton	FBI Radiation Forensics Lab	7.17
Goetz, Simon	Stully Lennocks alias	8.11
Grainger, Marion	Family	2.03
Grayson, Jared	FBI, Philadelphia, PA	7.08
Grissom, NFN	FBI, Washington, DC	1.05
Hardens, NFN	Immigration and Customs Service	6.16
Healy, Frank	WAR driver	7.06
Heneryt, Neal	FBI, Frankfort, KY	2.01
Herrera, Luis	Delivery driver, victim	5.06
Holloway, Jerry	RAP team member	2.11
Horner, Donald	WAR Lieutenant	8.20
Jameson, Gary	Delta Force HAHO Team	9.07
Jeffers, George	WAR driver	7.15
Jeffers, Gerald	WAR driver	7.15
Jerrick, Kelly	NSA Tier 1 Analyst	8.03

Kalbaugh, David	Fire Chief, DCA Airport	4.05
Kraus, Kevin	FBI SAC, Chicago, IL	5.04
Levine, Stefanie	FBI ASAC, Louisville, KY	2.08
Lloyd, William	Victim	4.05
Logan, NFN	Intelligence Collection Office	3.09
Lohman, Walter	US Army IDC	3.08
Maloney, Sean	FBI, Orlando, FL	5.08
McAllister, Wilson	WAR driver	2.10
McKinnon, Larry	Los Alamos National Lab	8.15
Melli, Chuck	CIO, U.S. Army IDC	5.13
Mellon, Chad	CIA, Islamabad, Pakistan	3.12
Metcalfe, Byron	FBI SAC, Norfolk, VA	1.02
Mooney, Jennifer	Family	7.08
Mooney, Pam	WAR driver	7.04
Morse, Bill	WAR driver	1.08
Nevins, Carson	DoJ Analyst	3.13
Ng, William	FBI, Washington, DC	9.16
NLN, Al	Bar owner	7.05
NLN, Art	RAP team member	2.11
NLN, Bill	Lt. Governor, KY	2.16
NLN, Bruce	U.S. Attorney's Office, Louisville	2.08
NLN, Dhakir	AQNA soldier	1.04
NLN, Fida	AQNA soldier	1.04
NLN, Howard	RAP team member	2.11
NLN, Jalal	AQNA soldier	1.04
NLN, Janine	Gillette, WY Police Department	3.15
NLN, Malaki	AQNA soldier	2.06
NLN, Margery	Chuck Melli's secretary	5.13
NLN, Martha	Alby Pearson's Secretary	3.09
NLN, Pauline	Colin Avery's assistant	7.14
NLN, Pete	Commander, KY National Guard	2.16
NLN, Pat	WAR driver	9.14
NLN, Roshan	AQNA soldier	8.01
NLN, Sushonna	Waitress	1.12
NLN, Sayed	AQNA soldier	2.03
NLN, Stanley	KY Finance Secretary	2.16
NLN, Veronica	DOE Watch Team	2.02
NLN, Willy	Manager, Queen Anne Marina	2.05
O'Donnell, Perry	FBI, Boston, MA	6.09
Ortiz, Daniel	Delivery driver, victim	5.06
Owens, Alan	WAR driver	9.08

PASTOR, GINELLE	FAMILY	3.03
PASTOR, PATSY	FAMILY	1.06
PEARSON, ALBY	INTELLIGENCE COLLECTION OFFICE	3.09
PENTON, GABRIELLE	STROGER/COOK COUNTY HOSPITAL	5.05
PHILLIPS, NFN	FBI, LOUISVILLE, KY	2.13
RAHMAN, ATIYAH	AQAP LIEUTENANT	3.01
RANDALL, BILLY	PEARSON'S DHS CONTACT	3.09
RANDALL, GLORIA	WINSLOW AIDE	4.05
REYNOLDS, NFN	FBI, BOISE, ID	7.05
RIAZ, JAVED	SENIOR AGENT, PAKISTAN ISI	3.12
RICE, NFN	IMMIGRATION AND CUSTOMS SERVICE	6.16
RODRIGUEZ, VICTOR	PA STATE POLICE	8.21
SALTERS, NFN	SYBRIUM DOCK FOREMAN	8.21
SAMEER, FAISEL (MAHDI)	AQNA SOLDIER	1.04
SATTERS, NFN	FBI, HOUSTON, TX	7.02
SAVIDGE, RICHARD	U.S. ARMY IDC	6.06
SEWICKLEY, NFN	FBI, HOUSTON, TX	7.02
SIMMONS, JEFF	WAR DRIVER	7.08
SIMON, BRENDA	VICTIM	4.05
SPARKS, EDDIE	FBI, HOUSTON, TX	8.08
SPENCE, GERRY	FBI COUNTER-TERRORISM	2.19
STEIN, HERSH	COMMANDER, DCA AIRPORT POLICE	4.05
GOODWYN, RAOUL	FBI, BOSTON, MA	6.09
TRAYNOR, MARK	FBI, WASHINGTON, DC	9.09
TUCKER, PETER	U.S. CONSUL, BRITISH COLUMBIA	8.06
WACHS, NFN	FBI, SALT LAKE CITY UT	8.22
WARNER, JOHN	AMERICAN SECURITY PROJECT	10.07
WERNECKE, NFN	INTELLIGENCE COLLECTION OFFICE	3.09
WILEY, MITCH	HEAD OF SECURITY, ORNL	2.04
WILKINS, DARLENE	WAR DRIVER	7.03
WILKINS, MILTON	WAR DRIVER	7.03
WILKINS, SALLY	FAMILY	7.03
WILKINS, TOM	FAMILY	7.03
WILLIS, LES	WYOMING STATE POLICE	3.15
WILSON, DONALD	WAR SUV OWNER	9.03
WINSLOW, EVAN	CONGRESSMAN, R-OKLAHOMA	4.05
WOLFSON, NFN	FBI, SPRINGFIELD, IL	3.06
ZARDOOZ, SAMI	VICTIM	4.05
ZARTOORI, AHMED	AL JEZEERA NEWS READER	5.10

NFN = NO FIRST NAME;   NLN = NO LAST NAME